'The world of this novel appears as many scholars see that of Homer: a rich melange of different eras ... It has suspense, treachery and bone-crunching action ... It will leave fans of the genre eagerly awaiting the rest of the series'

Harry Sidebottom,
author of the best selling Warrior of Rome series

'Iliffe is a talented storyteller'

Times Literary Supplement

'A ripping swords-and-sandals treatment of *The Iliad*'

The Telegraph

'A thrilling adventure full of bloody battles, vibrant characters and the heart-stopping romance that makes ancient Greece so universally appealing. Dazzling drama on a grand scale'

Lancashire Evening Post

'A must read for those who enjoy good old epic battles, chilling death scenes and the extravagance of ancient Greece'

Lifestyle Magazine

'The reader does not need to be a classicist by any means to enjoy this epic and stirring tale. It makes a great novel and would be an even better film'

Historical Novels Review

'Another gripping and thrilling tale from the new demi-god of the genre, one which fans will relish getting stuck into'

The Catholic Herald

THE VOYAGE OF ODYSSEUS

Glyn Iliffe studied English and Classics at Reading University, where he developed a passion for Greek mythology. Well travelled, Glyn has visited nearly forty countries, trekked in the Himalayas, hitch-hiked across North America and had his collarbone broken by a bull in Pamplona.

He is married with two daughters and lives in Leicestershire. *King of Ithaca* was his first novel, followed by *The Gates of Troy*, *The Armour of Achilles* and *The Oracles of Troy*. He is currently working on the concluding book of the series.

For more information visit www.glyniliffe.com

Also by Glyn Iliffe

King of Ithaca
The Gates of Troy
The Armour of Achilles
The Oracles of Troy

THE VOYAGE
OF ODYSSEUS

GLYN ILIFFE

ISBN: 1523645954
ISBN 13: 9781523645954

FOR KATIE

ACKNOWLEDGEMENTS

I would like to thank Richard Sheehan for editing the original text and suggesting improvements.

I am also indebted to Justine Elliott for designing the cover and her patience with my constant tinkering.

Finally, for their proofreading skills, I would like to thank Saleh Abdulhadi, Kevin Beard, Maureen Corderoy, Jane Davies, Simon Jenson, Kenneth Kiffer Fong, Pierre L'Eplattenier, Sebastian Lockwood, Prashant Malikpuria, Kevin Marlow, Steven A. McKay, Nick Metcalfe, Nicholas Oxman, Dean Rodgers, Joseph Sofaer, Daniel Southall, Sam Stockdale, Rhys Thatcher, Sherwin Titus and Bruce Villas.

GLOSSARY

A

Achilles	– renowned Greek warrior
Acheron	– greatest of the rivers in the Underworld
Aeaea	– island home of Circe
Aeolia	– island of Aeolus
Aeolus	– ruler of the Winds
Aethiopes	– peoples from northern Africa
Agamemnon	– king of Mycenae, leader of the Greeks
Ajax (greater)	– king of Salamis, killed himself after being sent mad by the gods
Ajax (lesser)	– king of Locris
Alybas	– home city of Eperitus in northern Greece
Androcles	– eldest son of Aeolus
Antenor	– Trojan elder
Anticleia	– Odysseus's mother
Antinous	– Ithacan noble, son of Eupeithes
Antiphates	– king of the Laestrygonians
Antiphus	– Ithacan guardsman
Apheidas	– Trojan commander, father of Eperitus
Aphrodite	– goddess of love
Apollo	– archer god, associated with music, song and healing
Arceisius	– Ithacan soldier, murdered by Apheidas
Artemis	– moon-goddess associated with childbirth, noted for her virginity and vengefulness
Astynome	– daughter of Chryses, a priest of Apollo
Athena	– goddess of wisdom and warfare
Aulis	– sheltered bay in the Euboean Straits
Autonoe	– Penelope's body slave

B
Baius   — Ithacan helmsman

C
Calchas   — priest of Apollo, adviser to Agamemnon
Calypso   — island-dwelling demi-goddess
Charybdis   — a monstrous whirlpool
Cicones   — northern allies of the Trojans
Circe   — witch possessing the power to turn men into animals
Clytaemnestra   — queen of Mycenae and wife of Agamemnon
Cocytus   — the River of Lamentation found in the Underworld
Cyclops   — one-eyed giant
Cythera   — island off Cape Malea
Chelonion   — flower native to Ithaca

D
Dia   — daughter of Aeolus
Diomedes   — king of Argos
Dolius   — Ithacan slave
Drakios   — Ithacan soldier
Dulichium   — one of the Ionian islands under Odysseus's rule

E
Elpenor   — Ithacan soldier
Epistor   — Ithacan soldier
Eperitus   — captain of Odysseus's guard

Eupeithes	– member of the Kerosia
Eurybates	– Odysseus's squire
Eurylochus	– Ithacan soldier, cousin of Odysseus
Eurymachus	– Ithacan noble, henchman to Antinous

H

Hades	– god of the Underworld
Halitherses	– former captain of the Ithacan royal guard, given joint charge of Ithaca in Odysseus's absence
Hecabe	– Trojan queen, wife of King Priam
Hector	– Trojan prince, killed by Achilles
Helen	– queen of Sparta and wife of Menelaus
Hippasos	– Ithacan soldier
Hyperion	– god of the sun

I

Ilium	– the region of which Troy was the capital
Iphigenia	– daughter of Eperitus and Clytaemnestra, sacrificed by Agamemnon
Ismarus	– land of the Cicones
Ithaca	– island in the Ionian Sea

K

Kerosia	– Ithacan council meeting

L

Laertes	– Odysseus's father
Laestrygonians	– race of giant cannibals

Lethe	– the River of Forgetfulness found in the Underworld
Lotus Eaters	– a people addicted to the lotus fruit
Lyrnessus	– Trojan city sacked by the Greeks

M

Malea	– cape on the south-eastern tip of the Peloponnese
Maron	– Cicone priest of Apollo
Melanthius	– Ithacan goatherd and henchman of Antinous
Melantho	– Ithacan maidservant
Menelaus	– king of Sparta, brother of Agamemnon and cuckolded husband of Helen
Mentor	– close friend of Odysseus, given joint charge of Ithaca in Odysseus's absence
Moly	– flower native to Aeaea
Mycenae	– most powerful city in Greece, situated in north-eastern Peloponnese
Mydon	– Ithacan soldier

N

Neoptolemus	– son of Achilles and Deidameia
Neriton (Mount)	– highest point on Ithaca
Nestor	– king of Pylos

O

Odysseus	– king of Ithaca
Oenops	– member of the Kerosia

Oicles	– Ithacan soldier
Omeros	– Ithacan soldier and bard
Ophelestes	– Ithacan soldier

P

Palladium	– sacred image of Athena's companion, Pallas
Paris	– Trojan prince, killed by Philoctetes
Parnassus (Mount)	– mountain in central Greece and home of the Pythian oracle
Peiraeus	– friend of Telemachus
Peloponnese	– southernmost landmass of Greek mainland, named after Pelops
Pelops	– grandfather of Agamemnon and Menelaus
Penelope	– queen of Ithaca and wife of Odysseus
Pergamos	– the citadel of Troy
Perimedes	– Taphian soldier
Phaeacia	– island on the cusp of the known world
Philoctetes	– Malean archer, deserted by the Greeks on Lemnos
Phlegethon	– the River of Flaming Fire found in the Underworld
Polites	– Ithacan warrior
Polyctor	– member of the Kerosia
Polyphemus	– a Cyclops, son of Poseidon
Poseidon	– god of the sea
Priam	– king of Troy
Proreus	– Phaeacian sailor
Pylos	– city in south-western Peloponnese
Pythoness	– high priestess of the Pythian oracle

S

Samos — westernmost of the Ionian islands under Odysseus's rule

Scamander — river on the Trojan plain

Scylla — six-headed monster

Selagos — Taphian warrior

Sirens — monsters with the body of a bird and the head of a woman

Sisyphus — condemned to the Underworld for boasting he could outwit Zeus

Styx — the River of Hatred found in the Underworld

T

Talthybius — squire to Agamemnon

Tantalus — great-grandfather of Agamemnon and Menelaus, condemned to the Underworld for serving his son to the gods in a stew

Tartarus — the Underworld

Taphians — pirate race from Taphos

Teiresias — blind seer

Telemachus — son of Odysseus and Penelope

Telepora — wife of Aeolus

Tenedos — island off the coast of Ilium

Theano — priestess of Athena and wife of Antenor

Thrinacie — island where Hyperion keeps his cattle

Tityus — Giant condemned to the Underworld for attempting to rape the mother of Apollo and Artemis

Troy — chief city of Ilium

X
xenia   – the custom of friendship towards strangers

Z
Zacynthos   – southernmost of the Ionian islands under Odysseus's rule

Zeus   – the king of the gods

book
ONE

Chapter One

DEDICATING THE ANCHOR STONES

Eperitus, son of Apheidas, looked across the Scamander valley at the ruins of Troy. Countless fires pumped slanted pillars of smoke high into the sky, where they congregated and drifted west to befog the late afternoon sun. The walls of the great city, which had stood for so long in defiance against the besieging Greeks, were now broken and charred, the once impenetrable gates stretched out in the dust like slain giants. From his viewpoint on the ridge, Eperitus could see the destruction within: the hovels of the lower city still burning the best part of a day after the first torches had set them alight, the mansions and temples of the citadel – Pergamos – blackened and roofless as the fires gorged themselves on the delicate furniture and rich tapestries that had filled the halls of Troy's elite. King Priam's palace had borne the brunt of the Greeks' vengeance. One whole wing had exploded when the flames had reached the giant pithoi of oil and wine, blowing out the walls and killing Greek and Trojan without discrimination. Not satisfied with that, King Agamemnon had ordered his soldiers to tear down the walls of his enemy's home stone by stone, so all that remained now was a pile of scorched rubble. Before it, in the centre of the courtyard, a huge pyre fed on the corpses of the fallen. There were other such pyres throughout the ruined city, for despite their hatred of the Trojans, the Greeks would not abandon their bodies to be feasted on by dogs and vultures, leaving their spirits to remain on earth instead of being led down to the Halls of Hades. Ten years of war had made savages out of the Greeks, but they were not yet monsters.

Halfway between the Scaean Gate and the walls of the citadel, wreathed in smoke, stood the great horse that had brought death and destruction to Troy. Had it only been last night, Eperitus thought, that he had sat hidden inside its wooden body with the best of the Greeks, waiting for the moment to leap out and wreak chaos on the unsuspecting Trojans? It had been a fearful gamble – the idea of his friend and king, the ever-resourceful Odysseus – but after ten years of deadlock the Greeks had been willing to risk anything to end the war. And by the will of the gods they had succeeded. In one terrible night Troy had fallen. Men, women and children were slaughtered in their sleep or chased from their homes and hunted down like swine until the streets ran with their blood. Only the females were shown any mercy, if rape and the murder of their families could be considered merciful. They were useful slaves, an essential part of any economy, but were a poor recompense for ten years of war. With Troy's wealth exhausted, the only men who had gained from the conflict were the sons of Atreus: Menelaus had recovered his wife, the incomparable Helen, from the clutches of the Trojans, while Agamemnon, the most powerful of all the Greek rulers, had destroyed his greatest rival and ensured the Aegean trade routes would belong to Mycenae. As for the rest of the kings, their rewards were less tangible: freedom from the oaths that had bound them to the war, until Troy was defeated or death had claimed them; and immortality through their illustrious deeds, the aspiration of every fighting man. Though Eperitus doubted whether any thought the price they had paid was worth it.

For his own part, he knew it had been too much. He had started the war seeking glory in battle, and his lust had been well satisfied – glutted, even, to the point of sickness – in a ten-year orgy of blood and death. He had also been keen for revenge against his treacherous father, the king slayer who had sought refuge among the Trojans. That desire, too, had been met, though he had felt little satisfaction in seeing Apheidas take his own life. And the price of glory and vengeance had been the lives of his daughter, his squire and countless comrades in arms. But there was *one* compensation for all that he had suffered in the bloody, decade-long conflict.

'What are you thinking?'

A soft hand slipped into his and he turned to see Astynome beside him. Her cheeks were smeared with dirt to conceal their softness, while the leather breastplate and long woollen cloak she wore hid her womanly curves from unwelcome eyes. Only the tresses of her black hair, tied into a messy bun at the back of her head, betrayed her true sex.

'Come on, tell me what's on your mind,' she insisted with a smile, her Trojan accent broad and exotic to Eperitus's ears.

She reached up with her other hand and ran her fingers along the unfamiliar smoothness of his chin. He took the hand and raised her wrist to his lips. The fine, sun-bleached hairs of her forearm were soft against his newly shaven skin.

'Ithaca. I was thinking of Ithaca. Of you and me and the farm I'm going to build for us. A team of oxen, some pigs, a couple of slaves to help me about the place –'

'And our children? Of little Arceisius sitting on the oxen's back while his father drives up the ground with the plough? Of Iphigenia holding the distaff while her mother spins the wool?'

'So we'll call her Iphigenia then?'

'Of course we will. But you weren't thinking of Ithaca at all, were you? Your eyes betray you: there's no joy in them, only sadness.'

'I wish I *had* been thinking of Ithaca,' he said, gazing once more at the smouldering ruins of Troy. 'But how can I look to the future when we're still here?'

Surrounded by the ghosts of the war, he thought. As he stared down at the rolling meadows that led to the fords of the Scamander, his mind's eye could still see the great battles that had taken place there. The Greek and Trojan armies grinding against each other like great millstones. The long ranks of spearmen locked in the centre and the cavalry swarming on the flanks. Kings and captains riding this way and that in their chariots, bringing death wherever they went. He recalled the duel between Menelaus and Paris, fought as the armies sat in rows watching them. And the time Achilles had herded hundreds of Trojans into the fast-flowing Scamander, slaying them without compassion among the tamarisks and willows, forcing them down the banks to drown under the weight of their own armour. He had witnessed Achilles kill Hector before the Scaean Gate, only to be killed there himself a few days later by an arrow from Paris's bow. The same ground had drunk Paris's blood after he had been shot down by Philoctetes. And so the killing had gone on, death after death, until the gods brought the war to its conclusion. The gods and Odysseus.

Eperitus looked a little further along the ridge to the temple of Thymbrean Apollo. It was formed from a double-ring of plane trees, dense enough to block all but a few glimmers of light from the westering sun behind them. Its roof was formed from their closely intertwined branches, and in the breeze the leaves whispered like the voices of the dead. An ox and cart waited a few paces from the narrow entrance, the beast's head bent low to the parched grass. Beyond it Eperitus could see the sunlight glinting on the expanse of the Aegean, the great sea that separated the Greeks from their native lands and which would soon be bearing their fleets back home again.

Astynome must have been thinking the same thing.

'We won't be here much longer,' she said. 'And then we can forget all about Troy and start again.'

'But Troy's your home.'

'Troy no longer exists. From now on my home is wherever you are. But if we're to start again – build a home and have a family – then you must leave the shadow of the past.'

'My father's dead,' he answered. 'And if you're worried that I still blame you for luring me into his trap –'

'I'm not talking about Apheidas, or what *I* did. I'm talking about Agamemnon. Has there been a single day since he murdered your daughter that you haven't longed to take revenge? Though Iphigenia's mother made you swear not to kill him, I know the thought of his going unpunished still haunts you. So now I'm scared you'll do something rash before the fleets go their separate ways and you lose your chance forever.'

Her intuition caught him unawares. She trapped his gaze with her own, challenging him to refute her accusation, but he forced himself to look away once more to the tumbled and fire-blackened remains of Troy. He stared hard at the hundreds upon hundreds of beached and anchored galleys in the large harbour, their denuded masts moving gently with the motion of the water, like breeze-blown stalks of corn. Inevitably his eyes were drawn towards the mass of tents that had been pitched that morning on the plain before the city walls, and to the largest tent of them all. The tent of Agamemnon.

As he looked he saw a horseman splashing across the ford and onto the soft, watery meadows of the plain. He kicked his heels back and sent his mount galloping over the battle-bruised and debris-strewn grass to the foot of the ridge. Pausing to shield his eyes from the sun and look up at the temple, he was soon urging his horse up the slope again, clearly driven by some urgency.

'Who is it?' Astynome asked.

'Talthybius, Agamemnon's herald,' Eperitus answered, picking up her bronze cap from the grass and pushing it onto her head. 'So unless you want to be recognised, keep your head down and try to stay out of the way.'

Agamemnon had once claimed Astynome as a spoil of war but had forced to relinquish her when her father, a priest of Apollo, had called a plague down on the Greek camp. Knowing that the Mycenaean king would not be denied a second time, the Ithacans had disguised her as a soldier to prevent her presence being discovered. Eperitus waited while she threw the cloak about her shoulders, picked up her spear and shield and walked towards the temple. Before he could call a warning, a figure emerged from the ring of trees into the late afternoon sun. He was a stocky man with broad shoulders and short legs that gave him a top-heavy appearance. His beard and hair were red, and his green, clever eyes blinked in the sunlight. Unlike Eperitus, King Odysseus of Ithaca wore no armour. As far as he was concerned the war was over and the peace could not start soon enough. His only weapon was the dagger in his belt, which he had used for the sacrifice of a lamb to Apollo, while over his shoulder was the skin of water he had brought to wash the blood from his hands.

Odysseus was followed by three men. The most prominent was Polites, a giant Thessalian recruited into the Ithacan army before the war. He carried an anchor stone under each arm, which he heaved one after the other onto the back of the cart, making the dust leap from its seams. Odysseus had brought the stones to be dedicated before the long journey home. It was a vital ceremony – in rough seas an anchor stone was often all that stood between a ship and destruction – and with the temple of Poseidon in Troy a smoking ruin, the temple of Thymbrean Apollo was the only sacred place left. The other two men looked like children next to Polites. Indeed, Omeros, Eperitus's squire, and Elpenor, his friend, had barely reached manhood before arriving in Ilium a few months earlier with the reinforcements from Ithaca. War had aged them quickly enough, but with their downy beards shaved off, they had the appearance of young boys again.

Odysseus raised his hand in greeting towards Eperitus and Astynome. Eperitus waved back and pointed urgently down the slope at the approaching horseman. At this distance the figure would still have been a blur to the king's eyes, and only the supernatural sharpness of Eperitus's senses – a gift from Athena many years before – could discern the rider's features.

'It's Talthybius,' he said, joining Odysseus.

'Get inside the temple,' Odysseus commanded Astynome. 'I don't want to risk him recognising you.'

She disappeared into the gloom of the temple as Polites emerged with two more anchor stones. He swung them onto the back of the cart – which sank heavily and pulled the ox back a step – then joined the others as they watched the horseman picking his way up the gradient. Eventually the herald looked up and, seeing the figures atop the ridge, jabbed his heels back and sent his grey mare quickly up the remainder of the slope.

'Here you are,' he said, addressing Odysseus with a touch of impatience. 'Agamemnon's called a meeting of the Council. Your presence is required at once.'

'The Council only met this morning.'

'That was to divide the spoils; this is to discuss the return home. Do you have horses?'

'We have a cart,' Odysseus answered, deliberately provoking Talthybius's irritation.

'Then I would suggest you run, my lord.'

Odysseus slipped the waterskin from his shoulder and offered it up to the sweating herald.

'Why the urgency?'

Talthybius drank deeply, then looked down at Odysseus. He debated with himself a moment, then passed back the water.

'There's been a difference of opinion about when the fleet should leave and the route they should take.'

'A difference of opinion?' Odysseus asked, cocking an eyebrow. 'You mean an argument.'

'Yes, between Agamemnon and Menelaus. Come as quickly as you can, Odysseus. You might be the only man who can stop them from killing each other.'

Chapter Two

THE FLEET DIVIDES

The new Greek camp was a sprawling, chaotic mass of dirty white canvas, smoking campfires and thousands of jubilant warriors still revelling in their victory of the night before. Unlike the old site to the south-west, where the army had been ensconced for ten years and which had witnessed so much strife and sorrow, this transitory encampment pulsed with noisy, triumphant energy. The stench of woodsmoke, roast meat and unwashed bodies filled Odysseus's nostrils as he splashed across the fords of the Scamander, where eels swam between the slippery-smooth stones and tendrils of green weed trailed in the current. Clambering up the far bank with Eperitus, he pushed his way into the crowd by the outermost tents and entered a masquerade of light and shadow caused by the dying glow of the sunset. Soldiers he did not know called his name and thrust skins of wine towards him as he shouldered his way through the drunken throng. Here and there, groups of men threw dice as they gambled the meagre possessions they had plundered from the city. In one group a naked woman tried to cover herself as a Spartan and an Athenian haggled over her fate. She looked pleadingly at Odysseus, but he looked away. He had too many troubles of his own to take pity on a captured Trojan. Close to the shoreline he saw Agamemnon's palatial tent. A company of fully armed Mycenaeans stood guard over the piles of treasure and hundreds of slaves that Agamemnon had awarded himself, but the tent looked empty.

'Over there,' Eperitus said, touching Odysseus on the shoulder and pointing towards the ruins of the Scaean Gate.

A circle of war-torn banners thrummed the air, marking the spot where the Council of Kings had convened. The dolphin of Ithaca was among them, brought there from the ships, but Odysseus did not expect the debate had been delayed for his sake. Soon, he and Eperitus were barging their way through the crowd of attendants to take their places on the benches where the commanders of the Greek armies had gathered. A large fire at the centre of the circle threw up hundreds of sparks that eddied in the evening breeze. Nestor, the grey-headed king of Pylos, stood a few paces from the edge of the flames, his splendid armour gleaming from between the folds of his rich cloak. He clutched a golden staff in both hands and was using one end of it to trace lines in the dry earth.

'Has anything been decided?' Odysseus whispered, leaning in towards Diomedes.

'No,' the king of Argos replied. 'All you've missed is wine, prayers and a lot of scowling between the Atreides brothers.'

He indicated two men sitting on opposite sides of the circle. To Odysseus's right was King Menelaus of Sparta, the younger of the brothers. His auburn hair and beard were shot through with grey from years of worrying about Helen, the wife who had been stolen from him by the Trojans. Regaining her did not seem to have lightened his anxieties. He sat with his elbows on his knees and the fist of one hand clasped in the fingers of the other, glowering through the heat haze at his older brother. For his part, Agamemnon reclined in his fur-draped throne and refused to meet Menelaus's glare. The king of Mycenae's scarlet cloak was thrown back from his shoulders to reveal the breastplate gifted to him by King Cinyras of Cyprus, its highly burnished bands of blue enamel, tin and gold running red with the light from the fire. His blue eyes were cold and passionless as they regarded the flames, deep in thoughts that would soon be revealed to the Council. But where he had once been their elected leader and his word had been law, with the war over and the Council's oaths fulfilled, he no longer held any power over them. Unless it was by the influence of his wealth and the force of his vast army.

Nestor finished drawing his curious lines and circles in the dirt and looked up. The low murmurs on the benches carried on, forcing him to beat the speaker's staff three times on the ground.

'Troy,' he announced, tapping a spot between his feet. 'Tenedos, Lemnos, Samothrace,' he continued, stabbing the base of the staff into three of the circles he had traced in the dirt. 'To the north we have the Ismarus Mountains and the Thracian coast, looping around and down towards Euboea. To the south-west the open Aegean, with the island of Scyros the only stepping stone to Euboea. To the south, Lesbos, Chios and the Cyclades, which lead back up to northern Greece, or across to the Peloponnese. The northerly passage is out of the question: it's the longest route of all for most of us, and any fleet leaving from Troy will have to row against the prevailing current and the wind. We shouldn't forget, either, that our ships have been beached for the best part of ten years. The repairs we've carried out have barely made them seaworthy again and few would survive that course. The southerly route is safest. The fleet can hug the coast, sail around Lesbos and then on to Chios, Icaria, Myconos and so on, heading north towards Euboea and Attica or west to Melos and Malea. That route will be slow but offers plenty of shelter if the gods decide to send storms; it also has many places to gather fresh food and water if becalmed. But if you'll be guided by me, the fleet should head straight across the Aegean to Euboea. It's a risk in foul weather, of course, but it's the quickest route of all. And I, for one, want to see my homeland again as soon as possible.'

'We all do,' said Odysseus. 'And we should lose no time getting home to our wives and families.'

A loud chorus of agreement echoed from the benches, with only a few faces showing no enthusiasm for Nestor's suggestion. These were the northerly kings and captains, whose quickest route home would be to Lemnos and then directly west to the triple-pronged headlands of Paeonia. Then Menelaus stood and held his hand out to Nestor. The old king passed him the staff and returned to his seat beside Agamemnon.

'When the two wisest men in the army speak, the rest of us should listen. Nestor and Odysseus have proved themselves time and again to be right, and if any of us know the will of the gods it's them. And now that Troy has fallen at last, who among us isn't thinking of returning home without delay, to see the ones we love and restore order to the kingdoms we have neglected because of Zeus's stubbornness in keeping us here? So I say yes, let's take the quickest route back to Greece, and by all the gods on Olympus, let's leave while there's still a westerly wind to take us home. No tarrying – we've endured ten years of that – let's sail with the first light of dawn tomorrow.'

He turned his fierce gaze upon his brother while all around him the Council responded with a loud cheer. Odysseus's heart lifted at the idea of leaving Ilium in the morning and sailing his crimson-beaked ships back home across the Aegean. The thought of holding Penelope in his arms again made him tense with nervous anticipation, and to see the son he had left behind as a baby filled him with excitement. He turned to Eperitus, unable to suppress a smile, and saw the captain of his royal guard staring hard at Agamemnon. Whatever part of Eperitus was looking forward to starting his own family on Ithaca, a greater part was still mired in the past and the death of Iphigenia. As quickly as it had come, Odysseus's enthusiasm dropped away and his heart sank into his stomach. The echoes of his own past still stood between him and Ithaca. The words of the oracle given to him so long ago by the Pythoness in her cave beneath Mount Parnassus whispered through the back of his mind. *If ever you seek Priam's city, the wide waters will swallow you. For the time it takes a baby to become a man, you will know no home. Then, when friends and fortune have departed from you, you will rise again from the dead.*

It was a prophecy he had lived with for half his life, and though he refused to accept that he was a prisoner to such a fate – that he was unable to pilot his own destiny – its promise of doom had always tormented him. And yet how *could* it come true, he asked himself. The Pythoness had said that if he went to Troy he would not see Ithaca for twenty years; against all expectation ten years had passed without sight of his home, but surely the war could not spring back into life for another decade? No, the oracle had to be false.

Then he remembered Athena.

The goddess had been his protector since boyhood, even appearing to him at times to save him from an early death or offer him guidance. But that was before he had betrayed her, stealing the sacred Palladium from her temple in direct defiance of her orders. For that she had promised him her wrath, declaring that the Pythian oracle would be played out to the full. He ran a hand through his thick hair and sighed heavily.

'What is it?' Eperitus asked.

Before Odysseus could answer, Agamemnon rose from his high-backed throne and strode towards his brother. Menelaus almost growled as Agamemnon thrust out his hand and seized the speaker's staff. For a long moment the Spartan king refused to relinquish his hold, but as the clamour about them died down and the kings, princes and commanders of the Council turned their eyes on the contest of wills before them, Menelaus eased his grip and let his hand fall. With an open sneer, he returned to his seat.

'My brother has got what he came to Troy for,' Agamemnon announced grandly, 'and now he wants to scuttle back to Sparta so that he can reacquaint himself with his wife. Indeed, who can blame him? Helen's beauty is something to die for, as too many of our comrades would testify – if we could hear their voices from Hades. But in his haste Menelaus has perhaps forgotten his debt to the rest of us. After all, he isn't the only one who was deprived of his wife for ten years – didn't we also give up our loved ones so he could recover his? But though we're all keen to return home, let's not be so hasty that we leave behind a legacy for our own children to suffer from. Are we in such a hurry to depart that we will leave these mighty fortifications for a new enemy to occupy? The walls of Troy still stand,' he reminded his audience, pointing the golden staff towards the battlements that had defied the Greeks for so long. Efforts had been made all day long to throw down the great stones that Poseidon and Apollo had placed there, but tens of thousands of men had barely succeeded in toppling their lofty parapets. 'I say we cannot go as long as one of those stones stands upon another. My friends, wait a few more days until our job is properly finished, then we'll take whichever route will get us back to Greece the quickest. Let us finish the war as we have fought it – together.'

A few members of the Council nodded at his words, though most of these were the weaker kings who still had something to gain from keeping Agamemnon's favour. Others looked about doubtfully, trying to weigh what the general opinion might be. But many crossed their arms in defiance, or looked into the flames to avoid Agamemnon's keen stare. These did not want to remain a day longer than they had to, and the first to put a voice to their collective reluctance was Diomedes.

'Not me,' he declared. 'I want to go now. But if you're so concerned, Agamemnon, why don't you leave a garrison of Mycenaeans here?'

His words educed a mixture of agreement and denial.

'Why should Mycenae gain from our hard work?' demanded Little Ajax, leaping angrily up from his bench. 'We Locrians fought as hard as anyone else. Harder than most. The last thing I want is Mycenaean strongholds on both sides of the Aegean dictating whose trade can or can't pass.'

'Don't be a fool, Ajax,' Nestor said. 'Will you see the Greeks return to the petty squabbles and civil wars that divided us before Troy?'

'Giving Mycenae full control of the Aegean is a sure way to start another civil war,' called another voice.

'There will be *no* garrison!' Agamemnon shouted, raising the speaker's staff to silence the sudden din of voices. 'Do you think I hadn't thought about this a long time ago? Of course I had – and division among the Greeks is one of the *lesser* problems it would cause. No, we must raze Troy to the ground and go home. But if all most of you care about is getting back as quickly as possible, then consider this also: if men are at the mercy of the gods on land, how much more so are we on the waves? We have yet to honour the gods fully for our victory or appease them for the temples we have destroyed. Do you think the few hasty sacrifices we offered them this morning are going to see us home safely? *Do you?* Then launch your galleys and see how quickly you get home, if at all! But we Mycenaeans will stay and offer proper sacrifices, and when we're done we'll remain until the walls of Troy are destroyed. If you have any sense then you'll stay with us.'

This brought further squabbling from the benches, with fingers pointed and voices raised.

'I take it you won't wait,' Eperitus asked, leaning in towards Odysseus.

Before Odysseus could reply, Diomedes, who had caught Eperitus's words, swung about on his seat and faced the king of Ithaca.

'I say we go at first light tomorrow, Odysseus. What do you say? The fleets of Argos and Ithaca together, alongside Menelaus and his Spartans. Isn't this what you've been waiting for for ten years?'

Menelaus stood again and entered the circle of benches. Agamemnon tossed the speaker's staff into the dust at his feet and returned to his chair. Not bothering to retrieve the symbol of authority, the Spartan king raised his hand and the Council fell silent.

'Then there's no other option: the fleet must be divided. The gods will have *my* sacrifices the moment I set foot on Spartan soil again, and I will make sure they receive all that's due to them and more. But I'll not stay in this place a day longer, for all my brother's honeyed words. Sparta sails at dawn; who is with her?'

He extended a hand to the Council, but was met with silence. Agamemnon, reclining once more on his fur-draped throne, allowed himself a smile. Odysseus glanced at Diomedes, whose face was a torment of indecision. But Odysseus's own hesitancy had nothing to do with the fear of offending Agamemnon, whose icy gaze swept the benches daring anyone to disagree with him. Nor was it out of a desire to appease the terrible Olympians that ruled over every aspect of a man's life. It was to do with just one god: Athena. Did he stay and give her back the one thing he knew she wanted, or did he sail with the morning breeze that would come down from the mountains and send the Spartan fleet homeward to Greece? The anxiety tore at his insides, but for once he decided to ignore his head and follow the will of his heart. He took a deep breath and prepared to stand, but another rose to his feet before him.

The Council seemed to hold its breath as all eyes turned to the last man anyone expected to flout Agamemnon. King Nestor of Pylos, Agamemnon's closest adviser and most loyal ally in ten years of war, looked briefly down into the Mycenaean's shocked eyes, then across at Menelaus.

'I will sail with you tomorrow, Menelaus. If the gods choose to punish an old man in his haste to return home, then so be it. But my men are weary for Pylos and I won't deny them any longer.'

'I'll sail, too,' Diomedes announced.

'And me,' said Odysseus, standing beside him.

None of the others spoke. Perhaps they believed in Agamemnon's arguments, or perhaps they had their own reasons for not rushing home. But Odysseus did not care for them. As he and Eperitus walked back to the Ithacan galleys, where doubtless rumours of their departure had preceded them, he looked at the sun sinking into the Aegean. A third of its yellow orb had already melted into the waters and the sky above it was banded into different shades of deepening purple. As it touched the horizon, its reflection extended a golden carpet across the waves, as if inviting him to hurry back to Greece. Maybe it was a good omen, he thought. Maybe not.

Chapter Three

SELAGOS

I t was still dark when the Ithacan ships were hauled down the beach and into the great bay, where they joined the fleets of Argos, Pylos and Sparta. The moon had long since slipped beneath the Aegean but Eperitus could clearly see the hundreds of galleys heading for the mouth of the harbour, pulled gracefully forward by rows of slowly moving oars. The swish of water was accompanied by the creak of rigging and the sound of low voices uttering words of command in the darkness – distractions that Eperitus tried to filter out as he stood in the prow of the ship, focussing his senses on the quiet hulks of the fleets that were staying behind. Agamemnon and Menelaus had parted on bitter terms, leaving Eperitus with the uncomfortable suspicion that Agamemnon might try to prevent any early departure from Troy. But the hundred ships of the Mycenaean fleet were still firmly beached on the grey shore, with their cross spars stowed and their benches empty. The galleys of the other Greek nations were similarly dormant, though Eperitus watched them all closely until the last Ithacan ship had sailed into the wide strait that led to the open sea. Even then, as he turned to look at the thicket of naked masts and the broken walls of Troy looming up beyond them, he still felt as if he were attached to this place by an invisible cord that at any moment would run out of slack and jerk him and his comrades irresistibly back to Ilium.

There was a last moment of tension as they turned the spur of land dividing the harbour from the sea, then he felt the current take hold and pull the galley south towards the black hump of Tenedos. A pale outline was forming above the eastern mountains when a series of orders barked out from the ships ahead. Hundreds of grey sails unfurled in the gloom, shuddering briefly before filling out with the clean, south-westerly breeze that swept the surface of the water. The voice of Eurybates called from the stern of the ship. An instant later the sails of the Ithacan galleys were tumbling heavily down from the cross spars and billowing out as they caught the wind. A short period of activity followed while the rigging was adjusted and the pine oars were hauled in and laid down between the benches. Then there was silence as the crews returned to their seats, shook out their tired limbs and waited for dawn to arrive.

Eperitus glanced down at Astynome, asleep on a large sack of grain. She had not been woken by the activity around her, so he kissed her on the brow and left her to her slumber. The journey to the stern – where Odysseus was manning the twin steering oars – was difficult, not least because of the constant motion of the deck that would doubtless take him days to get used to. He also had to negotiate a route through the densely packed stores of food and drink that crammed the narrow space between the benches. Among the sacks of wheat and barley and the different clay pithoi of wine and water were live pigs in reed baskets, goats with their hooves bound – that bleated at him as he stepped over them – and even a bony, long-horned cow that had been coaxed onto its stomach and lashed to the deck with leather ropes. Packed amid these provisions for the voyage home was Odysseus's share of the spoils from Troy: precious metals; reams of expensive cloth; bails of wool and other goods, all covered with leather tarps. Most numerous of all were the slaves. This human plunder was exclusively female, the men and boys having been slain on Agamemnon's orders. Chief among them was Hecabe, King Priam's wife, whom Odysseus had chosen to serve as a maid to Penelope. Eperitus saw her lying with the other slaves among the carefully arranged cargo, her proud status so utterly destroyed that she was now barely a shell of flesh and blood. Her mind had been emptied by grief at the loss of her husband, her many sons and the impenetrable city that had been her home. Several of the other women and young girls were disturbed by Eperitus's clumsy progress and complained loudly. He expected to find Odysseus amused by his efforts, but the king's face was sombre and he hardly seemed to notice his captain's arrival. Eurybates stood close behind him, equally silent and ready to take the oars if needed.

Eperitus looked up at the long, grey clouds that barred the sky.

'A bright day ahead, but autumn isn't far away. All the more reason to have left when we did. And yet, even now I feel –'

'Feel what?' Odysseus asked, diverting his gaze briefly from the sea ahead of the galley, which was now gleaming with the first true light of dawn.

Eperitus plumped himself down on a sack of grain. 'As if any moment now something's going to happen to take us back. After all this time it doesn't seem possible we're finally heading home.'

'I feel the same, and I know exactly why,' Odysseus replied. 'It's been haunting me ever since we left the belly of the horse, the moment I knew Troy had fallen. Twenty years the Pythoness said I'd be away from Ithaca. That's another ten years before I see my family again.'

'But she was wrong. By all the gods, she has to be,' Eperitus said. 'Helen's safe and Troy wiped out. Ithaca's a few weeks' voyage away at the most. There isn't a force in the world that can put another decade between us and home.'

'Perhaps you forget the one force you've just called upon: the gods. What can twelve small galleys do against the power of Zeus or Poseidon? Or Athena? You heard what she said the night we took the Palladium.'

Odysseus's eyes burned with the certainty of his own doom as he spoke, but at the last word he seemed to check himself and turned his face back to the sea. Eperitus followed his gaze, wondering what had distracted him, but all he could see were the white sails of two hundred ships and the growing bulk of Tenedos getting ever nearer, its eastern flanks orange with the light of the rising sun. Then he noticed the sack at Odysseus's heels. At first it looked like another bag of wheat or barley, but it was too bulky and angular for that. Leaning forward, he flipped back a corner of the rough weave before Odysseus could stop him.

It only took a fleeting glance of the blackened, misshapen object for Eperitus to recognise it. Odysseus replaced the cloth quickly and looked at Eperitus, more in guilt than anger.

'The *Palladium*?' Eperitus hissed.

Odysseus glanced across at the rowing benches where his cousin Eurylochus and three of his cronies had been casting dice. Their game forgotten, they were staring at the king and the sack by his heels. Odysseus glared at them and they returned to their game.

'You told me the Palladium had been placed in the head of the wooden horse,' Eperitus said in a low voice.

'I lied. You think I'd give it back to the Trojans after the lengths I went to to steal it from them?'

The Palladium was a burnt and disfigured effigy of Pallas, whom Athena had killed in a hunting accident. It had no beauty or value, but the Trojans had cherished it more than any other treasure, for it was said Troy would not fall as long as the figure was held within its walls. Desperate to end the war and go home, Odysseus had tricked his way into the city to steal it. When Athena had appeared in her temple and ordered him not to remove it, he defied her and took it anyway.

'You didn't have to bring it with us! You should have burned it, or buried it, or just left it lying in the ruins. Do you think it's going to somehow preserve you from Athena's wrath? Do you? More likely she'll destroy us for certain if you keep it! Throw it overboard.'

'Never,' Odysseus snapped. 'I'll take it back to Ithaca and re-dedicate it in a temple of my own. If I don't do something to appease her, we're doomed for sure.'

They had almost forgotten the presence of Eurybates, who had tried to move out of earshot of their whispers. But as the wind changed and Tenedos loomed closer, he called out for an alteration to the sail. Odysseus and Eperitus fell silent and moved apart.

'Selagos, it's your throw.'

Selagos was sitting on one of the rowing benches, his fore-arms resting on his thighs as he stared beneath his thick eyebrows at Odysseus and Eperitus, watching their whispered argument over the contents of the bag. From the moment Eperitus had foolishly revealed its contents, Selagos had forgotten the game of dice and let his thoughts trickle down through the possibilities forming in his uneducated but sharp brain. Reluctantly he turned towards his impatient comrades and looked down at the seven wooden cubes on the mat between their feet.

'Five to beat,' Eurylochus announced.

There was a sheen of sweat on the round, pink face of Odysseus's cousin, who licked his thick lips in anticipation as he stared at Selagos.

'You?' Selagos asked.

Eurylochus shook his head and nodded towards a skinny man with red-rimmed eyes, who grinned at Selagos through crooked yellow teeth. The smile quickly withered under the Taphian merce-nary's savage glare. Scooping the dice up in his broad hands, Selagos shook them once and tossed them back onto the mat.

'Three!' Eurylochus announced.

He pulled the matching dice aside and, picking up the remain-der, placed them into Selagos's open palm. He shook again and rolled. A moment's silence as four pairs of eyes scanned the faces of the dice, then shouts of laughter and derision as they counted a total of six matches.

'You win,' Eurylochus congratulated him.

But Selagos had already forgotten the game and was frowning at the sack that contained the Palladium. He tugged at the top of his left ear, where it had been severed by a Trojan sword, then scratched at the tangled red beard that he had refused to shave when the rest of the crew had removed theirs. With the war over and the fleet sailing back to Ithaca, the time had come for him to fulfil his mission. And if he was to find an opportunity, he had to buy as much time as he could with as much disruption as possible. The unexpected presence of the Palladium had given him his first chance.

He stared at Odysseus and felt the old, comfortable hatred swell within him. The king's eyes were fixed on the water ahead of the galley, unaware that one of his own men was patiently awaiting the right moment to strike him dead. But how could he know that, when Selagos had been so careful in keeping his emotions hidden? Though driven by loathing for the Ithacan, he was neither irrational nor reckless. He would not gamble away his chance for vengeance in a hot-blooded moment, or even risk it on a favourable chance. No, he would wait until retribution was guaranteed, when he could face Odysseus alone and let him know why he was about to take his life. His blood had burned with the desire for revenge for over ten years, but he would not let rash anger give Odysseus the slightest opportunity to escape his doom.

'Take your throw, Selagos,' Eurylochus said beside him.

Selagos looked down at the pile of barley cakes at his feet, his winnings from the last throw. More cakes had been placed at the edges of the leather mat, the pathetic stakes in a meaningless game. He shook his head.

'I don't want to throw dice,' he answered in his broad Taphian accent and slid further along the bench.

The flames of his hatred hot within him, he glanced at Odysseus and their eyes met. Immediately he regretted it. He forced his attention back to the game, feigning interest while seeing from the periphery of his vision that Odysseus was still watching him, doubtless questioning the look of disdain he had encountered in the mercenary's eyes. Cursing himself for a fool, Selagos waited until the king was staring out at the ocean again and then let his gaze drift back to the sack containing the Palladium. As he mulled over what he would do, he risked a glance at Eperitus. Since reaching the shores of Ilium with the replacements a few months earlier, in every plot and scheme he had considered for the demise of Odysseus, Eperitus had been the greatest obstacle in all of them. The captain of the royal guard was fiercely loyal, but not just because Odysseus was his king. Odysseus was also his friend, and their friendship had been forged through years of trial and danger, not just in war. As a warrior himself, Selagos knew how intense the bond between fighting men could be, so if he wanted to kill Odysseus he first had to remove Eperitus. And that, he knew, would not be easy. He had watched him in the fierce battles that had raged across the Trojan plains and knew his skill as a warrior was fearsome. That skill was enhanced by his acute senses – the gift of a goddess, or so Eurylochus had claimed during one of his tirades about the man he felt had prevented him from becoming captain of the guard.

But Selagos was also a man to be reckoned with. He had honed his weapon skills every day since boyhood, and as a pirate and a mercenary – and since on the battlefields of Ilium – he had proved himself many times as an outstanding warrior: quick, ferocious and ruthless. He was taller and stronger than either Odysseus or Eperitus, with a burning hatred that had proved the bane of all that had faced it before. But there was one other quality that gave him an edge. Just as the gods had gifted Eperitus his supernatural senses, so they had gifted Selagos with a childhood spent in poverty – and the keen instinct for survival that had come out of it. It was a gift with many facets: unbreakable hardness; pitiless brutality; deadly cunning. Hunger had driven him to murder before he was ten and his thieving had caused him to be beaten to within a heartbeat of Hades on several occasions. Survival had also cured him of his fear, so that he cared little whether he was caught or not. But brutishness and an indifference to pain did not make him dangerous: even an ox could boast those qualities. The thing that made him a perilous enemy was his willingness to get his way at all costs. And if Eperitus stood between him and Odysseus, then Selagos knew how to overcome him. For despite the man's many strengths, Eperitus also had one weakness – Astynome.

At that moment, the northern flank of Tenedos loomed up over his left shoulder. He looked at the tree-covered slopes, now a dark green in the first light of day, and made his decision.

'Eurylochus,' he said, lowering his voice and forcing a look of concern. 'We have to turn the fleet around and go back to Troy. At once.'

Despite the long years of war on land, the Ithacan galleys had been kept in good repair ready for the day when they would be able to return home. This seaworthiness showed now as the dozen ships slowly slipped past the eighty under Diomedes's command and closed on the sixty vessels of the Spartan fleet ahead of them. With the ninety craft from Pylos leading the way, the surface of the Aegean was covered with sails displaying the motifs of their respective nations: the white maiden of Sparta, the leaping fox of Argos, the eagle of Pylos and the dolphin of Ithaca. Such a spectacle had not been seen since the coming of the Greeks at the beginning of the conflict. The only time it would be seen again was when the rest of the army had finished the destruction of Troy and Agamemnon led them back to their homeland. It was a sight to put fear into the heart of any enemy, but its power was transitory. Within a few days the fleets would divide and head for different parts of Greece. As they limped into the neglected harbours from which they had launched a decade before, the bulk of each army would dissolve with the departure of homesick men to their villages and farms. Only a small core of soldiers would remain to restore their king's authority to whatever remained of the countries they had abandoned. The great army that had defeated Troy would melt away and its like would never be seen again.

Eperitus looked back as they passed the western slopes of Tenedos. The houses of the islanders looked empty now that the Greeks had abandoned their occupation. Only the handful of fishing boats in the harbour below suggested anybody might still be living there. But they were there, watching the departure of their enemies and wondering what new dangers freedom would bring. At least they had been more fortunate than their neighbours in Troy, Eperitus thought. Seagulls hovered like kites in the galley's wake, screeching at nothing as they glided and turned. Below them, dolphins arced through the glittering waves, playful as children. Eperitus glanced at Odysseus, stern and uncommunicative, then wondered whether Astynome was awake yet. He gazed towards the prow where she slept and he noticed a group of sailors on the nearest benches. They were leaning in towards each other and talking in low voices. An argument about dice, he wondered. But then the men rose as one and turned to face the helm with angry expressions. Eurylochus was at their head.

Eperitus touched Odysseus on the arm, but the king had already noticed them. He ordered Eurybates to take the steering oars and stepped down to face his cousin.

'What's this?'

'We want to know what's in the bag?' Eurylochus demanded, tipping his forehead towards the grain sack where Eurybates now stood.

'Nothing that concerns you, Eurylochus. Nothing to concern *any* of you. Now go back to your benches.'

Eurylochus's gaze wavered under Odysseus's clear green eyes, but there were a dozen men behind him and the rest of the crew were now looking on with interest, their boredom relieved by the unusual show of insubordination. He narrowed his small eyes and stared back at the king.

'I think the Palladium concerns us all, my lord.'

As he had expected, the mention of the effigy sent a stir through the ranks of Ithacans. Mild interest turned to anxiety, and Eperitus wished Astynome were behind him, rather than lying asleep in the prow with Eurylochus and his cronies standing between.

'The contents of the bag are my business, not yours,' Odysseus hissed.

'Do you deny you have the Palladium when we *saw* it with our own eyes? Open the sack and let everyone know the danger you've put us in.'

'If I want to bring the Palladium on my own ship then who are you to question me? Do you think our shared blood gives you the right to challenge my judgement before the whole crew?'

'I'll challenge the folly of any man if it puts me in danger. And having *that* on board,' Eurylochus said, stabbing a finger towards the misshapen sack, 'will imperil us all. It belongs in the temple of Athena, not here or anywhere else. Unless you return it, Odysseus, the goddess will destroy us before we get anywhere near Ithaca.'

'I took the Palladium from Troy and it's coming home with me, whether you like it or not.'

'Not if we refuse to sail the ship.'

Several voices broke out in agreement, not just among Eurylochus's followers. Some pleaded for Odysseus to take the effigy back to Troy. Others were angry and more forceful. Sensing the danger, Eperitus placed a hand on the hilt of his dagger and walked forward to face Eurylochus. Polites followed him, pulling aside his cloak to reveal the sword hanging from his waist.

'You heard the king,' Eperitus said, pressing his face so close to Eurylochus's that they almost touched. 'Sit down now, unless you want to find yourself marooned on Lemnos like Philoctetes. And I'll make sure you don't get a bow and arrows to hunt seagulls with.'

Eurylochus took a step back, only to find his retreat blocked by Selagos. Eperitus raised his eyes to the big Taphian, whose scornful smile was backed by a hard, unrelenting stare. There was no fear in that gaze and Eperitus could sense the cold violence behind it.

'Turn the ship around! We're heading back to Troy.'

Eperitus turned in astonishment to Odysseus, who had taken the steering oars from Eurybates and was wearing the ship about while the crew followed his order and adjusted the angle of the sail.

'What are you doing?' Eperitus demanded. He retreated to where Odysseus stood and spoke in a low voice. 'Back down now and you'll lose your authority in front of the whole crew.'

'I'm not backing down,' Odysseus answered. 'The crew are right, so I'm simply doing what I should have done all along. The Palladium belongs in Athena's temple, and unless I return it we'll never make it back to Ithaca.'

'But –'

'But what? Didn't you advise me to burn it, bury it or throw it in the sea? If I'm backing down, it's as much to you as Eurylochus. We're taking it back.'

Eperitus looked away in silent exasperation. The men who had defied Odysseus were seated again and Eurylochus was bathing in the plaudits of his cronies. Tenedos was now ahead of them once more, and on either side the other Ithacan galleys were turning about to follow their king, looks of confusion visible on the faces of their crews. Within moments they were passing the Argive fleet. The sailors of the numerous vessels were shouting at them and pointing westward, perplexed by their sudden change of course. Finally, bringing up the rear was Diomedes's own galley with the king leaning across the bow rail at the stern. His hands were cupped about his mouth and his voice came rolling across the restless waters.

'Where are you going?'

Odysseus raised the sack and pulled back its coarse material.

'Returning this to where it belongs.'

Diomedes was surprised to see the blackened figure, but gave a nod and waved. He had helped Odysseus steal the effigy – one of many trials they had fought through together – and was in the temple when Odysseus had defied Athena's orders. He would understand.

'May the gods be with you, my friend!' he shouted.

Odysseus raised his hand in farewell.

'He's a good man,' Eperitus said. 'One of the few to come out of that war with any integrity. I wonder when we'll see him again.'

'I don't think we ever shall,' Odysseus replied.

Chapter Four

THE FUNERAL OF
ANTICLEIA

The afternoon sun was mercilessly hot. The mourners sweated beneath their black clothing as they watched Anticleia's bier pass by, borne on the shoulders of four slaves to the sound of female lamentations. The grave-clothes were brilliantly white in the sunshine and it hurt Penelope's eyes to look at the shrouded body. It was strung about with garlands of flowers and with the eyes and mouth shut – the last duty Laertes had performed for his wife – the old queen looked as if she were merely sleeping. How different to the last months of her life when longing for her absent son had finally driven her insane. She had woken the palace almost every night with her dreams of Odysseus's death, running around the corridors with wild eyes and lips that babbled about the terrible things Morpheus had revealed to her. Penelope's love for her mother-in-law had turned to hate then. She had wished the old woman dead so that she would not have to listen to her premonitions of doom. Moreover, it seemed to Penelope that others were looking at Anticleia's suffering and wondering why their present queen did not show the same anguish for Odysseus. How little they understood. Open displays of grief were a luxury she could not afford to indulge in. She had a palace to run, a kingdom to administer. Whenever a decision needed to be made about matters of trade, or if an agricultural dispute needed settling, or if the priests felt this god or that needed appeasing, she was the one they came to. And if she allowed her fears for Odysseus to undo her, what then for Ithaca? No, when her husband returned – be it in a month or ten years – he would find her waiting for him with his throne safe and his kingdom intact. That was *her* duty.

The cries of the women on either side of her grew louder as the pallbearers reached the passage cut into the hillside. The shadows of the overhanging trees dimmed the lustre of the shroud and the crowd of mourners grew suddenly restless. Laertes raised his shaven head for one final look before Anticleia passed out of his life forever. Eurycleia, Odysseus's old nursemaid, folded her arms over the top of her head and sobbed openly. Beside her was Melantho, the gorgeous maid with a sluttish heart. She glanced carefully about herself, then rushed forward to toss more flowers on top of the body, wailing loudly as she did so. If a mere slave could feign grief, Penelope thought, why was it impossible for her to do the same? Then the bier descended into the shadow of the tomb and was gone. A procession of household servants followed with jars of wine and baskets of food to sustain Anticleia's spirit on her journey to the Underworld. They brought oil lamps, silver cups, gold plates and other objects for her comfort, while Dolius – Laertes's faithful slave and father of the faithless Melantho – carried a polished bronze mirror. What pleasure such a thing would bring to a tormented phantom, Penelope could not guess.

As the last figure passed into the vault, she reached out and laid a hand on Laertes's shoulder. He did not acknowledge her touch, just as he had refused all gestures of consolation since his wife's death, but remained standing with his eyes on the tomb's entrance. *At least you have a corpse to grieve over*, Penelope thought. *My husband was taken from me ten years ago, yet my broken heart must mourn without a grave to kneel beside. Because your hope is gone your suffering will fade with time, but mine continues in the knowledge Odysseus might yet come back.* And if he found peace in death or in the arms of another woman, she would never know about it. Instead she would have to keep her vigil in ignorance until the day she died.

She lowered her unwanted hand from Laertes's shoulder, only to have it taken up in the warm fingers of her body slave. Autonoe was a plain-looking girl with a kind smile that endowed her with a beauty beyond anything Melantho could boast. She kissed her mistress's hand and laid it back at her side.

'He means no insult, my lady,' she whispered. 'He's just afraid of facing his remaining years without Anticleia. But fear of loneliness will make him appreciate what family he has left.'

'I don't think so, Autonoe. Dolius tells me he intends to retire to his farm permanently and leave palace life behind.'

'What about his seat on the Kerosia?'

'What does it matter? Eupeithes and his cronies already have the majority on the council. Indeed, they rule the island in all but name.'

Autonoe shook her head.

'Not yet, my lady. Eupeithes may desire the throne, but he doesn't wear the crown and he won't dare do anything drastic as long as he thinks Odysseus will return. And the king *will* return one day.'

'I'm glad you have faith in him,' Penelope said. 'So few do any more.'

Autonoe had only been her body slave for three months, since the death of her previous maid, but it seemed as if they had known each other for much longer. She had already become the closest thing the queen had to a friend. And yet what could Autonoe really know about the pressure of defending Odysseus's throne against the political machinations of Ithaca's nobility? What could she begin to understand of the terrible loneliness of power? What help could she offer against the enemies who were growing in strength every day?

The pallbearers and slaves were emerging from the tomb, some holding up their hands as shields against the bright sunshine. Dolius went to Laertes's side and hooked his arm through his master's elbow, leading him down the path back to the palace. Melantho joined them, taking Laertes's other elbow and offering whispered words of comfort. The former king nodded and patted her hand, brightening at her presence in a way he would not for Penelope. As they passed, Melantho put her tongue out at Autonoe.

'She still hates you then,' Penelope said.

'She doesn't like people getting in her way,' Autonoe replied. 'When Actoris died she expected to be made your body slave, so when you picked me she resented it.'

'As if I could have chosen her when everyone knows she's sleeping with Antinous,' Penelope said with a laugh. 'She'd have told him all my secrets and he would have told them to his father. And Eupeithes already holds too much power over me.'

'I'm afraid it's not just Antinous, my lady. The kitchen girls say she's sleeping with Eurymachus too.'

'Antinous's best friend? Isn't it bad enough she married poor Arceisius before he sailed back to the war?'

Penelope watched Melantho helping Laertes along with the eyes of every male mourner following her lithe figure. Melantho knew that power was shifting from the throne to the nobility, and if Odysseus never returned to claim his kingdom then it was the younger nobles – the likes of Antinous and Eurymachus – who would eventually rise to the top. And she intended to be there with them.

Several men began blocking up the entrance to the tomb, the clack of the stones marking the end of the ceremony. All that remained now was the funeral banquet in Anticleia's honour. Laertes distrusted the nobility and had only invited a loyal core to the burial, but many more were certain to show up at the feast. Indeed, some were beginning to treat the palace as if it were their own home. It gave them the sense of power they felt they had been deprived of for so long, and which a few – Eupeithes chief among them – believed they were entitled to.

Penelope tipped the hood of her cloak back from her head and sighed. The thought of Eupeithes and his followers crowding her home filled her with dismay, but she could hardly excuse herself from her own mother-in-law's funeral banquet. Reluctantly, she joined the trickle of mourners returning to the palace, wondering how she would cope for a whole day in the presence of so many of her enemies. For if her life had been difficult since Odysseus's departure, it was unbearable without Telemachus. The fact her son would inherit the throne if his father did not return had always put him in danger, but with Eupeithes reviving his ambition to rule, that danger had become acute, forcing her to send Telemachus to safety in Sparta. And yet without him she felt lost. She could not hold him in her arms and forget for a while the responsibilities and pressures of being the queen. She could not look at his face and see the shadow of Odysseus staring back at her, reminding her that one day her husband would return to put things right. And if for ten years she had felt like a candle holding back the darkness, without Telemachus she wondered how much wick remained.

So she had done the only thing she could do that would allow him to return to Ithaca in safety. She had publicly promised to re-marry if Odysseus did not return from the war before Telemachus came of age, thereby giving her new husband the right to the throne ahead of her son. It was all part of the game she had to play to pre-serve Odysseus's kingdom for his return. And for now it had worked. Eupeithes had nothing to gain from killing Telemachus, so Penelope had sent word to Sparta for her son to return. But if Odysseus did not come back before Telemachus was twenty-one then they would lose everything.

As she approached the gates in the outer wall of the palace, a large grey boarhound ran out to greet her. He barked loudly, turned back to the gates, then changed his mind and came bounding to-wards her again.

'What is it, Argus?' she asked, kneeling to embrace him. 'What's got you so excited?'

'Mistress,' Autonoe said. 'Look.'

A tall, grey-haired man was watching her from the gateway. He wore a brown tunic and a travel-stained cloak, and a short sword hung from a baldric at his side.

'Halitherses?'

The man opened his arms and gathered Penelope up like a child as she ran to meet him.

'When did you get back?' she demanded joyfully.

'The galley's still unloading in the dock, my lady.'

'Where is he?'

'In his room, I expect. When they told him where you were – that his grandmother had died – he ran off. Too proud to let anyone see him cry, of course.'

'I'll go to him now,' she said, pausing briefly to kiss the old man on the cheek. 'Halitherses, thank you for keeping him safe.'

He smiled and nodded. 'Go and see your son; we'll talk later.'

It was as much as she could do to keep herself from running across the inner courtyard and through the palace doors, but with so many slaves around she had her dignity to maintain. As soon as the doors closed behind her, though, she ran along the darkened corridors and up the stairs to the living quarters. Telemachus was in his room, spread across his bed with his face in the furs. She sat down beside him and laid a hand on his shoulder.

'Telemachus?'

He lifted his head at the sound of her voice and she caught only the merest glimpse of his tear-filled eyes before he sat up and buried his face in her chest. At last, she felt almost whole again.

Chapter Five

THE TEMPLE OF ATHENA

Troy was no longer recognisable as the great city it had been just two days before. From the ruin of the Scaean Gates, which had witnessed the deaths of Hector and Achilles, to the entrance to the citadel on the mound above, the streets were strewn with charred rubble and the remains of ordinary things: smashed furniture, shattered pots, torn clothing, discarded sandals. Their former owners were now either enslaved or their blackened bones smouldered on the numerous pyres that filled the air with the stench of burnt flesh. Here and there, in the dirt or sprayed across the walls of the destroyed hovels, were the bloodstains that marked where they had fallen. The devastation within the great citadel of Pergamos was even worse. Here the violence had reached a climax as the Trojans had fled to find sanctuary among the palaces and the temples, and Priam's soldiers had fought to defend their king against the hated Greeks. But their resistance had only provoked a greater fury in the victors, who murdered, raped and plundered without pity. And when the last of the defenders were dead, they had taken out their rage upon the very stones about them, first with fire and then – when the flames had burned themselves out – with their bare hands, pushing and pulling at walls until they collapsed in swirls of dust.

Eperitus and Odysseus stood at the foot of the ramp that led to the second tier of the citadel and looked at the ruination before them. It was hard now to recall the rich and glorious city they had first encountered before the war, when as young men they had joined

Menelaus's embassy to demand the return of his wife. Now the high roofs had fallen in on themselves and the muralled walls were cast down, leaving nothing to obscure the ring of broken battlements about the citadel or the wide blue skies beyond them. The poplar trees that lined the ramp were burned and the palace at the top was transformed into a pile of debris. Everything was coated with dust, so that even the stunted walls that had survived the conflagration were not black but a powdery grey. And still the crash of stone echoed through the desolation as teams of soldiers, following Agamemnon's orders, tore down what remained of the ramparts.

'Come on,' Odysseus said.

Eperitus followed him up the rubble-littered ramp to the second tier. By now the sun was high above them, teasing out beads of sweat from beneath his arms and the middle of his back that trickled slowly down his skin. Little remained of the temple of Athena: its marble columns had fallen and lay at angles across the broad steps; its high roof was gone, and the remnant of its thick walls was blackened with fire; the painted statue that had stood before the temple lay toppled and headless on the rubble-strewn cobbles, its gaudy purple robes and golden trim dimmed by a thick coating of dust.

Odysseus stood over it and shook his head. 'May the gods forgive us.'

Clutching the bulky sack under his arm, he mounted the broken steps and passed through the open doorway to the temple beyond. Eperitus followed. The last time he had been there was on the night they had stolen the Palladium. Then their torches had nudged back the shadows to reveal walls painted with frescoes, a high ceiling supported by twelve thick columns and an oversized statue of Athena seated on a throne at the back. Now the columns had collapsed and brought the ceiling down with them, allowing broad sunlight to shine on the piled debris. A haze of dust still filled the air, preserved somewhat from the wind by the remnant of the walls. These were scorched, and much of the limestone plaster had fallen away, though a few murals survived. These, too, were cracked and dust-covered, the stories they told obscured and disjointed. Only in one place did Eperitus see anything recognisable: a depiction of Athena springing fully formed from the head of Zeus. But it was the only image of the goddess that remained. Even the seated statue had been destroyed by the flames and the collapse of the roof. All that remained now were its skirted knees and sandalled feet.

Odysseus glanced sidelong at Eperitus.

'We should have prevented this. I could have ordered a company of men to stand guard over the temple. That's all it needed, a bit of forethought. But I was too busy plotting an end to the war to give mind to anything else.'

Eperitus stooped down and picked a broken roof tile from the wreckage of the temple. He rubbed idly at the scorch marks with the heel of his thumb, then tossed it aside.

'You can't think of everything, Odysseus, and you certainly couldn't have prevented this. Even if you'd ordered a hundred men to defend the place while the rest of Troy burned, Agamemnon would have had it destroyed afterwards. He commanded the city to be razed, and whatever Agamemnon wants he gets. Even the gods seem powerless to prevent him.'

'They may not have stood in his way,' Odysseus replied, 'but they won't forgive him for what he's done. That's precisely why *we're* here now. I fear Athena's wrath on the journey home if we don't return the Palladium. And what man can survive the ocean with the gods against him? But if I can put it back where it belongs, she might let us sail unhindered.'

'She might and she might not,' Eperitus said. 'I suppose there's no danger if we let Troy have her talisman back, though. She'll never rise to challenge Greece again. Not from *these* ruins.'

'A foolish thought,' answered a voice from among the rubble, speaking in the Trojan tongue. 'A foolish thought, indeed. A new Troy *will* rise to face the Greeks, if not here then somewhere else. And if it doesn't, then the Greeks will go in search of one. And when the Greeks are no more, other nations will find their own Troys to face. It's the nature of nations and the nature of men. If you don't confront the Troy that lies beyond the next horizon, then you're left with the Troy within, and that might just prove the better of you.'

Odysseus laid the Palladium at his feet and placed a hand on the hilt of his sword.

'Who are you? Come out where we can see you.'

'I'm here, in plain view.'

The men turned to see the figure of a woman standing on the plinth beside the knees of the broken statue. She was short and plump, with a long cloak about her shoulders and a shawl over her head. The white wool was stained grey with the dust of the temple and her old face had an equally grey pallor. Eperitus recognised the high priestess of Athena and wondered that he had not seen her standing there before.

'Theano,' Odysseus said. 'I thought you and Antenor were with Menelaus. It's not safe for you here.'

'My husband and sons sailed with the Spartan fleet at dawn, but I slipped away in the confusion at the last moment. Athena commanded me to wait in her temple.'

'Wait for what?' Odysseus asked.

'For you, of course. My mistress knows you better than you think, and far better than you think you know her. Do you really believe returning the Palladium will be enough to appease her anger? It has saved your life – you would not have survived any voyage with it on board – but you have yet to earn the goddess's forgiveness. You betrayed her, Odysseus, and that is not something to be overlooked. Those chosen by the gods for special favour must put the gods before everything else. When she warned you not to take the effigy and defile her temple, you put your desire to return home before the will of the goddess.'

Odysseus hung his head.

'Then you remember what happened,' Eperitus asked the priestess, 'after Athena took possession of your body, here in this temple?'

'I recall finding you here and threatening to call the guards, and I remember Odysseus's sword point pressed against my throat. After that, nothing until I woke gagged and bound the next morning. But

I am not a priestess for nothing, Eperitus, son of Apheidas. My mistress communicates with me as well as through me. I understand much more than you imagine. I know she loves your king dearly, more than he deserves. Certainly more than many other men of greater power and higher renown than him.'

'Then will she appear to us again?' Eperitus asked.

'If you mean will she take possession of me, then no. You will not see the goddess until your return to Ithaca,' she said, turning back to Odysseus. 'And that will no longer be easy, my lord. Your voyage will be beset with difficulties and trials. As you were a bad guest in Athena's house, so you will face many bad hosts on your return journey.'

'Then will the oracle prove true?' Odysseus said, bitterly. 'Am I doomed not to see my family and home for ten more years?'

'That depends on what you believe. Do you now accept a man's destiny is pre-ordained; that the Pythoness is a prophet of doom? Or do you stand by what you used to believe: that his fate is dictated by his actions and the priestess's words are nothing more than a phantom of the future, a warning of what could be? If the former, then why did you disobey the goddess, knowing you were doomed not to see Ithaca for another ten years? If the latter, then the speed of your return – even whether you will see your home again or perish on the way – depends entirely on how you meet the challenges before you.'

Odysseus moved closer to the plinth where Theano stood, crunching the rubble and broken tiles beneath his sandals.

'Then I will be home soon, for my desire to see my wife and son is greater than any obstacle that stands between us.'

'That remains to be seen,' Theano replied. 'First you must learn that the will of the Olympians has to be obeyed. After all, if a king defies the gods then where does his own authority come from? To teach you the meaning of obedience, therefore, Athena has set rebellion into the hearts of your crew – all but Eperitus, whom she gave to you long ago as a friend and guardian, and a handful of others. The rest will remain disobedient unto the end, whenever or whatever that may be. What is more, she will turn their loyalties to your royal cousin, Eurylochus.'

'That oaf?' Eperitus exclaimed. 'Not even a fool would follow him.'

'The gods often make fools of men,' she retorted. 'But whatever opposition Eurylochus offers you, Odysseus, you are not to kill him.'

'I may not like the man, Theano, but I would never stoop to murdering him.'

'Never? Not even if he stands between you and your return to Ithaca?'

Odysseus did not answer, but let his gaze fall to the rubble at the priestess's feet.

'All the same, Athena will make him a thorn in your flesh, a constant reminder of your rebellion against her. You are commanded not to kill him, maroon him, chain him up or restrict his freedom in anyway, for through him she will test your loyalty to her. Do you understand?' The king nodded and Theano continued. 'But the greatest obstacles you will face are already inside you. You have become a liar, a thief and a murderer. Where is the home-loving king of a modest country now? Where is the husband and father that set sail ten years ago? You have lost yourself, Odysseus, and for a while it will be your fate to be lost from the world, both in body and name. But not forever.'

'*Then, when friends and fortune have departed from you, you will rise again from the dead,*' Odysseus said, quoting the words of the Pythoness given to him two decades before. 'So I'm to be forsaken then, by heaven, my crew, even by myself.'

Theano shook her head. 'You may have lost the goddess's protection, Odysseus, but she still favours you. In time she will forgive you, and for that you should be grateful. Many of the other kings have offended the gods and will pay for it with their lives. And though she has cursed your men to disobedience, she may yet send you help in unlooked for places. But have you forgotten Eperitus? Athena once told him to follow you to the ends of the Earth, and he has not let you down yet.'

'Nor will I,' Eperitus replied. 'Even if every last man in the army turns their back on the king, I won't.'

'It's true Athena has spared you from her curse,' Theano said, 'but disobedience does not have to be imposed by the gods. Many things can provoke it, and you are ignorant of the tests that lie ahead. Have you also forgotten that you have other loyalties, now, in Astynome?'

Her words raised a question Eperitus had not considered before: if he had to choose between his friend and his lover, where would his first allegiance lie? It was impossible to answer until he was faced with the choice, and he offered a silent prayer to Athena that he never would be.

'Here,' Theano said, moving to the edge of the plinth and beckoning to Odysseus. 'Give me that.'

Odysseus pulled the sack away to reveal the charred, misshapen lump that had caused him such trouble. He approached the plinth and passed the Palladium to Theano, who gathered it quickly but reverently in her arms. She placed it atop a mound of rubble where its wooden cradle had once been. Then, bowing her head and raising her arms in supplication to the goddess, she began to pray.

Odysseus stepped away and watched her for a moment. Perhaps he was pondering the strange outcome of his decision to defy Athena and steal the Palladium, Eperitus thought. Though his disobedience had advanced the end of the war, possibly by many years, he had lost any hope of a smooth journey home. But was he doomed not to see his beloved Ithaca for another ten years, or would he overcome the challenges without and within himself and find a swift way back? And what of those whose fates were tied up with their king's? Eperitus only knew that all things were possible with Odysseus, and for his own part he would do whatever it took to get his friend, the fleet and Astynome back to Ithaca.

'Come with us, Theano,' Odysseus said, as the old woman finished her prayer and laid her chin on her chest in silence. 'Our route will pass the mouth of the Eurotas, which leads up to Sparta.

We'll be able to return you to Antenor and your sons, if that's where Menelaus was taking them.'

Theano shook her head.

'Thank you, but my place is here in Athena's temple, ruin though it is. Antenor will understand; he has known me long enough. Make sure you come to understand, too, Odysseus. Put the gods first and everything else will come after.'

'But you'll starve.'

'The goddess will provide.'

Odysseus hesitated, then returned to the plinth and slipped the waterskin from his shoulder, laying it at Theano's knees. Fishing in the leather bag at his hip, he pulled out some oat cakes and pushed them into her hands. Eperitus followed, leaving his own waterskin with the priestess.

'You see,' she said with a smile.

'Come on,' Eperitus said, laying a hand on Odysseus's arm. 'Let's get back to the ships. We've fulfilled our obligations and I don't want to remain in this city of ghosts any longer than I have to.'

They picked their way over the mounds of broken masonry and shattered roof tiles, heading for the empty doorway. All around them they could hear the sounds of destruction from the city walls, but somewhere a bird was singing. Then, as they reached the splintered remains of the temple doors, Theano called out to them

'Wait! I have something else to say. To you, Eperitus.'

Eperitus turned and saw the priestess standing in the sunlight, surrounded by the devastation of her temple. He wondered for a moment whether he wanted to hear the words she had for him, or whether he should leave before she could prophesy a crippling doom that would only bring despair. Too many Greeks and Trojans had been destroyed by such glimpses of the future, seen darkly through the eyes of priests and prophets. And yet he knew he must listen.

'For ten years you have suffered under the oath that Agamemnon's wife extracted from you,' she began. 'When Clytaemnestra knew her husband would offer their daughter as a sacrifice to the gods, she made you swear to protect his life until he returned from the war, so that she could exact her own revenge upon him.'

Eperitus felt his heart race and a nervous sickness enter his stomach.

'How did you know about the oath?'

Theano smiled, though sadly. 'The goddess revealed it to me. I also know that you slept with Clytaemnestra ten years before in the foothills of the Taygetus Mountains, but when she realised she was pregnant she told Agamemnon the child was his.'

'I didn't know she had conceived,' Eperitus said, holding his hands out imploringly to the priestess. 'I didn't know I had a daughter. How could I? It was one night and I didn't see Clytaemnestra again for another ten years. And it was only after she made me swear that she told me Iphigenia was mine. By then it was too late to save her.'

'Agamemnon plunged his dagger into Iphigenia's heart,' Theano said. 'And you have had to suffer his presence ever since, even saving his life when you could have let him die at the hands of his enemies.'

'I have kept my oath,' Eperitus answered, coldly. 'And it is some comfort knowing Clytaemnestra will avenge our daughter's death; she brought Iphigenia into the world and has a greater claim for vengeance than I, who only knew her a short while.'

'But it is difficult for you, Eperitus – a warrior used to imposing your will by force not being able to make Agamemnon pay for his crime, or even to have a hand in his destruction.'

Eperitus felt his anger rise at what seemed to be her provocation. He nodded slowly.

'Then listen to me,' Theano continued. 'You can yet play a part. Indeed, unless you *do*, Iphigenia's murder will never be avenged. Leave now and go to Agamemnon's tent, alone. There you will find your chance for retribution.'

Chapter Six

THE CALL OF JUSTICE

A strong wind blew through the ruins of Troy, chasing clouds of dust along the narrow thoroughfares and sweeping away the columns of smoke that rose from the funeral pyres. From the gates of the citadel Eperitus could see over the battlements to the Scamander valley and the great harbour into which the river fed, now filled with the beetle-like galleys of the Greek fleet. The sky above was clean and blue, made bright by the warm mid-morning sun. It was a day full of hope and the promise of freedom, a day for raising anchors and dropping sails for the homeward voyage. But now it had come to it, Eperitus was reluctant to leave. Not for any love of Ilium, his prison for the last ten years. With the war over, there was still one thing to be done before he could take ship with Odysseus. Astynome knew it and feared it. Theano had commanded it, if only for his own sake. And Odysseus was against it.

The king leaned against the sloped wall of the tower that had once guarded the gateway. His arms were crossed and his eyes fixed obstinately upon Eperitus.

'You aren't going –' he began.

Warning shouts from further along the walls were followed by the crash of falling stone. A billow of dust rolled up the street, forcing a group of warriors to raise the corners of their cloaks to their faces. After a moment's silence, the sound of metal upon stone resumed.

'I won't allow you to go, Eperitus,' he continued. 'As your king I forbid it.'

'And as my friend?' Eperitus asked. 'How would you feel if Agamemnon had murdered your son? Will you *order* me to carry this burden for the rest of my days?'

'The question is what will killing Agamemnon achieve? It won't bring Iphigenia back to life. Even if you weren't oath-bound not to take your vengeance, murdering him will only result in your own execution. It's time to turn from the past and look to the future. And you *have* a future now, Eperitus. With Astynome. Don't sacrifice that for some hollow victory.'

Eperitus scowled and looked to where the smoke-blackened wooden horse still towered over the remains of the city it had conquered.

'I hope that after all these years you aren't intending to *forget* your oath, Eperitus?'

Eperitus shook his head. The years of war had taken much from him, but it had not taken his honour. And he would not surrender it now.

'Then what can you hope to accomplish by going to Agamemnon's tent?' Odysseus insisted.

'I don't know. Maybe I'll confront him, let him know that Iphigenia was *my* daughter, not his. I've hated living this lie for ten years. If I can't kill him I'll at least have the satisfaction of letting him know Clytaemnestra betrayed their marriage bed. Perhaps he'll begin to wonder whether Orestes is really his son, too.'

'So you'll risk his anger for petty vengeance. Is that the sort of man you've become, Eperitus? For Astynome's sake – and mine – let it go. Come back to the ships and let's sail for home.'

'No. I can't leave without seeing justice for my daughter. *That's* the sort of man I am, Odysseus. Athena knows it, even if you don't, and she commanded me to take retribution. Would you have me disobey her like you did?'

Odysseus's eyes darkened momentarily then were calm and thoughtful again. He sighed and stared at his captain.

'Theano is not Athena –'

'Odysseus!'

Three men came running up the road that led from the Scaean Gate, the gleam of their leather armour dulled by a thin layer of dust. The first was Antiphus who, despite the war being over, still carried his customary bow over his shoulder; the others were Omeros and Elpenor.

'My lord, we've been looking for you everywhere,' Antiphus said.

'What is it?'

'Hecabe's raving again. She's calling down curses on the Greek kings, including you, and it's making the men nervous.'

'Then let Eurybates deal with it,' Odysseus snapped. 'I left him in charge to deal with this sort of thing, not so that I'd be called away from more urgent matters just to play nursemaid to a madwoman.'

'A mad *queen*!' Antiphus protested. 'I'd rather take on a company of fully armed Trojans than face that old harpy. She keeps calling for Priam and her dead children, and it's making the other women cry out for their own dead. Eurybates is afraid she'll kill herself.'

Odysseus turned to Eperitus.

'That settles it. We need to leave at once and get them away from this place before they go insane with grief. As soon as we're on the open sea they'll have other things to worry about. And so will you, Eperitus. Forget Agamemnon and look to the journey home – that's an order. Come on.'

He set off at a jog down the sloping road towards the remnants of the Scaean Gate, followed by Antiphus, Omeros and Elpenor. Eperitus hesitated, debating hurriedly between the command of his king and his instinct for revenge. A shouted warning followed by the crash of another great block from the walls of Pergamos snapped him out of his thoughts and he set off in pursuit of the others. They ran beneath the shadow of the great horse and down to the gates, passing scores of Greeks busy razing the buildings where the citizens of Troy had once lived and worked, and in which many of them had died. They hurried through the gateway that had defied Agamemnon's armies for so long and which, in the end, the Trojans had torn down themselves. Reaching the plain beyond, they were confronted by the vast camp of the victors, stretching from the skirts of the city to the shores of the bay. Somewhere on the far side were the twelve ships of the Ithacan fleet.

Odysseus led the way into the mass of pitched canvas. Seeing the towering peaks of Agamemnon's tent to his right, Eperitus hesitated. A group of Trojan captives was seated nearby, among whom was a girl of nine or ten years old. Her hands were cupped in a begging gesture towards some soldiers. Irked by her pleading, one of the men kicked her into the dirt and spat on her prostrate body. After a moment, the child wiped away the tears and blood, pushed herself to her knees and held her hands out to the other soldiers.

'What's the matter with you?' the first man grunted. 'Are you stupid? We don't feed dogs; we let them scavenge for themselves.'

His comrades laughed, but the girl did not understand Greek and turned her hands back towards the man who had struck her. Angrily, he raised his fist to strike her, but before the blow could connect, Eperitus caught his wrist and held it fast. The soldier turned to him with a look of surprise that quickly turned to fury. He grabbed his sword, but before it could leave the scabbard Eperitus butted him hard in the face. The man's nose split and blood gushed down over his lips and beard. As he fell unconscious in the dust, Eperitus pulled out his own sword and pointed it at the man's comrades, whose hands were already reaching for their weapons.

'Don't be fools,' he warned them.

'You're the fool, my friend,' scoffed the tallest, Thessalian by his accent. 'There's four of us and one of you. And soon there'll just be the four of us.'

'I've faced worse odds,' Eperitus replied, glancing coolly about himself. There was no sign of Odysseus or the others. 'Now, put your weapons away and we can all go about our business.'

'Our business is with you,' said the Thessalian, casually tossing his sword from one hand to the other and back again.

The four men spread out and prepared to attack Eperitus from all sides. By the scars on their armour he knew they were seasoned veterans and that bloodshed was inevitable. Then the man whose nose he had broken groaned and sat up. Before his comrades could take another step, Eperitus grabbed his mop of black hair and pulled him to his feet, holding the blade beneath his chin.

'Stop where you are or he dies.'

The Thessalian's eyes narrowed and his lip curled up in a sneer.

'Now you really *are* being a fool,' he said, stepping forward.

'By all the gods, man, he means it, *he means it!*' squealed the first as Eperitus pressed the sharpened bronze against his throat, breaking the skin so that a trickle of red ran down the blade.

His comrades stopped. Two began edging backwards.

'Sheathe your weapons and return to your camp,' Eperitus insisted. 'When I think you're far enough away I'll release your friend.'

'And why should we trust you?' asked the Thessalian.

'What choice do you have?'

'For mercy's sake, Tekton, do as he says before he murders me,' the first man implored.

With a scowl, Tekton slid his weapon back into its scabbard, then turned slowly on his heel and walked towards the tents. The others followed. When they were no longer visible Eperitus withdrew his sword and brought the pommel down hard on his hostage's head. He collapsed for a second time and lay still.

'Sir,' said a voice at Eperitus's side.

There was blood on the Trojan girl's lip where she had been kicked, and though she now stood at a respectful distance, her hands were cupped in the same gesture she had used earlier.

'You're persistent,' he replied in her own tongue.

She's starving, he thought.

Over the unconscious soldier's shoulder was a bulging leather satchel. Eperitus cut the strap and pulled it free. Inside were several cakes of flatbread.

'Here,' he said, handing it to the girl. 'Eat your fill.'

She pulled out a cake and crammed it into her mouth, before tucking the rest inside a rip in her dress and running back to the fragile safety of the other slaves. Eperitus watched her share the meagre food between them, then signalled to an armed man stand-ing at the edge of the encampment.

'Whose slaves are these?' he asked as the man approached.

'They belong to my master, King Agapenor of the Arcadians.'

'Then keep a better watch over them, unless Agapenor wants to lose what little he's got to show for ten years of war.'

'Yes, my lord.'

The Arcadian called to two more men loitering by the edge of the camp, who picked up their spears and shields and joined him. Eperitus looked over to the gap in the tents where the Thessalians – and Odysseus before them – had disappeared. They would return at any moment; or worse still, Odysseus would appear first and prevent him from doing what he now knew must be done.

Sensing a presence behind him, he turned to see one of the slave women.

'Why did you help my daughter?' she asked.

'She was hungry.'

'That's not it. After all these years of war and hatred, why would a Greek risk his life for a Trojan?'

He saw the loss and despair in her eyes. And yet there was a glimmer of hope, too; hope that after the brutality of the past ten years some humanity might remain in the world. If not for her own sake, then for the sake of her daughter, who would grow up a slave subject to the will of her masters.

'For pity then,' he replied. 'And justice. I had a daughter of my own once, and she received neither. Until now.'

He pushed his sword into its scabbard and moved past the Trojan woman towards the outermost line of tents. Agamemnon's great pavilion was clearly visible on the far side of the encamp-ment, close to the edge of the bay. As Eperitus looked, the banner of Mycenae was opened up by a gust of wind, revealing the golden lion with its jaws buried in the throat of a fallen deer. It was an image he had always hated, reminding him as it did of his own inability to prevent Iphigenia's murder at Agamemnon's hands. Feeling a sense of urgency, he plunged into the maze of rope and canvas only to find himself blinded by the smoke of unnumbered campfires and lost in the crush of soldiers moving to and fro. It was as if they were trying to prevent him from reaching Agamemnon's tent; as if the king himself was directing them like unconscious pawns to hinder his path. As he pressed on he kept hearing Odysseus's voice. *I won't allow you to go… What will killing Agamemnon achieve? It won't bring Iphigenia back to life… Murdering him will only result in your own execution.*

'Watch where you're going, you damned idiot!'

Eperitus saw an angry face glaring at him and looked down to see a basket and several loaves in the grass at his feet. He said nothing and pushed on towards the golden lion on its field of blood, which seemed to be getting no closer. And what would he do when he got there? He grasped the pommel of his sword. Would he have to kill the guards to get to Agamemnon? For what? To taunt the king with the truth about his wife's infidelity? Or would he go further? The questions mocked his resolve, yet he pressed on, letting his instincts guide him.

Then the words of Clytaemnestra came back to him, spoken ten years ago on the clifftops overlooking the bay of Aulis where the Greek fleet was gathered for the coming war. *I promise you, the time will come when you can take your revenge on Agamemnon – the gods have revealed it to me. His downfall will begin at Troy, by your hand.*

'But how?' he asked, speaking aloud. 'How can I have revenge when your oath has tied my hands?'

For a moment his vision was blinded by a billow of thick smoke from a nearby fire. He raised his hand to swat it aside and caught his foot on a guy rope, falling to his knees. His hands plunged into warm sand, but as the smoke blew away he saw the white sails of Agamemnon's tent ahead of him, separated only by a stretch of beach.

He sat back on his heels and gazed about himself. Behind him, a slave woman was throwing clutches of dry grass onto the fire that had blinded him. She stared at him boldly, as if she knew what had brought him there. Scanning the crescent of tents that bordered the beach, he counted fewer than a dozen Mycenaean warriors, all of them busy with their mundane duties. Only two men were guarding Agamemnon's tent, where normally there would be at least ten. Their attention was fixed by the game of dice they were playing on an outstretched cloak. It could only mean one thing: the king was not in his tent. Why then had Theano ordered him to come here on the promise of retribution? He looked back at the slave woman, but she was nowhere to be seen. Thinking quickly, he retreated among the tents and circled back to a point further along the beach, beside the creaking mass of the Mycenaean fleet. There were men on the galleys repairing the neglect of a decade stuck on land. He walked down the sand to the water's edge, amid the sound of falling hammers and splitting wood, then splashed ankle-deep through the breakers until he reached the shadow of the pavilion. After another cursory glance, he approached the sail walls, knelt, and drew out two of the wooden stakes that were holding the flax into the sand. The taut material relaxed and – with a final look over his shoulder – he rolled beneath the hem and was inside.

Chapter Seven

CALCHAS'S LAST VISION

Rising onto his haunches, Eperitus pulled out his sword and looked around the tent. His eyes quickly adjusted to the gloom, revealing that he was in Agamemnon's bedroom. The tension in his muscles eased a little as he realised it was empty, but the relief was temporary. He looked down at the sword in his hand, knowing that to be caught in the king of Mycenae's private chamber with a drawn weapon would be enough to get him executed. He returned it to its scabbard, unbuckled the strap and, for want of somewhere better to hide it, lifted the corner of Agamemnon's fur-laden mattress and tossed it underneath.

'Now what?' he asked himself. *Hide behind a tapestry until he returns, then leap out and confront him? And if tempers rise, pull out the sword and defy the oath I've kept faithfully for ten years? Or wait in the main chamber like the man of honour everyone thinks I am, ready to reveal the truth about Iphigenia in front of whichever kings and commanders might be with him? Is that Athena and Clytaemnestra's idea of revenge?*

The truth was he did not know what he should do. He had expected to come to the tent, find Agamemnon and let his desire for justice lead him. But here he was with no target for his anger and no plan. Odysseus would have known what to do, of course, but then Odysseus would not have been stupid enough to be standing in the king of Mycenae's tent hoping the Fates had laid out his path for him. And Odysseus had already told him to let his head rule his heart and balance a past that was beyond his control with a future that was still his to call. A future with Astynome.

'Damn my stupidity,' he hissed, and moved to the side of the tent where he had entered.

A noise made him stop. It was something his senses had been aware of for some time, like the background sounds of hammering from the ships and the hushing of the breakers in the bay, but which had suddenly sharpened and become more urgent. It came from the main chamber of the tent, as if an animal was whimpering in pain or a child was crying for its mother. As the sound grew louder, Eperitus found his curiosity drawing him to the curtain that separated the two halves of the pavilion.

A large fire circumvented by a ring of stones crackled and spat at the centre of the vaulted chamber, smoke trailing thinly up towards the hole in the apex of the roof above. The glow from the flames was lost in the pale light that forced its way through the sides of the tent and gleamed on the captured armour and weapons displayed on its walls. Even now, though the tent had only been up a day, Agamemnon insisted on displaying his war trophies, as if to remind himself he was still the conqueror of Troy. The humble benches where the heroes of Greece had once gathered to take their orders from the King of Men remained in a circle about the hearth, flattened at one edge where the heavy wooden chairs of Agamemnon, Menelaus and Nestor sat in a line. The floor between and around the benches was layered with thick furs that left no glimpse of the sand beneath. And in their midst, lying on his back before the throne of Agamemnon, was a man in a black robe, his contrastingly white hands clutching his face and stifling his groans as he shook uncontrollably.

Eperitus watched, fascinated but uncomprehending, as the man's fists clenched and he released a long cry of anguish. Suddenly afraid that the guards outside would hear and rush in, Eperitus leapt the nearest bench and threw himself down at the man's side, seizing him by the wrists and fighting the force of his convulsions.

'Calchas!' he said urgently, recognising the priest. 'Calchas, do you hear me?'

Calchas's eyes were open but he seemed not to see Eperitus leaning over him. Froth was trickling from his mouth and down his chin, and as Eperitus tried to contain his spasms, he began thrashing his head from side to side. His back arched in protest and he kicked out with his bare feet, displacing the furs and nearly pushing one into the fire.

'Witch!' he cried, his voice hoarse but loud enough to fill Eperitus with alarm. 'Witch!'

Eperitus slapped him hard across his face and he went limp, his head lolling to one side and his eyes closed. Looking around, Eperitus saw a wineskin hanging against a wall of the tent and ran to fetch it. He raised it to his lips and took a swallow. The contents were strong and undiluted, but the powerful taste seemed to clear his thoughts. After a glance at the tent entrance, through which he expected the guards to come rushing in at any moment, he returned to Calchas and poured some of the dark liquid over his lips. The priest's tongue flicked out in response and his mouth opened like a babe seeking its mother's nipple. Then he grabbed the neck of the skin and drank greedily. Eperitus had to tear it from his grasp.

Calchas looked up in protest, his eyes in a fog until, slowly, something of his waking consciousness returned.

'Eperitus?' he croaked. 'What are you...? Where am I?'

'Agamemnon's tent.'

'Agamemnon's tent? Of course. He summoned me. Wanted to know the auspices for the return voyage, whether the gods would be with him or not. He still trusts me, you know. And why shouldn't he? Didn't I predict the war would last ten years and end in victory for the Greeks? Didn't I?'

His breath stank of wine, and not just from the mouthful Eperitus had given him. He looked at Eperitus with his black eyes, seeking reassurance as his ailing mind struggled to find some reason for his continuing existence. Eperitus stared back at him, remembering that it was Calchas who had led Iphigenia to the altar to be sacrificed. But he had never hated Calchas for his part in her death. Only ever Agamemnon.

'Yes, you did,' Eperitus acknowledged. 'But where is Agamemnon?'

Calchas clutched at Eperitus's arm with his bony hand, trying to pull himself up so he could look around the tent. As he did so, his hood dropped back to reveal his skull-like face and bald head, pale in the filtered sunlight.

'He's not here? No, that's right. He went to inspect the destruction of the walls while I made the sacrifice.'

For the first time, Eperitus noted blood on the palms of Calchas's hands. More traces were on his neck and the white robes that showed beneath his cloak. For the first time he saw the decapitated body of a snake lying close to the fire. There was no sign of its head, but a small knife gleamed among the bloodstained furs. He had heard that priests of Apollo would drink the blood of snakes to invoke visions.

'Here,' he said, reaching for a cushion and placing it under Calchas's head. 'You should rest a little –'

Calchas's hand shot up and seized Eperitus's wrist, his fingers tightening around it with a strength that seemed impossible in a body so thin and wasted. He stared at Eperitus with a look of dismal terror.

'He's in danger. Agamemnon's in danger. I have to warn him.'

'What danger? What do you mean?'

Calchas tried to pull himself up, but Eperitus held him where he was.

'Let me go!'

'Not until you tell me what you mean. Did Apollo give you a vision? What did you see?'

'Blood and death! Now take your damned hands *off* me! I have to see the king at once.'

His voice began to rise again and once more Eperitus slapped him hard across the face. He fell back onto the cushion, his whole body shaking uncontrollably. Eperitus hit him again and he lay still, staring up at the ceiling with unseeing eyes.

'Calchas. Calchas! Snap out of it man.'

Eperitus cast another glance over his shoulder at the tent door, sure the guards must come this time. But they did not, perhaps because the cries of the mad priest were nothing new to them. Then he laid his hands on Calchas's shoulders and shook him gently. He was heavy, the way a body feels when the spirit has left it and nothing remains to animate the flesh. Fearing he had hit the frail priest too hard, he was about to reach for the wine again when Calchas blinked and drew a sharp breath.

'I drank the blood of the snake,' he whispered. 'Sometimes it leads to darkness, a horrible, tormented darkness of hidden voices and half-seen shadows. But this time the god was waiting for me. He took me to a walled city on a hill overlooked by two mountains. It was a rich city once, but its wealth has dwindled with its people. An army was camped around its walls, an army returned from the war upon Troy. I passed through them to a gate guarded by two stone lions –'

'Mycenae!'

'Yes, Agamemnon's city,' Calchas said with a shudder. 'I entered the great hall where many tables stood laden with food. But the bread and fruit were shrivelled and black, the platters and cups shrouded with cobwebs. The fire had burned itself to cold ash and there was no longer any life in the heart of the palace. Then I saw a carpet, as red as Agamemnon's cloak, poking like a tongue into the hall from a side entrance. I followed it through empty corridors where the torches had long since died, up stairs and along more corridors to a doorway. The doors opened into a large bedroom, a place so cold and dark that I feared to enter. But the carpet continued to the foot of an archway at the far end of the room, disappearing beneath long red curtains that concealed whatever lay beyond. There were great slashes in the cloth like the claw marks of some dreadful beast. Blood was seeping through the gashes as if from a living wound, pulsing slowly with the dying beats of a hidden heart. It flowed down to the floor and over the threshold until I saw that I was no longer standing on a carpet but in a river of blood. If I could have cried out I would have; and if I could have turned back I would have, too. But I could not. This was not my vision to control. I was but a witness to the horror of it, a herald summoned by the gods to receive their message. And so I was drawn closer, feeling the still-warm blood between my toes and watching in fear as the curtains towered up before me. I reached out and slowly pulled them aside to reveal a small room, gloomy and silent but for a slow, monotonous dripping. As my eyes adjusted to the darkness I could see a stone bath against the far wall with something long and pale hanging from it. To my horror I realised it was an arm. A man lay up to his chest in blood, which was dripping onto the floor. His head was cloven down the middle and his pupils had rolled up into their sockets so that the eyes were white orbs in a mask of gore. Even then I knew him. It was the king, Eperitus. Agamemnon! And he wasn't alone.

'A figure stood in the corner of the room. I did not see her at first, but she was there, watching me with her dark, murderous eyes. "Are you shocked?" she asked, her beautiful face spattered with blood. "Shocked that the mighty Agamemnon should fall at the hands of a woman? The conqueror of Troy murdered by his own wife? What of the glory and honour that are due to him, you say? Here then," she said, dipping her hand into the bath and trickling the blood over Agamemnon's mutilated head. "See, I pour a libation over him, just as he would have poured a libation to Artemis before he sacrificed my daughter to her."

'Then I saw the axe hanging from her other hand, double-headed and heavy to her womanly arm. She noticed my eyes upon it and smiled as she took its weight in both her hands. I turned to run, but my foot slipped in the blood and I fell. Then she was astride me, the axe above her head. I turned and looked up at her. And then... And then –'

He looked at Eperitus and his eyes grew wide with terror, as if seeing Clytaemnestra standing over him again.

'Mercy!' he squealed, throwing his hands before his face. 'Mercy!'

'Quiet!' Eperitus demanded. 'It's me, Eperitus.'

But Calchas was out of his mind. Eperitus seized his wrists and felt his limbs shaking with a terrible force. As the priest looked back at him, he knew Calchas was still looking into the vengeful eyes of Clytaemnestra.

'No, no, no!'

Eperitus slapped him across the face. When his pitiable moaning grew in volume he clenched his fist and punched him. The seer's nose broke with a crack and blood spurted over his lips and cheeks. But the blow did not silence him. Instead he stared into Eperitus's eyes – recognising him again – and took hold of his tunic.

'Eperitus! Thank the gods. Agamemnon is in great danger. His wife plans to murder him when he returns to Mycenae! We have to warn him at once. Guards! *Guards!*'

Gripped with sudden panic, Eperitus snatched the pillow from behind Calchas's head and pressed it over his face, desperate to stifle his shouts. He looked again towards the tent entrance, all the time conscious of the priest's muffled cries and the strength of his fingers as they clawed at Eperitus's tunic and ripped the wool.

'Be silent, damn you!'

But Calchas refused to obey. His body began to thrash about and his muted shouts grew in fury, forcing Eperitus to sit astride him and push the cushion ever harder over his face. Calchas fought back, his fingernails gouging Eperitus's chest. The pain made his temper flare. He thought back to the day ten years ago when he had failed to stop Agamemnon sacrificing Iphigenia to Artemis. He remembered afresh his agony and despair, the sense of his own weakness and impotence. Gritting his teeth, he pushed harder on the cushion. He would not allow the king of Mycenae to escape justice, even if it was to be meted out by Clytaemnestra and not by his own hand. He would not allow Calchas to forewarn him!

His anger lent strength to his muscles, forcing the cushion ever tighter over the priest's face until his nails had stopped tearing into his flesh and his suffocated yells had ceased. As quickly as it had come, Eperitus's anger slipped away to leave him empty and confused. He tossed the cushion aside and looked at the dull eyes and gaping mouth of the dead man.

'Calchas? *Calchas!*'

He shook him furiously by the shoulders, then bent down and held his ear against his lips. Nothing. Pushing himself away, he staggered to his feet and stared down at the priest's corpse.

'Forgive me, Calchas, I didn't mean for this. And maybe you didn't deserve death, tortured soul that you are. But at least I know now that Iphigenia will receive justice. And before Clytaemnestra strikes Agamemnon dead, I hope she lets him know why.'

The clank of arms and a tumult of approaching voices brought him back to his senses. He dashed to the wall of the tent and, throwing himself to the floor, eased up the lip of the canvas. A large number of soldiers were marching towards the pavilion with Agamemnon at their head. Eperitus glanced back at Calchas's body and saw the blood from his broken nose and on his fingernails where he had clawed at Eperitus's chest. One look would tell Agamemnon what had happened, and the king's retribution would be swift. He looked around for somewhere to hide the body, then, seeing nowhere, felt for the place where his sword would normally have hung, instinctively resorting to thoughts of self-defence. As his hand groped at his empty hip, he heard the rustle of canvas and saw sunlight spill onto the furs by the entrance to the portico.

Chapter Eight

HECABE'S MADNESS

C alchas,' Agamemnon called. 'Where are you man? Did the gods speak to you?'

A strong hand seized hold of Eperitus's shoulder, pulling him through the curtain into the king's quarters. Another hand clapped over his mouth.

'It's me,' Odysseus hissed in his ear. 'Have the gods robbed you of your senses?'

Eperitus pulled his hand away. 'How did you know I was here?'

'Because you're as predictable as a sunrise, of course. Now, let's get out of here.'

Eperitus snatched his sword from beneath the mattress, then lifted the hem of the canvas where he had entered earlier. At that moment a shout of dismay rang out from the main chamber, causing Odysseus to take a step towards the curtain. Eperitus grabbed him by the wrist and almost pushed him under the tent wall, following behind as quickly as he could. Blinking in the bright sunlight, he looked around and saw that there were no Mycenaeans on the beach.

'Come on, Odysseus, we have to go.'

'That was Agamemnon calling out. He could be in danger –'

'He's safe. I'll explain everything later.'

They ran down the beach, following Eperitus's earlier footprints and those Odysseus had left as he had followed his captain to the tent. The trail took them to the edge of the water, where they sprinted through the surf as quickly as the wet sand would allow. Shouts of alarm from the Mycenaean camp followed them, though only

Eperitus's keen senses could distinguish the words: *Murder! Scour the tents! He can't be far!*

They turned aside, back up the beach and into the anonymity of the crowded camp. As they passed a group of men braiding strips of leather into rope, Eperitus felt Odysseus's hand on his arm, pulling him back.

'Slow down, unless you want to draw everyone's attention to us,' he said, falling into step beside his captain. 'Now, tell me what you've done and quickly.'

Eperitus described what had happened as they made their way to their own camp at the other end of the bay, glancing occasionally at the king's face for the expected look of condemnation. None came, though there was a brief wince at the mention of Calchas's death. Then, as the tragic tale ended and they saw the masts and cross spars of the already seaworthy Ithacan galleys ahead, Odysseus stopped and looked his friend in the eye.

'It's a pity for Calchas, but perhaps there's more to this than your recklessness. The gods had a hand in it, I think. Why else would Theano have sent you to Agamemnon's tent?'

'But why would they want to destroy Agamemnon? And you forget that Apollo warned Calchas of his fate.'

'Apollo has always favoured the Trojans, so Calchas's vision wasn't given out of any love he might have for Agamemnon. Perhaps he wanted you to kill the priest who betrayed Troy to help the Greeks? Perhaps Athena sent you there so you could have some part in avenging the murder of your daughter? Who knows? The gods are fickle and we are simply pieces in their games, risked and sacrificed for their petty whims. One thing's for certain, though, there's no god that will rescue you from Agamemnon's wrath if he finds out you killed his favourite seer. Those scratch marks on your chest are enough to give you away, so if you want to live as much as *I* want you to live, then we need to set sail at once.

'Eurybates!' he called out as they saw the king's squire inspecting the hull of one of the beached galleys. 'Get everyone aboard. We're leaving now.'

Odysseus's ship led the way out of the crowded harbour. Eurybates stood at the prow, ordering the oarsmen to row when there was enough space between the anchored vessels of the other fleets, or to pull in their oars and let their momentum take them through where the gaps were too narrow. Slaves sat in silent groups on deck, crammed in between the supplies and piles of plunder that had been taken from their once proud city. The faces of the women were stern as they looked upon their homeland for the last time. Eperitus was sitting on a bale of hay in the stern with Astynome beside him. Her long hair was hidden beneath the helmet she still wore and her breasts were strapped down beneath her leather cuirass, but her disguise did not fool the captive women whose bitter glances would often fall upon her. Eperitus wanted to put his arm about her, to reassure her against the resentful stares of her former compatriots, but did not want to catch the eye of any of the sailors on the vessels they were passing between. It was bad enough knowing that any moment Mycenaean galleys could be sent in pursuit of them, demanding justice for the death of Calchas, but the thought that a moment of carelessness on his part might risk the woman he loved being taken back by Agamemnon was unbearable. Besides, they did not have long to wait until they reached the open sea. Then Astynome could shed the armour that encased her beauty and together they could throw off the invisible fetters that had bound them to the war for so many years. He looked round at Odysseus standing by the twin rudders. The king smiled as he steered a way through the anchored fleets, knowing that he would soon be on his way home.

A murmur of voices caused Eperitus to look back at the deck. Hecabe had risen to her feet and was looking back at the ruin of Troy. She was a small woman, unremarkable in many ways, but her face was so tight with sorrow at the loss of her once numerous family that she commanded attention. As Eperitus watched, the old queen tore open her chiton at the shoulder and began to wail, a prolonged, ululating sound made by rapid movements of her tongue. She beat her fist against her breast while tears of anger rolled down her face. One by one the women and girls joined her, until their high-pitched lament was repeated by the slaves in the other ships of the Ithacan fleet, the sound of it rolling out across the bay to chill the blood of all who heard it. Eperitus sensed Astynome bow her head beside him and saw the tears splash over her cuirass as she began to thump the heel of her hand against the hardened leather. He felt suddenly helpless, as if at this last moment of farewell to her nation he might lose her after all. Odysseus's smile had given way to a look of grim endurance. He glanced at Eperitus, saw the doubt in his captain's eyes and shook his head.

'Let them say their goodbyes,' he said.

After what seemed an eternity, the twelve galleys rowed clear of the enclosed bay and out towards the open seas.

'Set sail!' Eurybates ordered, his voice cutting across the Trojan lament and silencing it.

The crew pulled in the oars and rushed to their stations – barging their way roughly past the captives – and muddled through the half-forgotten routine of releasing and trimming the sail to distribute the wind pressure. Eurybates strode through the chaos to join Odysseus and Eperitus at the helm.

'The north wind's not so strong today. We should have gone with Nestor and the others when we had the chance.'

There was a hint of criticism in his tone, but Odysseus brushed it off.

'All the better if we're heading north. We don't want a strong wind fighting us all the way.'

'North?' Eurybates and Eperitus asked together.

'But my lord,' Eurybates continued, 'that's against the current. We'll have to row and it'll tire the men out. It'll be much quicker to go south.'

'That was Nestor's recommendation,' Eperitus agreed. 'Heading north'll add days to the voyage. I thought you were desperate to get home.'

'I am,' Odysseus said with a look that warned him not to question his desire to see Ithaca again. 'And even a few more days will be an agony. But how can I go back with a handful of slaves and what few trinkets the Trojans didn't sell off to fund the war? Ten years and hundreds of Ithacan lives for this?' He waved his hand towards the slaves and tarpaulin-covered treasure on the deck. 'No, at the least I intend to raid the coast as we go, attacking Priam's Thracian allies and taking enough plunder to save our faces when we return. Now, Eurybates, set the correct course and if necessary get the men back to their oars. Am I clear?'

His squire nodded and turned to call out the orders. The crew understood at once what they meant and for a hesitating moment looked at their king for confirmation. Eperitus noted the rebellious light in Eurylochus's eyes, but as he opened his mouth to speak, Selagos laid an oversized hand on his shoulder and pushed him down onto one of the benches. The Taphian gave Eperitus a strange look, then took his seat beside Eurylochus and reached for the oar. Eperitus looked down at Astynome.

'Are you alright?'

The tears had washed a path through the thin layer of smoke and grime on her face, but her expression was determined.

'I feel better than I have in a long time, my love. And now, am I allowed to take this cursed war gear off yet? I'm sick of the smell of leather and someone else's –'

She fell silent. Not noticing at first, Eperitus looked over at the mouth of the straits they had just left behind. The masts of the once mighty Greek armada were still visible in the harbour beyond. The other eleven galleys of the Ithacan fleet were following behind Odysseus's ship, their oars slipping out into the waves again as they beat northward against the current. To his relief there was no sign of any pursuit.

'Yes, take it off –'

Astynome's hand wrapped about his wrist and squeezed it. Following her gaze, he saw Hecabe walking towards them. A woollen cloak had been thrown about her shoulders to cover her torn chiton, but she seemed not to notice it and it fell away as she approached. Astynome stood, her eyes wide with uncertainty as the queen came closer. Hecabe passed her and climbed onto the bale of hay, looking out at the coast of Ilium and the green sea that lay between.

Odysseus rushed forward and laid a hand on the old woman's arm.

'Hecabe,' he said, his voice calm and gentle. 'Hecabe, come down.'

She looked back down at him, her expression lost in personal torment. Then something inside her recognised him, and a look of pity entered her eyes.

'We are cursed, you and I. Cursed to suffer. Do you think that because your ships are laden with Trojan plunder you have somehow been justified by the gods? Do you think that your survival where so many have perished means their favour is upon you? No, Odysseus. I remember my happiness each time I gave birth to one of Priam's children, my pride as I watched them grow into princes and princesses, my joy when Hector returned from his first battle with blood on his armour and the light of victory in his eyes. I thought then that the gods had blessed me above all women. Only now do I see that by raising me up, they simply intended to make my fall all the greater. Fifty children I bore my husband; now not one remains to give me comfort. *Not one.* The same fate awaits you, Odysseus, great king though you are. The gods will take everything from you – your fleet, your plunder, your friends – before you find their favour again. But they will never give me back my children. Never!'

Odysseus, seeing what was in her mind, grabbed at her arm. But Hecabe was too quick. She leapt onto the side of the ship, tried to balance as she stared out one last time at the pillars of smoke that marked her beloved Troy, then lost her footing and fell. Eperitus leaned against the rail, with Astynome, Odysseus and many others pressing either side of him. Hecabe was in the water, her face and limbs pale amid the dark waves as they thrashed about in the last instinct that remained to her – to save her own life. Odysseus threw aside his helmet and tried to unbuckle his armour, but it was too late. The current was pulling her away rapidly, though her screams still came to them on the wind. Within moments she had fallen beneath the oars of another galley, the spray from the blades briefly turning pink as the last queen of Troy sank beneath their murderous strokes.

book
TWO

Chapter Nine

THE LAND OF THE CICONES

Hecabe's death subdued any spirit of resistance that might have remained in the Trojan women. From that point on they sat despondent on the deck, between the protesting livestock, the sacks of grain, the clay pithoi and the precious plunder beneath its leather tarps. Their mournful eyes looked out at the hills on the peninsula to the east, watching as they slipped away from the home they had known all their lives and plunged further on into an unfamiliar world. With the queen's demise, though, the fortunes of the Ithacans seemed to change. The usual north wind fell away and a new breeze blew in from the south-east, filling out the sails and allowing them to ship their oars. Through what remained of the afternoon, they sailed across the mouth of a great bay with the island of Samothrace to the west, until they reached the inlet of a large river. Here they beached the galleys and made camp as the sun was setting.

While the men slaughtered goats and sheep, Odysseus asked Eperitus to join him by one of the fires. As they sat beneath a red sky and ate the food their men brought them, the king traced lines in the sand to show where they were. A little further down the coast was the island of Thasos, and on the mainland opposite were the towns and villages of the Cicones, Priam's former allies. But they were allies whose warriors had perished inside the walls of Troy, leaving their homes virtually defenceless. Easy prey even for a single galley, Odysseus suggested with a grin, let alone twelve.

They discussed their plans until dusk and then summoned the captains of the other ships to explain the details of the next day's attack. The night sky was awash with stars by the time Eperitus found the pile of furs where Astynome was sleeping. She woke at his touch and they made love silently before falling asleep in each other's arms.

Eperitus gripped the rail and watched the beak of the ship slicing through the waves below. The beach was getting rapidly nearer and he braced himself for the impact that would soon come. Glancing up, he could see the walled city nestling between tree-covered hillsides. Thin trails of smoke drifted up into the clear sky while flocks of goats picked their way across the surrounding fields. Everything gave the impression that the city's inhabitants were blithely going about their daily business, ignorant of the Ithacans' approach. Then the gates banged open and a flood of men rushed out. The midday sun glinted on their armour and Eperitus felt the old, familiar tug of nerves in his stomach.

'Get ready,' Odysseus shouted.

The galley scraped against the soft beach below and then thudded to a sudden stop. Eperitus used its momentum to throw himself over the side and land waist-deep in the water. His legs buckled with the impact and the spears almost slipped from his hand, but somehow he staggered on and regained his footing as he splashed his way up through the breakers. For a moment he felt alone, with the empty beach ahead of him and the army of the Cicones filing into their ranks on the plain beyond. Then he heard the screams of fear from the women and children in the galleys behind, followed by the low roar from the throats of the other Ithacans on either side of him. A quick glance over each shoulder revealed a sea full of men, their legs kicking up white spray as they rushed to gain the beach. Polites was among them, towering head and chest over the others. Antiphus was already fitting an arrow to his bow, while beside him Omeros and Elpenor were struggling beneath the combined weight of their armour and weaponry.

'Form up on those dunes,' Odysseus shouted from behind Eperitus's right shoulder. 'I want a wall of shields before the Cicones can get anywhere near us.'

A familiar whickering sound filled the air above, followed by the hiss of arrows hitting the water. Others rattled onto the galleys behind, where a woman cried out in sudden pain and was silent. Eperitus told himself it was not Astynome and ran on, his sandals finding the beach and sprinting up the slope towards firmer ground. It had been a hasty volley, fired at long range and with no audible casualties among the men, but the solitary shout from the ships had put a spark in the kindling of his temper. He thrust his shield before him. Its half-moon shape offered less protection than the shield he had left behind in the ruins of Troy, but over its upper rim he could clearly see the ranks of the Cicones marching towards him. His experienced eye estimated three ranks of a hundred men each, a greater force than they had anticipated, though still only half their own number. He could also see many grey beards among them and an equal number whose clean jaws betrayed their youth. The glint of armour he had seen from the prow of the galley had been deceptive, too. Not one in three wore breastplates and only half carried shields; the second and third ranks probably had none at all. He winced. It would be a massacre.

'How many?' Odysseus asked, falling in beside him and locking his shield alongside Eperitus's. Omeros arrived on his other side, followed by Elpenor and Antiphus.

'Three hundred. A mixture of old men, boys and farmers.'

Odysseus sensed the disdain in his voice.

'The easier the fight, the less of our own dead there'll be.'

Another badly aimed rain of arrows fell, clattering off the wooden hulls of the ships. A man further down the hastily forming Ithacan line fell heavily onto the sand. Eperitus glanced at him, then back at the galleys where the women and children were crying out in fear.

'We're too close to the ships,' he said. 'We need to attack now.'

Odysseus looked across at his small army. Many were still jumping from the ships or wading through the surf. He had seen the danger, though, and must have known what lay at the heart of his captain's anxiety. Reaching down to his belt, he touched the old, dry chelonion flower that had been there since the war began – a reminder of home – and raised his sword.

'For Ithaca!' he shouted.

The men roared their response and advanced. Another wasteful volley fell among them, easily parried by their upraised shields. But Eperitus recalled the woman's scream that had rung from the galleys after the first arrows had fallen and he quickened to a jog. They were still a distance away from their attackers, who were on higher ground, but the Ithacans picked up the pace easily. The ground thundered with their footfalls and the air rang with the clank of armour. As they closed, the others could see what Eperitus's eyes had picked out from the beach: the frightened faces of their enemies, a force stripped of true warriors by their alliance with Troy and leaving behind only boys and old men, the crippled and the cowardly. At their backs was a one-armed man on horseback, shouting orders in a dialect Eperitus could not understand. But he heard the authority in his voice and knew that – for now at least – the men under his command still feared him more than they did their enemies.

More arrows sprang out from behind the Cicones' front rank, the range closer now but their aim panicked by the fast-approaching Ithacans. A black-feathered barb thumped into Eperitus's shield, its bronze tip piercing the fourfold leather and nosing through the wicker lining. Behind him a voice cried out in sudden agony but was quickly lost beneath the war cry of six hundred warriors. Soon they would be within range of their enemies' spears, the moment when they were most vulnerable. The man on the horse knew it, too, and rode rapidly behind the lines of his men, calling out encouragement in his booming voice. He raised his sword in his remaining hand, ready to give the order.

'Spears!' Eperitus shouted.

Without stopping, the Ithacans readied spears in their hands and hurled them at the Cicones. The range was long and their target uphill, but many found targets among their poorly armoured enemies. All along the Cicones' ranks men fell or shrieked in pain as sharp bronze tore through flesh and shattered bone. Against a better opponent the volley would have come too early, but against the frightened militia it was enough. A cry of panic rose up and men began streaming away from the rear ranks, back towards the safety of the town. Their commander shouted at them to hold, even bringing his sword down onto the head of a fleeing boy and slicing away the top of his skull. But it did no good. A few spears were thrown hastily from what remained of the front rank and then they, too, turned and ran.

A victorious cry erupted from the Ithacans. Desperate to catch the Cicones before they could reach the gates, they forgot the weight of their armaments and broke into a sprint. The commander of the militia, deserted by his men, watched them advance with eyes that showed no fear. Raising his bloodied sword before him, he spurred his horse down the slope towards the Ithacans. The blade fell once, removing a man's forearm in a spray of blood, then dozens of hands seized hold of him and pulled him from his mount.

Eperitus was the first to reach the line of dead and dying Cicones. Clutching his remaining spear, he ran after their fleeing comrades, desperate to reach the gates before they could be shut against him. But while the Cicones were still streaming across the plain, unseen hands closed the heavy wooden portals with a bang that shook the dust from their thick planks. Shouts of protest erupted from the betrayed militia, quickly turning to pleas of desperation as they heard the Ithacans rushing up behind them. Many realised they could expect no mercy and turned with weapons raised.

An old man pulled the sword from his belt and ran at Eperitus, who knocked the thrust aside with the flat of his shield and drove the point of his spear through the man's chest. Drawing it out again he swung the shaft into the face of a second attacker, who crashed to the ground with a grunt. Weapons clashed all around as more Ithacans joined the fray. A young Cicone threw himself at Eperitus's feet, clutching at his legs and pleading incoherently for mercy. Eperitus struck at him with the lower edge of his shield but the boy clung on, tears of pain and fear flowing down his cheeks. As Eperitus raised his shield to strike again, two more Cicones rushed at him with their spears levelled. The first pierced his shield and almost tore it from his arm; the second he turned aside with his own spear, before slashing at the Cicone's woollen tunic with the return stroke. The man's stomach opened, spilling blood and intestines over his legs as he crumpled into the dust.

The first attacker had abandoned his spear and now rushed at Eperitus with a dagger. Eperitus caught the man's wrist and dropped his own weapon as he struggled to prise the blade from the Cicone's hand. For a moment their faces were so close he could smell the wine on the man's breath. Pushing him away, he aimed a punch at the side of his head. The Cicone blocked it with his forearm, then closed quickly and butted Eperitus in the face. Stunned, Eperitus staggered back and caught his heel on the boy who was still clinging to his leg.

He fell heavily, pulling his assailant on top of him. The point of the dagger was now pressing against Eperitus's side, held back only by the thick leather armour that had turned so many other blades in his years of fighting. The man grunted something, his bearded cheek pressed against Eperitus's face as they matched their strength against each other. In desperation, Eperitus bit into the exposed flesh, driving his teeth through the hair and skin until he felt the warm blood burst into his mouth. The Cicone tore himself away with a bellow of pain and rage, releasing his hold on the dagger and wrenching free of Eperitus's grip as he pressed his hands to the wound. Eperitus spat out the flesh he had torn off and drove his fist into the man's face, sending him rolling aside in the dust. Grabbing his discarded spear, he stumbled to his feet ready for the next attack, only to see his adversary staggering off through the confused melee. Then an instinct warned him of danger. Turning, he saw the boy who had pleaded for mercy with the abandoned dagger in his hand. Eperitus instinctively raised his weapon, impaling the boy as he leapt. His body slumped to the ground, the spear buried in his chest.

'Eperitus!' Antiphus was beside him, an arrow fitted in his bow. 'We need you.'

Without waiting, he ran towards the town. The last of the Cicones were being dealt with by the Ithacans, so Eperitus followed the archer to the walls. These were low and poorly maintained, but they were still twice the height of an ordinary man and the Ithacans had brought no ladders. Polites crouched with his back against the wall and his hands cupped beneath Odysseus's foot. Then, standing to his full height, he threw the king up towards the ramparts. Odysseus caught the top of the wall with both hands and began pulling himself up. A lone figure appeared and ran along the top of the battlements towards him, his woodman's axe raised over his head. Antiphus's bow twanged and the man fell backwards, his dying scream silenced by the arrow in his throat. Odysseus spared the archer an appreciative glance before hauling himself onto the parapet. Another Ithacan stepped up to Polites and was thrown upwards in the same manner, but before the next man could follow, Eperitus pulled him back by the shoulder and placed his foot into Polites's hands. A moment later he was being launched up towards the ramparts, catching hold of the rough stone and hoping it would not crumble away before he could pull himself onto the battlements.

Two pairs of strong hands grabbed him under the armpits and lifted him up.

'All we need to do is open the gates and the city is ours,' Odysseus said. 'This way.'

He pointed to a flight of stone steps leading to the town below. A quick glance showed Eperitus several dozen stone buildings, the streets between them filled with people fleeing towards another gate on the far side of the encircling walls. He pulled his sword from its scabbard and followed Odysseus and the other soldier to the top of the steps. Below them a handful of Cicones were leaning their weight against the town gates, trying to relieve some of the pressure on the crossbar. The Ithacans sprang down the stairs and attacked them, killing a man each before they could draw their weapons. Eperitus stooped and pulled the shield from the back of his victim, slipping it onto his arm just in time to fend off a blow from one of the remaining Cicones.

'Greek pig!' the man said, speaking in a barely intelligible form of the Trojan tongue. He spat into the dust and pointed to the left side of his face, where the cheek was hideously scarred and the ear missing. 'A Greek gave me this at Troy. Now *you* can pay for it!'

He threw his weight onto his front foot and thrust the point of his sword at Eperitus's chest. Eperitus knocked the attack aside with his shield, fell onto his right knee and swung his own weapon in a low arc at his opponent's legs. The blade sliced through his ankle and the man – a look of disbelief frozen onto his face – fell sidelong onto the dusty flagstones. Eperitus dispatched him with a sword thrust to the heart. Odysseus and the other Ithacan had already finished the two remaining Cicones and were lifting the crossbar from its brackets on the back of the gates. At once, the doors were pushed inward by a surge of Ithacans. Eurylochus and his Taphian henchman, Selagos, were at their head.

'The town's ours, lads,' Eurylochus called out, not noticing Odysseus. 'Take whatever you want – gold, women, *wine!*'

The men behind him cheered and flooded into the streets, already littered with the flotsam of a population that had fled for their lives. Odysseus leapt halfway up the stairs to the battlements and called out in a booming voice, stopping the Ithacans in their tracks.

'*I* command this army, *not* Eurylochus. No-one is to get drunk. I will not have a repeat of what happened at Troy. Captives are valuable and will be treated with respect. All plunder – women, children, wine, gold, *anything* – is to be taken down to the beach for fair distribution among the ships later.'

'Fair by whose standards?' Eurylochus challenged. 'The standards of kings? We saw how Agamemnon shared out the plunder from Troy – half for him and half for everyone else!'

'We want what we've fought for,' another voice shouted to murmured agreement.

'So long as I'm your king you'll follow my orders!' Odysseus said. 'And if anyone else wants to question my authority let him do it at sword point or keep his silence. That includes you, cousin.'

He stared at Eurylochus, who met his gaze with a glimmer of rebellion in his eyes. Selagos stood behind him like a tower of rock, his face hard and fearless. Eperitus tightened his grip on the hilt of his sword, sensing trouble. But at the moment before Eperitus thought Odysseus's patience would break, Eurylochus broke eye contact and turned to the men around him.

'Come on, lads. We have our orders. No wine. No women. Your reward is to collect the king's plunder, won for his glory alone.'

They began to disperse in groups, some of them grumbling aloud, others casting sullen looks over their shoulders as they went. Eperitus joined Odysseus on the steps.

'Did you hear him? He speaks as if the army's his, not yours.'

'Eurylochus is a fool,' Odysseus replied. 'It's the men I'm worried about. Too many were ready to take his side.'

'The war has got to them. We've been too long away from home, paid too high a price.'

'It's true. And no man should be exposed to his king for too long. They begin to see his weaknesses. But this is more than war-weariness, Eperitus. This is the beginning of Athena's curse. Their disobedience will grow in time, and as it does they will turn to Eurylochus for leadership.'

'Well, better him than someone with intelligence, I suppose. But I still can't believe they'll choose him over you, not after all you've brought them through.'

Odysseus sheathed his sword. 'If the gods make them tire of me then they'll follow anyone with a shred of legitimacy. And Eurylochus has royal blood.'

'But he's a buffoon.'

'Maybe so, but he's being guided by someone with a sharper mind.'

'You mean the Taphian, Selagos?'

Odysseus put a hand on Eperitus's shoulder and led him down the steps.

'Come on, I need to see the captives are being well treated.'

'You realise, of course, there won't be anyone left but the old and the crippled,' Eperitus said with a smile. 'The ones worth capturing left through the other gate while the battle was going on, taking their wealth with them. Hardly worth taking the long route home, in my opinion.'

'Perhaps you were too busy fighting old men and children to notice Eurybates and a hundred warriors going around the hills to the northern gate,' Odysseus said, returning Eperitus's smile. 'After all, there's always another gate to any town. Unfortunately for the Cicones, Eurybates will have been waiting for them when they left.'

They moved into the press of single-storey mud brick houses, following a narrow street lined with empty animal pens and the abandoned stalls of farmers, fishermen, potters, sandal makers and other merchants. The smells of woodsmoke, raw fish and freshly baked bread told Eperitus their attack had caught the townsfolk completely by surprise. He had not been this close to normal, civilised life for a long time and regretted his part in frightening away the men, women and children who should have been thronging the streets. In his youth he had disdained everyday human existence and thirsted for the excitement and glory of battle. But here, in this place that had only a short while before been filled with life, he understood what men really fought for. Encamped beyond the walls of Troy he had only known a war of honour and renown, not the war of preservation that the Trojans had fought. And their war was the more honourable one. If the achievements of Hector and Paris had earned them glory, it was for the love of their homes and families that they had fought. Could there be any better reason for a man to take up arms and kill his enemies?

Of course, Odysseus had known that all along.

The sights and sounds of a city in turmoil were becoming rapidly more obvious. A jar flew out of a doorway and smashed against the wall opposite, splattering it with olive oil and shards of clay. A chair followed, followed by a peal of laughter. Further along the street, wooden stalls had been turned over and the goods on them left to spoil in the dust. From the alleys on both sides came shouts and sounds of destruction. Odysseus picked up a wheel of flatbread, brushed away the dirt and tore off half for Eperitus.

'We should be thankful the battle wasn't harder,' he said. 'The men would have been torching the place by now and looking for blood.'

As the king spoke, a woman's scream tore the air. Eperitus's muscles tensed and he drew his sword.

'Leave it,' Odysseus said. 'We need to find the other gate and see to the safety of the prisoners.'

'Let Eurybates take care of them,' Eperitus replied, trying to calculate where the scream had come from.

'You can't save every woman that falls victim to a lust-filled warrior.'

The woman screamed again.

'Well, I can save this one,' Eperitus said.

He ran off down a side alley. Footsteps behind him told him Odysseus was following. The narrow passage twisted confusingly between recently deserted hovels, crossed a street filled with Ithacans and continued on the other side.

'You'll never find her,' Odysseus called after him.

The woman screamed again, just a little way ahead now, and was followed by the wail of a child. Eperitus stumbled into a small square surrounded by large houses with porticoed entrances. A walled well was at the centre. On the floor was the body of a man dressed in white robes. A soldier stood over him with his sword drawn, while by the well was a half-naked woman, her chiton hanging in shreds about her waist. She was clutching a small boy to her chest, but another soldier tore him from her arms and flung him aside. As the woman cried out, a third soldier seized hold of her and pressed his mouth to hers, his hand fumbling against her bared breasts.

It was a sight Eperitus had seen many times before, but the woman's scream had reminded him of the shriek from the ships as the first volley of arrows had overshot the beach. All he could think of was whether the scream had belonged to Astynome, and the thought enraged him. With a shout, he raised his sword and ran at the Ithacan standing over the dead man. The soldier turned with an expression of confusion, then fear, as he saw the sword in Eperitus's hand. Eperitus swung with all his strength, intending to kill the man, but before the blade could slice through his neck a shield blocked its path.

Odysseus threw Eperitus's sword back and turned to the three soldiers.

'Go, before I kill you myself.'

'Yes, my lord,' said the man whose life he had saved, before scuttling away with his comrades.

As they fled, the woman ran to her child and took him in her arms, comforting him with her kisses. Eperitus took control of his rage and sheathed his sword.

'Odysseus, I'm –'

'Don't be,' the king said, kneeling by the dead man. 'They deserved death, but if news of it had reached the other men... Zeus's beard, he's alive!'

The man, who had been lying on his front covered by his white robes, coughed hoarsely and pushed himself up onto his elbows, his forehead still resting in the dirt.

'Maron!' the woman shouted.

She ran over with the child still clutched in her arms, then held back out of fear of the red-haired warrior kneeling over her husband.

'Go to him,' Odysseus said in the Trojan tongue, which she seemed to understand.

The man sat back on his heels and raised his head groggily. There was a wound on his bald scalp and blood had trickled down in dark rivulets over his face. As he saw his family he burst into tears and opened his arms to receive them. The woman kissed his forehead repeatedly and then began to fuss over his wound. After a while the man spoke to his wife, who moved away with the child still in her arms.

'Why did you save us?' he asked in Greek, looking at Eperitus.

'I… I heard a scream and –'

'We were told to look for you,' Odysseus interrupted, winking surreptitiously at Eperitus.

'You were *told* to look for me?' Maron asked.

'We were sailing home from Troy when I saw the smoke from your city. I ordered my galleys to attack at once, but as we prepared to land a voice spoke to me. It said the city would be given into our hands as a punishment upon its people. They'd neglected their sacrifices to Apollo –'

The bald-headed man looked up to the heavens and groaned.

'I *told* them to sacrifice the best of their herds, but they didn't listen. They thought they could cheat Apollo with a few scrawny offerings, and now they have paid the price.'

'But not you,' Odysseus said. 'You *are* Maron, son of –'

'Son of Euanthes. Yes, that's me.'

'Apollo has ordered me to spare you because of your faithful service. In return he said you would reward us with rich gifts.'

Maron stood and laid his hands on Odysseus's shoulders.

'My friend, you will have gold and silver worthy of a king. And something *better* than gold and silver.'

Eperitus laughed. 'What is better than gold or silver?'

'A dozen jars of my best wine, that's what. The gold and silver for my life and the greatest wine in all of Ismarus for the lives of my wife and child. When you taste it you'll agree it's better than any precious metal. And it's potent, too.'

'Then take us to your house and we'll celebrate your deliverance,' Odysseus said, placing his arm around Maron's shoulders.

'My home is beside a sacred grove on that hillside,' the fat priest said, pointing to one of the low peaks that surrounded the walled town.

Eperitus saw a thin trail of smoke rising up from a ring of trees close to the summit.

'It's a long way, Odysseus,' he said. 'Shouldn't we stay here and watch over the men?'

'Eurybates will take charge,' Odysseus replied. 'They won't miss us while we escort Maron and his family back to the safety of their home.'

Eperitus listened to the sounds of destruction and revelry from the middle of the town, but knew Odysseus would not be parted from Maron's promise of treasure. He shrugged his shoulders and nodded his agreement.

Chapter Ten

SACRIFICES ON THE BEACH

The cart's axle had been well greased with pig fat and barely made a squeak as the two oxen pulled it slowly along the road that led down to the town. Out of boredom, the slave on the bench between Odysseus and Eperitus whacked his stick across the beasts' backs. He was an Aethiope, tall and thin with grey hair and a face that seemed incapable of expression. Ahead of them the sun had almost disappeared behind the hills, leaving a trickle of red gold visible through the trees. The town was in shadow, but the plain to the south was alight with scores of campfires. Eperitus could see hundreds of figures moving between them and smell the familiar aromas of roast meat, freshly baked bread and woodsmoke. The Ithacan galleys remained where their prows had bitten into the sandy beach, though the sails had been stowed and the masts were bare.

'The city would have been safer,' Odysseus said. 'We still don't know who else inhabits this country.'

'It's getting close to dusk, too,' Eperitus agreed. 'A good time to attack, if anyone had a mind to.'

'I can't see guards on the walls.'

'There aren't any,' Eperitus confirmed. He glanced at the slave, whose face was as impassive as ever. 'But Eurybates is sure to have posted lookouts on the hills.'

'I hope so.'

Nobody had stopped them, though, Eperitus thought, looking back up into the trees they had left behind. He watched the shadowy boles, half expecting to see enemy warriors moving stealthily between them. The only sign of life was the thin trail of smoke coming from the hearth in Maron's house, hidden behind the rise of the slope above.

He looked into the back of the cart. Beneath the tarpaulin were seven talents of gold, a silver mixing bowl and twelve jars of the priest's wine. Maron's boasts about its potency had not been exaggerated. One cup, heavily watered down, had been enough to convince Eperitus he should drink no more, despite the powerful desire to taste it on his lips again. Odysseus, too, had resisted all Maron's attempts to get them drunk, knowing as well as Eperitus that for all his rich gifts the man was still an enemy whose people they had slain or taken into slavery. Eperitus's spirits still felt light, though they had drunk the wine at midday, and even now the smell from the jars made his mouth water for more.

He looked back at the town. The rutted track from the hills had levelled out and they were following it towards the north gate.

'Go around,' Odysseus told the slave, pointing to a fork in the road that followed the circuit of the walls.

The Aethiope tapped his stick hard against the flank of one of the oxen and slowly the pair moved to the right. They heard the sounds of the camp long before they saw it: singing; a woman's scream met by male laughter; the cries of distressed livestock. Odysseus gave Eperitus a concerned look. When eventually the cart edged round the walls, the sight before them was worse than either of them had feared.

'This is Eurylochus's work,' Eperitus said.

Odysseus sat in silence, staring at the shambles before them. Large numbers of Ithacans were staggering about arm in arm, singing and laughing as they shared skins of wine. Others had women in their arms, though whether Trojans or Cicones Eperitus could not tell. Not a few had already passed out from the drink and were lying here and there like dead men, while some had taken women to the edges of the camp and were forcing themselves upon them.

Odysseus shook his head.

'No, this is *my* work. I should have known better than to leave them to their own devices.' He laid a hand on the Aethiope's shoulder. 'Take the cart down to that ship at the centre of the beach. You see those men standing guard? Tell them to load everything on board and once they've finished go straight back to your master. Do you understand?'

The slave nodded, and as soon as Odysseus and Eperitus had jumped down from the bench he smacked his stick across the oxen's backs and moved off in the direction Odysseus had ordered.

'This is dangerous,' Eperitus said. 'If we go in and start knocking some heads together there's some who might not take it so well. I saw it enough times back at Troy, especially in the last months.'

'True, but *they* weren't Ithacans. And there's still some order here. There must be a hundred men standing guard by the galleys, and I see women on deck. These ones in the camp must be Cicones.'

'I hope so. If any man has laid a hand on Astynome he'll pay with his life.'

'She's safe. There are good men who would lay down their own lives for her sake – Polites, Antiphus and Eurybates among them.'

'So, what do you suggest we do?'

'Find my cousin,' Odysseus answered. 'He'll be at the heart of this mess, like you say, but above all we must keep our tempers. Whatever you do, don't draw your sword.'

They marched towards the nearest campfire, where a dozen soldiers were singing loudly. Three women sat forlornly on the outer edge of the group, their nakedness barely covered by the cloaks they wore. As the two men approached, the singing stuttered to a halt and the soldiers glanced guiltily at the king.

'Who gave you permission to drink wine?' Odysseus asked.

Most looked down at their sandals, but a few dared to hold his gaze.

'Everyone else was, so why shouldn't we?'

'*My lord*,' Eperitus hissed.

'My lord,' the soldier added.

'After ten years fighting we've earned it,' said another.

'Maybe, but not without my permission. Is that clear? There'll be other towns beyond those hills, neighbours to these women.' Odysseus pointed to the three Cicones seated behind the Ithacans. 'They could be mustering their forces right now, ready to avenge their countrymen. Instead of drinking yourselves stupid you should have been loading these women onto the ships and making ready to sail.'

'So why weren't you here to give the orders, my lord?'

The speaker was a squat figure with a low forehead and deep-set eyes. Eperitus tore the wineskin from his hands and slammed his fist into his face. The man fell where he had sat and lay there unmoving, blood pumping from his nostrils. Eperitus poured the wine over his face and he sputtered back into consciousness.

'Clean yourselves up and get back to your galleys,' he snapped. 'We're leaving before nightfall. And find those women some clothes if they're to join the rest of the slaves on the ships.'

The men nodded sulkily, while two of their number helped their comrade to his feet.

'That *wasn't* what I meant by keeping your temper,' Odysseus said as they walked away.

Others had witnessed the scene and the singing and laughter close at hand had faltered into silence. Eperitus noticed men tossing away their wineskins or pointing their women in the direction of the ships, but many more were either too drunk to realise what was happening or had no intention of giving up their revelry. They looked sullenly at Odysseus as he walked by, while some stared with open defiance.

'Amphion,' Odysseus addressed one of them, a burly warrior holding a wineskin in each hand. 'Where is Eurylochus?'

Hearing the king speak his name, the soldier's insolence seemed to fade and he pointed towards the line of ships.

'That way, my lord. Making sacrifices on the beach.'

Odysseus's eyes narrowed, a rare sign of anger, but he checked himself quickly.

'You're a good man, Amphion. One of the best. Can I trust you to remind some of these men that they're warriors and get them back into some kind of order?'

Amphion looked about himself and nodded. 'I'll do what I can.'

Odysseus patted his arm and moved on through the crowd of soldiers. A guilty hush descended on the camp as he passed, broken only by the lowing of cattle and the bleating of sheep from the beach ahead. As the way cleared before them, Eperitus could see men flaying dead animals or busily butchering the carcasses, while others roasted the meat on spits. Here, where the beach reached up to the grassy plain, the drinking and feasting carried on in ignorance.

'Odysseus!' called a voice.

Eurybates pushed his way through a group of men and ran to the king.

'What's happened here?' Odysseus demanded. 'Why aren't the ships ready to sail?'

'I've done everything I could in your absence, but it hasn't been easy. The royal guard were the only ones who kept their heads after the town fell and you disappeared. The rest found whatever wine was to be had and that's the result.' Eurybates pointed to the undisciplined mass of men on the beach. 'It was as much as we could do to collect the plunder into one place. As for the women and children, most of them are under guard inside the town. Though we couldn't save them all. When we tried, swords were drawn and there was nearly bloodshed. I had to call off the guard.'

'You did the right thing, Eurybates,' Odysseus said, forgetting his sternness and taking his squire by the hand. 'Where have you put the spoils?'

'On the beach by your ship. We found more than we'd counted on: gold, silver, copper, iron, cloth, livestock. By my reckoning it's more than our share of what was left in Troy. You were right to attack the town.'

'And yet I nearly lost it all for the sake of a few more trinkets,' Odysseus replied wistfully.

'The cartload brought by the black slave?' Eurybates asked.

Odysseus nodded. 'Have that loaded onto my ship. The rest is to be divided up equally between the fleet. Tell the captain of each ship they're to take a tenth for themselves and share what's left between their crews.'

'Is Astynome safe?' Eperitus asked, unable to hold back any longer.

'She insisted on leaving the ship and helping with the Cicones we captured. She's still with them now, but Polites is with her.'

That reassured Eperitus, who for the first time since the volley of arrows had fallen among the slave-packed galleys felt a weight lift from his heart – something even Maron's wine had not achieved.

'We lost six men in the fight,' Eurybates continued. 'A fair price for all the plunder we took. I'm sorry, my lord, but we didn't wait for your return to bury them.'

He pointed to a small mound on the western side of the plain, in which six spears had been planted. Eperitus guessed the much larger mound beside it was for the Cicones.

'Unless we get these ships ready to sail tonight I fear there'll be a lot more to bury by morning.'

'Look about you, my lord,' Eurybates said. 'The army's in no fit state to do anything. Some may have come to their senses since your return, but there's plenty more who've already taken up their wine-skins again. You won't get them back in the ships tonight.'

'Eurybates is right, Odysseus,' Eperitus said. 'Zeus himself couldn't get the fleet back to sea by nightfall.'

Odysseus scratched at his beard for a moment and then turned to his squire.

'Have you posted lookouts on the hilltops?'

'One on each of those peaks,' he said, pointing at the two tallest summits behind the town. 'They'll see anything coming from the other side, as long as there's light to see by. And tonight the moon will be near to full.'

Odysseus looked unconvinced and Eperitus shared his doubts. A bank of purple cloud was gathering to the south. If it rolled in overnight there would be no moon to see by and the lookouts would have to rely upon their hearing alone.

'I'd have sent more, but I needed every man I could spare here,' Eurybates said, sensing the king's scepticism. 'They both have mounts and orders to ride back the moment they see anything.'

'Are there any more horses?'

'Yes, my lord.'

'Then send two riders to the temple on the hill,' Odysseus ordered, 'where that trace of smoke is rising up between the trees. The priest there gave me those gifts, but he'll send inland for help if there's any to be had. Have the riders count his slaves: two men, including the Aethiope, and four women. If any are missing tell them to come back immediately; if not, they're to keep watch over the household until dawn, when they're to come straight back here if they don't want to be left behind.'

Eurybates nodded and ran off to carry out his instructions. Odysseus glanced at Eperitus.

'Time to speak with my cousin.'

Selagos spotted them first. He raised himself to his full height and watched warily as Odysseus and Eperitus pushed their way through the crowd surrounding the large fire. Eurylochus was beside him with a bloody knife in his hand. He wore a black robe, thrown back over his shoulders to expose a red-stained tunic. His eyes were tightly closed and his thick lips were moving in prayer. At a kick from Selagos his mutterings ceased and he stared in momentary shock at his cousin.

Odysseus refused to meet his frightened gaze, turning his eyes instead on the calf that stood between Eurylochus and the blazing fire. Its horns had been wrapped with beaten gold and were held fast by two Taphians, while Elpenor knelt before it with a bowl to catch the sacrificial blood. The sandy grass where the plain met the beach was already stained black with the blood of earlier sacrifices. On every side men were butchering carcasses or sprinkling the meat with ritual salt and roasting it over the fire. At the king's arrival they forgot their tasks and waited to see what would happen next.

Eperitus was tense with anger. By leading the sacrifices, Eurylochus had taken on the role of king, an act of rebellion deserving of death. But he was not such an imbecile that he would affront Odysseus without being certain of his own support first. Things must have grown serious in their absence, Eperitus realised, and that Eurybates had managed to avoid a confrontation up to now was greatly to his credit. Or perhaps Eurylochus had waited for Odysseus's return before striking his blow. Not that Eperitus considered him capable of planning a coup, but Selagos was. He looked at the Taphian and saw the cold intelligence in his eyes, an intelligence that knew how to hide all emotion and thought. It was what Selagos would do, not Eurylochus, that worried Eperitus.

Without a word Odysseus stepped forward. Eurylochus stood his ground, holding his knife purposefully before him. Eperitus's hand fell to the pommel of his sword and he noticed Selagos do the same. Then, as quick as a viper, Odysseus seized his cousin's wrist and prised the blade from his grip. The circle of Ithacans tensed, as if ready to spring to the aid of one man or the other. Taking the knife, Odysseus grabbed Eurylochus by the chest, and for a moment Eperitus thought he would plunge it into his cousin's bulging stomach. Instead, he pushed him into Selagos's arms and turned to face the calf.

'Has it drunk?' he asked one of the men holding the horns, pointing to a wooden bowl on the ground.

The man nodded, confirming the beast had bowed its head in consent to the sacrifice. With practised skill, Odysseus snicked off a tuft of hair from its head and tossed it into the nearby flames. Signalling for Elpenor to come closer, he placed the blade under the calf's throat and opened the flesh with a quick jerk of his arm. A stream of dark blood gushed out over Elpenor's hands and into the bowl. The animal twitched its head and then staggered sideward, where a handful of men rushed forward to prevent it falling.

Odysseus stepped away and turned to Eurylochus.

'You are not king *yet*, cousin,' he said, pushing the gore-spattered knife into his hand. 'Until you are, sacrifices are my prerogative and mine alone. Do you understand?'

Eurylochus nodded dumbly.

'Now, have those campfires near the trees on either side brought closer into the beach and set up a picket line,' Odysseus ordered. 'If the gods are with us, we'll get through the night unmolested and can sail away safely in the morning. If not, I hope you're the first to die.'

Selagos lay beneath his blanket, listening to the crack and spit of the fire and the drunken snores of his comrades. As he waited, a bank of fog rolled in from the sea to blot out the stars and shroud everything in grey vapour. If any god had ever noticed the few sacrifices he had made in his life, they were repaying him now.

He pulled the blanket aside, strapped on his sword and crawled away on his hands and knees so as not to be silhouetted by the flames when he stood. He had deliberately picked the fire furthest from the beach and closest to the town gates, and had personally selected the men who were to guard that part of the perimeter. The mist covered his approach to the town and, as he expected, the two guards were propped up against the walls either side of the gates, sleeping off the wine he had sent them. With a final glance over his shoulder, he passed between the open portals.

The street was empty, but Selagos slipped into the shadows and waited. When he was certain there were no footsteps on the battlements above or signs of life from the surrounding buildings, he broke cover and set off through the dark streets, moving from alley to alley until he found the main square. Even in the fog he could see the chaos of broken jars and sticks of furniture that the Ithacans had tossed out of the houses in their hunt for wine. The outline of the temple where the townswomen were being held was visible directly opposite, but rather than risk treading on a shard of pottery and giving himself away to the guards, he decided to skirt round and approach from the side.

Moving from one doorway to the next, he made his way carefully to the other side of the square. Through the shifting fog he glimpsed a lone soldier standing before the doors of the temple. Unlike the guards Selagos had set, this man had been chosen by Eurybates. He carried a shield on his arm and a spear in his hand, and was sober and wakeful. Silently, Selagos drew the dagger from his belt and crept to the nearest corner of the temple, looking around for other guards in the fog. There were none.

The Ithacan seemed to sense Selagos's presence a moment before his large hand closed over his mouth and the point of his dagger sliced open his throat. The man struggled briefly and then slumped heavily into Selagos's arms. The Taphian dragged his body into the shadows and hid it beneath an overturned cart, then ran back to the temple. Before he could push open the doors, they swung back and an armed soldier stared out at him. The Taphian was first to react, seizing the man's cloak at the shoulder and pulling him out into the street. The wool tore and the guard staggered free of Selagos's grip, drawing his sword as he regained his footing.

'Telephus! Telephus! Where are you, man?' he shouted.

'He's dead,' Selagos answered, tossing away the ripped cloak and freeing his own sword.

'*Selagos?*' the Ithacan said, squinting at him through the fog. 'What's all this about?'

Selagos did not answer. Adjusting the grip on his sword, he stepped forward and swung at his chest. The man had been half expecting the blow and stepped back out of range. He raised his sword but did not counter-attack, still reluctant to fight a man who that morning had been his comrade.

'Put away the sword, Selagos! We're both Ithacans.'

'I'm a Taphian.'

Selagos skipped forward, knocked his opponent's sword aside and thrust at him with the point of his blade. The Ithacan pulled nimbly aside and fell back.

'If it's gold you're after, or wine, then you're in the wrong place. There're only slaves in there.'

Selagos attacked again. Their swords met with a ring of metal, sparking in the darkness. This time the Ithacan did not retreat but forced Selagos back against one of the stone pillars, grimacing as he matched his strength against the Taphian's. Then Selagos plucked the dagger from his belt and sank it into the man's stomach. He fell backwards, choking blood. Selagos finished him with his sword.

'What is this?' a woman's voice asked.

One of the Cicones was standing in the open doorway. She was young, maybe fifteen or sixteen years, but she was clearly used to giving commands and having them obeyed. Other female faces skulked in the shadows behind her.

'Who are you?' she demanded, stepping out onto the portico.

Selagos stooped to pick up the discarded cloak from the dirt and proceeded to wipe the blood from his sword.

'Are there more of your people nearby?' he said.

'Why? So you can raid more towns? Kill more old men and boys and take their womenfolk into slavery?'

'Are there more Cicones nearby?' he asked again, this time raising the tip of his sword to the base of her throat.

She swallowed, then seemed to remember her pride and raised her chin a little higher.

'They will not be as easy to conquer as we were,' she answered. 'Their towns are bigger and their walls higher, and the king of Ismarus did not send all his fighting men to Troy. If you attack, they will defeat you.'

Selagos lowered his weapon and slid it into its scabbard.

'Good. Do you want to avenge your dead sons and fathers?'

'Who *are* you?'

'*Do you?*'

'Yes.'

'Then come with me.'

The woman wore a light dress, but its rich material was stained and torn. He threw the bloodied cloak about her naked shoulders and took her by the upper arm, almost dragging her from the portico.

'Where are you taking me?' she insisted, struggling against his grip.

'Up to the hills. There are men with horses, keeping watch for enemies. I'm going to kill one of them and you're going to take his mount and ride to the city of your king. When you get there you will raise the alarm and bring an army back here to rescue the other women. Is that clear?'

She looked into his hard face and knew he was not lying.

'Find me a horse,' she said, 'and I can have the king's army here by sunrise.'

Chapter Eleven

CHARIOTS IN THE FOG

Eperitus sniffed at the cold air: lingering woodsmoke and roasted meat; wine; fresh sweat mingled with old from the mass of sleeping men; the blood of wounds; the sea; the aroma of pine trees on the hillsides; and the dampness of the mist. He had left Astynome asleep on the beach as soon as he sensed the fog approaching, fearing what might be hidden within its thick white fronds as they crept over the plain and around the city walls. The perimeter guards would be blinded by it and vulnerable to a knife in the dark, leaving the camp open to attack. So he had walked beyond the picket line to familiarise himself with the smells of Ismarus at night, letting them form a background against which he could search for anything new. The noises, too, of waves lapping over the beach, tired men snoring heavily and the pop and hiss of the handful of watch fires had faded to a low hum in his mind. Instead, his ears were attuned to the irregular sounds that sometimes broke through the softening effect of the fog: animals moving, the rustle of bat wings or the squeaking of a mouse. At each small noise his mind would instinctively calculate whether the fall of a stone on the hillside was from the light tread of a goat or the heavier footfall of an armed warrior, or if the repeated hunting calls of an owl were in fact imitations sending a different kind of message. And most of all he listened for anything from the men posted on the hilltops. Though they were above the ocean of mist, they would see little moving beneath it until it was too late. A shout of sudden fear or the last cry of a dying man was all Eperitus could hope for in such an event. But he had heard or smelled nothing alien, and now his instincts were telling him that dawn was not far off.

After finishing a fourth circuit of the town walls, he approached the glow of a watch fire at the edge of the plain and coughed.

'Who's there?'

The voice was forceful but controlled.

'It's me, Eperitus.'

The figure of a man stepped before the fire, his silhouette limned by the flames. A bow was ready in his hands.

'You may be able to see through this cursed fog, Eperitus, but I can't. Now come closer before I put an arrow in you to be safe.'

Eperitus laughed and moved into the glow cast by the fire.

'Lower that arrow, Antiphus. I'm soaked through and chilled to the bone with this fog; all I want is a bit of warmth.'

Antiphus unfitted his arrow and beckoned him forward. Together they stood with their palms held out to the flames, occasionally rubbing their hands or stamping their feet.

'Hear anything out there?' Antiphus asked.

'Not a thing. I'd have been better off staying under the furs with Astynome.'

'Can't beat another warm body on a cold night. But you've reassured me, at least. If *you* can't sense anything then there's nothing to worry about.'

'I wouldn't say nothing,' Eperitus cautioned. 'It's the old soldier's instinct that kept me from sleeping in the first place. You know, that sense you get before something happens. It's probably just this fog and the fact three-quarters of the army is asleep with a hangover on a hostile shore when we should have been away before sunset.'

'That's most likely it,' Antiphus concurred. 'Odysseus fell asleep the moment his head touched the sand. And if anyone worries about the fate of these damned fools it's him.'

Eperitus took a few logs from a pile and threw them on the fire, causing a swarm of glowing embers to rise up and swirl away in the chill air.

'But that's the problem. He's exhausted. Now the war's over it's started catching up with him. He hides it well, of course, but *I* can see it. If you asked me I'd say we can't get home soon enough.'

'So why did he take us north when the route south is so much quicker?' Antiphus said. 'I don't know a single man who wouldn't give his share of the plunder we've taken from the Cicones just to be back home.'

'Fatigue can do strange things to a man. I can't count how many times I've taken needless risks in battle just because of some perverse urge to test my luck. Perhaps it's something like that.'

'Perhaps,' Antiphus replied, scratching his large nose with the stumps of his missing fore and index fingers. They had been cut off in his youth as a punishment for poaching, but he had simply learned to shoot with his other hand. 'The war is over, though, and the time for taking risks is too. We've all done things during the past ten years, things we'd never have dreamed of doing on Ithaca – some of them to our glory and some to our shame. But now I'm ready to go home. I want to see my father, again – if the gods have spared him. And it's time I got myself a wife. A man needs someone to bear his children, someone…' he looked Eperitus in the eye, '…someone to make him feel human again. Do you think that's possible for us? After all we've done? All those years of killing. Can we ever find peace and go back to a normal life again?'

It was a question Eperitus had asked himself many times. All through his youth he had dreamed of going to war and creating a name that would be remembered long after his soul had descended to Hades. And for a while war had excited him. But the siege of Troy had lasted too long. There was no honour left in it by the end, just suffering and treachery. They had all done so much to be ashamed of that he wondered if any of them could ever find happiness again. But then he remembered how he felt when Astynome was in his arms and when she told him that she loved him. If a woman like that could love him, then there was hope. There was something worth living for.

'Yes, Antiphus, we can. I know it in my heart. Gods willing, we'll be home soon and you'll find yourself a wife to bear lots of little Antiphuses. And we'll all be able to sleep again at night.'

'I hope so,' Antiphus said.

Eperitus looked to the west. The fog was beginning to thin, and somewhere in the distance he could make out the sable bulk of the hills against the lightening sky. And then he heard the sound he had been dreading all night long: the soft clank of armour, the tread of cloth-covered hooves and the trundle of wheels sheathed in sacking. It was the noise of an army approaching by stealth, using the cover of night and the fog, and Eperitus could tell they were already moving through the trees that covered the hills around the town.

'Zeus's beard, Antiphus. While we've been talking about peace another battle has crept up on us. Run back, man, and wake Odysseus. Tell him we're being attacked!'

'Are you sure?' Odysseus asked.

'Certain,' Eperitus replied. 'They're on the other side of the town.'

'How many?'

'It's hard to say but they've got plenty of chariots.'

'They're not just scouts, then,' said Eurybates. 'It's an army.'

The three men were crouched on the damp grass of the plain, looking out into the treacherous curtain of fog that still hung over the land. The walls of the town were visible as a dark presence a spear's throw away and the dozen fires of the picket line burned like orange flowers in between. The Ithacan army had been hurriedly roused from their sleep and were lying on their stomachs in two rows facing the town. Most were still groggy from the night before and few had been able to don their full armour in the rush, but they were armed and ready for whatever would soon emerge from the mist. The picked veterans of the royal guard were formed into a phalanx behind their commanders, ready to reinforce any weaknesses in the line once the mysterious enemy showed themselves. On Odysseus's orders, every man was to remain prone until told. Their attackers were expecting them to be asleep, and he wanted to maintain that illusion for as long as possible.

'There!'

Eperitus pointed to figures emerging from the fog near the town walls. They were moving slowly and at a stoop, creeping towards the nearest watch fire. More groups appeared, each one converging on the different points of the picket line where the Ithacan sentries should have been keeping watch. In the scramble to wake everyone up and prepare for the attack, Omeros had shown his intelligence by suggesting they throw blankets over piles of firewood to make it look as if the guards were asleep. The ruse had succeeded and the attackers drew their weapons, the blades gleaming orange as they plunged them into the blanketed shapes around the fires. They knew at once they had been fooled and looked out into the mist beyond the firelight, the uncertainty in their faces visible to Eperitus's eyes.

He raised his hand, and scores of Ithacans clambered up from where they had been lying. They fitted arrows to their bows and took aim at the figures silhouetted against the watch fires. There was a hiss as they loosed their strings, followed by the cries of several men as the missiles found their targets. One man fell into the flames and screamed horribly as he pushed himself free and ran blindly towards the Ithacans, his whole body alight. Antiphus fitted a second arrow and brought him down into the grass, where he lay like an abandoned torch. His surviving comrades had already disappeared back into the mist.

'Stand!' Odysseus ordered.

The Ithacans shambled to their feet, turned their shields to face the fog and lowered the points of their spears. They did not need Eperitus's ears now to hear the thunder of hooves and wheels approaching from the darkness. Dozens of chariots now burst from the milky vapour, drawn by two horses apiece with nostrils wide and teeth bared as their drivers whipped them on. Orders were shouted along the Ithacan ranks. Men instinctively drew closer to their neighbours for protection. Then the chariots veered left and right, driving along the face of the line as archers in each car loosed arrows rapidly into the closely packed soldiers. Eurybates raised his shield at the last moment as an arrow sailed over the men in front, catching its bronze head in the fourfold leather. Others were not so lucky. Here and there men cried out or fell heavily into the grass.

'Archers!' Eperitus shouted, but the chariots had already slipped back into the mist.

The sky was now dark blue above the hills to the east. In the woods beyond the town a few birds were greeting the coming day, but Eperitus did not share their joy. Instead his thoughts strayed to the beached galleys behind, where Astynome would be anxiously staring into the fog and wondering what was happening. He did not know what the daylight and the lifting of the fog would reveal, but by the number of chariots that had attacked he knew the attacking force was large. They would be hard pressed to defeat them, or even escape with their lives. If they were defeated that would mean rape, a life of slavery for Astynome, even death. This was why the Trojans had fought so hard to defend their city.

The sound of hooves beating the ground, the squeal of wooden axles and the rattle of iron-shod wheels warned him of the next attack.

'Take aim!' he shouted, as the chariots sped free of the fog and raced down the slope to where the Ithacans were waiting.

Again they veered left and right, the bowmen in the back firing with speed and skill as they passed, felling more Ithacans. Antiphus and his archers returned fire from behind the shields of their comrades, but without effect. The arrows that did not fall into the long grass simply bounced off the wicker cabs and yokes of the chariots, or sprang back from their wooden wheels. As quickly as they had appeared they were gone again.

'Word must have got out to the towns and cities inland,' Odysseus said.

'They're no militia, either,' Eperitus added. 'Not with this many chariots. There'll be hundreds of spearmen waiting in the mist. We need to launch the ships and get away while we still can.'

'They'll massacre us as we push off from the beach. No, we have to teach them to fear us before we show our tails and run. But as long as those chariots can keep picking us off from out of the fog their main force won't come anywhere near.'

'Then we use the fog to our own advantage,' Eperitus said.

He ran back to where the royal guard were waiting.

'First four ranks, step forward,' he ordered.

Behind him he heard the rumble of the chariots and the twanging of bows as the Cicones delivered more volleys into the helpless Ithacans. Again Antiphus's archers fired back without result, and again the chariots disappeared into the mist that covered the battlefield.

'Follow me,' Eperitus ordered the sixty men standing before him.

He turned and ran past Odysseus and Eurybates, through the line of spearmen and onto the empty plain. The first hint of light was in the sky now, but the fog remained stubbornly thick. He sprinted towards the watch fires, conscious of the heavy footsteps following behind. Signalling for the guards to spread out, he had almost reached the old picket line when he heard the sounds of horses and chariots approaching once more through the fog. He dropped to one knee and readied his spear. Two men fell in on either side of him, their breathing heavy and fast as they adopted similar poses. From the corner of his eye Eperitus could see the beginnings of a skirmish line forming, which he could only hope was stretching along the length of the plain. The royal guard were the best men in the army; they did not need to be told what was on their captain's mind.

He felt the pounding of the hooves through the ground, smelled the breath of the horses and the sweat on their flanks, heard the snapping of the drivers' whips across their backs. He had picked a spot behind one of the watch fires, knowing the chariots would pass on either side of it. Then a pair of black horses charged out of the fog, pulling a bouncing chariot behind them. By the time the driver and bowman had spotted the waiting Ithacans it was too late. Eperitus ran forward and rammed his spear into the chest of the archer, sending him tumbling from the back of the car. The driver tried to steer to the right, but as he turned two guardsmen hurled their spears into his back and he fell dead into the grass. The panicked horses ran into the path of another chariot and both were brought to the ground in a tangle of splintered wood and screaming animals.

Eperitus could not see far in the fog, but he could hear the sounds of men dying and the crash of more chariots coming to grief. He did not know how many they had killed, but he knew the Cicones would not dare ride their chariots into the mist again without the support of their spearmen.

'Back to the lines,' he shouted, hoping his voice would carry in the damp air.

As they sprinted back, they were greeted by a cheer from the waiting Ithacans. Odysseus took Eperitus's hand and patted him excitedly on the back.

'They won't come again,' he enthused, 'not while this fog lasts and they don't know our numbers.'

'Then we should spare some men to get the galleys into the water. If the gods are with us we might be able to slip away before they know we're gone.'

Odysseus nodded.

'Eurybates, take one in five men from the line and get the ships into the sea. We need to leave before this fog lifts.'

'It might be too late for that, my lord,' Eurybates replied, pointing at the plain.

They looked back towards the watch fires, where a long line of armoured men was emerging from the mist, their spear points gleaming in the grey dawn.

'I think you've underestimated their resolve, Odysseus,' Eperitus said. 'They're not going to let us go without a fight. And there's a lot more of them than there are of us.'

The Cicones continued to pour into view, rank after rank with unknown numbers behind. All were men of fighting age and well armed, nothing like the collection of old men and boys they had defeated the day before.

'Eurybates, pick some men from the guard instead – take the ones who fought the chariots – and have them push the galleys out one by one. Be as quick as you can about it.'

'Yes, my lord.'

Eperitus looked along the line of Ithacans and spotted Polites's great bulk standing head and shoulders over the rest. He had followed Eperitus up the slope to attack the chariots, but rather than rejoining his comrades in the reserve phalanx he had taken a place beside Omeros and Elpenor. Elpenor looked up as Eperitus pushed in to the shield wall beside them.

'Odysseus has sent men to push the ships back into the water,' Eperitus told him. 'Once that's done we'll be away from this place and heading home again.'

'I'm not a child,' Elpenor replied, staring straight ahead. 'I don't need reassuring. And I know the Cicones won't let us go without a fight.'

'They won't. But if you're going to correct a captain of the guard, you should at least call him sir.'

A horn sounded from the enemy army and their ranks began to move.

'You don't need to be here with me, sir. I can look after myself.'

'I expect you can,' Eperitus said, 'but this is as good a place as any to die so I'll stay. You can move if you want to.'

Elpenor shook his head.

'No thanks. I like it here just fine.'

The disciplined tramp of feet echoed through the mist. It was an ominous sound, as if the relentless beat would roll straight over the ranks of the Ithacans and on to the galleys behind. Eperitus wondered whether Astynome was worrying about him as she sat among the Trojan slaves on deck. He heard the grunting of men behind him, followed by the soft splash of a ship sliding into the waves. The Cicones were closing fast when a voice called out and they came to a sudden halt.

A shout of 'Spears!' was repeated along the Ithacan line and men crouched as best they could behind their leather shields. Seeing

Polites standing with his shield held nonchalantly at his side – knowing it would provide minimal cover for his vast torso – Eperitus decided to do the same. Strangely, he realised his bravado was as much about impressing Elpenor as it was the rest of the men. The volley came quickly. Hundreds of spears darkened the grey air, punching trails through the vapour and sounding like a great wind rather than the hiss that arrows made. It was a sound Eperitus had heard many times before, and as the missiles began to fall, again he whispered a prayer to Athena for protection.

The goddess must have heard him, for a wind began to blow, tearing the fog to rags and lifting the volley of spears so that they carried over the heads of the Ithacans. And yet many still fell and the air was assailed with their cries. A spear landed with a thump between Eperitus and Elpenor. Eperitus plucked it from the dry earth, pushed his own weapon into the ground, and called out in a loud voice.

'On my command!'

The Cicones began to jog down the slope towards the foreigners who had invaded their land and slain their countrymen. As Eperitus took aim he could see their faces clearly. They were hard faces, experienced in battle, and yet that very experience had taught them to fear the moment of vulnerability when a massed volley of spears fills the air and rains destruction.

'Now!'

He cast his weapon at a man in splendid armour, but so many spears fell among the Cicones and so many were brought crashing into the grass that he could not tell whether his throw had counted. But the slaughter did not stop the attackers. Many hundreds came charging down the slope towards the Ithacan line, driven by a fury that was written into their bearded faces. Eperitus gave a last, side-long look at Elpenor, noted with satisfaction that he was sufficiently frightened – though not terrified – then drew his shield across his body, plucked his spear from the earth and took aim. All around him men whispered prayers to Ares, asking for his protection in the coming fight or a death with honour. Then the Cicones were upon them.

Eperitus put a foot back to brace himself as a thickset man with dark, unintelligent eyes rushed at him. He charged through the hedge of spear points and drove his shield against Eperitus's with a brutal jolt. Eperitus pushed back, testing the man's strength and finding it a match for his own. All around them the sounds of battle filled the air. Men grunted or shouted insults in their different languages. Some cried out as weapons tore at flesh and took life. Oxhide shields ground against each other and below the heaving mass of bodies came the scuffing of feet scrambling for footholds in the dew-damp grass. It was a familiar sound, both terrifying and exhilarating to Eperitus as he sensed the nearness of death and with it the immediacy of life. He felt his heart beating hard, the sweat running in rivulets beneath his armour and the tension in his muscles that turned soft flesh to rock. With it came a passion to cling on to his precious existence; that overruling desire to survive and destroy anyone who threatened to take it from him. He stared into the eyes of his opponent and hated him, knowing the Cicone felt the same. They strained shield against shield, swearing at each other and stepping on each other's feet in the tussle for the small patch of earth that was theirs to dispute. Realising the other man was not wearing greaves, Eperitus raised his foot and scraped the leather sole of his sandal down his unprotected shin and onto his foot. The man's face contorted with sudden pain, but he held his position and pushed harder in response, trying to employ the same trick against Eperitus but failing against his bronze greaves.

'Move your head!' a voice behind him commanded.

Eperitus ducked aside and watched his opponent's expression change to horror. An instant later the point of a sword was pushed into his neck above the protection of his breastplate, opening the flesh and releasing the dark blood within. The man choked and fell, opening a gap in the ranks of the Cicones. Another man moved to fill it, but Eperitus pushed the point of his spear into the gap below the rim of his shield, piercing the soft flesh between his thigh and his groin. He screamed horribly and fell backwards into his comrades. Hands pulled him out of the way and more shields rushed into the hole that had been created. Desperate to widen the small breach in the enemy wall, Eperitus met two of the shields with his own and pulled out his sword. A spear stabbed at him from the mass of Cicones, but an Ithacan sword from the rear rank hacked at it and split the shaft.

'Help me,' Eperitus grunted to the soldiers behind him.

Two men squeezed themselves into the narrowing gap and began to push the Cicones back. From the corner of his eye, Eperitus watched Polites throw a punch at one of the two Cicones who were struggling to hold him. The man fell and was trampled beneath the mass of struggling feet. The other man's strength gave before the colossal Ithacan and he stumbled back. Though they were four or five ranks deep, the Cicones' line began to bend. Eperitus threw his weight behind his shield and pushed, opening the flank of the man fighting the Ithacan to his right. He stabbed up into his armpit, almost severing his arm at the shoulder. The man roared with pain and fell beneath the feet of the Ithacans, to be speared through the stomach by a man in the second rank.

With their shield wall perilously close to breaking, more Cicones launched themselves into the fray. Eperitus looked back and saw Odysseus at the head of the royal guard. But the king had already seen what was happening and understood at once what was needed. With a loud command he led the reserve into the fight. Scores of heavily armoured men threw their weight behind the thin ranks of their countrymen and, heaving and grunting, began to push the Cicones back. The man opposite Eperitus shouted and spat at him in frustration, his face filled with rage as he tried to resist the momentum behind the Ithacan shields. With the spittle running down his cheek, Eperitus pulled his sword free from the crush of bodies and sank it into his opponent's neck. As the man fell, the point of a Cicone spear thrust into the gap and caught Eperitus in the shoulder. His leather armour held it for a moment, then with another push from the unseen spearman the point broke through and tore into his flesh.

A burning sensation raced through his chest and arm. His vision darkened and he shouted at the pain that threatened to undo him.

Twisting away from the spearhead so that it slipped from his shoulder, he hacked at the wooden shaft with his sword and broke it. The wound continued to send an almost unbearable fire through his flesh, but rather than weakening him it filled him with rage. He slammed the pommel of his sword into a snarling face, knocking the man's eye from its socket. He swung the blade at another enemy's head, feeling the force of the blow dampened by the man's leather helmet but seeing him go down nonetheless. Then the Cicones' resistance broke like a dam before a swollen river. Men were suddenly running back into the mist, some throwing away their weapons or shields, others pausing to turn and ward off blows from their attackers. Now was the time when men would die. In the confines of the shield wall few fell, but once the struggle was won and one side cracked under the pressure, then swords and axes could be swung with malicious freedom and spears could find their victims with impunity. As one section of the Cicones' line gave way, so the rest quickly fragmented and the whole army began retreating back up the slope towards the town walls. The Ithacans followed, shouting triumphantly and striking down every man who was not quick enough to flee.

Eperitus raised his sword to join the rout but felt his body weaken and his arm fall to his side. As the sounds of the battle faded, a calm voice – his own, he thought – told him that he must not succumb. He blinked, felt the sharpness of the pain and allowed it to bring him to his senses again.

'Hold your positions!' Odysseus shouted. 'Remember the chariots.'

As if he had summoned them himself, gaps formed in the fleeing ranks of the Cicones and a dozen chariots came racing down the slope. This time the men in the cars did not carry bows but long lances. Eperitus watched three or four Ithacans charged down beneath the hooves of the horses or thrust through by the lances before the remainder fled back to the safety of the lines.

As the army reformed and the chariots retreated, he moved to the rear and knelt by the body of an Ithacan. Tearing off a strip of his cloak, he folded it and slipped it under his leather armour to cover the wound.

'You're hurt,' said a voice behind him.

Eperitus turned to see Elpenor. His sinewy limbs and armoured chest were spattered with gore, and though a beardless youth, his eyes were confident and unafraid. There was a hint of arrogance in them as he regarded his wounded countryman.

'I'm amazed *you're* even alive,' Eperitus returned.

'That's more than can be said for the man who faced me in the shield wall.'

Elpenor raised his sword, which was dark with blood. Eperitus looked at it and nodded.

'Good work. Who taught you to use a sword?'

'My uncle back on Ithaca. He's a fine swordsman, but I'm better.'

'Did you get your pride from him too, lad? What's his name, this uncle of yours?'

'Eperitus!' Odysseus appeared, helmetless and with his shield strapped across his back. 'Are you alright?'

'I'll live. I was caught in the shoulder and it stings like Hades, but it'll heal quickly enough. What about the Cicones?'

'They're forming up again,' Odysseus answered, untying his friend's cuirass and lifting it away from his torso. The tunic beneath was sodden with blood and the king gave an involuntary frown as he peeled away the makeshift bandage. 'The moment we try to board the ships they'll attack again, I'm sure of it. Not that it matters to you what they do. you're going back to the beach to get this looked at. The Trojan women are tending to the wounded there –'

'I'll stay and command the reserve.'

Odysseus ignored him and turned to Elpenor, who had barely taken his eyes from the king since he had arrived.

'Help the captain back to the beach, lad. You can carry his armour for him.'

But Elpenor simply turned and ran back to the waiting Ithacans.

Chapter Twelve

THE ESCAPE

The fog dissipated quickly as the sun rose above the hilltops. Blue cloudless skies stretched from the edge of the sea to the peaks of the northern mountains. From where he sat on the beach, having his wound cleaned by a Trojan slave, Eperitus could see the Cicones mustering their strength in the shade of the city walls. The casualties they had taken in their first attack had not deterred them from throwing themselves at the Ithacans a second time soon after. Odysseus had just pulled a further hundred men from the line and ordered them to help the guards push the galleys back into the water, but they were forced to rejoin their comrades as the Cicones came yelling down the slope. The assault had been beaten off, but the king would not risk pulling men from the army again, leaving the handful of guards to complete the task themselves. So far they had only succeeded in getting four ships into the water.

The old nurse muttered something in her native tongue and indicated for Eperitus to sit down. Placing his folded cloak beneath his head, she produced a bone needle threaded with animal gut and began to close the wound. He winced as she tugged the edges of broken skin together, but it was over quickly. Moments later she was sitting him back up and wrapping a clean bandage around the cut. As she knotted it – none too gently – a female voice called Eperitus's name. He turned to see Astynome running across the sand towards him.

'How bad is it?' she asked, kneeling beside him.

'It's nothing.'

Astynome shook her head and put the same question to the nurse, who called her a traitor and walked away. Astynome watched her go, then turned and placed her lips on Eperitus's cheek.

'I looked for you in the fighting but couldn't see you. Then a man told me you had been wounded. Will this killing ever stop, my love? I thought we were going to Ithaca to make a home of our own, not raid more towns and kill more people.'

'There'll be no more raids,' he answered, stroking her hair. 'In a few days we'll reach the Peloponnese and then we'll be almost home.'

'Home,' she repeated, savouring the word. 'I can hardly bring myself to believe it, as if doing so will just push it further from my grasp. After all these years of war I can't imagine peace.'

'As a boy I used to hunger for stories of war told by my grand-father or the travelling bards. Now war is normal and peace is the thing we dream of.'

She sat beside him on the sand, hugging her knees to her chest while he placed his arm around her. A strong breeze pulled her clothing tight about the contours of her body. For a moment his desire for her made him forget the irritation in his shoulder.

'It's as you say, though,' she said. 'In a few days we'll be home. I've never seen Ithaca, but I know I'll be happy there. How can I not when I have you?'

But whenever Eperitus thought of Ithaca he remembered Theano's warning that their return would see many trials. The Cicones, he sensed, were not the last ordeal they would face before they reached home.

A whisper of arrows shook him from his thoughts. The volley fell among the line of Ithacans and was returned almost instantly. Then the Cicones let out their war cry and charged down the slope for a third time.

The Cicones quickly learned that the Ithacans were stubborn, hard-fighting men. But the Ithacans, too, realised that their opponents were just as obstinate and would not give up the fight until every one of the invaders lay dead. Despite the carpet of their own slain, which thickened with each assault as the day dragged on, the Cicones were ready to launch a fresh charge every time the Greeks showed any sign of retiring to their ships. Sometimes Odysseus would feign a withdrawal to provoke an attack, in the hope their enemies' casualties would break their resolve to continue the fight. But like vultures eyeing a wounded animal, they refused to leave. The bloody nose Odysseus had intended to scare them off with had been delivered time and again as morning gave way to afternoon, but each blow just seemed to increase their determination. And so he and his men had been forced to hold fast and wait.

Odysseus watched the chariot of the sun sinking towards the west. Being trapped at the head of a narrow beach with no room for manoeuvre and in full sight of the enemy, there was no trick he could play to make good his escape. The only hope would have been to run for the ships and count on the rearguard to hold the Cicones while the rest of them boarded and slipped away. But that would require sacrificing at least a hundred men on top of the thirty who had already fallen. So he had waited, letting his mind stray time and again to Penelope and Telemachus. He pictured them standing hand in hand as they watched him bring the fleet safely into anchor. His wife was as beautiful as the day he had left her all those years ago, while his ten-year-old son was smiling as he waved to him from the shore. They seemed so agonisingly close and yet as distant as if the walls of Troy still stood between them.

With the twelve galleys now laying at anchor in the water – manned by skeleton crews of mostly wounded men – he settled on a plan and gave out his orders. After night fell the Ithacans would be able to slip away unseen, so the Cicones were certain to attack before last light. They would throw everything they had at their enemies, and if the Ithacan line broke then the survivors would have to make the ships as best they could in the twilight. It would be a massacre, and so Odysseus had decided on an orderly withdrawal before sunset to shorten the distance to the fleet. It might also draw the Cicones out before they were ready. The disadvantage was that the nearer his men were to the safety of the galleys, the stronger the temptation would be to run if the Cicones pressed them hard. And if just a few men left the shield wall then they would all be in danger.

'Eurybates, on my command we will march back to the water's edge. If the Cicones launch an attack, every man is to turn and fight. We have to hold them until dark and then I'll give the order to board, but no-one puts a foot in the water without my permission. Understood?'

'Yes, my lord.'

The double rank of the army began their march, crossing the plain with only an occasional glance over their shoulders to see whether the Cicones were following. They were not. Instead, the densely packed enemy remained beneath the town walls, staring over the rims of their shields at the backs of the retreating invaders. Perhaps, Odysseus thought, he had misjudged them. Perhaps they had suffered enough and were content to let the Ithacans go without a fight. How he wished Eperitus were with him, whose far-seeing eyes would tell him what the Cicones were doing.

'Shorten the line. Form three ranks,' he called out.

The order was followed in a stumbling fashion, but soon the line was only a little wider than the stretch of beach where the galleys were waiting. The army was still on the grassy plain, though, with its flanks exposed. Now would be the moment for the Cicones to commit their chariots, forcing the Ithacans to turn and defend while they brought their spearmen down upon them. But still the Cicones did not move.

More men were glancing over their shoulders now. The gap between them and the beach was closing rapidly, and with no sign of pursuit their anxiety was giving way to relief and hope.

Eurybates joined the king.

'What are they doing? They've pressed us all day and pressed us hard, and now they're just going to let us go?'

'Maybe they're beaten,' Odysseus replied. 'Perhaps they're afraid to attack us again and are only staying to defend the town.'

'Then the gods have favoured us,' Eurybates said. 'I only wish we could have given our dead a proper burial.'

'Their memories will be honoured,' Odysseus said, looking at the large new mound alongside the barrow of those who had fallen the day before. 'We can do no more than that.'

An urgent shout made him turn. Eperitus was standing at the prow of the centremost galley and pointing towards the two mounds. Then a horn blew from the town's battlements and hundreds of Cicones rose up from the long grass on either side. While Odysseus had been watching the spearmen and chariots at the top of the plain, large companies of their countrymen had crept up under cover of the vegetation and folds in the ground to outflank the Ithacans. It was only a matter of luck that he had withdrawn his men when he did, or the Cicones would have surrounded them and cut them off from the galleys.

As the long, rolling horn call died away, a dozen chariots came hurtling down the slope from the town walls. Dense ranks of spearmen followed in their wake. At the same moment, the warriors on either side of the Ithacans lowered their spears and charged, shouting as they came. Odysseus thought quickly. To hold an attack on three sides was impossible, even for seasoned fighters. But the trap had been sprung too soon and one hope remained. The ships were close in and several gangplanks had been run out into the shallow water. If they were quick, half of his men could make it on board before the Cicones reached them. The rest would be hacked to pieces in the surf, but it was better that a few survive than the whole army be trapped and cut down one by one. He gave the order to break ranks and run.

At once, the disciplined lines dissolved and every man sprinted for the beach, Odysseus with them. The Cicones closing on either side hurled volleys of spears in desperation, some finding targets among the Ithacans, but the majority, thrown hastily, missing their aim. A few men threw away their shields and weapons as they fled, frantically trying to lighten their load as they dashed for the ships. Odysseus saw Antiphus in the chaos and shouted to him to get as many archers up the gangplanks as he could, to cover the retreat of the army from the decks of the galleys. Antiphus raised his maimed hand in acknowledgement and disappeared into the throng. Odysseus glanced back over the heads of his men and saw the chariots gaining on them rapidly, the horses' hooves thundering over the dry ground and raising a wall of dust behind them.

'Get to the beach!' he shouted, waving the last few soldiers past. 'The chariots won't follow us onto the sand.'

He watched the foremost vehicle catch a straggler. With great skill the driver steered the horses slightly to the left, while his companion plunged the point of his lance between the fleeing man's shoulders. He tumbled to the ground and was ridden over by a second chariot. A third was closing on two other Ithacans, one of whom was struggling beneath the burden of his armour and weapons. Odysseus recognised Eurylochus at once. Despite his dislike for his cousin he felt an anguished wrench as he watched the spearman in the chariot aim the head of his lance at his back. He shouted a warning to Selagos, Eurylochus's companion. The Taphian turned in mid-flight, swung his spear and deflected the lance downward into the ground. The Cicone was too slow to release his hold on the shaft and was lifted out of the chariot to fall into the long grass. Selagos seized Eurylochus by the elbow and dragged him towards the beach.

Afraid of becoming bogged down on the soft sand, the rest of the chariots peeled off and returned up the slope. By now the bulk of the Ithacans had reached the beach. Many were already running up onto the galleys, while the rest crowded behind, some fighting each other to get onto the gangplanks. But the flanking companies of the Cicones were close behind them. Many Ithacans had turned to meet the threat, fighting them on the beach or waist-deep in the water where the surf was already pink with blood. Knowing the spearmen from the town would soon be upon them, Odysseus ordered the rearmost ranks to turn and form a defensive line. As he joined the shield wall he felt a shadow fall over him and looked up to see Polites. Omeros was beside him, and the sight of their calm, determined faces was reassuring. And yet he wished Eperitus was at his side.

The ring of bronze and the thump of sword against shield were joined by the twang of bowstrings as more and more Ithacan archers lined the decks and found targets on the flanks of the battle. Then a wall of shields and spears appeared at the top of the beach and with a triumphant shout the main force of Cicones dashed down upon the rearguard. A volley of arrows thinned the charging warriors but did not halt them. An instant later they crashed into the Ithacans. Odysseus stopped a man with the point of his spear through his throat, while Polites flattened another with a blow from his shield boss. The air around them was full of the shouts of men fighting and dying, but all the time more Ithacans were pouring up the gangplanks and more arrows were finding targets among the Cicones on the beach and in the water. The rearguard fell back, pushed by their enemies into the vacuum left by their retreating countrymen. Odysseus felt the water washing over his feet and sucking away the sand beneath his sandals. He parried the thrust of a spear and replied by slashing his own weapon across his attacker's face. The point sliced through his eye and sent him staggering backwards, howling with pain. Others were falling all around him, Cicones and Ithacans. Now they were thigh deep in the surf, struggling to stand as the water ebbed and flowed. Odysseus's heels kicked against something hard and a voice called down to him. He glanced back to see a soldier standing on a gangplank and waving to him to come up. As Odysseus watched, a spear caught the man in the chest and brought him down into the water.

'Omeros, get on the ship,' he ordered, seeing the bard still at his side. 'I'll follow.'

Omeros drove back his opponent with his spear, then turned and ran up the gangplank. The Cicone tried to follow but was knocked back into the water by a blow from Polites's shield. The giant Ithacan thrust his sword through another man's chest before following Omeros. Halfway up he paused and offered Odysseus his hand. The king took it and was hauled onto the slippery walkway. A furious shout erupted behind him and he felt the thick wood bouncing beneath his feet as the Cicones followed, almost at his heels. Then he heard the hiss of arrows and the cries of his pursuers as they fell back into the sea.

He reached the deck and turned to stare at the scene below. The water was thronged with the bodies of the dead and the living, but of the latter almost none were Ithacans. Those few that were left were surrounded by foes and could not hope to reach the ships. Instead, the walkways were being mounted by the Cicones, trying desperately to gain the decks of the galleys above while dozens of spear points drove them back again. The enemy's archers had now reached the top of the beach and were sending volleys of black-fletched arrows into the crowded ships. Odysseus heard the death cries of slaves behind him, at least one of them a child. Already two of the galleys were being rowed out to sea. Knowing there was no hope for anyone not already aboard, Odysseus ordered the gangplanks to be dropped into the water and for all but a few archers to man the benches. The anchors were cut and the oars fed out into the sea, slowly driving the bulk of the galley away from the enraged Cicones.

Chapter Thirteen

CAPE MALEA

A final volley of arrows fell into the waves astern of the galley. Eperitus slung his shield across his back and offered his hand to Astynome, who was taking cover with some of the other women behind sacks of grain.

'It's safe now,' he said, pulling her up to stand at his side.

All twelve ships had escaped, but it had been a close fight. Many Ithacans had died and the survivors were mixed and scattered across the fleet, but if Odysseus had not commenced the withdrawal when he had, they would all have perished. Even Eperitus, from his elevated position on deck, had been too focussed on the Cicones before the town walls to notice the hundreds of men crawling on their bellies through the grass on either side of the plain. Only when Odysseus's order to withdraw had caused a few of them to raise their heads did he spot them and call out a warning.

The curses of the Cicones could still be heard, carried to the ships on the back of a strong northerly breeze. Then a lone voice answered them. It was the voice of Odysseus from one of the other galleys, smooth and forceful, calling out a lament for the men who had fallen. As the sound of it rolled across the water, his enemies on the beach fell silent and the sobbing of the women in the galleys was hushed. Across the fleet, men pulled in their oars and stood to listen as their king extolled the skill and courage of their comrades, his words as stirring and powerful as any bard's. As he shouted out the ritual salute to the dead, they raised their fists and echoed it in a great roar, filling the air with their pride and grief. Twice more the salute was repeated and then the crews fell silent, many slumping to the benches and sobbing openly as they mourned their countrymen.

Sails now fell open like great white flowers among the ships, as the different captains took advantage of the wind to take them as far away from Ismarus as possible. The helmsman on Eperitus's galley, an old mariner with skin like leather and a beard like snow, called out the order to release their own sail. Soon the vessel was darting across the open waves like a dolphin, competing with the ships on either side.

'Where to?' the helmsman shouted over the wind and the snapping of canvas.

'Follow Odysseus,' Eperitus called back.

'And which one is that?'

'Whichever takes the lead.'

Astynome placed a hand on his unhurt shoulder and lowered him onto a nearby bench. He was not wearing his breastplate, and as she peeled back the bandage from his wound her eyes narrowed a little.

'You're fortunate the stitches haven't broken. But you should have left the fighting to the others. And where's that sling I prepared for you?'

'You talk as if we're already married,' he replied with a smile.

'Sorry,' she said, returning his smile and flushing a little beneath her tanned skin. 'But you need the sling to rest your arm – if you *want* the wound to heal, that is.'

He pulled the strip of knotted cloth from a fold in his tunic and tried to loop it around his neck and arm. She took it from him with an impatient tut and, after replacing the bandage, fitted the sling gently and efficiently. She was right of course, he admitted, and not just about the bandage. When the Cicones had tried to storm the gangplanks there had been more than enough Ithacans on board to throw them back. Perhaps it had been the frustration of standing helplessly on deck while his comrades were being cut down in the water, or perhaps it was the sight of Selagos exulting over his killing of two Cicones that had provoked his pride and drawn him into the battle. But he had overestimated his strength, and the first man he had faced had barged him aside with his shield, pushing it into Eperitus's wounded shoulder and knocking him onto the deck. It was Antiphus who had come to his rescue, plunging his sword into the Cicone's stomach before hurling him overboard.

'Can't have you die lying on your back, can we,' he had said, smiling at Eperitus before helping him to safety.

'I'll fetch you a little wine,' Astynome said.

'No. Take some to each of the men. They've had a hard day and they need something to raise their spirits. Get a few of these women to help you, too. Then you can bring a cup to me.'

She did not demur, but set about his request as if it were an order. Eperitus joined the helmsman in the stern, noticing with concern the clouds descending upon them from the north. They had appeared a short while before the retreat to the ships, nothing more then than a dark fringe spreading over the hills. But now they filled the evening skies above land and sea, whipped into an angry mass by the ever-strengthening winds.

'I don't like the look of that,' he said to the helmsman, Baius, pointing to the ceiling of cloud that was already overtaking them.

'Neither does Odysseus,' he said, tipping his chin towards the lead galley. 'He's changed course for that island, but if I know anything about weather – and I've been thirty years at sea, not counting the war – then the storm'll catch us before we've covered half the distance. We'd be safest steering for the mainland.'

'At the risk of being found by the Cicones again. I'd take my chances with the sea.'

Baius raised a white eyebrow, but said nothing. Eperitus leaned back against the bow rail and watched Astynome and three of the younger women taking wine to the men on the benches. Their shoulders were hunched and their heads hung low with exhaustion and grief, only stirring as cups of wine were pushed into their hands. By now the ship was beginning to pitch and yaw on the restless sea, making it difficult for the women to pour the wine. Then the galley plunged into a trough and threw Astynome forward. Eurylochus – as sure-footed as any Ithacan on a ship – stood and caught her. When she turned from his grip and tried to struggle free, his grip tightened.

'Steady now,' he laughed, raising a pink fleshy hand to her breast.

As Eperitus ran forward from the stern, Astynome stamped her heel on Eurylochus's foot and thrust an elbow into his ribs, causing him to cry out. At the same time the ship lurched heavily again, sending her stumbling forward against the mast and beyond the range of Eurylochus's arms. Before Eperitus could throw himself at Odysseus's cousin, a bellowed command from Baius had the ship's crew springing from their benches and running this way and that across the deck to alter the angle of the sail. One of them stumbled into Eperitus, jarring his hurt shoulder and provoking a shout of pain. Pushing the man aside, he staggered forward across the swaying deck towards Eurylochus.

Selagos got there first, thrusting his great bulk between them and laying his hand on Eperitus's already stinging wound, squeezing it hard. Eperitus reeled back, just as the galley plunged into another trough and a large wave broke across the deck. Selagos and Eurylochus disappeared behind a wall of spray and Eperitus was thrown against the mast. A hand took hold of his and, wiping the seawater from his eyes, he saw Astynome staring back at him.

'We'll be safer in the stern,' she shouted.

The edge of the storm was now upon them. The wind howled in Eperitus's ears and the deck beneath his feet sloped and bucked like an angry colt, tipping him this way and that as he struggled to keep hold of Astynome and she of him. Women and children were huddling together for shelter, while all around them men were trying to secure the supplies of grain, wine and water that were on deck. The bleating of goats mingled with the shrieking gale as they were trussed up to the bottoms of benches and then left to the mercies of the storm. As they reached the helm, Eperitus pulled Astynome down onto a pile of canvas-covered sacks. Reaching for a coil of spare rope, he tied one end around her waist and the other to a wooden bollard used for attaching the braces.

'What if the ship sinks?' she protested.

'It won't.'

'She may yet,' Baius shouted beside them as he pulled on the twin rudders, his muscles bulging with the strain. 'And if she does then we're all as good as dead anyway, tied up or free.'

'I'm more worried you'll be swept overboard,' Eperitus said. 'And while you're here you can pray to Poseidon to deliver us safe and sound on that island.'

As he spoke, the wind rose to a scream, tugging and snapping furiously at the sail. Baius knew what was coming and, cupping a hand around his mouth, bellowed out an order. A wave washed over the side of the ship as it was sucked down into another trough, nearly sweeping several of the crew into the sea. Men clung to benches and the mast, holding on with all their strength while the slaves hugged the deck and each other in desperation. Then with a great tearing sound the sail flew apart into two halves. One of the braces snapped and the heavy spar swung in the gale. Eperitus rushed forward with several others and took hold of the halyard, the wet rope rough against his palms. Others seized the braces and tried to steady the two ends of the yard.

'Swing it round!' Baius yelled. 'Swing it round before it has us over.'

Eperitus felt the vessel's sudden instability as the men struggled to sway the heavy spar lengthways across the ship. Their bare feet slipped on the wet deck and it was not until Selagos threw his great strength onto one of the braces that they were able to get the yard and the tattered remnants of the flaxen sail under control. Together they eased it round so that it was fore and aft, then, on Baius's command, Eperitus and the men on the halyard began to ease away. More men rushed forward to catch the falling yard, while yet more threw rope around the sail to secure it to the spar. All the time, the galley pitched and rolled and waves swept over the sides to drench everyone in seawater. Overhead and from horizon to lurching horizon the sky was black with cloud, from which sheets of rain swept down to add to the misery of the Ithacans. Eperitus glanced back to see that Astynome was still safely in the helm, where she was now holding on to two pale-faced children. Beyond the confines of the ship the rest of the fleet had disappeared, though here and there he caught glances of distant objects that might have been galleys. He thought of Odysseus and the others he had come to love over the years, and prayed to Athena she would protect them.

A hand on his arm pulled him towards the benches. He sat down heavily and lifted the oar into place, sliding it out into the water. Looking along the length of wood, he saw the black waves rise up to swamp the blade, then plunge down beyond its reach again. How the oars were to bite and pull in such an ocean was beyond him, but without a sail they had no choice but to row. And even if they made the island they had seen rising up from the horizon, the chance of finding a landfall that was not beset by rocks and other perils seemed impossibly small.

'Put your backs into it!' Baius hollered.

Ignoring the pain in his wounded shoulder, Eperitus thrust the oar into the waves and pulled.

They stayed on the island for two days and two nights, repairing the sails and the damage to the ships but mostly sleeping. The men were exhausted, and Odysseus – also heavy with fatigue – let them rest and regain their strength. Even then he resented putting two more days between himself and Ithaca. He was already furious with his decision to raid Ismarus, a folly undertaken in the belief it would give him an easy victory and plenty of plunder. In truth he was ashamed of the little that had been allotted to him from the remnants of Troy's wealth. But he should have realised that no quantity of gold, silver or slaves could compensate them for what they had lost. Could Penelope ever love him again like she did when they were young? Could Telemachus come to love the father he had never known? Could his people ever trust him as king again, after they had spent so many years governed by the Kerosia? Not all the wealth in Troy – let alone his paltry share – could purchase back what the war had stolen from him. Only time and patience would restore such things, and each day away from home was invaluable.

But though he was anxious to depart, he had no choice other than to let the men rest. Eperitus and Eurybates had counselled him not to hurry them. A mutinous temper had settled over the army, fuelled by the disastrous raid on Ismarus. Few cared that every man was twice as rich as before, and it was their own drunkenness that had led them to being ambushed. But in their tired minds Odysseus had led them to a defeat in which seventy-two of their comrades had died, and so there would be little to gain from pushing them before they were ready.

He consoled himself with the thought that he needed them at their best for the return home. With the prevailing north wind and a favourable current, two days' sailing south-west would bring them to Euboea, where the Greek fleet had gathered for the attack on Troy ten years ago. From there they would pass through the channel that separated Euboea from the island of Andros, then on to the southern tip of Attica and finally the eastern coast of the Peloponnese. Here they would round Cape Malea before heading west on the once familiar route to Ithaca. With fair weather, a little over a week's sailing was all that was needed.

On the morning of the third day they set sail. The cloudy skies and rain that had followed the storm lifted and they were able to see the white peak of a mountain on the western horizon. They sailed towards and then past it, and when the afternoon saw the return of a low belly of cloud – which grew blacker towards the south – they found a headland and took shelter for the night. After the chaotic retreat from Ismarus, the crews had returned to their own galleys and Eperitus had rejoined Odysseus's ship. As it lay at anchor and the men had gone ashore to eat and sleep, the two old friends remained at the helm and discussed the course that would take them home. After nightfall it began to rain, a fine drizzle that quickly soaked their woollen cloaks and left them cold to the bone. Further south, lightning was flickering across the invisible horizon, though too far away even for Eperitus to hear the report of the thunder.

'The gods are angry with someone,' he commented.

Odysseus nodded, but did not reply.

The next day they set sail again under clear skies and with a strong wind filling their sails. The coastline of northern Greece was just visible in the west, while ahead of them were the clustered islands of the Sporades. They passed to the east of these and in the afternoon saw the outline of Scyros on their left. The island was home to King Lycomedes, whom Odysseus knew would not give him a warm welcome. They sailed on until the rugged coastline of Euboea came into view. And with it the first corpse.

For some time Odysseus had watched pieces of wood drifting past the hull, guessing at what they signified, but it was Eperitus whose sharp eyes saw the body floating towards them. It was a man in a brown tunic lying face down over a broken spar, his limbs pale against the dark water as he swept towards them. Two of the crew tried to reach him with an oar, but as if reluctant to be disturbed he moved away from the outstretched blade and passed on. As the rocky shore came closer they saw more driftwood and, dotted among it, the bodies of more sailors.

'By all the gods, do you see that?' asked Eperitus.

It was some time before the king was able to make out the wreckage of a galley on the distant shore, its hull impaled upon a black rock and its broken mast pointing upward at an angle. Before long they could see another, and then a third. The crew's silence as they watched the ghastly flotilla of drowned sailors pass by was ominous. Though they did not know them, they knew that but for the whims of the gods their fates could have been the same. One night less on the island – as Odysseus had wanted – and they might all have been caught up in the same storm that had destroyed the unknown fleet whose remains they were now passing. A fleet, Odysseus thought, that had endured ten years of strife at Troy only to be destroyed by the gods on their return. It was a grim omen.

Omeros called out from the bow where several of the Ithacans were gathered.

'Odysseus! My lord, come quickly.'

The crowd of men parted to let Odysseus and Eperitus through. Omeros was leaning against the bow rail, pointing to a body floating in the water. It was of a short, stocky man whose milky eyes gazed out from his pale face, a face that Odysseus recognised immediately. The sight shocked him.

'Get an oar and pull him out, now!'

But for all the efforts of the crew, Little Ajax's body refused to be coaxed towards the galley. After the fourth attempt, one of the blades hit him in the face and his corpse rolled under the water and disappeared.

'A shame for the men who perished with him,' Omeros said. 'Better to have died in battle with glory and honour than to be swallowed up by the sea.'

'One death is much the same as another,' Eperitus replied.

Odysseus nodded. 'Either way, they'll never see home again and their families will be left watching and waiting.'

They passed easily through the straits that separated Euboea and Andros, sped on by the current and the north wind, and by nightfall were dropping their anchor stones in a sheltered bay at the foot of Mount Ocha. Ten years before, Odysseus and Eperitus – in the company of Menelaus – had spent the night here on their return from the failed embassy to Troy, before entering the Euboean Straits the next morning and sailing to Aulis. For most of the Ithacans it was the first time they had touched Greek soil since the start of the war. Yet their mood was strangely subdued as they made campfires along the shore and prepared the evening meal. They sang songs of home – melancholy tunes filled with sentiment – while the women and children gazed into the fires and remembered Troy. Now they were in the land of their enemies they were forced to accept they were no longer free. Those of high birth who had owned slaves pondered the fickleness of the gods; the rest prayed that their new masters would treat them with kindness.

Odysseus kept himself apart from the rest, even Eperitus, wandering along the wooded shoreline and through the trees to the foothills of Mount Ocha. In a clearing on top of a knoll he gazed up at the stars. The full moon hung low and bloated above the spurs of the mountain. Its light strangled out the eastern constellations, but above him they still shone brightly. He wondered whether Penelope was looking at the same stars, and as he thought of her, a tightness gripped his stomach. Soon, gods willing, they would be together. It was the one thing he had longed for all these years, fighting each day of the war in the hope it would be the last and that he would soon be restored to his family. But now their reunion was within his grasp he felt sick at the thought of it. Was it the same nervousness that had blighted him ever since they had turned their prows away from Troy and towards home: that he would arrive home only to be rejected by Penelope, Telemachus and his people, whom he had deserted for the war? Yet the more he pondered it, the more he knew it was not that. What he actually feared was far worse. Something weighed on his spirit, something terrible and beyond his control, a feeling that his own fate was being slowly prised from his fingertips. Unbidden, the words of the Pythoness came back to him: *the wide waters will swallow you. For the time it takes a baby to become a man, you will know no home.* As the words mocked him he knew the baby was Telemachus, the son he had left behind, who would not be a man for another ten years.

'You're wrong!' he shouted at the stars.

But the stars were gone. A bank of cloud had slipped quietly across the night sky, shrouding everything in darkness. Odysseus felt the first spots of rain on his face and the winds of change fanning his cheek.

The next morning was grey and wet. The sunrise was sensed more than seen, a faint lessening of the blackness that had settled over the land and the sea. The Ithacans took to their oars and pulled the galley out into the choppy waters of the bay, all the time the thin sheets of rain settling over them like watery cobwebs. It soaked everything and chilled them to the marrow of their bones. Their only good fortune was that the northerly wind continued to prevail, filling the sails and taking them southward at as great a speed as they could have hoped for in the restless seas.

Eurybates was at the twin rudders, his face a mask of concentration as he steered the galley across the waves and silently fretted about the increasing strength of the wind. They sped over the sea in a south-westerly direction, the western shore of Attica a dark line on the western horizon, steadily growing closer. Before long they approached a large island and, after skirting around its northern tip, saw a spur of land jutting out into the sea ahead of them.

'Cape Sunium,' Eurybates announced, as if Odysseus needed telling.

The southernmost tip of the Attican peninsula was a familiar sight to any Greek sailor, being the final marker on the return voyage to the Peloponnese. Despite the persistent rain and the oppressive clouds, a great cheer greeted Cape Sunium as the men realised they were passing the threshold of their home waters. With a friendly wind, Ithaca would be no more than two days' sailing away.

'Only Cape Malea to go,' Eurybates added, his voice so low he could have been speaking to himself.

His grudging comment echoed Odysseus's own thoughts. Malea was the final test in their journey, the pivot from which they would swing from south-east to north-west and skirt the coast of the Peloponnese for home. But Malea was also treacherous and unpredictable. It was such a narrow point of rock that the northerly winds that swept a galley down towards its tip would meet it again on the other side. As the vessel turned the Cape its crew had to somehow claw its way north-west against the same force that had taken them there, and either succeed or be driven southward and out to sea. For one ship alone it was a perilous task, for twelve it would take all their skill and every last drop of their luck. But the challenge was unavoidable and they had to overcome it.

The galley forged on across the expanse of grey water, driven by a near gale-force wind to whatever fate the gods had prepared for them. They reached the easternmost point of the Peloponnese, the lands of the Argolis where Diomedes ruled and from which he had drawn his vast army. Odysseus wondered whether his friend had made it safely home, and whether he, too, would have reached

Ithaca by now, had he not headed back to return the Palladium to the ruins of Troy.

'The wind's too strong,' Eperitus said, joining his king in the stern. 'Shouldn't we find somewhere to shelter until there's a change in the weather?'

'That could be a while,' Eurybates answered. 'The summer's gone and the best of the weather with it. We're on the cusp of winter, and the winds around the Cape are strong at the best of times. Hesitate now and we could be waiting for days, even weeks.'

He looked at Odysseus as he spoke. He had offered his opinion as helmsman, but given it knowing the decision lay with the king. But it was not an easy one. Both men were right: the force of the winds, mixed with the already dangerous current around the Cape, would make successfully weathering it difficult; but if they tarried and the winds decided to worsen, their chance might not come again for a long time. The thought of the already unruly crews penned up in a small cove on an inhospitable coast was not one he savoured.

'Keep going,' he commanded. 'If we stay on this heading we should reach the Cape in good time before sunset.'

They turned south with the wind now full behind them. On their right they could see the mountains of the Peloponnese like a distant wall. As they drew closer, Odysseus could pick out the details of the hostile shoreline, where waves crashed continuously against the rocks to form a white mist. Had there been any sun he would have glimpsed circular rainbows in the spray; but the sun had not shown its face all day long, adding to the heaviness in his heart. They passed a final peninsula – a shoulder of rock thrusting upward from the sea that offered their last chance of shelter – then saw the bleak hump of Malea ahead of them. The sight of it filled the whole crew with anticipation.

Odysseus moved to the prow, followed by Eperitus. Shielding his eyes against the westering sun, he gazed at the white-capped waves beneath the Cape, where different forces drove the waters into a frenzy and smashed them against the rocks in great arcs of spray. As he watched he felt the wind building in strength behind him, forcing his cloak against his legs and blowing his hair in long strands before his face. It howled like the Furies, catching the sail with a bang and almost lifting the vessel over the crests of the waves. Eurybates shouted for the sail to be hoisted halfway, aware that a sudden gust could tear it in half and leave them at the mercy of the currents. Odysseus turned, squinting against the wind and spray, and looked at his fleet. They were closing in on each other, huddling together like sheep in a storm, but as he watched their sails half furled, he knew they were still under control. Like many Ithacans, their captains and helmsmen were used to the sea in all its treachery, and if anyone could master it, they could. But the Cape would test them to their limits.

'There's an island on the horizon,' Eperitus said, his voice barely audible amid the gale.

'It's Cythera. We need to claw our way up the channel between the Cape and the island. Pray these winds calm down enough to allow us.'

'And if they don't?'

'Then we'll beat them all the same,' Odysseus answered. 'Come on.'

They returned to the helm, Odysseus ignoring the anxious looks on the faces of many of his men. Eurybates's teeth were gritted as he struggled with the steering oars.

'What do you want me to do? Head out into the channel before we turn her?'

Odysseus nodded. 'When the time comes, make the turn as smart as you can. We don't want to lay across this wind any longer than we have to.'

They were approaching the eastern flank of the Cape now. Odysseus glanced over his right shoulder at the tip of the peninsula, rising tall and grey beside them. It reminded him of a short, angry man, sitting on his haunches as he glared out at the sea. Shredded clouds flew low past its western cheek, an indicator of the winds that were awaiting them on the other side. Eurybates called out an order and several men moved to the stays. A second order saw the rest of the crew lifting the long oars up onto their knees, ready to feed them out into the choppy waters on either side of the galley. Odysseus stood firm on the deck, watching the crew and resisting the urge to bite his fingernails, knowing that it would be an outward sign of nervousness and indecision. He also refused to look over his shoulder at how the rest of the fleet were coping. It would not help them to show he was worried about their fate.

The deck was rolling uncomfortably beneath his feet now. The Cape had sheltered them briefly from the worst of the wind, but as the galley moved past it he could feel the gale picking up rapidly again. Out in the channel where the battle would be fought, he could see the white crests of the waves like the shield walls of a distant foe. At last, Eurybates gave the order.

'*Turn her about*!'

Until then the wind had been their ally, sending them coursing south-west over the choppy waves. Now it became their enemy. As they turned, a furious gust caught the wooden flank of the galley and drove them sideways over the water. The crew fought to master it but failed, and the vessel swung back to continue in the same direction. Again, Eurybates gave the order. It was all Odysseus could do not to repeat it or to rush to one of the stays and throw his own strength into the battle. Behind him he knew the helmsman's muscles would be straining at the twin oars, desperately trying to make them count in the confused waters below. Again the ship refused to turn, caught once more by a fierce gust that turned it back to the south-east. Odysseus ran back to the helm and wrested the oars from Eurybates's grip, signalling for the helmsman to join the men on the ropes. He looked out at the waves and felt the wind on his cheek, letting his sailor's instincts guide his mind as he waited for the right moment to give the order.

'Now!' he hollered.

He leaned upon the twin oars and immediately felt the strain on the wood as they fought against the sea's resistance. His arms ached under the tension, but as the galley turned he felt the force of the wind catch her and try to spin her back again. He battled against it with all his strength, making the oars vibrate so much he feared they would break. If they did, or if his strength gave first, they were lost. The gale would drive them one way onto the rocks of Cythera, or the other way onto the equally dangerous shoreline of Crete beyond the southern horizon; or between the two into the open sea. Then, as he felt his muscles begin to weaken, one of the stays parted and the sail began to swing round. He was losing mastery of the ship. Calling on the last reserves of his strength, he fought to regain control. At the same time, Eperitus seized the tail of the severed rope and with a handful of others hauled the sail back round into the wind. Eurybates shouted for the oars to be lowered into the sea and slowly – painfully slowly – the crew began to pull the ship around. The wind resisted them, but they fought back ferociously. Odysseus began to feel the tension easing from the blades of the steering oars. Then the turn was complete and they were facing into the wind.

Eurybates ordered the sail furled and then returned to the prow and took the steering oars from Odysseus. The king spared him a slap on the shoulder and ran down between the benches. Men on both sides were grimacing under the strain now that the ship was turned into the face of the wind. They had won the first part of the battle, but the worst was still ahead. They would have to wrestle the galley past the Cape and into one of the bays on the western shore of the peninsula, fighting the prevailing current the whole way. Odysseus fixed his gaze on the round peak of the Cape, trying to measure their progress. It was woefully small. His men would tire long before they could pull out of the channel and into the shallower, less tempestuous waters along the coast. And if they failed? In a clear but all too brief moment he pictured Penelope and Telemachus standing on a fog-shrouded beach. Then they were gone again. A shadow fell across his spirit, threatening to crush the fight out of him.

'Odysseus! Odysseus! The fleet!'

He turned to see Eperitus, his face wet with spray and his features set in a look of alarm. Odysseus followed the direction of his finger and saw the dark seas astern, hissing in their natural turmoil as curtains of rain drifted across them.

'The fleet's gone,' Eperitus exclaimed. 'They didn't make the turn.'

Odysseus felt panic closing like a hand about his windpipe.

'They must be there.'

'They're not. They've been swept away.'

Odysseus turned to the men around him.

'*Row*!' he yelled. 'Put your backs into it if you ever want to see your homes again.'

'We have to go back for the others,' Eperitus said, grabbing his arm. 'We can't just leave them.'

The thought of going back – of abandoning the fight – stirred Odysseus to anger.

'No! I'm not giving up now. The others have good captains and strong crews; they'll make it home in their own time. *We're* heading back to Ithaca. And unless you want us to suffer the same fate as the rest of the fleet, then find an oar and get rowing.'

Eperitus stared at him for a moment, then took his place on the benches. Odysseus looked once more at the Cape, shrouded now in rain but still visible. They had barely made any progress since the last time he had checked.

'Row, damn it!' he yelled, drawing his sword and scowling at the men. 'I'll strike down any man who doesn't pull his weight. Now *row*!'

The galley was rolling awkwardly as it struggled over the waves, some of the crew crying out as they struggled at the oars. Only Polites on one side and Selagos on the other seemed not to be hurting, but many around them were beginning to flag. Omeros, his lips pulled back in a grimace and his eyes closed tightly, had to battle his way through every stroke. Beside him Elpenor was in tears, shouting at the pain that coursed through his limbs. The next moment he had fallen back from the bench, hitting the deck with a thud. Odysseus seized him by his tunic and slapped him across the face.

'Row, damn you!' he screamed. 'I won't lose this fight because you're not man enough to pull an oar.'

But Elpenor just groaned and rolled his eyes like a wild animal, not caring whether he lived or died. Odysseus drew his sword, his fury urging him to drive the point into Elpenor's throat. Then he tossed the weapon across the deck, took the boy's place at the oar and began to heave at it with all his strength.

Chapter Fourteen

PAST THE RIM OF THE WORLD

'Ship,' the little girl said, though the Greek word was barely distinguishable through her Trojan accent.

Astynome smiled, nodded and pointed above her head.

'Sail.'

'Excellent,' Astynome said brightly, smiling again. 'And what about that?'

She indicated a goat tethered to the base of one of the benches. The girl sighed, her shoulders slumping.

'G –,' Astynome prompted her.

The child shook her head and said the animal's name in the Trojan tongue, an obstinate tone infiltrating her small voice.

'Goat,' Astynome corrected, patting her head.

The child had clearly had her fill of learning the language of her new masters, so Astynome handed her a little piece of wood that – at her request – Antiphus had whittled into the shape of a person with two legs, two arms and a smooth head with no features. Astynome had made the doll a dress from a piece of old flax, with a hood that hid the fact it had no hair. The girl took the wooden figure and hugged her with a rocking motion.

The sail rumpled a little in the persistent north wind. The spar had been lowered halfway down the mast to keep the galley steady, while the white canvas with its dolphin motif had been brailed into small loops to prevent the ship being driven further away from Greece than it had to. The sky was blue with a few high clouds and

Astynome thought again that it was peculiar that this same wind should have lasted for so many days without abating. A north wind blew most of the year round back in Ilium, but she had always been under the impression that at sea it was more changeable. Perhaps the gods were at play again, she mused, and gave it no more mind. Craning her neck a little from her sitting position she could see a handful of other ships dotted over the surface of the sea, but as ever there was no sight of land. Eurybates would have called out if there had been, of course, but boredom had made her look anyway. Perhaps they had sailed beyond the borders of the ocean. Plenty of the men had said as much, whispering in groups on the benches. Especially after that mist and the unknown stars that had followed it.

She looked down at the four children seated around her. Each had a toy – the doll Antiphus had carved, a bear for the girl's sister and horses for the two others, which Astynome thought ironic since their fathers had been slain by the massacre Odysseus's wooden horse had unleashed on Troy – but they were all bored. No amount of toys or lessons in Greek could keep a child entertained for long. At home, the streets of Troy had been their world, which they had enjoyed with a freedom denied to the besieged adults around them. But here, on the claustrophobic deck of the galley, they were all prisoners, hemmed in by wooden walls and the constant moaning of the wind.

There were other children on board, but, unlike these four, they were not orphans. Their mothers considered Astynome a traitor and would not allow their daughters to go near her, though they were happy enough for her to take charge of the four girls whose parents had not survived the chaos of Troy's last moments. It was a responsibility she had taken up gladly, grateful to have a sense of purpose during the monotony of the voyage. She was convinced it was better for the orphans, too, for they received the attention of Eperitus, Omeros, Antiphus and Polites, and sometimes the king himself. Whereas the other children were kept close to their mothers, these four were spoiled with toys, titbits of extra food and even lessons in sword fighting. Neither would their ears be filled with poisonous thoughts of a lost homeland; not for them the bitterness of knowing they were the last survivors of a proud but extinct race. They would grow up aware of nothing else but Ithaca and their own servitude.

As one of the girls rested her head in her lap, Astynome looked across at Eperitus sleeping on the sacks by the helm. It was over a week now since the winds and currents around Cape Malea had defeated them. The crew had fought hard, cajoled by their desperate king, but in the end they had failed. The force of the gale had driven them helplessly past the shores of Cythera and out into the ocean. In the darkness of night their misery had been compounded by an unyielding downpour of rain that left them wet through and seized by a deathly cold. To the women and children huddled on deck amid the supplies and tethered animals it had been unbearable; to the men, shattered by their exertions, it must have been an unending nightmare. Many had given up the struggle and collapsed. Others, though physically stronger, had been defeated by despair, knowing that their chance of returning home had been lost for days, maybe weeks. But a core of men endured, led by Odysseus, Eurybates and Eperitus and the examples of Polites and Antiphus, sailing the galley through the storm until the morning light brought some deliverance.

The next day's sun had never been more than a dull luminescence showing itself through the cloud. Though the storm abated somewhat, the strong winds did not, preventing them from returning to the Peloponnese and driving them further away across a sea devoid of landmarks. Not even Odysseus or Eurybates had sailed this far south. No-one knew what islands or shorelines they could expect to sight, though all had heard that – once past the stretch of water between Cythera in the west and Crete in the east – there was nothing but ocean for many days.

The four orphans had been a blessing to Astynome then, their tearful fear a spur that prevented her from succumbing to her own misery. For their sake she had to forget her increasing anxiety that she and Eperitus might never find their little farm on Ithaca or have children of their own, and the other dark thoughts that grey skies and an empty ocean were nurturing in her. Instead she had to become a source of reassurance, smiling into their sadness and telling them they were on a great adventure that would be sung about until the end of time, while comforting them that their troubles would only be brief and they would soon find their new home. When the mention of Ithaca brought doubts and worries, she told them it was a beautiful island with snow-capped mountains and grassy plains filled with little white flowers, just like the dried ones that the Ithacans wore in their belts. That was how she had always imagined it in her own dreams, and the children's concerns grew less as she told them about the place she had never been to.

And all the time she had felt Eurylochus's eyes upon her, weighing her on the scales of his lust.

By evening of that second day, the clouds had begun to fray at the edges, breaking up above the horizon and allowing sight of the sun as it slowly sank into the sea. Astynome's heart rose briefly at the sight of it and the hope of warmth that it suggested, but it was quickly absorbed again by the waiting ocean. The night that followed was black and moonless, though the ceiling of shifting cloud was rent by great holes that gave glimpses of the stars above. By their light she could see the shapes of the sailors on the benches around, oblivious to the rocking of the galley as they snored. The women and children, too, were asleep, and for a while she had felt as if she were alone on that great expanse of sea. Then she had heard a movement behind her and turned to see a figure silhouetted against a field of stars. Eurylochus, she had thought, her muscles tensing as she pulled her damp cloak tighter about herself.

'Astynome?' Eperitus's voice whispered her name.

'I'm here,' she answered, stretching out a hand.

He took it and guided himself to her side. They embraced and kissed, his arms warm and solid as they closed around her. It was the first time they had spoken in a day and a half, though to Astynome it had felt much longer.

'How are the children?' he asked, his features faintly visible in the starlight.

'Full of terrible fears and inconsolable worries that they'll forget at the first sight of land or sunshine.'

'If only our fears and worries would leave us so easily.'

'They will soon enough, when we find our way to Ithaca.'

It was as if she was talking to one of the children, though this time she was seeking comfort rather than giving it.

'Of course,' he said flatly, looking over his shoulder at the ever-present figures of Odysseus and Eurybates at the helm. Neither had left their positions since Cape Malea. 'Though right now any land would be welcome. Somewhere to light a fire and get warm. Here.'

He unclasped his double cloak and draped it around her shoulders. She protested that he would get cold but he refused to listen.

'We *will* find Ithaca, won't we?' she asked.

'I… I don't know. If it's within our power to, we will, but we're not even sure where we are any more. Look at the stars. They seem the same. All the familiar constellations are there, and yet they're different. A star out of place here and there, some dimmer where they used to be bright or brighter where they used to be dim. Eurybates noticed it first.'

'What does Odysseus think?'

'He's hardly spoken a word since the Cape. You don't know how desperate he is to get home to Penelope and Telemachus. I've tried speaking to him, tried to lift his mood, but most of the time it's as if I'm not even there. The one time he said anything was to mention the old prophecy the Pythoness gave him,' his voice fell further, 'that he won't get home for another ten years. I reminded him of what he always used to say, that a man can master his own destiny regardless of what the gods say. But he didn't want to listen. This thing with the stars has only made him worse.'

Astynome looked across at the northern horizon, now almost clear of clouds, and saw that Eperitus was right. The constellations were different. The one thing that had remained constant throughout her fragile life – beyond the reaches of man, nature and even, it seemed, the gods – had somehow become distorted, subtly but undeniably. And it filled her with fear.

'There's something else.'

'What is it?'

Eperitus's dark eyes flicked from side to side at the sleeping figures around them.

'One of the ropes parted when we were rounding the Cape. I managed to catch hold of it and haul the sail back round into the wind, not that it did us any good.'

'I remember. What of it?'

'The rope didn't snap, Astynome. It was cut.'

'What do you mean? By a knife?'

He nodded.

'But why? Who did it?'

Her voice had risen above a whisper and he had placed a finger to her lips.

'I don't know who. One of the men on the stays: Polites was one, and Omeros, but they wouldn't have any reason to cut the rope. I didn't see the others. As for why – why else? To stop us getting home.'

Astynome frowned.

'That doesn't make any sense. Every man wants to get back to Ithaca, don't they?'

'Eventually, perhaps, but not yet. I haven't mentioned it to Odysseus, but I've thought long and hard about it myself, and it strikes me the only reason someone doesn't want us to get back home is –'

'They want to kill Odysseus first,' Astynome finished.

'Someone doesn't want him to take up his throne again, and they know that once he's home he'll be beyond their reach. But here, out at sea on a small galley, they can get to him.'

'A knife in the dark –'

'Why do you think I've hardly slept? Someone has to keep an eye open.'

'Then tell Odysseus.'

'Not yet,' Eperitus said. 'It might be nothing.'

'And it might be Eurylochus,' Astynome hissed, her voice barely a breath now. 'You know he's ambitious and unscrupulous, and that he has some claim on the throne.'

'He was on the benches, as was his Taphian. It could have been one of his other cronies, but for some reason I don't think this is his style.'

Astynome looked over at Odysseus's cousin asleep on one of the benches, his large stomach rising and falling slowly. Whatever Eperitus's instincts, she believed otherwise.

Though the whole crew seemed to have slept until dawn, the next morning everyone was talking about the stars. Voices spoke of being cursed by the gods, and a few, in whispers, blamed Odysseus. Eurylochus monopolised on this, attracting small groups of unhappy men who were angry about the failure at Cape Malea and superstitious about the distorted constellations. But as more men came and went and Astynome began to suspect that Eurylochus and Selagos were stirring up mutiny, something had happened to change the mood on board the galley.

'Ship! Ship to port!'

Odysseus, ever conscious of the loss of the rest of his fleet, had positioned a lookout atop the mast. The man now called out with all his strength and pointed to the east. As if in response, the sun emerged from between two stacks of white cloud and poured warmth and light down on the beleaguered occupants of the galley, nearly all of whom had rushed over to the port side to get a better view. An angry bellow from Eurybates brought most of them back again and restored the ship's balance.

'I see it,' Eperitus announced. 'It could be Ithacan. They're unfurling the sail and turning towards us. There's a dolphin on it!'

His words brought a cheer from the crew. More orders from the helm brought the galley about on a diagonal path intended to cut across the front of the other ship. The strong winds caught the sail as it fell open and drove the vessel forward.

'There's another,' cried the lookout. 'And a third.'

Astynome doubted the Ithacans could have been happier if they had spotted their homeland. Before long, eleven ships had been counted, all of them changing course to meet the lone galley of their commander.

When the fleet was reunited, the different captains had come across in small rowing boats and joined Odysseus at the helm, where they informed the king of how they had been swept inexorably out to sea at Malea and driven south by the strong winds ever since. All agreed it had been a miracle they had ever found each other again, but the initial joy of being reunited soon faded as they discussed what to do next. They talked loud enough for Astynome to overhear almost every word, and there was no hiding the fact they were lost and unable to do anything but let the persistent gale take them where it would. One man suggested they had sailed past the rim of the world, pointing out the difference in the stars that they had all noticed. Eperitus was dismissive, but Astynome noticed that Odysseus said nothing.

That night, after the captains had returned to their own ships and torches were lit at the helm and prow of each galley so they would not lose each other in the darkness, everyone but the children stayed awake until late. The men had sat in groups on the benches, looking at the constellations and quietly discussing what it could mean. Astynome joined Eperitus, Antiphus, Polites and Omeros, though she did not feel like adding to their conversation as they pooled their knowledge to decide what was different about each grouping of stars. Eventually they came to accept that the constellations *were* different and there was nothing they could do to explain or correct it, so Omeros produced his lyre and began to sing a poem he had been composing about the death of Achilles. A few others joined them, drawn like moths to the young bard's music, and slowly Astynome and Eperitus drew away to the end of their bench. She placed her hand over his cheek, where the beard had grown back full and thick, then leaned across to kiss him.

'I don't think we should,' he said, easing his lips from hers. He glanced over at the lone figure at the twin steering oars, his stocky, triangular shape outlined by the mass of bright stars. 'At least not in front of Odysseus.'

'He's not a prude,' she said, smiling.

He shook his head.

'When we get back to Ithaca we'll get married, buy a farm and have a dozen children just like we've always planned. But until we do, I don't want to remind him of his separation from Penelope. The nearer we get to home, the more he misses her.'

'Oh,' she said, withdrawing a little.

She had hoped to spend the night in his arms, but he returned to the helm shortly afterwards and left her wondering at this man who could kill an enemy without compunction but worry so much about causing a friend anxiety. Instead she found the four orphans, who were snuggled closely together, and lay down beside them, her body protecting them from the cold. And so it had carried on, every night for over a week, with Eperitus standing watch by his king and only sleeping when the morning came and the threat of an assassin's blade was diminished by the light of day.

The ninth morning of the voyage since Cape Malea had arrived cool and bright without a cloud in the sky, though the wind remained strong out of the north. Astynome's eyes remained on Eperitus as he slept on the sacks of grain, tired of the endless voyage and wishing she could be alone with him, just for a while. She felt trapped and restless, yearning for his touch and the release it would bring.

'There's always room under my blanket.'

Astynome felt a chill run down her back. She turned and stared into Eurylochus's small, mean eyes. Selagos, as ever, was standing behind him.

'If Eperitus sees you anywhere near me, he'll slice open your fat pig's throat and toss your carcass into the sea.'

The smile barely faltered on his heavy-jowled pink face.

'You have a temper on you. I like that. Are you as passionate in bed?'

'You'll never know.'

'What's wrong?' asked one of the children, raising her head from Astynome's lap.

'Nothing,' she replied, lifting her to her feet and gently shooing her to one side. 'Go and play.'

'Yes, push off, you Trojan rat.'

'Leave her alone!'

Astynome glowered at Eurylochus but sensed a group of men gathering behind her. She hoped they were merely attracted to the spectacle, yet suspected they were deliberately forming a screen between her and the helm, where Eperitus and Odysseus were both asleep and Eurybates was busy with the twin oars.

'You should be a little friendlier,' Eurylochus continued, 'or you'll find worse things can happen to you than having your throat cut and your body thrown overboard. There are plenty here would like to see a bit of your passion. Resistance makes it more fun for some, if you know what I mean. But show me a little kindness and I'll see to it no-one else touches you.'

'You tried to take me all those months ago in Lyrnessus, but Eperitus sent you running like the coward you are. Next time, he'll kill you.'

'So you keep saying. Let's see, shall we?'

He stepped towards her, reassured by the giant presence of Selagos behind him and his other henchmen in the crowd. Some of them she recognised from the sacking of Lyrnessus, where they had tried to rape her.

'You wouldn't dare, not in front of a ship full of witnesses.'

But she sensed he would. Perhaps to attack her would inflame the mob instincts he had been busy exciting in the crew, the spark he needed to provoke a fight and turn them against Odysseus. A hand shoved her in the small of her back and propelled her into Eurylochus's arms. For a moment he was as surprised as she was. Then he placed his hand on her buttock and squeezed it hard as he pressed his mouth clumsily against hers. Suddenly her anger flared up inside her and she bit down fast and hard upon his lower lip.

Eurylochus let out a high-pitched squeal and pushed her away. As she fell into the arms of a man behind her, the wall of onlookers was torn open and Eperitus appeared, flanked by Polites and Omeros on one side and Antiphus and Elpenor on the other. He turned questioning eyes towards her.

'I'm alright,' she said, wiping Eurylochus's blood from her lips.

'She tried to kiss me,' Eurylochus protested. 'She's nothing but a whore!'

'You'll die for that,' Eperitus told him, scraping his blade clear of its scabbard.

Eurylochus drew his own weapon and met the first blow with a ringing clash. Selagos lunged forward and was met by the even greater bulk of Polites, who pulled him aside into the crowd of onlookers, scattering them like hens before foxes as the two giants crashed to the deck. Another man pulled out his sword, only to find Antiphus's bow drawn and the arrow pointed at his heart.

Astynome was barely conscious of anything other than the fight between Eperitus and Eurylochus. To her surprise, the latter was quick with his blade, parrying every angry blow that Eperitus threw at him and returning them with determined attacks of his own. Neither wore a shield or armour, and with a thrill of fear Astynome realised the first successful strike could be fatal. She also saw the pain written on Eperitus's features every time his blade met Eurylochus's, a sign his shoulder was still weak.

Eurylochus aimed his blows higher to test the damaged shoulder muscle. Then Eperitus struck hard and fast, knocking the blade from Eurylochus's hand. He stumbled backwards and tripped over one of the benches. Eperitus's foot was on his chest in a moment, his sword in both hands and held point-downward over Eurylochus's chest.

'Don't, Eperitus!' Astynome shouted, rushing forward. 'He's still the king's cousin.'

Eperitus looked at her, then back at the surrounding crew as if Odysseus would step out from among them at any moment. But there was no sign of the king, only the expectant faces of the Ithacans. Eperitus shook his head at her and raised his sword.

But before he could plunge the point into Eurylochus's chest, a voice rang out from a nearby ship. A second followed and then a third. Then the man atop the mast lifted his eyes from the fight and out towards the horizon.

'Land!' he shouted.

Chapter Fifteen

A SMALL VICTORY

Telemachus sat on the edge of the dock swinging his feet over the water. His fine features, the male mirror of his mother's, were sullen as he watched the merchant galley slipping out into the strait between Ithaca and Kefalonia. A couple of the crew waved to him from the benches where they sat pulling at their oars. He raised his hand half-heartedly and saw them lean in and share a comment that made both men laugh. Doubtless they thought him a curious boy, running as fast as he could down the path from the town and asking them breathlessly for news from Troy. Had the Greeks taken the city yet? Was the war over? Had they met any returning warriors? Did they have any news at all?

But just like every other merchant vessel that brought its cargo from foreign shores, they could tell him nothing of value. A few rumours, some of them contradicting what he had been told by previous crews; nothing to ease the hunger of a ten-year-old desperate for news of his father. It had been even more frustrating in Sparta. Though its glory had dimmed greatly – according to Halitherses – it still teemed with merchants and travellers, and should have been full of reports from the war. Instead, the people seemed to have forgotten about it. A few had bitter comments about their absent king, abandoning his city for the sake of a faithless harlot. Some rued the loss of loved ones. More were angry that Sparta's wealth had been stripped to fuel the war and that the people were poor and hungry. The few crippled soldiers he had found – limbless beggars no longer able to fight in Menelaus's army – could tell him little of worth for the food he gave them. Without revealing that

Odysseus was his father, he would ask whether they knew anything of the king of Ithaca. But too often their replies were scathing or ignorant. *Brave enough* was the best he could get from them, but *scheming, dishonourable* or *too clever for his own good and ours* were more common. So Telemachus had returned from Sparta more frustrated than when he had arrived. It seemed his whole life had been spent in frustration, waiting for something that would never come. Sometimes he wondered whether his father even existed – at least the great man his mother spoke about. Such a man would have found a way home by now.

The merchant galley had reached the straits and was unfurling its sail. Telemachus watched it head south for a moment longer, then started the walk back. Climbing the road towards the spring where the townsfolk fetched their water, he heard laughter from beneath the shade of the poplar trees. With a sinking heart he recognised the voices of Melantho, her brother Melanthius, and her latest lover, Eurymachus. Antinous's braying tones could also be heard as he made mock of Melanthius. Telemachus could see them sitting with their backs against the poplars, Melanthius smiling stupidly as Antinous compared him to one of the goats he looked after. Then, as Telemachus approached with his gaze fixed on the road, the laughter stopped.

'It's the young pretender,' Antinous scoffed, though there was more menace than mockery in his voice now. 'Any news from Troy today?'

'Is your daddy dead yet?' Eurymachus sneered. 'It'd be good to have a real king around here. One we can actually *see*!'

Telemachus clenched his fists tightly and forced himself to walk on, but Melantho blocked his path.

'Don't *you* want to be king, little Telemachus?' she asked, inclining her head slightly and looking at him with an expression of sympathy. 'Oh, I forgot. You can't. Not since mummy sold your birthright.'

Telemachus did not understand what she meant, but her giggling irked him.

'You won't be laughing when Arceisius finds out you've been sleeping with half the men on the island.'

Her smile stiffened. Then she bent down and looked him in the eye.

'With any luck my husband is already dead, along with your father and the rest of the idiots who followed him off to war.'

'Get out of my way, whore!'

'What did you call her?'

Eurymachus's fist crashed into the side of Telemachus's face. He fell to the ground and his vision went black. When he came to, a moment later, it was to see Eurymachus's fearsome bulk standing over him – twice his age and twice his size – with his fists bared and his low forehead contorted into a frown.

'Kill the little runt and let's be done with him,' Antinous goaded, standing at his shoulder.

It was Melanthius who saved him. Whether from a grain of concern or from fear of the consequences of beating up the young prince, he stepped in front of Eurymachus and gestured Telemachus to his feet.

'Run home, little boy, and in future learn not to insult your elders and betters. Not if you know what's good for you.'

Telemachus picked himself up, seething with shame and anger, and marched off towards the town. Their laughter followed him to the first bend in the road, after which he ran – his eyes burning with tears – until he saw the busy marketplace and the palace gates beyond it. He desperately wanted to run into the inner courtyard and find a place to hide, but he knew some servant or other would stop him and demand to know what was wrong. So he joined the throng milling around the stalls of the fishermen and farmers and threaded his way to the far corner of the palace wall. Slipping out of sight, he slumped down beneath its shadow and hid his face in his hands.

But he had not gone unnoticed. Hearing footsteps, he peered between his fingers and saw a pair of sandalled feet stop before him. There was a pause, then the man knelt and placed a hand on his shoulder.

'What is it, lad?'

The hand and the voice belonged to Halitherses. Telemachus felt the tears return. Reluctantly he told the story of his humiliation at the spring, not daring to look the old man in the eyes.

'I'm not worthy of him, Halitherses.'

'Your father? Of course you are.'

'No I'm not!' Telemachus insisted, shaking his head. 'He's brave. He's strong. He can fight. And he has authority. I'm none of those things. I'm a weakling and a coward.'

He felt the hateful tears again. More hateful still was the part of him that wanted Halitherses to go back to the spring and give Eurymachus the beating he deserved; that wanted someone else to fight his battles for him. Frustratingly, Halitherses neither refuted his self-accusations of weakness and cowardice nor agreed with them; nor did he offer to beat up Eurymachus on his behalf. Instead he slumped down beside him with a grunt and a sigh that spoke of weary bones.

'What has Mentor spent the past few weeks teaching you, Telemachus?'

'Lots of useless things. Stories about the gods. How to sacrifice animals. The seasons for farming and fishing. How to win an argument. The rules of *xenia* –'

'He's teaching you how to be a king.'

'Then he's wasting his time and mine!'

'And he's been teaching you how to fight.'

'So what do you want me to *do*? Take a sword and stab Eurymachus in the *stomach*? What does a one-handed man know about sword fighting anyway?'

'Lots, and don't you ever think otherwise,' Halitherses admonished him. 'Now, think of the things he's been teaching you and take away the sword.'

'I don't understand –'

'You have to, Telemachus. Mentor's teaching you these things because one day the fate of Ithaca may rest in your hands. You have to be ready for when that day comes. And it will. But right now you're at a crossroads.' He held out his hand and tipped it from one side to another, as if on an invisible pivot. 'You've faced a challenge and failed. You can let it pass and live with the humiliation, or you can go back to that spring and do something about it. Let it pass and the only thing you lose is your self-belief; face up to it and you'll probably get a few bruises and a broken bone or two for your courage. But you'll know you took it like the man you're going to be one day: your father's son.'

Telemachus looked at Halitherses and understood this was a choice the old man had made many times in his life. That was what it meant to be a warrior or a king: to choose every day between courage and cowardice, danger and safety. As he considered the choice before him, he remembered the sting of Eurymachus's fist and felt the fear of it. But more terrible was the thought of running away and not being able to face himself any more. He stood up.

'Thank you, Halitherses.'

'Good lad. But don't forget, you *are* Odysseus's son, and that means using more than brawn to gain a victory.'

He tapped the side of his head to emphasise the point and winked.

Telemachus almost ran back to the spring, more afraid that Eurymachus and the others would have left than he was of the beating that surely awaited him. He was determined now, and his deter mination refused to listen to the voice of caution that warned him against rash decisions.

'I thought I told you to go home.'

They were still there, all four of them, sitting on the grass and sharing wine from a goatskin. Eurymachus saw him and jumped to his feet with frightening readiness. Telemachus remembered what Mentor had taught him, trying to apply his words to the fact he did not have a sword in his hand.

Controlled aggression.

'One punch not enough for you then?' Eurymachus snarled.

Act swiftly and act first.

Melantho seemed to recognise something was different.

'Be careful, Eurymachus,' she warned.

Eurymachus saw it too, but too late. Telemachus threw a punch at his stomach. The hard muscle yielded and Eurymachus spat the air out of his lungs. Telemachus aimed a second punch at his brick-like jaw but missed and caught him in the throat. Eurymachus gagged and staggered backwards, eyes agog as he clutched at his neck. That was not what Telemachus had expected. More unexpected was Melantho throwing herself onto his back and bundling him to the ground as she tried to drive her sharp fingernails into his face. Instinctively he threw his elbow back and caught her in the cheek. She screamed and rolled over, dragging Telemachus on top of herself. They stared each other in the eye, but in that moment of indecision it was Telemachus who thought fastest. Gripping her hair so she could not move, he lowered his mouth to her ear and spoke in a low voice.

Then Melanthius pulled him from his sister and locked his arms behind his back. Antinous appeared before him, his fists balled up and his face twisted with rage.

'You've been asking for this for a long time.'

He punched him in the stomach, knocking the breath from his lungs so that he hung from Melanthius's grip. Eurymachus pushed Antinous aside and readied his own fist. But before he could land the first blow, Melantho leapt between them and prised her brother's hands from Telemachus's arms. The prince dropped to the grass.

'Leave him alone,' she screamed. There was fear in her eyes, enough to convince them not to ignore her. 'Leave him alone before you do something we'll all regret. Let's go.'

Telemachus lay on his side and watched them run off. The few words he had whispered in Melantho's ear had worked. If the pain had not been so overwhelming and if there had been enough air in his lungs, he would have laughed.

Chapter Sixteen

THE LAND OF THE LOTUS EATERS

Eperitus was furious. The brief trial was over and the crew were already dispersing across the sand to make fires and prepare food with the crews of the other galleys. Eurylochus slung his shield across his back and shouldered his spear, and with a mocking smile at Eperitus he went to join two similarly armed men at the top of the beach. Despite Astynome's testimony and the statements of several crew members, Eurylochus's punishment was laughable. He had dared to lay his hands on Astynome – not a mere slave, but the woman of another Ithacan – and for his affront had been made to forfeit a quarter of his share of the plunder. He had also been ordered on a scouting mission to explore the new coast. Eperitus felt as if *he* were the one being punished, not Eurylochus.

Strangely, Astynome did not share his anger. Rather she seemed relieved as she placed a hand on his shoulder and stood on tiptoes to kiss his cheek.

'It's nothing,' she said, softly, before turning and running barefoot across the sand to where her orphans were waiting.

Eperitus looked at Odysseus, who was eyeing him with his arms folded.

'Say it then,' the king challenged, wistfully.

'Why bother? You know exactly what I think of that farce.'

'So what would you have me do? Execute my own cousin?' Odysseus raised his hands in despair. 'And you heard what Theano said: Athena has forbidden me to lay a finger on him.'

'Then punish some of his cronies,' Eperitus replied, trying not to raise his voice. 'Execute the Taphian and do us both a favour! Show them you're still the king.'

'Execute him on what charge? Perhaps getting rid of Selagos would save me a lot of trouble, but at worst he defended his friend in a fight. I can't kill him for *that*, even if I'd like to. And I *am* the king. I have a duty to show justice. When I corrupt that justice to satisfy a friend's anger – even if it's righteous – then I give up my privilege as king.'

'Kingship isn't earned, it's a birthright.'

'Say you, the son of a king slayer!' Odysseus snapped. 'You, more than most, should know how easy it is to topple a ruler. I'm flesh and blood, too. All I need to do is make a few bad decisions to get myself stabbed in the dark, or, worse still, strung up by a mob of my unhappy subjects. And what if I hadn't burst in and stopped you from cutting Eurylochus's throat? What would you have thought of the king's justice then, if I'd been forced to execute you for murder? I'm just thankful to the gods that we sighted land when we did and it stayed your hand long enough for me to reach you. Now, whether I've earned your loyalty or you just respect my birthright, please get a few men together and go find some fresh water. The casks are almost empty.'

It did not take long to find an inland stream and replenish their supplies. As he supervised the teams of water-carriers, Eperitus looked up at the flat-topped mountains that they had first seen from the sea and wondered whether this unknown coast was inhabited. There were no dwellings or fishing boats and no land had been cleared for farming. The only smoke trails came from the Ithacans on the beach and he could not hear the telltale bleating of goats or sheep. Yet the place did not feel entirely wild. There were places along the banks of the stream where the grass had been trampled bare, and not by animals. Four large, flat stones crossed the waterbed at one point, and here and there he found what looked like olive stones in the dust, though there was no sign of an olive tree anywhere. And then there was the faint scent that suggested the presence of people. It was different to the odour of the men around him – just as the Trojans had smelled differently to the Greeks – but it was there nonetheless. He did not like the thought they were not alone, especially after their experience with the Cicones, and the sooner Eurylochus and the other two scouts returned, the sooner he would be encouraging Odysseus to set sail again.

But the three men had not returned by the time he returned to camp, so he found Astynome and sat with her orphans while she fetched some broth. They looked at him uncertainly in his leather breastplate with its many battle scars and with the short sword hanging in the scabbard at his side. They had seen enough soldiers in their short lifetimes and were most likely the children of soldiers, but in the death throes of Troy they must have witnessed what such men could do, and it left them quiet and uneasy despite his clumsy efforts to entertain them. Only when Astynome returned did they relax again, eventually accepting him into their simple, foolish games.

'You'll make a good father,' Astynome said as he threw knucklebones in the sand with the oldest girl.

'You're joking, aren't you? They're terrified of me when you're not around.'

'All warriors scare them. If you didn't have all that war gear on they'd have been running circles round you. And it will be different with your own children.'

He thought of Iphigenia and how she had seemed to warm to him from the start. But the memory of her just reminded him of how he had failed her. Briefly he questioned whether he had the right to bring other children into the world, then pushed the thought from his mind. Astynome would not give him a choice in the matter.

'Duty calls, Eperitus. Odysseus wants you.'

Antiphus had appeared with his bow in his hand and his quiver slung across his shoulder. Eperitus passed the last of his broth to the smallest of the girls, who took it greedily, then, after saying farewell to Astynome, he picked up his shield and followed the archer across the beach. They found Odysseus with Polites, Omeros and Eurybates and half a dozen others, all of them except Eurybates fully armed.

'What's wrong?'

'Nothing for certain,' Odysseus answered, smiling at him as if their earlier altercation had never happened. 'But it's late afternoon and Eurylochus's party haven't returned yet. I ordered them to seek out signs of habitation and report back the moment they found anything. Either way, they should have been back by now.'

'With Eurylochus in charge they're probably lost.'

'Whatever's happened, I'm going to look for them,' Odysseus replied. 'Eurybates, you're in command until we return. If we don't find them by nightfall, we'll make camp and continue the search at first light. Give us until noon tomorrow and then send out another search party. If they don't find us – or don't return themselves – then set sail without us and make it back to Ithaca as best you can.'

Eurybates nodded and said nothing. The others tightened the straps on their shields and made ready to go.

'Wait,' Eperitus said, signalling for Odysseus and Polites to join him. Polites's left eye and cheek were black from his fight with Selagos, though the Taphian had received a cracked rib and lost a tooth. 'I want Polites to stay here.'

'I'm not staying,' the giant warrior said with a dismissive laugh.

'We might need him,' Odysseus agreed.

'I need someone to watch over Astynome. If Eurylochus comes back while we're out looking for him, I don't want her left with no-one to protect her. Even if he doesn't return, I don't trust Selagos near her. And there's only one man in this whole camp can guard her from him.'

Polites's eyes narrowed in thought, then he nodded.

'You're right. I'll do it.'

He looked at Odysseus, who conceded with a shrug and went to join the others. Eperitus reached up and laid a hand on Polites's shoulder.

'This isn't a one-time favour either. I don't know how long it'll be before we find our way home, but until then I need you to keep an eye on her when I'm not around. She means everything to me.'

'She'll be safe. I give you my word.'

He gripped Eperitus's hand as a token of his promise, then turned and marched back down the beach.

'I'd have let you stay behind if you're worried about Astynome's safety,' Odysseus told him as he caught up with the others.

'Of course you would,' Eperitus said. 'But then who would look after you?'

They followed the general direction that the scouts had taken that morning and soon picked up their trail by the wanton hacking of trees and bushes along the way. After a while Odysseus halted by a path running east to west through the scrub. No plants grew there and the ground had been smoothed by the regular passing of many feet.

'A trail?' Omeros suggested.

'Looks like it,' Odysseus said, drawing his sword. 'We'll follow it west towards that high ridge. Eperitus, walk with me if you will.'

The two men went side by side along the narrow track with the others behind them. Eperitus quickly picked up the distinctive scent of other people. It was the same faint odour he had noticed by the stream, though more evident. As they approached the ridge he noticed the sour tang of communal latrines that marked every settlement he had ever known. But if there was a town or village over the crest of the hill, why could he not detect roast meat, baked bread, woodsmoke and the other smells that indicated the presence of man? Then he stopped and held up his hand.

'I can hear people,' he said. 'Beyond the ridge.'

The Ithacans readied their weapons and advanced cautiously up the slope, preferring the cover of the scrub to the open path. There were no lookouts and soon all four men were lying on their stomachs on the top of the ridge. Below them the reverse slope fell away to an open plain with a walled town at its centre. But it was not like any other walled town Eperitus had ever seen before. There were no towers or gates, just a large gap in the eastern battlement where a gateway must once have stood. The ruined walls would only reach a man's head at the highest points and would be little higher than his knee in others. Eperitus had seen enough sieges to know their destruction was not the result of war, which would have seen one or two breaches with the rest of the circuit more or less intact. Neither had they been brought down by one of Poseidon's earthquakes, which left heaps of fallen masonry on either side. Instead the ramparts had been pulled down stone by stone to build the ramshackle buildings that surrounded the old town. These seemed not to have been constructed to any plan, but were more like the dens of children – idle fancies thrown together in a day's work, with little thought for appearance or comfort. Their roofs looked to have been made from driftwood or old pieces of sail, held in place by blocks of stone. The houses inside the town walls had been properly erected but were in need of repair. Some had collapsed altogether, while most had roofs that had fallen in and been replaced with wood or canvas arrangements, similar to the hovels outside. From his vantage point on the ridge he could see a temple and a palace facing each other across an open space in the centre of the town. The temple was a roofless shell with empty plinths at the foot of its steps where the images of gods would once have stood. The palace was rectangular with an opening at its centre in which trees grew wild and unchecked. The far side of the building had collapsed, while on the near wall his keen eyes could make out the remains of flaking plaster still decorated with the faded outlines of elaborate murals. The square that separated the two buildings had once been paved with great flags of stone. These were now cracked and thick with dry grass.

He would have taken it for a city that had been deserted long years ago, were it not for the people that lined the walls and filled the doorways, or strolled through the many streets and thoroughfares that criss-crossed the town. They were dark-skinned with black hair and wore nothing but plain skirts around their waists. That was the oddest thing of all. In every town or city Eperitus had ever visited, clothing was what marked a person's place in society: the wealthy and high-born in their brightly dyed cloaks and dresses, the jewellery glinting off the women's necks and wrists; the warriors with their armour and the swords hanging from their sides; the craftsmen with their rough tunics and leather aprons; the slaves in their plain clothing, carrying jars of water or baskets of bread balanced on their heads. But here everyone was the same: no adornments, no tools marking their different professions, no colour – just simple skirts of grey wool. There were none of the normal sounds of a town, either – the cries of merchants selling their wares, the rumble of cartwheels straining beneath wagons loaded with goods, the lowing of cattle and the whack of the herdsmen's sticks across their rumps. Even the children that Eperitus could see sitting among the ruins seemed quiet. Instead of the healthy sounds of an active town, all Eperitus could hear was the settled hum of voices in conversation.

'I don't like it,' he told Odysseus, lying at his shoulder. 'Something feels wrong.'

'Something *is* wrong,' Antiphus agreed. 'There isn't any structure. What sort of town doesn't have soldiers to protect it? I know there's not much to defend, but every man, woman and child here should have become the slaves of the first armed band to come across them. And where are the farmers selling their crops, or the shepherds with their flocks? Where are the smiths, the bakers, the wine merchants? That temple doesn't look like it's seen a sacrifice in a hundred years. And the palace! What ruler would live *there*? It's not as if there aren't enough idle hands to tidy things up.'

'I think that's the problem,' Odysseus said. 'Maybe there aren't any rulers. Not in the way we understand them.'

'No *rulers*?' Antiphus exclaimed. 'Everyone has rulers. If they didn't, then somebody would put themselves in charge. It's the way of the world.'

'Exactly,' Eperitus said.

He was as disturbed as Antiphus by the notion that a body of people could exist without someone governing them. Men were not like birds, flocking together and then migrating according to a collective instinct. Men needed laws and laws needed makers and upholders. Without law the world would slip into chaos, just as it was in the days before the Olympians came to power.

'We'll soon find out,' Odysseus said. 'Eurylochus and the others are in there somewhere, and we're going to find them. But keep your weapons to hand. There's something here I don't understand, and that usually means trouble.'

They rejoined the path and followed it down the slope towards the town. The people outside the walls had already spotted them and were watching their approach. They did not flee in terror, but stood in groups and eyed the heavily armed newcomers with bold curiosity. A single child was sent running back to the town, which was the most activity Eperitus had observed among its strange inhabitants.

As they reached the first makeshift hovels, a woman left the group of onlookers and walked towards them. Like every other adult, she was naked to the waist and barefoot. Smiling, she indicated the way to the town and spoke a word that Eperitus did not understand. When she did not receive a response, she smiled again.

'Welcome.'

'You speak Greek?' Odysseus asked.

'Welcome,' she repeated and again gestured him towards the town.

They carried on towards the gap in the broken walls, all the time regarded listlessly by groups of men and women from the ruins around them. The women's eyes lingered on the Ithacans, while their men merely smiled and nodded dumbly. Several spoke words of welcome as the warriors strolled past. They seemed benign and without aggression, and yet Eperitus felt uneasy as he sensed them leaving their tumbledown homes and following in their wake.

As they entered the town they were met by another large crowd that gazed at them with languid curiosity, rather like a herd of cows. Eperitus noticed there was not a single elder among them and they were all younger than him. The realisation only increased the feeling of disquiet that had haunted him since he had first seen the town from the ridge. Then a man with oddly pale eyes and long brown hair came forward and spoke a few words in a language Eperitus did not know. Several women left the circle of onlookers and walked towards the Ithacans. One laid a hand on Eperitus's upper arm, stroking the bulge of his muscle as she looked him in the eye.

'Come lay with me,' she said and tried to lead him away to a nearby house.

He pulled free of her grip and she turned in confusion to the pale-eyed man. Meanwhile, one of the other women had taken Odysseus's hand and was guiding it towards her naked breast. He snatched it away and drove her off with a fierce stare.

'Now I know why they don't need an army,' Antiphus said as another woman draped her arms over his shoulders and kissed his neck.

Behind him Omeros was being led uncertainly into the crowd by two girls.

'Enough!' Odysseus snapped. 'We're here to find Eurylochus and the others, nothing else.'

The women released their hold on the Ithacans and looked to the pale-eyed man, who waved them back and spoke once more in his unknown language. This time four men stepped forward. One took Eperitus by the hand and raised his fingers to his lips. A moment later he lay in the dust, clutching at his cheek and wailing pathetically. The others retreated back into the crowd, and the murmur of voices that had surrounded the newcomers since their entry into the town fell suddenly silent. Eperitus unclenched his fist and let his hand fall to the pommel of his sword as he looked around at the blank faces staring back at him. Odysseus, too, had slipped his fingers to the handle of his sword and was eyeing the hushed throng. Then one of the women began to laugh, pointing at the man lying on the ground and saying something in their strange, melodic language. Slowly the rest of the crowd joined in, some of them kicking dust at him as he crawled away through the wall of their legs.

'We want to speak to your king,' Odysseus said, raising his voice above their laughter. 'Who is your king?'

Their mirth faded and they became docile again as they turned their eyes on Odysseus.

'I asked you who your king is,' he repeated.

'We don't understand,' the pale-eyed man answered, staring at Odysseus with curiosity.

'Who *leads* you?'

The man smiled, intrigued by the notion.

'Why do we need to be led?'

'Who makes your rules? Who enforces them?' Eperitus said.

'There are no rules. We do as we please.'

'Rubbish. Without the rule of law there's no cohesion, no society.'

'We're looking for three men,' Odysseus interrupted. 'Three men who dress like us. They came this way this morning. Have you seen them?'

The pale-eyed man smiled again.

'There have been no others. You are the only men we have seen. But you can stay here with us and wait for your friends if you wish. We will be pleased to share our home with you until they come.'

Odysseus's eyes narrowed pensively.

'No. If you haven't seen them then they must have headed south, or up into the mountains. We need to go look for them.'

'Stay a while. Maybe the Old One can help you.'

'The Old One?'

'Of course. If there are things we don't know, we go to him and he helps us. He knows very much and perhaps he knows something about your friends.'

'Why would he have seen them if you haven't?' Antiphus asked, sceptically.

'His mind travels further than ours. You'll see. Come with me.'

Odysseus glanced at Eperitus and Antiphus and gave a small nod.

'We'll come.'

The crowd parted and they followed the pale-eyed man through the streets, past well-made buildings lost to years of neglect and between hundreds of the strange, lethargic youths who inhabited them. Long shadows fell across the cracked flagstones as the sun set over the tumbled walls and fallen roofs ahead of them. Shortly, they reached the marketplace they had observed from the high ridge. But instead of being taken to the palace as Eperitus had expected, they were led into a stone hut built against a wall of the ruined temple. Fresh hay lined the floor and several bowls of fruit had been placed on a rough table in the centre of the single room. A bowl of water and some wooden cups had been set out beside the food.

'Eat and drink,' their guide said. 'Maybe sleep a while. I will tell the Old One you wish to see him.'

'Sleep a while?' Antiphus said when the man had gone. 'How long does he expect us to wait?'

'As long as it takes,' Odysseus answered. 'I've a feeling Eurylochus and the others are here and I'm not going until I know otherwise. Perhaps this Old One can give us some answers.'

'I knew they had to have a leader,' Eperitus said, picking up an orange-coloured fruit from the bowl and sniffing at it.

Eperitus opened his eyes and looked up through the broken roof to the skies above. The stars were fading as the grey tinge of dawn was creeping into the world. Somewhere he could hear birds singing, while further off he was conscious of the sound of waves rolling in on sandy beaches. The air was cold and he could smell pine trees and the pungent aroma of the skins they had peeled from the orange fruits. He almost did not notice the familiar smells of sweat and leather and the sound of snoring.

He lifted himself onto one elbow in the thick straw. His muscles were stiff and awkward and the chill from the flagstones below seemed to have penetrated into his bones. He yawned, stretched and sat up. Odysseus's large bulk was leaning against one of the door jambs as he looked thoughtfully out at the ruin of the once impressive marketplace beyond.

'Good morning,' the king said as Eperitus rose and joined him. 'Sleep well?'

'Not as well as I'd expected. After ten days at sea, my brain is still swimming around but my body won't go with it. How about you?'

'Couldn't sleep, so I relieved the guard. There's something about this place that keeps playing on my mind. I get a real sense of danger, but I don't know why. Much worse than the Cicones.'

'I have it too. At least with the Cicones you knew what the threat was. They had chariots and spears and bows and arrows, but we've dealt with that sort of peril many times. These people seem harmless, and yet –'

'And yet it's not the people,' Odysseus said, turning to look at Eperitus. 'It's what's happened to them. They're like human husks, as if their souls have been drawn out. The thing I fear is whatever made them that way.'

'Perhaps this Old One they talk of will know.'

'Perhaps he's responsible,' Odysseus commented.

'If he even exists,' said Omeros, pulling straw from his mop of hair as he joined them. 'I mean, why didn't he send for us last night? Don't they observe the rules of *xenia* in this country? What sort of people don't know how to show a proper welcome to peaceful guests?'

'The sort of people who don't know how to build a wall or repair a roof,' Odysseus said. 'You have to remember we're not in the Greek world now, Omeros.'

'And yet they speak Greek, some of them,' Eperitus said. 'Even the Trojans and the northern barbarians have languages of their own, so if that wind blew us beyond the rim of the world, why would they speak Greek here?'

'They have a language of their own, so if they can communicate a little in our language then maybe we're not the only Greeks to have visited them. Besides, take a look at the few repairs they've made to this town: old ship's planking and bits of sail. Others have visited before us – but they didn't sail home again.'

'Shipwrecks?' Omeros suggested.

'Not likely in this bay. Have you ever seen a friendlier shore to beach a galley on? Barely a rock in sight.'

'Then what happened to the crews?' Eperitus asked.

'That's what I'd like to know. And until we find out we need to watch each other's backs.'

The sun was visible above the hilltops before they saw any sign of their hosts. Then, as Eperitus was ready to suggest they start searching the town, a group of women appeared on the threshold of the palace and walked across the square. Despite the morning coolness, they did not think to cover their nakedness with cloaks. Eperitus thought there was a strange beauty about them, but not one that aroused desire. They were more like children than adults and their attraction was in their innocence. As they laughed and chased each other across the flagstones, they seemed oblivious to the fact their town was a ruin without walls, that at any time they could fall victim to pirates or invading armies, or that the strangers that they were coming to visit could slay them upon a whim. They seemed to have no worries at all, and an older part of Eperitus envied them.

'Odysseus,' he called over his shoulder. 'We have visitors.'

The king, who had been dozing in the straw while Omeros and Antiphus played dice, roused himself.

'I hear them,' he answered.

The women grew quieter as they saw the two men waiting for them. Eperitus recognised one as the girl who had wanted him to make love to her the evening before. She showed no recollection of him as she walked ahead of the others and stood before Odysseus.

'Do you wish to lay with us now?'

'We want to speak with the Old One,' Odysseus said.

'He knows that and is expecting you, but first he thought you would like to relieve yourselves of your burdens. The Old One is keen to speak with you, but says men cannot think or talk straight while their sacks are full.'

She cupped her hand over her crotch to indicate what she meant.

Odysseus smiled.

'Some of us have carried our burdens for a long time and we can manage for a while longer. Right now I'm more interested in talking to the Old One and finding out where our friends are.'

The girl shrugged her shoulders.

'Of course. He's in there,' she said, pointing to the ruined palace. 'You can follow us back if you like.'

Odysseus called for the others and made a point of telling Omeros to bring his lyre. The women did not wait, but set off towards the palace. Eperitus caught up with their leader.

'What's the name of this place?' he asked her.

'Name? It has no name.'

'Every town has a name.'

'If this one did, then we forgot it a long time ago.'

'Then did your ancestors build it?'

She smiled at him and shook her head. 'You ask such strange questions. Always thinking about names and who is in charge, yet you won't even lie with us.'

'I already have a woman.'

'Just one? Stay with us and you can have as many as you like and whomever you like. Lie with me when we reach the palace, if you wish. I like you, not that that matters. You are bigger and stronger than the men here, and you intrigue me with your strange way of thinking. The Old One has told us about the world you come from. It's violent and greedy and people work ceaselessly from the time the sun rises until the time it sets again. I don't think I would like it.'

She was more like a child than Eperitus had first thought.

'There is much violence and greed,' he replied, 'but that's because there are things worth fighting for. And everyone has to work. It gives us our purpose, our reason for living. Are you saying *no-one* works here?'

'Only if we want to – to pick fruit or fetch water, sometimes. But it is not why we live.'

'Then why *do* you live? Aren't you bored in these ruins all day long, sleeping with each other and eating fruit? What's the point of it all?'

She took his hand in hers.

'Why do you worry about such things? Here we have the lotus, and the lotus is enough. Nothing else matters. You'll see for yourself, in time.'

The other women had gone on ahead and were already entering the roofless portico where the palace gates used to stand. Odysseus and the others were several paces behind.

'What's the lotus?'

'It is pleasure,' she answered, letting his fingers slip. 'Nothing but pleasure. Embrace it as the others did and you will have no need for violence or work. No need for anything at all.'

'What others?' he asked, but already she was running towards the temple, her long hair flowing behind her as she laughed aloud.

A moment later Odysseus was at his side.

'Did you learn anything?'

'Yes. Your instincts were right: Eurylochus is here.'

Chapter Seventeen

THE OLD ONE

A s the front of the palace cast its shadow over them they were able to see that it had once been a building of beauty and opulence. Six broad steps led up to the portico, where a wooden pediment had been supported by four columns. One of the columns had since collapsed and lay like a slain serpent across the steps, while the pediment had sagged and its roof had fallen in. The high front wall of the palace remained, though it was sun-bleached and the painted frieze that ran along it was now barely visible. The doors to the palace were gone and all they could see inside was darkness.

They entered a large antechamber, where the light spilling in from the doorway revealed a floor covered in fallen masonry and plaster. The ceiling remained, though, and to their right was a flight of steps leading to an upper storey. Ahead of them was a pair of large doors that no longer seemed to fit their frame, as bold lines of yellow light were visible beneath them and along the seam where they met. Beyond them they could hear the sound of many voices.

Odysseus pushed open the doors. The Ithacans now stood at the threshold of what had been the great hall. It was spacious, with five wooden columns forming the points of a pentacle at its centre. The ceiling they had once supported was gone and sunlight from the open roof was spreading over the western half of the hall, leaving the eastern half in shadow. The walls carried murals depicting a forest on two sides and the sea on the others. Large chunks of plaster had fallen away in places, but to his left Eperitus could still see the painted figures of huntsmen chasing deer through the trees, while to his right long galleys of an exotic design he had never seen before sailed over dolphin-filled waters. Unlike the murals on the outer walls, these had retained their colour and vibrancy. At the centre of the hall, between the columns, was a circular hearth. But whereas every palace he had ever visited kept a large bed of embers burning day and night, all that remained in the centre of the stone ring were a few burnt sticks and a pile of ash.

Despite its decrepit state, the hall was filled with people. The rubble from the fallen ceiling had been pushed against the walls and the remainder of the floor had been thickly strewn with straw. Lying or kneeling on this were more than a hundred of the town's inhabitants. A group of four or five children were throwing straw into the air and shouting, while on a mound of broken stone in the shadowy half of the hall three boys were beating another with sticks. The adults seemed not to care, absorbed as they were with their private conversations or picking fruit from large piles that had been left here and there in the straw. Some couples were touching each other intimately, not bothering even to withdraw into the shadows. Eperitus glanced across at Odysseus, who raised a questioning eyebrow in reply.

'Come, join us,' said the girl whom Eperitus had spoken with on the way to the palace.

She came towards them with her hands held out, the sunlight a warm yellow on her bare torso. That children were allowed to run free in the great hall, even the ruined shell of one like this, and that women were permitted to sit as equals among the men did not surprise Eperitus after everything he had seen; so to be welcomed into the hall by a woman in opposition to every custom that governed the world he knew seemed appropriate. It was not only the buildings that had crumbled in this strange place, he thought.

'My friends,' the girl announced to the rest of the hall, after taking Eperitus's hand, 'make space. Pass food and drink for our visitors. Make them welcome.'

There were no chairs or tables and no place of honour for the newcomers to sit at. Indeed, there was no throne or place of authority they could be seated across from. The girl sat in the straw and tugged at Eperitus's hand, encouraging him to do the same. He looked at Odysseus, who remained on his feet.

'Where is the Old One?'

'That'll be me you're looking for,' answered a voice in perfect Greek from a corner of the hall.

Eperitus observed a pot-bellied man walking towards them from the shadows, his penis still in his hand as he shook off the last drops of urine. At least they do *that* away from the others, Eperitus thought sardonically. The Old One hid his manhood behind his loin cloth and stepped into the sunlight, opening his arms wide in greeting.

'Welcome fellow Greeks,' he said, folding Odysseus in an embrace. 'Your accent gives you away. Peloponnese? Pylos perhaps?'

'Ithaca,' Odysseus replied. 'And you're a Cretan.'

'I *was*.' The man gave another laugh, patted Odysseus on both shoulders, and then went to lie down between a group of women. 'Or at least I think I was, but that was a very long time ago. A past life! Now I belong to paradise.'

He turned and placed his bearded lips against one of his companions' breasts. She smiled and held his head as if he were a suckling baby. Despite the streaks of grey in his hair and the title conferred on him by the others, Eperitus judged that the man was no older than himself, maybe even younger.

'Then were you shipwrecked here?' Odysseus asked, sitting in the straw and accepting the small brown fruit offered by one of the men.

The Old One pulled his face away, a line of saliva sagging between his lips and the woman's nipple.

'Eh? Shipwreck? Well, let's say our vessel came to grief, shall we? And what of yourselves? You're no merchantmen, I can tell that. Warriors by your garb. How many of you?'

'Enough to look after ourselves.'

'You've nothing to fear from us,' said the girl beside Eperitus, pulling at his hand again.

As the rest of his companions were sitting, Eperitus conceded and knelt beside her.

'But much to gain,' added the Old One.

'Do you have a name,' Odysseus asked him.

'Not that I remember.'

'What about this town, this land, these people?'

The man rolled his eyes and gave a groan.

'Don't your kind ever change? Why does everything need a name? Ithaca, Crete, your name, my name... Names are meaningless.'

'Without our names we're nothing,' Odysseus countered with a smile.

'Then become nothing and set yourself free! Perhaps you were expecting me to ask your name? Oh yes, I haven't forgotten the old customs – enquire of a guest's name and family; invite him to share the purpose of his visit; feed him; give him a gift. But don't you see that *xenia* is meaningless here? In a place without names, a man's reputation is of no importance. And as we have already said, you have nothing to fear among us. Nor do we have swords or cauldrons to offer you as guest-gifts. So stop hiding behind your names and forget why you came here – neither of which interests us. Eat the fruit! Take a woman! Take a man! And when you've forgotten some of your inhibitions perhaps there *is* something we can offer you. Something better than swords and cauldrons, eh, my friends?'

He gave a knowing look to those around him, who raised their voices in excited agreement. It was the most animated Eperitus had yet seen them. The men clapped their hands and the women beat their breasts, and amid the strange cacophony Eperitus felt a hand pull at his tunic. Turning, he saw the young man whom he had punched to the ground the evening before.

'I must show you something,' he whispered.

Eperitus shook off his hand and looked away.

'So you have no names, no leaders and, it seems, not even a chair to share among you,' Odysseus was saying as he bit into the brown fruit. 'And you're as free as any people I've ever met. So free that you boast about it with as much pride as any king.'

'Here we are all kings.'

'Kings in a city without walls, without armies and without weapons. You don't even have the good sense to employ *xenia* in the hope strangers will spare you out of respect for good manners. And yet you *survive*. How is that possible?'

'You've seen our city, my friend. We have nothing worth taking. Nothing that the likes of you would value.'

'But you do. You have yourselves. In the absence of gold and silver, a warrior will take slaves. What's to stop me drawing my sword and herding off a score of your men to farm my lands or watch over my flocks, or another score of your women to be nursemaids to my children or playthings for my men? What is this hidden power that protects you? Are you telling me that no armed band has ever appeared unexpected over the hills that surround you, or that no pirate has ever landed on your shores looking for plunder to make his voyage worthwhile?'

The Old One smiled and shrugged his shoulders.

'There are more ways to defeat armies and pirates than hard bronze and a lust for blood. And as you say, we are still here without walls or *xenia* to protect us.'

'A man who rejects *xenia* rejects the gods, and without the favour of the gods you are doomed.'

Eperitus, half-stunned and half-appalled by what he was hearing, felt another tug at his sleeve. It was the young man again.

'Don't sleep with the women,' he muttered. 'They will weaken your will to resist.'

Eperitus frowned. 'I'm not interested in the women. Or you, for that matter.'

'Listen to me. You don't have much time left –'

'What does that mean?'

'Come with me, *now*, before it is too late.'

Eperitus felt a surge of anger and prised the man's fingers from his sleeve, though there was something in his eyes and urgent tone that worried him. Nevertheless, he turned away and saw that Odysseus was staring hard following something the Old One had said.

'You *truly* believe there are no gods? Then you're an even greater fool than I thought. But I haven't come to bandy nonsense. If you won't ask my name, then I'll not share it with you; but I will tell you why I'm here and you *will* tell me what I need to know. Three of my countrymen came this way yesterday morning and I haven't seen them since. These children you surround yourself with say they know nothing about them –'

'And so we don't.'

'Then how is it that when I slipped out of the room you gave us last night I found one of their cloaks lying in an alleyway?'

The Old One's smile faded slightly and his eyes narrowed.

'I can assure you that you did not leave your room last night.'

'Can you? Then why do your eyes doubt your own assurance? What's more, the cloak I found belonged to my cousin and I'm particularly keen that no harm has befallen him. Do you understand me? If I find he has been hurt in any way you will no longer find me so friendly.'

Eperitus wondered whether Odysseus had really found a cloak or whether he was bluffing. The Old One was uncertain, too.

'If you happened across a cloak then it must have belonged to someone else, not this precious cousin of yours.'

'And who would wear a cloak in this place? The most anyone has to cover themselves with is a strip of sailcloth. I know my cousin is here somewhere and you will tell me where or you'll find that hard bronze and a lust for blood are not as easily conquered as you think!'

The Old One rose to his feet and Eperitus laid a hand on the hilt of his sword. But the man's stern expression melted quickly into a smile as he stretched his open palms towards Odysseus.

'My friend, if my words have offended you then I apologise. Relax, be at peace. If you insist on following your custom then *I* must insist that we do it right. I will gladly answer your question, but first you must accept our hospitality. Isn't that how it goes? And we have a gift for you and your men that will surpass anything the great lords and kings of your world can offer.' At this the men and women began to clap and beat their breasts again, clearly agitated by the thought of what was to come. 'But first, I see one of you has a lyre? It's many years since I've heard music, and there are very few here have had the pleasure. Perhaps your friend will play for us?'

Odysseus beckoned to Omeros, who rose and came forward with his tortoiseshell lyre in his hand. In the same moment Eperitus sensed a presence behind him.

'I know where your friends are,' a voice whispered in his ear.

This time Eperitus did not ignore the man's words. He turned and looked him in the eye.

'If you've seen them then you'll be able to describe them to me.'

'One is fat, much fatter than the Old One. He has small, arrogant eyes and a boastful mouth. At least, he *used* to boast. Now he's more quiet.'

'Show me.'

Eperitus stood as Omeros struck the first cords. It sounded beautiful, like the call of a god amid the ruins, or the ghostly echo of a feast from the great hall's distant past. He looked at Odysseus and wondered whether he should let him know where he was going.

'Wait,' he told the young man, before leaning towards Odysseus. 'I'll be back soon.'

'Where are you going?'

'I don't know yet, but you should stay here or they'll suspect something. And whatever you do, keep the others away from the women. They'll weaken their will to resist.'

'Resist what?'

'I don't know that either.'

Eperitus turned and walked back into the shadows by the entrance, where the man was waiting for him.

'Follow me.'

'Won't we be missed?' Eperitus asked.

'They'll think we've left to be alone.'

'Even though I hit you yesterday?'

'We who eat the lotus are quick to forgive. The others will assume the same of you.'

'And you're not assuming I've changed my mind, I hope?'

The man half smiled and shook his head.

'I just want to take you to your friends.'

He disappeared through a doorway. Eperitus followed him into a dark corridor littered with fallen plaster and broken furniture. A grey half-light suffused the shadows at the far end, silhouetting the puny, underfed form of his guide, who was already some way ahead. Several doorways revealed themselves as black apertures in the darkness to the right, and for a moment Eperitus wondered whether he was being led into a trap. The lotus eaters may have been meek and unarmed, but all they needed to do was draw the Ithacans off one by one and murder them in gloomy corners of their ruined palace.

'Come on,' the man hissed at him. 'Don't be afraid.'

His words were not intended as a provocation, but Eperitus felt his natural courage challenged. He paused an instant longer, stretching out his senses for sounds of breathing or the smell of sweat that might indicate hidden foes, and on detecting nothing he continued down the narrow passageway, his hand resting on the pommel of his sword. As he passed each empty room, he could distinguish shapes in the darkness, all of them broken – the remains of chairs and tables, shards of clay, lumps of plaster, even sandals and torn clothing. There were bones, too, grey with age, and human skulls with black eye sockets that spoke of unknown horror.

He reached the end of the corridor, where the man was waiting for him. The pale glow was stronger here, though it remained ashen and ghostly.

'Through here,' his guide said, ducking beneath a low doorway.

They entered a spacious chamber with a wooden door at the far end. The light was coming through the cracks in its beams and the gaps between the jambs, where age and neglect had warped the wood. The floor in between was littered with more of the wreckage of whatever had befallen the town.

'There were skeletons in the rooms we passed,' Eperitus said. 'Who were they?'

'I don't know. They have always been there.'

'And how long have you lived here? How old are you?'

'I don't know. I have always been here, that's all I know.'

'Just like the bones,' Eperitus said, more to himself than his companion. 'How far now until we find my countrymen?'

'Not far.'

The man crossed the chamber and opened the door. A shaft of green-tinted daylight fell across the floor, forcing Eperitus to squint against its sudden brightness. There was a mass of foliage beyond the doorway and he could smell the pungent scent of earth, leaves and flowers. He followed his guide into what had once been the palace gardens. They were square with pillared cloisters on three sides, but now the pillars were twisted about with a form of ivy that boasted masses of purple, bell-shaped flowers. The trees that bordered the garden had run wild, sending branches into the cloisters and up through their sloped roofs so that many of the clay tiles had slipped off and fallen into the overgrown grass below. Shrubs that had once been carefully tended and kept at bay by the king's gardeners had grown large and monstrous, their white or yellow blooms dying on the bud and scattering their petals over the ground. The cloister to his right had collapsed long ago, leaving a broad gap in the palace wall that was smothered beneath the dark green fronds of creeping plants. In all that chaos of neglected nature, a single rough path was the only indication that anyone ever visited the place. Eperitus's guide did not wait for him, but took the path to the lowest point in the ruin of the wall and climbed over. Eperitus followed him into a narrow alley between the remains of a stone stable and the side wall of a large house. The rest of the town was quiet, and in the silence he heard a low moaning coming from a bend at the far end of the alley. His guide turned and beckoned to him.

'Come quickly. Your friends are here.'

He followed him into another, narrower alley that ended in a sunlit courtyard. On the other side of its cracked flagstones was a house with an open door, from which the low moaning was originating. Eperitus drew his sword and approached. The door opened into a low-ceilinged room. The floor was strewn with hay and in the middle were several bodies. Eurylochus was in the middle, naked but for his sandals. The hairy mound of his stomach was rising and fall-ing gently and he was staring up at the ceiling, oblivious to Eperitus's arrival. A naked woman lay on one side of him with her arm draped over his chest and her knee across his groin. A second woman, also undressed, lay face up with her head on his other shoulder. Her eyes were shut but Eperitus could see the rapid movements of her eyeballs beneath the lids. The other two Ithacans were also there, spreadea-gled on their backs with women beside them as they gazed vacantly upward. One was emitting a low moan, but by his empty expression Eperitus could not tell whether the sound was one of pain or plea-sure. Only then did he notice that their pupils were rolled up into their skulls to leave their eyes as featureless white orbs. The sight chilled him.

'What have you done to them?' he asked, seizing his guide by the arm.

The man winced beneath his powerful grip. 'It's the lotus. They've eaten of the lotus.'

'Are they in pain?' Eperitus demanded. 'Are they sick? What's wrong with them?'

'Pain?' the man laughed, despite the tightening grasp about his arm. 'Nothing could be farther from the truth. They are in a state of ecstasy! When a man eats the lotus he forgets his woes; all the pain of this world goes away. But he also forgets the world itself. Compared to the lotus, the world can offer nothing. It is meaningless.'

Eperitus released his hold on the man, whose laughter was now turning to tears. He slumped onto a stone bench against one of the walls of the courtyard.

'Why do you think we live like this: making nothing, repair-ing nothing, standing idle as everything crumbles around us? What need do we have of houses and rich clothing? What is the appeal of gold and wine when we have the lotus?' He looked up at Eperitus, his eyes suddenly passionate and sad. 'Why do you think we have no walls or army, even though we have many weapons hidden away? They are the weapons of our enemies! The men who came to raid us and conquer us were themselves conquered by the lotus, the humble gift we offered as we grovelled before them. And in the middle of their bliss, as their minds soared free of their bodies, we stabbed them with their own weapons and then burned their corpses on the beaches where their warships sat at anchor. It is what we have always done, with one exception – the Old One. Even he cannot remember why he was spared. But he has told us all about the world across the sea, with palaces and temples where men eat the flesh of dead animals and fight wars to enslave women. Can you deny it, when I have watched your own ships from the hillsides around the bay and seen the women serving food and drink to your warriors?'

'So you mean to drug my friends and slit their throats?' Eperitus said, looking anxiously back down the alley. 'By all the gods, I should have stayed with Odysseus in the palace, not here with you! You brought me here on purpose, didn't you? You separated me from my king when I should have been protecting him.'

He levelled his sword at the man's throat, torn between the need for answers and the desire to run back to the great hall, where at any moment Odysseus would be given the lotus and enslaved to its power. Eurylochus and his companions in the room behind him were forgotten. All that mattered now was getting back to his friends before the lotus eaters murdered them.

'Don't you see I had to bring you here?' the man pleaded. 'I tried to warn you but you wouldn't listen. The only way to get your attention was to tell you I knew where your friends were, and the only way to make you believe me was to show you.'

'Well I believe you now. But I have to go back to warn Odysseus.'

'Wait! Your friends here are in danger, too. My brothers and sisters will come soon to make sure they never wake from their dreams.'

Eperitus hesitated and glanced back into the shadowy room from which the low moaning was still emanating. He detested Eurylochus and would have gladly seen him dead, but the other two were good men and Eperitus had never abandoned a soldier he could have saved. On the other hand, Odysseus was more important than all of them, and every moment that passed led the king further and further into the lotus eaters' trap.

'There's something else you haven't told me,' he said, pressing the point of his sword against the base of the man's neck. 'Why didn't you leave me there in the hall to take the lotus and have my throat cut with the others? Why are you helping us?'

The man's face was screwed up with pain, his fingers folding timidly over the blade as if wanting but not daring to push it away. Tears flowed freely down his cheeks and he could barely speak to answer Eperitus's question.

'Because I hate this place. I hate what happens here. I hate the Old One and I hate the lotus. I want it to end. I want to be free of it.'

Eperitus knew he was looking at a child, a creature enslaved against its will and powerless to take control of its own life. His anger subsided and he eased the point of the sword away from the man's flesh.

'Then come with us, if that's what you want. If Odysseus lives then you'll have earned a place on one of his ships. But first I have to warn him.'

'And these men?' the lotus eater asked, rubbing his throat.

Eperitus looked through the doorway at the hated figure of Eurylochus, motionless in the straw. He entered and kicked him in the shin. He may as well have been kicking a corpse.

'You'll have to watch over them. I'll return shortly.'

The sound of approaching footsteps made him turn and look up the alley. Moments later, five lotus eaters turned the corner armed with short swords. At their head was the pale-eyed man who had led them to their quarters the evening before. He stared at Eperitus in surprise, then with a hateful scream he raised the sword above his head and ran at him.

Chapter Eighteen

TASTING THE LOTUS

Omeros had chosen to sing about the feud between Agamemnon and Achilles. He must have been working on it for a while, for Odysseus did not recognise the words but had heard the music many times during the long journey south from Malea. The song was evocative and beautiful and Odysseus was not ashamed of the tears that rolled down his cheeks as he recalled the bitter argument between the two great men and the consequences of their quarrel for all the Greeks. Antiphus was also wiping his eyes, while the young men and women around them – who had no understanding of the world outside their ruined town and for whom the words must have been meaningless – listened in rapt silence. Only the Old One seemed discomfited, perhaps regretting his request as Omeros's words stirred up memories of a life he had all but forgotten. When the poet reached the point where Patroclus begged Achilles to borrow his armour and ride out against Hector's victorious army, the Old One held up his hand.

'Enough now. My friends,' he said, speaking to the men and women about him, 'it is time to give our guests the gifts they have been waiting for.'

The spell of Omeros's song was broken and Odysseus felt a surge of anger at the interruption, but he bit it back as he saw the strange reaction that had seized hold of his hosts. All around him they were rising to their knees like slumbering dogs aroused by the smell of food. There was an excitement about them, nothing like the passionless detachment that had possessed them up to that point. And as they awoke from their docile stupor they became more aggressive, jostling each other with their elbows as they shuffled forward.

'Yes, bring it now,' said a woman.

'They must have their gifts,' said another.

'And us. We must eat too.'

'Yes, yes!'

Odysseus looked at Antiphus. The archer shrugged his shoulders nonchalantly, but his eyes could not hide the uncertainty he felt. It was a hesitation Odysseus shared.

'Your cousin,' said the Old One. 'Is he a fat man with the pride of a lion but the nobility of a dog? Yes, I remember him now. He and his companions were here yesterday.'

'And where are they now?'

A wiser man might have sensed the warning in Odysseus's tone, but the Old One seemed unconcerned.

'First we will eat.'

'We've eaten. Tell us where they are.'

'Bring the lotus!' shouted a voice.

Others echoed it. The Old One nodded and several men and women stood up and left the hall. The rest began to beat their chests with their hands.

'First, your guest-gift. The rules of *xenia* offer protection to the host as well as the guest, do they not? And you are the ones with swords and armour, not us. We are at your mercy and so I must insist you accept our humble offerings. Until you do you will learn nothing more from us about your friends.'

'I'll accept nothing until you give me your word they're not harmed.'

'On my oath they are safe and well. Indeed, they are the happiest they have been for many months.'

So they had succumbed to the sun-bronzed flesh of the half-naked women, Odysseus thought. That seemed like Eurylochus – putting his own pleasure before his duty. And yet he sensed the Old One was keeping something from him. Something he could not yet see, but which his instincts were railing against.

'If you've lied to me on oath, then *xenia* will not protect you.'

The Old One simply smiled and looked across to where the men and women were returning with large baskets under their arms. They were filled with brownish-red fruits a little larger than dates. Several of the others jumped to their feet and rushed forward, groping for the fruit.

'*Wait!*' the Old One shouted, sitting up suddenly. 'Our guests must eat first.'

The men and women scowled at him, but returned to their places.

'Tell me, Ithacan,' he continued, 'have you ever been offered wine as a guest-gift?'

'Of course.'

'And only the finest, no doubt.'

Odysseus thought about Maron, the priest of Apollo whose life he and Eperitus had saved. He had rewarded them with rich gifts, but the most precious had been the wine.

'Yes.'

'Then you will not be insulted if we don't offer you ingots of gold or copper tripods, of which we have none, but instead give you something more potent and pleasurable than any wine you will ever have tasted? The lotus.'

He stood and took a basket from one of the women. Walking over to the Ithacans, he handed them a fruit each, giving the last one to Odysseus. The men and women watched him greedily.

'Eat and be happy,' he said.

'After you, my friend.'

The Old One shrugged and smiled. Plucking a handful of the lotus from the basket, he tossed them into the straw. A group of men and women scrambled to snatch them up, fighting each other over the last few. Odysseus watched disdainfully as they bit into the fruit and sucked out the juice, while around them others wiped the juice from their chins and licked it from their fingers.

'I told you it was good,' the Old One laughed. 'Now, where was it I saw your friends?'

Odysseus took the hint and bit into the fruit. It tasted bitter and the flesh was tough. All around him the lotus eaters who had already taken the fruit were slumping to the ground, smiles spreading across their faces as they gazed up at the open skies where the ceiling had once been. Then there was a sound behind him and a voice boomed out across the hall.

'Spit it out, Odysseus. *Spit it out!*'

Odysseus spat the fruit onto the straw. Eperitus appeared before him, a bloody sword in one hand and a pitcher of water in the other.

'Here, swill it out. Don't swallow any of it.'

Odysseus took a mouthful of water from the pitcher and sluiced it between his cheeks before spitting it out again. Omeros, who had also taken a bite of fruit, coughed it out and snatched the water from Odysseus's hand. Meanwhile, Eperitus turned to the Old One and knocked the basket from his hand so that the fruit spilled over the floor. The lotus eaters pounced after it, but a shout from the Old One stopped them.

'Leave it. Block the doors. They mustn't escape.'

Eperitus hauled Odysseus up by his elbow.

'How do you feel?'

'Fine. Was it poisoned?'

'Worse than that. I'll explain later. First we must get out of here.'

Antiphus and Omeros were already beside them, their swords drawn. They looked at the doorway and saw the lotus eaters crowding before it. Their faces were twisted in anger as they fed off each other's emotions, reacting to the threat not as individuals but as a pack. Odysseus sensed its potential and knew he had to act before their rage found its momentum. He strode forward, pushing aside a young woman who stepped into his path. When a man lurched towards him he struck him hard with his fist, knocking him to the ground. Worryingly, the man seemed not to notice the pain and rose to his feet again at once, blood seeping from the gash on his cheek. The flash of violence sparked something in the once docile lotus eaters, who now pressed forward towards Odysseus. Eperitus appeared at his right shoulder, thrusting into the wall of bodies and pushing them back easily. Hands reached out for the drawn sword, gripping the blade and releasing it again with yelps of pain as the keen edge sliced through their skin. For a moment the mob wavered. Antiphus and Omeros appeared at Odysseus's other flank, shouldering their way into the crowd and driving them back. Odysseus and Eperitus joined them and together they pressed forward, ignoring the punches that were thrown at them. A woman tried to bite Odysseus's forearm, but he butted his forehead into her face and she collapsed with a groan. Fists were now beating at their unguarded backs and feet were kicking at their legs as more lotus eaters closed in behind them. Then their greater strength defeated the throng of weaker men and women before them and suddenly they were at the open doors of the great hall.

'Come on, quickly,' Odysseus shouted.

They ran through the rubble-strewn antechamber and out onto the portico, where the bright sunshine was almost blinding compared to the columns of dusty light in the hall. A roar of anger followed behind, driving them down the steps to the broad square below. Odysseus sprinted to the left, back in the same direction they had come the evening before. He was aware of the others on either side of him, but even more of the rush of naked feet on the cracked flagstones close behind.

People were appearing in the streets ahead, curious at the angry voices that were desecrating the usual silence. Eperitus could hear the cries of the lotus eaters as if they were at his very heels, though a glance over his shoulder showed him their thin legs were tiring and leaving them further behind.

'We're outpacing them,' Antiphus shouted. 'If these others don't cause us any trouble we'll soon be away and safe.'

They turned a corner onto the long avenue that led to the remains of the old gatehouse. More men and women were leaving the ruined houses before them and lining the sides of the street, though they seemed more bewildered than angry. That they would not oppose the Ithacans' escape was clear, but they were not the only obstacle standing between the handful of warriors and freedom.

'Stop,' Eperitus called. 'We can't leave yet.'

The others pulled up and turned to look at him.

'Why not?' Odysseus asked.

'Eurylochus is here, in the town.'

Antiphus and Omeros looked at the king, who after a moment's hesitation pointed to a nearby alley.

'Quick, down here.'

They crammed into the narrow gap and ran in single file between the high, crumbling walls. Eperitus was the last through and heard the clamour of voices burst into the avenue behind him, then surge past towards the ruined gatehouse. It would not be long before they realised their mistake and were directed down the alley by the other lotus eaters. His companions knew it too and followed the twists and turns of the passage at a sprint, not pausing until they reached another street. Without waiting, Odysseus turned left and led them in the direction of the palace. When they were sure they were not being pursued, Odysseus signalled a halt and pulled them into a doorway. Already the inquisitive but dispassionate eyes of other lotus eaters were watching them from the buildings on either side.

'Where is he?' Odysseus asked Eperitus.

'If we can get to the side of the palace I can lead you to him from there. But we need to be quick. If the lotus eaters get there before we do they'll murder them.'

'Murder armed warriors?' Antiphus scoffed. 'Not without dozens of their own being slain first.'

'When I saw Eurylochus and the others they didn't even have clothes, let alone their weapons and armour,' Eperitus answered. 'We have to keep going.'

Antiphus and Omeros set off towards the palace, but before Eperitus could follow, Odysseus took him by the arm.

'Why are you saving him? If you'd said nothing we would have carried on none the wiser and you'd have rid yourself of an enemy.'

'I don't give a damn about Eurylochus, but the others are good soldiers. They don't deserve to die at the hands of a mob.'

'So if it had just been my cousin you'd have left him to his fate?' Eperitus shrugged his shoulders.

'But it's not just him, is it. Now, let's go before the lotus eaters find us.'

They caught up with the others at the corner of a building that looked out on the large square. It was empty, though Eperitus sensed it was being watched. Without waiting, he dashed across the open space towards the side of the palace, where the overgrown garden was visible through the collapsed wall. The others followed him to the mouth of the alleyway where, after a glance over their shoulders at the still-empty square, they drew their swords. Cautiously they advanced to where the passage bent sharply to the right and led on to the house where Eperitus had found Eurylochus and the others. Several corpses lay piled across each other in the courtyard before it.

'We're too late!' Antiphus exclaimed.

'No we're not,' Eperitus said. 'Those bodies are my doing. I had no choice: they came to murder Eurylochus and when I stood in their way they attacked me.'

They entered the courtyard where the lotus eaters lay. The sight of their bodies filled Eperitus with shame. There had been no honour in slaying men armed only with daggers, but they had attacked with such frenzy that he had been forced to kill them all. His guide had also died in the fray – stabbed between the shoulder blades as he tried to run – and now lay in a pool of his own blood on the flagstones.

Odysseus stepped over the bodies and through the open door, where the three Ithacans were still in a stupor. He rolled one of the sleeping women aside and knelt down by his cousin, who was moaning gently. His pupils were staring up into the top of his head so that only the whites of his eyes showed. Omeros and Antiphus knelt beside Eurylochus's companions, while the king lifted his cousin's head into his lap and slapped his cheek gently.

'After I killed the lotus eaters I tried to revive him but couldn't,' Eperitus said from the doorway. 'They're all the same. It's the effect of the lotus. Had you eaten it, the same would have happened to you; and while your spirits went to wherever theirs have gone, the Old One would have ordered your throats cut. That's what they do to everyone who comes to this gods-forsaken town. They use the women to seduce them, then they drug them and murder them. If we hadn't arrived when we did yesterday I'm sure these three would already have been dead; it's my guess they didn't want the risk of us finding their bodies before they were sure of having us in the same trap.'

Odysseus's eyes narrowed with anger as he looked out at the pile of dead lotus eaters outside.

'Damned monsters. They got what they deserved. Here, pass me that waterskin.'

Eperitus picked up the skin that Eurylochus had taken with him as he had set off the morning before – which was lying discarded against a wall – and tossed it to Odysseus. The king tipped some of the water over Eurylochus's face. The shock of it made him gasp and jerk upwards with a groan of protest, before dropping back down into Odysseus's lap. Again Odysseus poured a slop of water into his open mouth, making him gag and forcing his body into a reaction that dragged part of his consciousness back with it.

'What is it?' he gasped, his white eyes staring blindly into a corner of the room. 'Who's there?'

'Eurylochus, it's me, Odysseus.'

'Leave me alone; I have to go back.'

A half-smile slid across his face and he slumped back into Odysseus's arms. The king slapped him lightly on the cheek.

'Listen to me, we're in danger. We need to get to the ships.'

'What ships?' he replied, groggily. 'Who are you? Why don't you leave me alone?'

He closed his eyes, but Odysseus poured more water into his mouth. He doubled up sharply, choking.

'Get up. We're leaving.'

Odysseus pulled at Eurylochus's elbow, but Eurylochus tore himself away and staggered to his feet, groping his way into a corner.

'I don't want to go with you,' he pleaded. 'You're ruining everything.'

'The lotus they gave you has done something to your mind, Eurylochus. Wherever it is you think you are, whatever it is you think you're seeing, it's not real. The only reality is that unless you come with us now you're going to die.'

At this, Eurylochus smiled, a look that, with his white, pupilless eyes, sent a chill down Eperitus's spine.

'Those that have shared the ambrosia of the gods cannot die, my friend.'

'It's driven him mad,' said Antiphus.

Eperitus turned suddenly and looked back through the open door.

'I can hear them. They're coming.'

Odysseus ran to join him. Moments later the end of the alleyway was crowded with lotus eaters, with the Old One at their head. The men were armed with swords, spears and bows.

'So what do we do now?' Antiphus asked, peering over Eperitus's shoulder.

'We can drive them back with our swords if we have to,' Eperitus answered.

Odysseus shook his head. 'If these men you fought earlier didn't turn and run, what chance this crowd will? There's something in the lotus that takes away their fear, and if they outnumber us fifty to one, we wouldn't stand a chance – warriors or not.'

A shout of anger erupted from the massed lotus eaters as they saw the pile of dead in the courtyard. Several bows twanged discordantly and a number of arrows rattled off the wall around them. Eperitus pushed the decaying door shut and propped his back against it.

'We're trapped.'

'No we're not,' said Omeros. 'There's another door at the back of the room.'

He ran over and pushed at it with his hands and then his shoulder until it began to edge open into silent darkness. Outside they could hear the shouts of the lotus eaters as they crowded into the courtyard and threw themselves upon the door. Odysseus joined Eperitus, thrusting his weight against the wood.

'Antiphus, your dagger!'

The archer pulled the blade from his belt and handed it to Odysseus, who fell to one knee and wedged it in the gap beneath the door.

'That should hold them. Eperitus, Antiphus, you'll have to carry the others. I'll bring Eurylochus.'

Eperitus ran to one of the Ithacan scouts and hauled his naked body onto his shoulders. Outside, the shouts were growing angrier and the door began to nudge open. A number of hands gripped the edge, but Antiphus drew his sword and hacked off several fingers. To a chorus of screams, he slammed the door shut again and kicked his dagger back into place before rushing over to the second Ithacan. By this time Eurylochus had slumped into a corner with his head lolling unconsciously onto his shoulder. Odysseus grabbed his wrist and slapped him hard across the face.

'Go away,' Eurylochus whined, almost weeping as he tried to drop back into the corner. 'I want to stay here!'

'You can't,' Odysseus growled.

He punched his cousin in the face, caught him as he slumped to the ground and threw him over his shoulder like a child. The door shuddered behind him and edged inwards.

'Come on!' Omeros shouted.

They ran into the room beyond the second door. Despite the near-total blackness, Eperitus could make out twisted shapes on the floor and smell the odour of dust and rotted cloth. Something crunched beneath his sandal and he looked down to see the grey outline of a human skeleton. Like those he had seen in the ruined palace, it must have lain there many years. Then he sensed movement in the air and knew there had to be another way out.

'Over there,' he announced as the lotus eaters forced their way into the room behind. 'Another door.'

He rushed shoulder-first towards the place where he guessed the door would be, barging it open and finding himself in a lesser darkness. At the far end of the room was another door, framed by a sliver of light. He ran across and kicked it open, stumbling out into the sudden brightness of a side street. The others piled out after him and fled headlong up the narrow thoroughfare, with the shouts of the lotus eaters echoing off the walls behind them.

'Which way?' Omeros shouted, as the side street fed into a broad avenue.

'Left,' Eperitus said.

A few arrows fell among them, one bouncing harmlessly off Eperitus's scabbard. He ran on, cursing the dead weight over his shoulders and wishing he could turn round and face his pursuers. But Odysseus was right. The lotus eaters he had slain in the courtyard had been men possessed. A terrible, inhuman anger had driven them against him; if he stopped to fight now he would have to kill every one of his attackers or die beneath the weight of their numbers – the latter most likely. He ran on.

Other lotus eaters were emerging from the ruins on either side and ahead of them now. Word of their escape must have spread, for this time their faces were not placid but dark and ominous. A child threw a stone as they ran past. A man and woman charged out into the street towards Omeros. With admirable speed, he drew his sword and swung the pommel into the man's face. Blood splashed across the lotus eater's cheek and he toppled back into the path of the woman, who jumped over him and ran at Omeros with her fingernails bared. She clawed the side of his head, drawing blood from his ear before he felled her with an instinctive blow to the stomach. For a moment he looked down at her in shock at what he had done, then Odysseus grabbed his arm and propelled him forward.

They ran on. Another street opened to their left and Odysseus led them down it. The lotus eaters were screaming like Furies behind them now, gaining all the time. Then, as Eperitus felt his legs tiring beneath the weight of the man he was carrying, they turned a corner and saw the remnants of the city wall ahead of them. The sight of it gave them new energy and they sprinted towards it, Omeros reaching the wall first and pulling himself up onto the broken battlements. Odysseus pushed Eurylochus's inert body towards him and Omeros dragged him up onto the rough stone. With the last of his strength, Eperitus almost threw the man he was carrying onto the wall. The Ithacan groaned as Omeros hauled him up, but did not emerge from his stupor.

'Get over the wall and head into the hills!' Eperitus shouted.

He turned to help Antiphus, only to see he had fallen in the street. His unconscious charge was lying across his legs and the horde of lotus eaters were almost upon them, snarling like a pack of dogs.

Eperitus drew his sword and charged towards them.

'They'll tear you to pieces!' Odysseus shouted after him.

He ran on. The first rank of the lotus eaters were armed with swords and spears. Antiphus tore the bow from his back, fitted an arrow and shot one of his attackers through the throat, tumbling him in the dust and bringing down a few others as they fell over his body. But the rest rushed on like a wave, unthinking and unstoppable. Leaping over Antiphus, Eperitus knocked the spear from the first man's hands, elbowed him aside and ran at the next. The lotus eater swung his sword clumsily and Eperitus hacked down at his wrist, severing it so that hand and weapon fell into the dust. Another rushed at him. He twisted aside and pulled the weapon from his attacker's hands, punching him hard in the face with the pommel of his sword so that he went flailing back into the men rushing up behind him. Eperitus now swung the spear in an arc, back and forth in the narrow street so that the lotus eaters were forced back before him.

'Kill him!' cried a familiar voice. 'Kill them all before they bring back their army to destroy us!'

The Old One was close behind the front rank, his face a mask of fury. Men and women reached out to grab at the spear, some screaming as the point slashed their fingers and hands, until they succeeded in taking hold of the shaft and pulling it from Eperitus's grip. He stepped back, balanced the weight of his sword in his hand and prepared to meet the onslaught.

A dozen lotus eaters rushed towards him. Then, with a loud shout, Odysseus appeared. He drove into them with a spear held crossways before him, throwing several back in confusion. Eperitus knocked the sword from one attacker's hand and punched another in the jaw, knocking him unconscious to the ground. Two or three bows twanged, but the arrows were badly aimed and flew wide or high. A figure ran out of the confusion and hurled a spear. Eperitus saw it from the corner of his vision and knew immediately that it would strike him in the chest. With all the reflexes his enhanced senses could lend him, he twisted his shoulders aside and arched his back. The head of the spear skimmed his breastplate and buried itself in the door of the building behind him. He stared with fierce anger at his assailant and saw it was the Old One.

'Kill him!' Odysseus shouted, swinging his spear as Eperitus had done to keep the lotus eaters back. 'He's the one driving them on.'

Eperitus pulled the spear from the door, balanced it over his shoulder and took aim. In the same instant the Old One snatched a sword from another man's hand and launched himself at the Ithacan. Eperitus's spear found the base of his neck and hurled him back into the crowd of his followers, the blood spurting from the wound as he kicked out the last of his life. With a terrible cry of grief, the lotus eaters forgot about the Ithacans and fell at his side.

Odysseus grabbed Eperitus's arm and pointed to Antiphus, who was with Omeros and the others by the wall.

'Come on. Let's go.'

Chapter Nineteen

IN THE CAVE

Selagos sniffed the night air. It was damp with the mist, but like every other seasoned sailor on board he could detect the unmistakeable scent of land. He could hear it, too, in the faint sound of waves breaking against a nearby shore. But what sort of shore would it be? Looking about himself, he could see the unsettled looks on the faces of the crew, knowing that any moment an unseen rock could tear a great hole in the hull and plunge them into life-threatening turmoil. Not that Selagos shared their fears. The gods were with him, helping him to plot his revenge on Odysseus. Until the moment came when he faced the Ithacan king alone in combat, he knew he was safe.

The wind had dropped a little after sunset, leaving the air still enough to carry the creak of rigging and the flap of canvas across the water from the nearest galleys. Every now and then he caught the glimpse of a sail through the thick fog, or saw the bulk of another ship's stern. Eperitus was in the bows with Polites, the former pitting his supernatural senses uselessly against the wall of vapour that had swallowed the fleet, the latter casting a weighted line to measure the depth of the water and calling out 'no bottom' at intervals in his deep voice. Other voices echoed his findings from the ships on either side, adding to the tensions of their crews.

The only other man who seemed careless to the danger was Eurylochus. He sat on the bench beside Selagos, his hands curled upwards in his lap and his expressionless eyes staring vacantly out at the billows of fog rolling over the bulwarks. When Odysseus had brought him back from the city of the lotus eaters he had been like a madman, filled with a raging desire to return and eat the fruit again. It had been necessary to tie him up and bundle him under the benches, as much for his own safety as those around him. The two men who had accompanied him on the scouting mission were the same, screaming and shouting to be released as the fleet had sailed away. Only when the shore was out of sight and night had fallen did they calm down. They sobbed uncontrollably like children until they fell asleep, then on waking they withdrew into a trance-like state and refused to eat or speak. Eventually Eurylochus's hunger brought him round, and as he ate he also answered the questions Odysseus had put to him. It soon became clear he could remember little or nothing of who he was or where he came from, which seemed to affect Odysseus deeply.

Selagos took upon himself the task of reminding Eurylochus of his identity, in the hope it would spark something in his memory and bring him back to himself. He had nothing but loathing for the king's weak-minded cousin. But until that point he had played his part usefully, stirring up antipathy towards Odysseus and presenting enough of a threat to Astynome to unsettle and distract Eperitus. So as he made Eurylochus repeat his name, the name of his father and the name of his country over and over again, Selagos reminded him that Odysseus was a bad ruler, that as his royal cousin he would make a better king, and that Astynome would be his queen. As he reiterated the latter, something stirred at the back of Eurylochus's empty eyes: a memory; an urging that had not been entirely lost to the lotus. And Selagos knew, smiling to himself, that he would win Eurylochus back.

Polites's voice boomed out urgently. His line had found the bottom. Moments later there was an outcry from one of the other galleys, followed by another. Selagos stood and looked in the direction of the voices. As it registered in his mind that there had not been an accompanying crash of wood splintering against rock, he heard the crews calling out again, this time in relieved joy.

'Sand!' Eperitus shouted back to the stern, where Odysseus and Eurybates were at the steering oars. 'Brace yourselves!'

An instant later the galley ground to a halt on the unseen beach, pitching everyone forward across the benches in a chaos of limbs and curses.

They could not have wished for a better landfall. On waking the next morning they saw that the curving beach was long enough to have accommodated twice their number of ships, and a freshwater stream fed into the bay from a cave among a knot of poplar trees. While they refilled their water casks, Eperitus called out and pointed up at the wooded hillsides that formed a crescent about the natural harbour. Long-horned goats were seen leaping among the crags, their bleats echoing from rock to rock. Men rushed to fetch their weapons before setting off in keen pursuit. Odysseus and Eperitus joined them, hunting the dextrous and elusive animals up the steep slopes into the thick woodland. Before long they found an opening in the trees. It allowed them to look out and see they were on a small island, not far from a much larger body of land. They studied it for a while, but after Eperitus had assured Odysseus he could see no signs of life, they carried on the hunt, bringing down an animal each. As they laughed and joked together, it seemed to Eperitus that for one morning at least – the first in a long time – Odysseus had put aside the pressures of kingship and rediscovered his carefree nature of years ago, before the clouds of war had cast their long shadow over him. When they returned to the beach, most of the others had already returned, several victorious in their endeavours. Antiphus and his bow had shot two of the creatures, both of which were slumped across Polites's broad shoulders. Eurybates, Omeros and Elpenor emerged from the trees shortly afterwards with a live goat trussed up on a thick branch that the two young men were carrying between them.

'It wasn't easy,' Eurybates declared as they strolled up to Odysseus, 'but here's your sacrifice.'

Odysseus was eager to recognise the gods for their safe landing the night before. He cut the animal loose and snicked off a lock of its hair, which he tossed into the flames of the nearest fire. Meanwhile Eperitus poured a slop of water into a bowl and placed it in the sand before the goat. It bowed its head to drink and unwittingly nodded its consent to the sacrifice, which Odysseus quickly and efficiently carried out, muttering prayers of thanks to the gods for their protection.

Later that evening the crews feasted on roast goat and the remnants of the wine they had taken from the Cicones. But through the songs and the laughter, Eperitus became aware of other sounds, distant but unsettling. He left Astynome with Polites and the children and went to find Odysseus. The king was standing at the edge of the beach, staring at the rippled reflection of the moon in the calm waters of the bay.

'You're not enjoying the feast with the others?'

Odysseus turned, caught unawares.

'No, I needed some time to myself.'

'I'm sorry –'

'It's fine. Stay, please. I was just thinking about the hunt earlier and how much I enjoyed it.'

'It felt like the old days,' Eperitus said. 'Before the war.'

'It did. For a while it was as if Troy had never happened. As if we were back on Ithaca or Samos hunting boar, not lost on an unknown island far away from home, in a place where even the stars are different. The moon, too. Every time I look at it, it seems strange. The same, but somehow changed. Am I wrong?'

Eperitus did not need to look up to know his friend was right. Just as the constellations had been distorted, so the face of the moon was altered too.

'In the daytime you can forget you're lost, but not at night,' Odysseus continued. 'Sometimes I wonder if we're all dead, a fleet of ghosts wandering the oceans of the Underworld. And then I think about what might have happened if you hadn't arrived when you did, back in the great hall of the lotus eaters. What if I'd swallowed the lotus? You've seen Eurylochus and the others. They can't even remember Ithaca.'

'They will, in time. The Old One knew where he was from, and he was as much a slave to the lotus as the rest of them. Besides, one way or another you'll get us home. There's no-one more determined to see Ithaca again than you; and if you can bring us through ten years of war, what's a few more days at sea going to do to us?'

'Don't tempt the gods,' Odysseus warned, with a smile. 'But you're right. Tomorrow we'll head over to the mainland. There must be someone there who can tell us where we are.'

'I'm not certain we should. I can hear strange sounds; I think they're coming from across the water.'

'Then let's go to back up into the woods and see what we can see.'

Aided by the moonlight, they found their way to the gap in the trees from which they had seen the mainland earlier. The woods were silent, but for the whispering of the wind in the dying leaves above them and the distant sound of the Ithacans on the beach. From across the water they could hear the bleating of penned-up goats and sheep, a sound that might have reminded them of their peaceful homeland were it not for the harsh voices that disrupted it. They were deep, booming and angry, like the cries of great beasts in the night. And yet, unmistakeably, there were words amid the roars. And from the glimmer of lights here and there among the trees it was clear there were fires burning

'So there are men there,' Odysseus said.

'But what sort of men?'

'What does it matter? Savage or civilised, they can tell us where we are. They can tell us the way home.'

Eperitus said nothing.

Eperitus woke before dawn to the sound of birds in the trees and the lapping of waves against the shore. He found Odysseus already aboard the galley, leaning against the bow rail and staring across the

water at the mainland. Eperitus joined him, but the king seemed unusually taciturn and only spoke to ask him to ready the crew. What was burdening his thoughts he could not guess.

Leaving the other ships in the bay, the men rowed the galley out into the channel dividing the island from the coast. The shoreline was too inhospitable for a landing, but Eurybates spotted a headland further up and steered towards it. After rowing past the narrow spur of rock they found a long, shingle beach backed by grey cliffs. Halfway along the shore a stone wall looped out in a semicircle from the cliff face. The mouth of a cave was just visible behind it, mostly hidden beneath a curtain of overhanging laurel.

'That wall is man-made,' Eperitus said. 'But the stones are too big to have been put there by a few fishermen or a bunch of savages. It's the work of a hundred men, at least.'

'Perhaps it's an old fortification,' Eurybates suggested. 'The foundations of a tower, maybe?'

'There are only two places built with stones that big,' Odysseus said. 'Mycenae and Troy; and the walls of Troy were built by gods.'

Gazing along the shoreline, he pointed out a small inlet scooped out of the cliffs some distance further on.

'Make for that cove.'

As they rowed, Eperitus scoured the wooded hilltops for any sign of men. There were several caves visible through the foliage, and here and there he noticed the stumps of felled trees. Winding its way down from the top of the headland was a rough path, but other than the wall in front of the cave there was nothing to indicate any kind of civilisation. From somewhere he could hear the bleating of goats and sheep, but there was no sound of the voices they had heard the night before. It seemed peaceful, and yet his every instinct told him it was a place of fear and danger.

Shortly afterwards they dropped their anchor stones into the shallow waters of the inlet.

'Take me,' Selagos said as Odysseus selected the men who would accompany him ashore.

'You can stay here and look after Eurylochus.'

'Your cousin is better now. I want to go with you, not stay here and play nursemaid.'

The king shook his head and pointed to Elpenor instead. Eperitus wondered at the decision to leave the Taphian behind, but the lotus had made Eurylochus such a shadow of his old self that he doubted even Selagos could goad him into starting another mutiny. Nevertheless, as Polites had been selected to join the expedition Eperitus had asked Eurybates to keep a close eye on Astynome while they were away. Odysseus also had orders for his squire: that if the expedition did not return after two days then it was up to him to lead the fleet back to Ithaca. Eperitus thought it was an ominous tone to part on.

'Take care while I'm gone and watch Eurylochus,' he told Astynome as they parted. 'The lotus may have taken his memory, but its effects won't last forever.'

'I can look after myself,' she reassured him. 'It's you I'm worried about. There's something about this place that frightens me. Something wild and savage, like in the stories about the world before the gods tamed it.'

'There's nothing here but a few goats,' he said with a smile. 'We'll be back by morning, empty-handed and hungry.'

He kissed her and then clambered into the waiting boat. The oarsmen rowed the party to shore, where Odysseus led them over the promontory that separated the inlet from the longer beach. The wall and cave were some distance away, but Odysseus set off with a determined stride. Eperitus caught up with him and they left the others to straggle behind in ones or twos.

'Is that wine?' he asked, indicating the goatskin slung over Odysseus's shoulder.

'It's some of the vintage Maron gave me.'

'The Cicone priest? Isn't it a bit too good for this place?'

'Something told me I should bring it,' Odysseus answered with a shrug.

'Then don't let Elpenor get his hands on it. The lad's nothing but a winebibber. Why did you bring him?'

'He needs the experience and a chance to prove himself. The thought that I chose him before others will do him a lot of good.'

'Selagos would have been better.'

'Selagos?' Odysseus asked, half turning to Eperitus as he strode over the shingle. 'You trust the Taphian?'

'I didn't say I trusted him. But I'd rather have him around than Elpenor if we got into trouble.'

'I wouldn't.'

'Because he's one of Eurylochus's cronies?'

'Because a god spoke to me in my dreams last night.'

Eperitus frowned and glanced over his shoulder, but the others were several paces behind, struggling across the loose wet stones.

'A *god* spoke to you? Is that why you've been so sullen all morning? What did this god say?'

'That one of my own men will try to kill me. I've always known Selagos hated me – I can see it in his eyes – and when he demanded to come with us I knew it had to be him.'

'But why would he want to kill you? Are you suggesting Eurylochus has put him up to it?'

'I'm not suggesting anything, least of all that – Eurylochus doesn't have the courage. But the dream troubled me. I'm not going to give Selagos the chance to put a knife in me before we get back to Ithaca.'

He said no more, and Eperitus was left thinking of the rope that had been deliberately cut as they had rounded Malea. But he also remembered that Selagos had not been one of the men on the cable when it had been severed.

The walk to the cave was quicker than he expected despite the thick shingle underfoot, and the sun had not yet reached noon by the time they arrived at the wall. They paused by the only opening, where a tall picket gate with leather hinges had been left half open. The carpet of dung on the pebbled floor inside and the sound of bleating coming from the mouth of the cave told them the enclosure was nothing more than a pen for livestock. And yet the scale of the high walls and the yawning blackness of the cavern – like a giant mouth waiting to swallow them up – had a belittling, oppressive effect that made Eperitus feel uneasy.

'It's even bigger than it looked from the ship,' Antiphus said, staring in awe at the huge blocks of stone and the roughly trimmed tree trunks stacked lengthways on top of them. 'Do you think someone lives here?'

'Someone or some*thing*,' Eperitus replied.

'A shepherd judging by the bleating coming from the cave and all these animal droppings,' Odysseus said.

Eperitus sniffed the air and nodded.

'I can smell cheese and fresh milk – it could be a shepherd's grotto. But it doesn't feel right, all the same. And what do you make of that?'

He pointed to a flat stone disc leaning against the cliff beside the cave entrance. It had been hewn from a single piece of rock and was as big as the mouth of the cave itself. A deep rut in the ground suggested the stone had once covered the entrance. The sight of it caused muttering among the rest of the men.

'No man could move that,' said Elpenor.

'*Fifty* men couldn't,' Polites corrected him.

'It would take a god or a titan to shift it,' Omeros said.

'Well the titans were locked up in Tartarus long ago and a god can be reasoned with, so I'm going to see if anyone's home,' Odysseus said. 'Come if you want, or wait here like frightened children.'

He crossed the dung-littered yard towards the cave. Despite the apprehension grating at every nerve, Eperitus followed at his shoulder. The crunch of pebbles behind them told him the others were not going to be left behind either. The mouth of the cave loomed over them, its apex as high as a galley's mast. A laurel tree rooted on one side had grown so tall that its trailing boughs hung like a beard over the entrance. Odysseus brushed them aside and walked through. As Eperitus entered he was met by a wall of cold shadow. The daylight barely penetrated more than a few paces into the gloom and for a moment his senses fumbled for purchase in the void. As his eyes adjusted to the faint light he saw the grey bodies of animals crowded in wooden pens to his left: spring-born kids and lambs nearest the entrance; the summer generation neighbouring them; and the new-borns almost lost in the shadows at the back. The cave floor was thick with dung and the stink of it mingled with the smells of cheese and damp rock. As the rest of the party stumbled into the cave – their spears and swords at the ready – the animals became agitated and jostled against each other, bleating nervously until the cave reverberated with their clamour.

'Is anyone here?' Odysseus called out. His words echoed back from the distant walls and high ceiling. 'We mean no harm. We're travellers trying to find our way home.'

'The place is empty,' Eperitus told him. 'If there was anyone here I'd have heard them.'

'Then why are you whispering?' Odysseus chided him with a smile. He turned to Elpenor. 'Light a fire and make some torches. I want to look around.'

Antiphus had walked over to the folds where the lambs and kids were settling down again.

'Look at these,' he said, leaning over a row of baskets against the wall of the cave. 'Cheeses the size of anchor stones and bowls full of whey and butter.'

'We should take them back to the ship,' said one of the others. 'The animals, too. I haven't had a bite of fresh cheese for months, and a haul like this'll be a handsome return for half a day's work.'

'Hippasos is right,' said another. 'I'd give my share of what we took from Ismarus for just half of one of those cheeses.'

'We're not here for cheese, Mydon,' Odysseus reminded him. 'We're here for information, and if you want to taste Ithacan cheese again you'd better pray to the gods we find someone who'll tell us where we are. Where's that fire?'

Elpenor found a pile of ashes surrounded by a ring of blackened stones not far into the cave. With Omeros's help he struck a spark and kindled it into a small flame at the centre of the hearth. After adding wood from a stack they had found at the side of the cave and dried dung from the floor, the flame was soon nurtured into a blazing fire. It churned sparks up into the darkness and threw back the shadows so that here and there the gleam of rock could be seen from the edges of the cave. Odysseus wrapped scraps of wool around lengths of wood to make torches and shared them with Eperitus, Polites and Hippasos. They lit them in the flames and ventured into the darkness at the back of the cave. Eperitus had heard nothing but the dripping of water on stone since entering, but above the odour of animals, cheese and wet rock he could smell something that unsettled him. It was the stench of sweat and faeces. It reminded him of Philoctetes's lair on Lemnos, but it was too powerful to belong to one man. As he walked slowly into the depths of the cave the reek became stronger, forcing him to hold a corner of his cloak over his face. Then Hippasos gave a shout of dismay, which was followed by the sound of retching.

'What is it?' Odysseus asked, rushing to join him.

Eperitus and Polites followed. By the shimmering glow of the torches they saw a recess in the wall of the cave where layers of broken branches had been laid over the pebble floor and covered with sheepskins. Around the pile of skins were heaps of animal bones, some yellow with age and others still matted with fresh gore.

'It looks like a bed,' Polites suggested, covering his nose and mouth against the stench.

'A bed?' Hippasos said, wiping away a string of vomit with the back of his hand. 'You could sleep twenty men on that, easily. And that *smell* –'

He turned aside and began to retch again.

'It's a bed alright, but not for one man or twenty,' Eperitus said. 'Whoever or whatever lives in this place, we should get out before it returns.'

'I think you're right,' Polites agreed. 'Odysseus, let's take some cheeses and a few lambs and go. We can't gain anything from staying here.'

The orange light from the king's torch cast deep shadows in the lines of his face.

'You talk like this is the lair of some monster, but ask your-selves this: what sort of monster keeps sheep and goats? What kind of bloodthirsty fiend takes time to milk his flock for cheese and whey? Have you ever met a dangerous goatherd or shepherd? And what are we here for? To steal a few wheels of cheese? To rustle a dozen lambs and kids? Or to discover where in Zeus's name we are! Until we find that out we're lost, and I don't intend wasting any more time drift-ing from one landfall to the next, hoping the gods will take it upon themselves to bring us home. We can't even navigate by the stars any more, since they're not the stars we used to know in the world we came from. So we need to find someone who can tell us where this place is and how we get back to Greece, and the only chance I see of doing that is waiting here until whoever lives in this cave turns up. Is that understood?'

Polites and Hippasos nodded sheepishly and slunk away to other corners of the cave, busying themselves with exploring the bare nooks and alcoves of its rough walls. Eperitus remained.

'And if this shepherd does turn out to be a monster?'

'Then we find a way to kill it or die in the attempt. And I'm sorry for losing my temper.'

'Don't apologise. They should be focussed on getting back home, not filling their bellies with cheese. Sometimes it seems they're more interested in what they find along the way.'

'That's what I'm afraid of,' Odysseus said with a sigh. 'Not for them but for myself! That raid on Ismarus nearly cost us ev-erything, but for what? I should have been the one thinking of home, but I gambled everything on a last quest for glory. I told myself the plunder we brought back from Troy wasn't enough for the lives and the years we wasted there – as if more gold and slaves would make everything worthwhile. But I knew it couldn't. So per-haps it's something worse, like when you risk your life needlessly in battle – when some madness in you wants to singe Hades's beard, to look over the edge into the depths of his Underworld and step back at the last moment. And with the war over and Ithaca near enough to touch, part of me keeps wanting to run away. I'm not waiting to see if whoever lives in this cave can tell me how to get back to Ithaca; I'm testing the Fates again, to see whether it truly is my destiny to return home.'

Eperitus looked at him concerned. He knew the temptation to risk life or limb in some pointless act of bravery. What warrior had not, in some heady moment when his blood was up, tried to coax fate and prove to himself he was invincible? But for Odysseus to gamble everything he had fought for over the last ten years on some mad test of destiny?

'If that's what this is about, then let's leave now.'

The king shook his head and smiled. His moment of self doubt had passed.

'And yet we still don't know where we are. We'll wait until the shepherd returns and see what he can tell us. If he observes *xenia* perhaps he'll give us a few of these cheeses as a guest-gift.'

He added the last with a wink, but Eperitus could see there was more bravado than humour in it. They returned to the fire where, to Eperitus's horror, the others were seated in a circle passing around large chunks of ripe cheese.

'What do you think you're doing?' he barked. 'Put the damned thing back.'

'Put it back?' Mydon scoffed. 'This is the best cheese I've eaten in ten years! And if you think I've braved Trojan spears and arrows and a thousand other dangers just to fret about offending some poor shepherd then think again. Besides, there must be three dozen of these things behind those pens. He won't miss one.'

Eperitus felt the anger surge through his veins and balled up his fists, ready to knock some discipline back into the insolent soldier. But Odysseus laid a hand on his arm and held him back.

'Forget about it,' he said. 'What's done is done. Let them eat their fill. Perhaps we can pay our unwitting host back with a little wine.'

He patted the goatskin hanging at his side then took the piece of cheese offered to him by Antiphus and sat down. A loud bleating was followed by the appearance of Hippasos with a lamb under his arm. He was accompanied by another guardsman, Ophelestes, who had his knife ready. Odysseus held up a hand and shook his head.

'If you're going to kill the beast, then at least let me offer it to the gods first.'

'And you expect this shepherd to observe *xenia* after you've helped yourself to his possessions?' Eperitus demanded. 'You should remember that a bad guest is as much an affront to the gods as a bad host.'

He turned his back on the warmth of the fire and the pungent smell of the broken cheese and walked out of the cave. Outside, he was surprised to see the chariot of the sun already descending towards the sea. After watching it for a few moments he leaned back against the stone disc and slid down onto his haunches. He soon forgot the laughter and the smell of roast lamb and let his anger subside into thoughts of Astynome and what awaited them on their return to Ithaca. He could barely recall what the island looked like, apart from a few details that his memory had clung on to over the years. And perhaps it was the weakness of his recollections that made it so difficult to imagine being home again. But then he was already finding it hard to remember Troy, or even the faces of the men he had fought beside for so long. Maybe it was the isolation of being lost at sea, in a world where the stars were different and everything else felt different with them.

A rustle of branches announced Odysseus's appearance. He held a piece of meat in one hand and a lump of cheese in the other.

'You should have some of this cheese, Eperitus. Ambrosia couldn't taste better.'

'When it's offered by the man who made it, I'll eat it. Not before.'

'But you'll happily take something if you've murdered its rightful owner first?'

'I won't sneak into his home and rob him of his property when he's not there like some thief in the night.'

'As proud and as stubborn as ever, then?'

'That's the price you pay for loyalty, Odysseus. Men who can steal from a stranger's home when he's not in can't be trusted.'

'Would you say that of Antiphus and Polites?' Odysseus asked, laying the food on a slab of rock. 'And me, after all we've been through? Say rather it's the curse of the gods on all of us. Now, don't waste the cheese.'

He patted Eperitus's shoulder and returned to the cave, welcomed by a peal of laughter as the leafy curtain was brushed aside. Eperitus picked up the cheese, took a long look at the ripe yellow flesh and then hurled it into a far corner of the compound. As it exploded into pieces against a rock, Eperitus's senses suddenly sprang to life. He had felt a pulse pass through the rock beneath him. He felt it again and then again, one tremor after another forming a slow rhythm like a giant heart beating in the earth. He heard the distant bleating of sheep and goats and picked up their scent on the breeze, pierced by the same odour of stale sweat he had found in the cave. Eperitus ran out into the compound and stared at the tree-covered hills above. Then he saw it: a movement high up in the foliage, shaking the leaves. Something tall and black was striding between the shadowy boles of the trees, its form lost in the gloom and yet terrifyingly large as it descended the hillside towards the beach. Eperitus glanced at the entrance to the compound and then back at the cave where his comrades were eating meat and cheese in blissful ignorance. He thought about running to the beach and drawing whatever it was away, but that would risk leading it towards the cove where the galley and Astynome were hidden. It was also possible it might not see him at all and would walk in on the Ithacans unexpectedly. No, he only had one choice.

He ran towards the cave, slipped on the pebbles and regained his footing. The first animals had reached the beach behind him and were followed by the thud of a heavy footstep. He pulled the screen of branches aside and stared at the dull glow of the fire, a mere ember in the all-consuming darkness. Several dimly lit faces looked up as he entered.

'Hide! Hide now if you want to live!'

They heard the fear in his voice, paused, then leapt to their feet and scattered into the shadows on either side. Eperitus risked a glance over his shoulder. Through the mesh of leaves he could see the sun setting beyond the compound wall. Then a figure blundered across his vision, blotting out the sun so that all he could see was the silhouette of something immense and terrible. He turned and ran into the cave, retaining wits enough to pick up a bowl of whey and toss it onto the flames. As he snatched up the spit with the remains of the lamb and threw it into a corner of the cave, he blundered straight into Elpenor.

'What is it?' the lad demanded, frightened and yet driven by an even more urgent curiosity. 'What did you see?'

Eperitus threw him onto his shoulder and ran into the darkness. Guided by his instincts, he sensed the approach of the cave wall and threw himself and Elpenor down onto the dung-covered floor. There was a low recess in the rock, which he slid back into, pulling the young Ithacan with him.

'Why are we –?'

'*Be quiet!*' Eperitus hissed.

He clapped his palm over Elpenor's mouth just as a large hand pushed through into the mouth of the cave and pulled the screen of laurel branches aside. Several fat sheep and goats trotted in, spreading out across the cavern floor and filling the enclosed space with their bleating. The lambs and kids pressed against the sides of the pens, calling out for their mothers as they pushed up against the wooden rungs or onto each others' backs. The entrance to the cave was now full of the largest sheep and goats Eperitus had ever seen, some of them spilling towards the side wall where he and Elpenor lay hidden. Then the hand that held the branches aside was followed by an arm and a great black head as the giant herdsman stooped to enter his lair. Elpenor stiffened and let out a muffled whimper before going limp. Taking his hand from Elpenor's mouth, Eperitus stared up in horror at the immense form silhouetted against the mouth of the cave. Even at a stoop it was as tall as four men, with thickset limbs covered in wiry hair that caught the light of the sunset through the laurel curtain. His features were in darkness, but it seemed to Eperitus that the monster was naked, his thick hair acting in the place of clothing as it hung like a pointed beard between the arch of his crooked legs.

Chapter Twenty

THE HERDSMAN

Laertes sat on a rock beside a row of vines. He wore a faded and patched tunic, leather gaiters tied about his shins with cord, and a pair of thick leather gloves. His pruning knife was still in his hand and his wide-brimmed goatskin hat was crushed firmly down on his head so that his eyes were but a gleam in its shadow.

'Well, go on lad, don't stop there. What did you tell the little strumpet to make them run off like that?'

Telemachus grinned at the memory.

'I told her a message had arrived that morning from Sparta, that the war was over and the kings were returning. They haven't been near me since.'

Laertes let out a thin crowing sound and slapped his gloved hand against his thigh.

'That's the finest thing I've heard since Eumaeus set his dogs on Melanthius. It's even funnier than you punching Eurymachus. Best of all they'll have told Eupeithes; I bet the old fool hasn't had a peaceful night's sleep since.' He rubbed his hands with glee at the thought of his old enemy's discomfort. Then, looking thoughtfully at Telemachus, he added, 'Your father would have been proud of that one, you know. Now, pick up that basket, will you, and follow me.'

Telemachus did as he was told and they continued down the row in silence. It was late afternoon and the only sounds were the calls of the seagulls overhead and the crashing of waves from beyond the cliff's edge. Every now and then his grandfather would shake his head and chuckle to himself, but Telemachus could not share his pleasure. All he could think about was Odysseus.

'Do you think he'll ever return?'

'Your father? Only the gods know that. But he's always had his wits about him and he's not one to let courage get in the way of common sense, so it's more likely than not.'

'Will I be made king if he doesn't?'

Laertes bent closer to his vines and grunted something indistinct.

'Because Melantho said something to me that I didn't understand.'

'You don't want to listen to her.'

'She said I wouldn't be king because mother had sold my birthright. Do you know what she means?'

Laertes sighed and stood up, pressing a hand into the small of his back to straighten himself. He saw a tree stump and sat down, indicating for Telemachus to join him.

'Then your mother hasn't told you yet? I thought not. Listen to me, lad. I love your mother as if she were my own flesh and blood. She's got a good heart, she's loyal and she's clever – qualities that most of the nobility seems to lack. What's more, if a man needs brains and brawn to rule a kingdom then a woman needs twice the brains because she hasn't got the brawn, if you follow.' He waited for Telemachus to nod before continuing. 'Now, she'll have wanted to say this to you herself at some point, but you've asked so I'm going to tell you. You already know your mother sent you to Sparta for your own safety, so why do you think she brought you back?'

'They caught the assassin?'

'They caught one assassin in a world full of them.'

'Then I don't know why. Am I still in danger then?'

'Not any more, your mother saw to that,' Laertes said. 'She's promised to remarry if Odysseus doesn't return before you reach manhood. So Melantho's right: unless your father returns, your mother will be forced to remarry and her new husband will become king, not you.'

Telemachus frowned.

'But why? Why would she do that?'

'Because she loves you enough to want to guarantee your safety. So long as you can never become king, Eupeithes and his cronies don't need you out of the way. I don't think there was much else she could do.'

'Then you're wrong about her,' Telemachus shouted, jumping to his feet and throwing the basket into the vines. 'You said she was loyal, but she's not. I was safe in Sparta; she betrayed me because she wanted me back home.'

He ran down the hillside to the track at the bottom and kept running. Eventually the need to think things through caught up with him and he slowed to a walk. His future, which had always been securely tied to the throne, was suddenly uncertain. For a boy with an absent father, like so many others on Ithaca, he had always felt empowered by the thought that one day he would be king. Now that had been taken from him. If Odysseus did not come back he had always known he would inherit the throne and have the power to make all the people and things he cared about safe. Now that power would fall into the hands of some unknown stepfather, most likely foisted on him by Eupeithes. Everything now depended on Odysseus returning and reclaiming his kingdom.

He still felt angry as he neared home some time later, though he had stopped blaming his mother, who he knew had done the only thing she could to ensure his safety. He would have welcomed the chance to encounter Eurymachus on the road though and vent his fury on the oaf, even if it meant a beating in return. Instead, as he walked the track along the side of Mount Neriton, he saw a tall boy strolling towards him from the opposite direction. The boy gave him an inquisitive look, then stopped and folded his arms.

'You're Odysseus's son.'

'So what? And who in Hades are you?'

'Peiraeus, son of Clytius.'

'Never heard of either of you.'

'Well you should have. My father went to Troy with the last shipload of replacements. If it wasn't for *your* father and his stupid war, *mine* would still be on Kefalonia and I wouldn't have been sent over here to live with my uncle.'

'It's not *my* father's war and you should speak about your king with more respect.'

'He's nobody's king at the moment, not while he's on the other side of the world fighting *somebody else's* war!'

Telemachus clenched his fist and swung at the boy, who stepped back from the blow and used his longer reach to punch Telemachus squarely in the face. Telemachus's legs gave and he found himself on his backside in the middle of the dusty track. But his anger propelled him back onto his feet and, remembering Mentor's training, he ducked beneath a second blow and punched Peiraeus in the chest. The boy staggered back, clutching his chest and coughing, then returned with fists flailing, a lucky blow catching Telemachus on the same spot where Eurymachus had hit him before. It stung and he felt his legs giving again, but seeing Peiraeus's guard open, he laid a well-aimed punch hard in his throat. At that moment his legs refused to go another step and buckled under him.

For a moment he lay on his back with a pounding head and looked up at the cloudless sky. Hearing the other boy moving, he sat up to see him also flat out on the track, propped up on one elbow and rubbing his neck.

'You've got a hard punch,' Telemachus said. 'If your father fights as well as you do the war'll be over soon.'

'I'm sorry I insulted the king,' Peiraeus replied. 'You had every right to hit me.'

Telemachus rose unsteadily to his feet and offered the boy his hand. Peiraeus shook it, then allowed Telemachus to pull him up. They looked at each other, secretly admiring the blood and dust that marked the start of their friendship, then, at Telemachus's suggestion, set off for the palace to see what food could be gleaned from the kitchens.

Under the Cyclops's arm was a bundle of firewood, which he tossed to one side with a startling clatter. Then he reached through the cave entrance with both arms, took hold of the stone disc that lay propped against the wall outside, and with barely a grunt rolled it slowly across the entrance. As rock grated against rock and daylight was quickly squeezed out of the cave, Eperitus felt he was being entombed. He reached down for the hilt of his sword and gripped it tight in an effort to control the shaking in his hand. It was then that he noticed the faint glow from the extinguished fire and the thin line of smoke that trailed up from it. A new wave of fear gripped him, for the Ithacans were trapped, and if the herdsman found them there they would be utterly defenceless against a creature of such size.

A small gap remained between the top of the stone and the apex of the cave, barely large enough for a man's hand. Through this a last beam of twilight filtered into the cave, by which Eperitus could see the herdsman's head turning this way and that as if counting the multitude of animals. When he was done, he took two ground-shaking steps across the cave and sat down on a boulder beside the sheep pens. Reaching behind himself into the blackness, he pulled out some large wooden bowls and laid them on the floor. As if reacting to a familiar routine, the animals began crowding towards him.

'Come now, don't push,' he boomed, his slow, heavy voice shaking the closed air of the cave. 'You'll all get your turn.'

One by one, he allowed them up to the bowls to be milked. After gently squeezing their udders with the tips of his enormous fingers, he lifted lambs or kids from the pens and put them to their mothers to feed. When all this was over he took half the bowls and with a patience that seemed unsuited to a beast of such savage appearance, he began curdling the milk. Finally, after Eperitus had grown stiff from lying motionless on the cold stone floor, the last ray of light faded away. The darkness was now filled with the noisy suckling of the young and the fidgeting of animals as they lay down to rest, but of their master Eperitus could hear nothing. He began to fear that the creature suspected their presence and was stalking the darkness for them; that at any moment a giant hand would reach out of the void and pluck him out of his hiding place to be devoured. And then with a loud crack of stone and a flash of light, Eperitus glimpsed him by the ring of stones where the Ithacans had made their fire. The noise startled Elpenor back into consciousness and Eperitus quickly closed his hand over the lad's mouth again. Another smack of stone upon stone and another spark of light seared a picture of the monster's face onto Eperitus's mind's eye, but it was an image so horrible he knew it could not have been possible. Another crack and flash followed. In the darkness he heard the herdsman blowing life into the spark of fire he had kindled, until slowly the glow of flame blossomed like an orange rose in the centre of the blackness. Before Eperitus could glimpse the hideous face again, the herdsman turned his back and sat cross-legged before the hearth, his shoulders hunched as he stared in dumb silence at what he had created.

After a while, he took a deep breath and spoke.

'Come out of the shadows. Let me see you.'

Eperitus felt his heart pounding faster and louder against his rib cage. He wanted to believe the monster was talking to his sheep again. But the tone was less gentle than when he had spoken to his flocks. Instead, his words were stern – a command rather than an invite. Peering into the tar-black recesses of the cave, Eperitus saw the slight sheen of the firelight washing over armour, but none of his comrades dared step out of their hiding places.

'Come now, do you take me for a fool because I'm big and clumsy to your tiny eyes? Do you think I didn't notice the smoke rising from the wet ashes when I entered? Can I not see the crumbs of cheese your little mouths have let fall around my hearth. And did I not notice that one of my children is missing, that one of my ewes is without her lamb?'

His voice rose so that the cave seemed to tremble with his anger, an anger that was as yet contained but which threatened to erupt with terrible consequences. While the echo of his words was still ringing from the stone walls, no-one moved. Then a man rose to his feet at the back of the cave and walked towards the edge of the firelight. It was Odysseus. Eperitus took his hand from Elpenor's mouth and stood. Though the giant's back was still turned to them, he had to wade through his own fear to cross the short distance to Odysseus's side.

'Only two of you?' the herdsman asked, as if speaking to the flames. 'Or only two of you brave enough to face the master of the home you have invaded? Yes, that's it: two brave men and eleven cowards. For thirteen men entered this cave. But what sort of men are you? Merchants? Well-fed merchants with big, fat legs, useless for running away but perfect for eating? No, you don't smell like seafaring traders. Too lean, too inquisitive, too reckless. Pirates then, with your pricking spears and your flimsy shields, and your unquenchable lust for what is not your own.'

'We are neither, my lord,' Odysseus answered.

In that dark prison, surrounded by cold stone and with a fiend as their gaoler, the king's voice sounded smoother and more reassuring than Eperitus had ever heard it before. It was like a warm light flickering into life amid the black hopelessness of their situation. And as Eperitus watched the hunched shoulders of the herdsman it seemed they were frozen, snared by the small voice that had emerged from the shadows. Behind him he heard the scuff of sandals on rock as more Ithacans conquered their fear and emerged from the shadows.

'We are Greeks, men of honour who respect the gods. We were returning from the siege of Troy where we were part of Agamemnon's victorious army. Ten years we fought for him, building his renown with the bricks of our dead bodies and the mortar of our blood, but from the moment we sailed for home we've had nothing but trouble. Recently the gods sent a storm to divide our fleet, and now we find ourselves alone in a strange land without any idea of how to find our way back again. When we saw your cave and its well-made wall, and when we entered and saw the carefully tended animals and other signs of a civilised mind, we decided to stay and throw ourselves upon your mercy. After all, in Greece a shepherd honours the gods as much as any other man, and anyone who honours the gods will show grace to a suppliant, if only because Zeus commands it.'

To Eperitus's mind, even a creature of such fearsome size and temper as the creature that sat before them could not refuse such a request. For a moment the shepherd sat in silence, then slowly – his shoulders shaking slightly so that he seemed to rock back and forth – he began to laugh. It was a deep, menacing sound that was felt rather than heard.

'I've been called many things, but civilised is not one of them. There's a threshold where flattery becomes obvious, and you, my little mouse, have crossed it. But after trying to flatter me you then dare to insult me! Do you think I am like you – small and weak, clinging on to life by grovelling before the gods? I am a Cyclops! The gods do not command me, for I am stronger than they are. And if I treat you as suppliants rather than thieves then it is because *I* choose to do so, not because *Zeus* commands it.'

'It wasn't my intention to offend you, friend,' Odysseus countered, calmly. 'If we stole from you then it was not due to base character, but because we were starving. We will gladly pay you back.'

'You have nothing I want, for I want nothing but to be left alone.'

'Then tell us where we are and how to find our way home. Do that and you will never hear from us again, you have my word.'

'We Cyclopes are not sailors,' the herdsman replied, picking up a large branch and stoking the flames with it before dropping it into the fire with a puff of embers. 'I could not tell you how to get home even if I knew where it is. Only Aeolus knows such things. But if you tell me where your galley is moored, maybe I could help you.'

'We have no ship. The storm that separated us from the rest of our fleet tore our sails and snapped our rudders, so that when we reached these shores we were driven helplessly upon the rocks. We are the only ones who made it to shore alive.'

'Liar!' the Cyclops boomed, rising to his feet. 'A sailor without a ship does not ask the way home.'

He turned towards the Ithacans, towering above them. With the light of the hearth behind him, he presented a terrifying silhouette, the shaggy hair of his head and limbs catching the orange glow of the flames. But as the men's eyes adjusted and his features became clearer, they fell away, some of them crying out in dread. Even Odysseus took a step back, colliding with Eperitus, who had remained rooted to the spot, staring up in disbelief at the hideous visage that stared down at him. For the herdsman had but a single eye in the centre of his face, a fierce, dominant orb that simmered with malevolent intelligence.

'And now that I think of it, perhaps you do have something that I want!'

With a roar that shook the air in the cave, the monster leapt towards them. Eperitus seized the hilt of his sword, but before he could draw it Odysseus caught him and bundled him backwards into the shadows. The others turned to run. From the corner of his eye Eperitus saw Omeros stumble and Polites rush back to help him. As Polites seized the back of the young warrior's tunic, so the monstrous hand of the Cyclops reached down towards them both. Eperitus drew his sword and rushed to help them. At the same moment, Mydon and Hippasos ran out of the shadows with their blades flashing in the firelight. Mydon struck at the Cyclops's outstretched arm, but the creature's thick hide turned the blow and the weapon flew out of the warrior's hand. Immediately the Cyclops' fingers closed about him and snatched him up into the smoky darkness. Hippasos charged the monster with a yell, aiming the point of his sword at his thigh. Before he could drive the attack home, the herdsman knocked him to the ground. Picking him up by his legs, he swung him high in the air and then back down against the floor, splitting his head open so that brains and pieces of skull exploded in an arc across the rock. Filled with rage for his comrades, Eperitus ran on, only to have his legs pulled from beneath him. A moment later, Odysseus was on top of him.

'I won't let you throw your life away,' he hissed. 'There's nothing you can do for them now.'

The king seized him by the elbow and dragged him back into the shadows. Eperitus caught sight of Polites doing the same for Omeros, who was now unconscious. Looking up, he saw the Cyclops drop the decapitated body of Hippasos onto the floor and turn his attention to Mydon. The Ithacan screamed, the cry of a man driven out of his mind with terror. Then the monstrous herdsman took hold of one of his arms and wrenched it from its socket, as if he was snapping a branch from a small tree. While Mydon's shouts rang back from the walls, the monster devoured his limb whole. Then, seizing the man's legs in his other hand, he tore him in two and put an end to his pitiful cries. Slumping back down onto the boulder where he had been sitting, the Cyclops gorged himself on the two Ithacans until his beard ran with blood and pieces of their flesh. Then, after draining one of the bowls of fresh milk, he gave out a large belch and threw himself down on the floor. Within moments he was asleep.

Odysseus had dragged Eperitus into the recess where Elpenor was still hiding. From here they had watched wide-eyed with fear as the Cyclops murdered and ate their friends. After convincing himself that the ogre's slow breathing and loud snores were not feigned, Eperitus mustered the courage to stand. He picked up his discarded sword and forced himself the few paces to where the ogre slept. Mortal dread sapped his strength, but he knew this would be his only opportunity to destroy the Cyclops and avenge his comrades. Yet every step was a trial, as if the air had solidified about him and could only be moved with the greatest effort. He had fought with selfless bravery against many terrifying enemies, but the sight of the fiend disarmed him. He tried to picture Astynome's face in his mind's eye but could not. The darkness of the cave and the horror of the Cyclops seemed to suck everything from him, so that only the instinct to slice open its throat or hack off its hideous head kept him going.

He passed its outstretched arm, barely daring to look at the huge hand that had dashed Hippasos to death and torn Mydon in half. He focussed himself on the great eye, now lidded, and as he advanced he felt a piece of skull crunch beneath his sandal. The bulge of the monster's pupil moved left to right beneath the brown, leathery skin – quick movements that showed Eperitus's approach had been sensed. Dreading that any moment the lid would rise like a sail to reveal the repulsive eye beneath, he called on the last of his courage and raised his sword high over his head.

A hand grabbed his wrist, blocking the blow he had meant to deliver.

'You can't kill him,' Odysseus hissed.

'This is our only chance! If we don't kill him now he'll devour us one by one.'

Odysseus prised the weapon from his hand.

'Come away before he awakes.'

As they retreated into the shadows, Antiphus, Polites and Ophelestes appeared beside them.

'Why did you stop him?' Antiphus demanded.

'It ate Mydon and Hippasos,' Ophelestes added. 'You should have let Eperitus kill it in its sleep.'

Polites drew his sword from its scabbard. 'I don't know why you want that thing alive, Odysseus, but you can't stop all of us.'

'There was a time when you trusted me,' the king said, looking at each of them in turn. 'Well, go ahead and kill him. He deserves to die and our friends should be avenged. But before you hack off his head or whatever you plan to do, tell me this: when the Cyclops is dead, how are you going to move that rock from the cave entrance?'

They looked at the colossal stone that blocked the only exit from the cave, and at last Eperitus saw what Odysseus must have seen from the very start. Polites returned his weapon to its sheath and bowed an apology, while Antiphus and Ophelestes looked from the stone to the monster and silently pondered the impossibility of their situation.

'I suggest we all find some hole or cranny to hide ourselves in and get as much sleep as our nightmares will allow us,' Odysseus said. 'Perhaps the morning will bring new hope, if the gods haven't forsaken us entirely.'

The others slunk away into the shadows and Eperitus followed Odysseus back to the overhang where they had left Elpenor. He was still there, his knees tucked into his chest as he stared at the sleeping monster.

'Tell me that great mind of yours has a plan to get us out of here,' Eperitus said quietly. 'I agree we can't kill the Cyclops without dooming ourselves, but if we do nothing he'll eat us all. I'd rather murder him than face that.'

'Do you realise how long it would take us to starve in this place?' Odysseus said. 'The animals and cheese alone would last us for weeks, and after that we might start eating each other. And all the time in almost complete darkness, slowly awaiting the inevitable. I'd rather be eaten than face that.'

'But the others would come looking for us, wouldn't they?' Elpenor suggested.

Odysseus shook his head. 'I told them to leave without us if we don't return within two days. They might disobey me and send out a search party, but I fear for anyone who finds us shut in here. Even if they could somehow move the stone, the noise would surely bring the other Cyclopes down upon them.'

'*Other* Cyclopes?' Eperitus asked.

'You saw the caves up on the hillsides, beyond the trees? And you remember the voices we heard shouting to each other last night? Yes, there are more of them.'

The thought left Eperitus cold. What if the other Cyclopes found the galley in its sheltered cove? The consequences were unthinkable, and in desperation for Astynome's safety he voiced the first half-formed idea that entered his mind.

'Perhaps if we were to wound the Cyclops so that he called out for help before we killed him, then the others would answer his call and remove the stone for us.'

'Then we would have a dozen giants to deal with instead of one,' Elpenor answered. 'Even I can see that.'

Eperitus could not deny the folly of his suggestion, even if Elpenor's arrogance piqued him. He looked at Odysseus, expecting to see the sympathetic expression he usually gave in response to his more ridiculous ideas. Instead he found the king gazing thoughtfully at him, as if ruminating over something. After a moment he shook his head and looked across at the sleeping Cyclops.

'No, the last thing we want is to bring the rest of his tribe down on us. Besides, I don't want him dead yet if I can avoid it. There was something he said that caught my ear, a name he mentioned: Aeolus. Only Aeolus can tell us the way home.'

'Who's Aeolus?' Elpenor asked. 'Another Cyclops?'

'I don't think so, but I'm going to find out. Cyclops or not, if this Aeolus knows the way back to Ithaca then I want to know who he is and where I can find him. At least then Mydon and Hippasos won't have given their lives in vain. And now I suggest we all get some sleep.'

With that, he threw his cloak about his shoulders and lay down on the bed of dried dung. Elpenor crept back into the farthest recess of the overhang and covered his face with his hands. Soon, both men were snoring gently. Eperitus looked at the one-eyed brute that had so easily slaughtered two Ithacan warriors, then lay down. He doubted he would dare to even close his eyes, let alone sleep.

He woke with a start. In his dream he had pictured Odysseus on a rooftop, looking over lush woodland towards an azure sea where seagulls cawed and swooped majestically, while all the time a figure with a drawn knife was approaching him stealthily from behind. He had called a warning but no sound had left his mouth. Whether it was the anguish of being unable to help his friend that had woken him, or the sound of bleating and the smell of woodsmoke, he could not say. Then he remembered the Cyclops and sat up.

Odysseus and Elpenor were already awake, sitting crouched beneath their cloaks in the darkness with the weak glow of the hearth reflecting on their faces. Both were staring at the Cyclops, who was sitting on the boulder he used for a chair. He had rekindled the fire and fed it more wood so that it was now ablaze and spitting merrily in that place of utter gloom. Only a thin beam of grey light coming in through the gap at the top of the stone door signified that day was approaching outside. The goats and sheep were pressing around their owner, impatient for their turn to be milked. One by one his fingers gently pulled at their udders before lifting out the young and placing each against its mother to feed. Eperitus glanced around the cave, spotting the other Ithacans in the shadows, entranced by the calm routine of the shepherd at his work, but knowing that those same hands – with such horrid strength – had last night torn their comrades to pieces. As the terrible moment came when the last lamb was plucked from its mother's teat and returned to its pen, and the Cyclops stood and rolled the stone away from the entrance – flooding the cave with light and momentarily blinding the Ithacans – Eperitus saw a movement among the flocks as they crowded towards the opening. He gripped Odysseus's arm and pointed at two men, Ophelestes and another he could not identify, crouching low among the herd. Both had pulled fleeces from the Cyclops's bed and thrown them over their backs. They only had to stoop to reduce themselves to the height of the abnormally large creatures surrounding them, and as the great flock pressed forward they moved with them.

'They'll never do it,' Elpenor declared, standing and gnawing at his bottom lip.

'Yes they can,' Odysseus said.

Only a slight widening of his eyes signified the tension inside as he watched the two men push forward, almost lost to sight among the jostling animals. But when the Cyclops had rolled the stone aside, he turned and planted his enormous legs either side of the entrance. His single eye stared down at the flock, counting each one as they passed beneath him.

'Somebody should warn them!' Elpenor urged, though not having the courage to stand and call out himself.

'No. That'll destroy any chance that remains to them,' Eperitus said. 'Their fate is in the lap of the gods now.'

'Pallas Athena, help them,' was all Odysseus could bring himself to say.

Ophelestes glanced up from beneath his fleece and saw the giant standing sentinel over the exit to the cave. He lost his nerve and tried to push his way back through the crowd of sheep and goats.

The Cyclops saw the hide slip from his back and, leaning forward, plucked him from the herd. Ophelestes had already drawn his sword and, despite the crushing pain of his captor's grip, slashed desperately at his hand. The Cyclops winced, then with his other hand he closed finger and thumb about the man's head and pinched him out of existence. The sword fell to the floor with a clang and Elpenor turned aside to vomit.

'Look!' Eperitus whispered. 'The other one's passing through. The Cyclops hasn't seen him.'

'But who is it?' Odysseus asked. 'Polites? Antiphus?'

'By all the gods! No!'

As the Cyclops buried his teeth into Ophelestes's corpse and the blood oozed between his fingers, he suddenly stopped and looked down. In an instant he had snatched up the second Ithacan, whom, as his fleece fell away, Eperitus recognised as Paion, a brave warrior who had often fought beside him at Troy. Paion barely had time to scream before the Cyclops's mouth closed over him and tore away his head and one of his shoulders. Odysseus lowered his face so as not to witness any more. Eperitus, unable to turn away, watched both men devoured limb by limb and mouthful by mouthful, until nothing remained but a matt of gore on the herdsman's beard. Then, when the last of his flock had left the cave, he rolled the stone back across the entrance and plunged the surviving Ithacans back into darkness.

Eperitus sat motionless, listening to the Cyclops's whistles fade into the distance as he herded his sheep along the beach and up to the hills above. Then a figure stood up in the darkness at the back of the cave and with a despairing cry ran at the boulder that imprisoned them. Antiphus threw his shoulder at the stone, only to be flung back onto the thick carpet of dung. Immediately he rose again and pressed both his hands against the rock, grunting loudly and pushing with all his might. He was joined by Polites, Omeros and a squat, muscular soldier named Drakios, all of them straining against the sole barrier to their freedom. Soon, Elpenor and the other two Ithacans were with them, crying out with the effort of their impossible task. Eperitus felt the tension in his own limbs, as if charged by the claustrophobia of his comrades, and ran over to thrust his weight against the cold, unmoving stone.

'It has to move!' Antiphus groaned. 'It *has* to move!'

'Keep pushing,' Polites said.

'You told us it would take fifty men to move this thing,' Omeros reminded him.

'I was wrong. It needs a hundred, but keep pushing anyway.'

Eperitus's feet slipped in the dung and the loose pebbles beneath. He turned his back to the rock, braced his shoulders against its rough, uneven surface and pushed with all the strength his thighs could lend him. Through the sweat pouring into his eyes, he saw Odysseus by the pens where the lambs and kids were kept. He was examining a long beam of wood. Eperitus stopped pushing and stood.

'What is it?'

'It's the trunk of a young olive tree. It's not seasoned yet, so the Cyclops didn't bring it here for firewood. A staff maybe? Here, Polites, Antiphus, Drakios: I need your help.'

Their fruitless efforts to shift the stone had already petered out. Antiphus and the others walked over and, following Odysseus's instructions, picked the bole up between them. Even with Polites's great strength it was too unwieldy, so Eperitus joined them and took the far end.

'What do you want us to do?' he asked. 'Batter the door down?'

Odysseus laughed, a strange sound in that place where the blood of their comrades was still fresh on the rocks.

'No. I want you to smooth the wood – leaving those branch stumps there and there – while I sharpen this end. And then I need four men to join me for a task that will put us in the greatest peril.'

'I'm with you,' Antiphus said, followed by all but Elpenor, who remained ashen-faced and quiet.

The four men were chosen by lot: Antiphus, Omeros, Drakios and Polites. When their work on the pole had been finished to Odysseus's satisfaction, they hardened the point over the flames of the fire and then hid it beneath a pile of dung. Another lamb was slaughtered and the Ithacans helped themselves freely to the

Cyclops's cheese. This time Eperitus was glad to share their meal as they swapped tales of their adventures together. They spoke as men on the threshold of great danger, reminiscing about the battles they had fought together and recalling their achievements. They could even laugh at the trials they had endured, though they had been less inclined to mirth when going through them. And they thought of home, too, each adding some memory to the tapestry they were weaving together. When the last had spoken they fell silent and each succumbed to thoughts of the homeland he had not seen for ten years. After a while their conversation revived and looked to the future, as if they were not prisoners of a man-eating terror but free men on their homeward voyage, with Ithaca just over the horizon. Eperitus declared he would marry Astynome the day after they returned and that they would start a farm together and raise a large family. Polites decided that, as Eperitus was going to leave the royal guard, he would offer his services to Odysseus as captain. Odysseus replied that he was not sure he would let Eperitus leave his service, but either way he would gladly yoke Polites to another ox and have him plough his fields for him. Omeros claimed to be the luckiest of them all, as he had seen enough of the world to keep him in songs for the rest of his life. He would travel all the courts of Greece, singing songs of the great war and highlighting the deeds of whichever king was his host. Antiphus said he did not have the heart to look into the future, but if the gods would grant him one prayer it would be that he could return home and see his father one more time. There was a finality about his tone that reminded them of their predicament.

When their talk had died down again, Odysseus explained his plan to them. They listened in sober silence, and then, after a few questions about detail, slipped away in ones or twos to the hidden corners where they had slept the night before. Only Odysseus and Eperitus remained. While Odysseus played idly with a wooden bowl he had emptied of curds and washed clean – though for what purpose he did not say – Eperitus listened for telltale signs of the herdsman's return. As the thin light from the gap above the door began to fade, he felt a tremor in the stone beneath him, then another. Before long he heard the bleating of sheep and goats. The Cyclops was coming back.

'If we were out there, Odysseus wouldn't just abandon us to our fate,' Eurybates protested.

Selagos was unmoved. 'He ordered us to stay here.'

Eurybates kicked the sand in frustration.

'What if they're in trouble? I say we send out a party to look for them.'

'Say what you like. Odysseus told us to wait two days then leave without him. That was his command and I intend to fulfil it at dawn tomorrow.'

Selagos's assumed authority was backed up by nods and murmurs from the crew. At Eurybates's request, they had formed a circle on the beach, but very few showed much inclination to search for their king. Eurybates held out his hands to them, imploring their support.

'We all saw those fires in the woods last night, the shadows moving in the flames. We all heard the shouts. What if whoever lives up on the clifftops has taken Odysseus and the others prisoner? Are we just going to leave them to be tortured and murdered? Where's your loyalty?'

'Yes we saw them,' said a man standing beside Eurylochus. 'Great big shadows like giants. And we heard them calling to each other in voices like thunder. If they've got Odysseus then there's not much we can do to rescue him.'

'So this is what we've come to, is it? The great Ithacan army, bane of Troy, is afraid of shadows in the dark.'

'We fear nothing,' Selagos said. 'But we haven't forgotten that Odysseus's greed led us into a massacre at Ismarus. Why should we follow him into a new disaster now? It's not cowardice to turn back in the face of folly.'

The agreement of the rest of the crew became more vocal, and at its height Eurylochus – who until that point had said nothing – stepped forward and proposed a show of hands in favour of sending out a party to find the king. Barely a dozen men raised their arms, and with a half-hearted cheer the assembly began to break up into little groups and drift apart.

Astynome, sitting on a grassy ridge at the top of the beach, watched Eurybates turn dejectedly away to converse with his few supporters. They did not even have a fire to comfort them in their failure, as the Ithacans did not dare risk attracting the attention of the spectral figures they had glimpsed the night before. With the twilight failing fast, the men now gathered into small groups and were served bread and cold meat by slave women, which they washed down with wine. Astynome rested her chin on her knees and pondered the implications of the debate. Eurybates was right: Eperitus, Odysseus and the others should have returned by now. That meant something had happened to delay them and that they were probably in danger – though she had a strong sense that Eperitus, at least, was still alive. But if they did not come back by first light then Selagos would see that the galley returned to the rest of the fleet. He was also certain to convey Odysseus's orders that they should assume he had perished and find their own way back to Ithaca.

But what would she do, she wondered? Slip away into the hills before the others could force her aboard and wait until Eperitus returned? Go looking for him herself? And if he and the others had perished, would she wander the coastline alone until she starved to death or fell into the hands of the savages that inhabited the hills above? Or should she go with the Ithacans and never see Eperitus again, forsaking his protection and doubtless falling prey to the slowly reviving lust of Eurylochus? Though the effects of the lotus had left him distant and even more lethargic than usual, there were signs that the old Eurylochus was returning. More than once she had caught him staring at her, his eyes alive with more than just a desire for the lotus fruit. She shuddered at the memory and looked up. Neither Eurylochus nor Selagos were anywhere in sight.

Disturbed by their absence, Astynome rose and brushed the sand from her dress. Two of the orphan girls were nearby, practising a dance together to an imagined tune. Astynome called them to her side.

'Girls, have you seen the fat soldier?'

'He went with the bad giant,' answered the oldest, pointing to the trees further along the beach.

The bad giant was Selagos, to distinguish him from Polites, the good giant. Astynome saw a solitary trail of footprints emerging from the tramplings of the crew and followed it in the direction of the trees. She was soon lost in the shadow of the eaves, and before long she heard voices. Slipping off her sandals, she trod gently through the sandy undergrowth until she saw Selagos and Eurylochus talking to each other in the gloom. She crouched behind a tree trunk and listened.

'I'm not so sure,' Eurylochus said. 'Perhaps Eurybates is right. Perhaps we should search for them in the morning. After all, if we leave and find our way back to Ithaca and then my cousin turns up with Eperitus and the others, it could prove, er, awkward.'

'Why? Because we followed the king's orders? Stop being a coward and seize the opportunity that's being offered to you. Don't you see this is a gift from the gods? With Odysseus out of the way and you his only male relative, you'll return to Ithaca as heir to the throne.'

'You forget Telemachus.'

'The boy? Boys die from all sorts of causes, even more so if they're princes.'

'Don't say such things,' Eurylochus warned. 'I won't murder a child just to become a king, especially the king of an island I can barely remember any more.'

Selagos folded his arms and looked down at Eurylochus.

'The effects of the lotus won't last forever. One day you will wake up and remember who you were – your desires and your ambitions. Until then I will look after your interests. We leave at dawn, whether Odysseus returns or not, and somehow we will find a way back to Ithaca.'

'What do you care about Ithaca?' Eurylochus snapped. 'You're a damned Taphian! And what does it matter to you whether I become king or not? Before you came to Troy a few months back, you'd never met me; now you want to place me on a throne that neither you nor I have any interest in. I sometimes wonder whether you're doing this for my sake or because you just want to see Odysseus brought down. Which is it?'

Selagos's eyes narrowed.

'Whatever I do is out of friendship for you.'

'Then let's leave at dawn, like you say. But if you're my friend, return me to the land of the lotus eaters. I don't care about anything else. Leave me there and then go your own way.'

'Perhaps I should,' Selagos replied, slapping the air between them in a gesture of frustration. 'And perhaps I would, if I knew how to get there. But I don't. Odysseus brought us here and only he can take us back.'

He turned away from Eurylochus and stared directly at the tree behind which Astynome was hiding. She did not have time to dart back behind the trunk and feared that any sudden movement now would reveal her presence. But the deepening shadow had engulfed her and, after a moment, the Taphian turned aside and reached for a goatskin propped against the roots of another tree.

'Let's not get angry with each other. Here, have a drink of this.'

Eurylochus took the goatskin and raised it to his lips. He lowered it briefly, looked at Selagos with surprise, then took another, longer swallow.

'Steady,' Selagos warned, reclaiming the goatskin.

'That's the best wine I've tasted in years. Where did you get it from?'

'I heard Odysseus talking about some wine he took from Ismarus, about how good it was. So I stole some.'

Eurylochus raised his fingers to his temple. 'It's strong, too. A krater or two of that every day and I could almost forget the lotus.'

'You don't need wine for that, Eurylochus,' Selagos said. 'After all, it isn't your only desire.'

'What do you mean?'

'You still have eyes for Eperitus's woman. I've seen you looking at her.'

'What of it?' Eurylochus snorted, reaching for the goatskin and taking another swallow. 'I've less chance of winning her from him than I do of returning to the land of the lotus eaters.'

'Not if Eperitus doesn't come back. If we leave at dawn then she's as good as yours.'

'She is?'

'Of course she is. And why wait until tomorrow when you have tonight?'

'Now what are you talking about?'

'You want her, don't you?'

'You know I do.'

'Then take her! Show her you're a man and perhaps she'll begin to respect you.'

Eurylochus chewed at his bottom lip for a moment, then shook his head.

'And if Eperitus comes back he'll kill me.'

'Eperitus isn't coming back. Whatever lives in those caves has murdered them all. Even Odysseus knew they were going to their doom, or why else would he have told us not to wait more than two days for them? Besides, you showed your courage on the galley, the day we found the lotus eaters. What's stopping you now with Astynome all alone? I'll even make sure nobody else interferes.'

Eurylochus took another swallow of the wine and belched loudly.

'When?'

'Midnight. We'll gag her and bind her in case she tries to call out or fight, and then we'll bring her here. Now, give me that wine before you unman yourself completely.'

Astynome watched them walk off towards the beach, Eurylochus swaying wildly even with Selagos's arm hooked through his. When they were lost to the darkness, she rolled back against the rough bark of the trunk and closed her eyes. Her first thought was that Eperitus had to come back. Her second was that she should run and hide, but she knew she would soon be missed and the whole crew would come looking for her. Perhaps Eperitus would return before nightfall, she told herself. But she knew he would not. The same instinct that told her he was alive also denied her any hope of his coming back that evening. There were more knots in the thread of her fate that had to be unravelled before that could happen. No, if she were to survive then it was up to her to save herself.

Then she opened her eyes.

She knew what she had to do. And it had to be done before midnight.

Chapter Twenty-One

NOBODY

S tone grated against stone as the door to the cave was rolled away. The Cyclops pushed the laurel branches aside and ushered his sheep and goats inside. They were led by a ram the size of a calf, with thick brown wool and horns so long they spiralled back on themselves twice. The animal jumped onto the Cyclops's stone seat by the fire and stood sentinel as the rest of the flock flooded in around him. From his hiding place beneath the overhanging rock – which he shared with Odysseus, Omeros and Elpenor – Eperitus's vision was temporarily blocked by the oversized creatures as they bumped and jostled their way into the recesses of the cave. When they had passed by, he could see the colossal herdsman standing over the hearth, his gruesome face lit by the orange flames. His lips were pulled back from his pointed teeth in a terrifying grimace and the single eye rolled this way and that as it searched the shadows for a sign of his prisoners. After a while he rolled the stone back into place, shutting out the last of the evening light and entombing the Ithacans in darkness.

Eperitus passed the wineskin to Odysseus.

'Do it now,' he hissed.

Odysseus reached for the neck of the skin and Eperitus saw that his hands were shaking. The king looked guiltily at his captain. Omeros and Elpenor were transfixed by the sight of the monster and did not appear to notice.

'Not yet,' Odysseus replied. 'Let him milk his animals first. I don't want him distracted by thoughts of that.'

The Cyclops waved the huge ram from the rock by the fire and sat down. Pulling up two large bowls, he began milking – first the sheep, then the goats. After he had squeezed enough milk from each animal, he plucked their young out of the pens and put them to their mothers, as he had done the night before and many hundreds of times before that. Then, while Eperitus was expecting him to begin curdling the milk, he leapt to his feet with a bellow that shook columns of dust from the ceiling and in three strides was at the back of the cave. He groped among the shadows and pulled out a man, whose shrill cries were even more intolerable to Eperitus's ears than the roaring of the monster.

'It's Drakios!' Omeros shouted, rising to his feet and aiming his spear.

The twang of a bowstring echoed through the cave, followed by another and then a third. In the darkness Eperitus could not see the fall of the arrows, but by his enraged scream he knew they had found their mark in the Cyclops's thick hide. In his fury, the herdsman clenched his fist about Drakios, crushing him to a pulp. Then, with his other hand he reached into a corner of the cave and plucked out another Ithacan. By the bow falling from his hand Eperitus knew it was Antiphus.

Omeros gasped in horror, and then lifted his spear and took aim. Before he could hurl it at the Cyclops, Odysseus pulled the weapon from his grip and threw it into a corner.

'Don't be a fool! Throw that and you'll be next.'

'But –'

'There's nothing we can do for him now.'

Eperitus did not share Odysseus's cool grasp of the situation. He could not. He had known Antiphus for twenty years, fought alongside him in countless battles, saved his life and been saved by him on many occasions. They were brothers. No, they were more than brothers, for Antiphus meant more to Eperitus than the family he had known back in Alybas. And as he saw his friend cry out in pain and horror, he abandoned all care for his own safety and

GLYN ILIFFE

dashed forward, sword in hand. An outcrop of rock lay halfway between him and the monster. Leaping onto it, he sprang high in the air, his blade already swinging in an arc towards the Cyclops's thick neck. But the creature had sensed his approach. Releasing Drakios's crushed corpse, he lashed out with his long, ape-like arm. The blow knocked the breath from Eperitus's body and sent him flying back into the shadows, where he hit the floor hard and rolled back against a boulder. Stunned, he fought the pain that threatened to overwhelm him and tried to push himself up on one arm. For a moment it held his armoured weight. In that instant he looked up and saw Antiphus, his limbs locked tight within the Cyclops's fingers and his face a mask of terror. Behind him was the great eye of the herdsman, a bloodshot disc with a saucer of deepest black at its centre. Then his mouth opened to reveal crooked yellow fangs, running with saliva as they closed over Antiphus's head. Eperitus's strength gave and he fell, sinking into the haze of his unconsciousness.

He did not know how long he had been insentient when he woke, but as he opened his eyes it was to the sound of Odysseus's voice. Not close at hand, but at a distance, his captivating tones followed by a stony echo.

'You may not be an honourable host, Cyclops, but my men and I – those of us you have left alive – respect the gods. I said we would pay you for what we have taken, and I'm a man of my word. Here, take this wine for the cheese and the animals we have eaten. You'll not think you've had the worst of the bargain when you taste it.'

Eperitus raised himself on one elbow and looked up, blinking and widening his eyes until they found their focus. A little to his right was the rock from which he had launched his attack on the Cyclops. It was spattered with black gore that glistened in the firelight. In its shadow Eperitus could discern a severed foot, though whether this belonged to Drakios or Antiphus he did not want to know. To his left the Cyclops was sitting cross-legged by the fire, his body bathed in flickering yellow light and his face a mesh of shadows. Standing before him, separated only by the blazing hearth, was Odysseus, a large olive-wood bowl held out before him in both hands.

'Do you think that because we Cyclopes don't work the land like men that we can't produce our own wine? My father is Poseidon; he sends the rain and parts the clouds for the sunshine, and the grapes grow by themselves. A fine crop year in, year out, without us having to lift a finger. I don't need your wine.'

'All the same, here it is. Take it or leave it,' Odysseus said, placing the bowl on top of the rock that the Cyclops normally used for a seat. 'We brought it as an offering in the hope you might treat us with kindness and tell us the way home. Doubtless Aeolus would have accepted it.'

'Aeolus? What do *you* know of Aeolus? He'd have turned you out like the beggars you are.'

'Then he doesn't honour the gods. Another Cyclops, perhaps.'

At this the Cyclops gave a roar of laughter and slapped his knee with his bloody hands.

'Ho, you clearly *don't* know Aeolus! A Cyclops he is not. More a man than anything, though not mortal like you poor wretches. And with powers greater than any king of men.'

'Surely not, my lord. For a king's greatness doesn't lie in his wealth or the size of his armies. It's in his respect for the gods. All the power in the world won't save a man if the Olympians are against him, but if they're for him then what other power does he need? Yet if this Aeolus would have turned suppliants away like beggars, then he despises the gods and has no real power at all.'

'Only the weak talk of power as something to be conferred or denied by the gods,' the Cyclops responded with a snort. 'But Aeolus's power is his own, as you would have found out for yourself if you'd visited his island. Like me, he is not one to be treated with disrespect.'

'We passed an island on the way here, half a day's voyage to the south-east. That must have been Aeolus's home.'

The Cyclops leaned forward on his knees and stared at Odysseus.

'You think to play games with me, little mouse? I don't know which is more insulting: that you believe me stupid enough to fall for your tricks, or that you still think you can escape and find your way to the home of Aeolus. You can't. You will die here, two by two. And if you insult me again tonight, then don't think I haven't room in my stomach for more human flesh.'

Sensing the threat, Eperitus rose to his feet and walked over to join his king. Only when he reached his side did he realise his scabbard was empty and that his sword must be lying somewhere in the shadows, among the layers of dung. Both Odysseus and the Cyclops barely seemed to register his presence.

'You shouldn't gorge yourself and ruin such a rich meal,' Odysseus said. 'And a costly one at that. They were two of my best men and one was a great friend. Something you'll never know living in this lonely hovel with nothing but sheep for company. The least you can do is honour their memory by drinking down their flesh with the wine I've brought you.'

'They did taste good,' the Cyclops conceded with a sneer, and picking up the bowl he drained it in one draft.

Eperitus saw the faintest flicker of a smile cross Odysseus's mouth as the monster dropped the empty bowl back down on the rock.

'That was good wine, my friend,' the Cyclops said, leaning back and taking a deep breath. 'Very good indeed. Give me another draught and in return I will give *you* a gift.'

'Fetch me some more,' Odysseus hissed, pointing Eperitus to where he had left the skin.

Eperitus grabbed the bowl from the rock – not wanting to spend any longer within arm's reach of the herdsman – and retrieved the wineskin, which he handed to Odysseus. The king filled the bowl almost to the brim and walked forward with it held out before him. The Cyclops licked his lips and took Odysseus's offering between thumb and forefinger, raising it carefully to his mouth so as not to spill any. Again he drained it to the dregs. This time, as he slapped it down on the rock, it bounced out of his fingers and rolled to a stop at Odysseus's feet.

'More!' the Cyclops demanded.

'I'm curious,' Odysseus said, picking up the bowl.

The Cyclops frowned.

'About what?'

'About this man, Aeolus.'

'He's not a man. Why don't you listen? I told you he wasn't a man.'

'But like a man, you said. An immortal, but not a god I think.'

'A favourite of the gods.'

'Then surely you are wrong about him. If the gods favour him then he must first honour them. And if he honours the gods then he would have followed Zeus's commands and treated us as his guests, not thrown us out like you suggest.'

'What does it matter?' the Cyclops shouted, throwing up his hands.

'Of course it matters! Either he respects the gods or he doesn't.'

'Then he respects them! But if he'd taken you under his roof to keep favour with the gods, then the last thing you'd have been was *welcome*. Know this, little mouse: he does not take kindly to visitors, unless they come from Olympus. Why else would he live on an island ringed with bronze walls?'

'You've visited this place?' Odysseus asked, refilling the bowl and offering it to the Cyclops.

The monster eyed it greedily, savouring the dark liquid before tilting back his head and pouring it down his throat.

'Visited? Don't you ever listen, you fool? Didn't you hear me say he hates visitors? Are you stupid?'

This time the bowl fell from his hands and bounced off the rock into the shadows. The Cyclops laughed as Eperitus ran to retrieve it.

'Ho, little men scuttling about like mice.'

'Then these bronze walls could just be a lie, invented by some sailor you devoured.'

'Who's lying?' the Cyclops boomed. 'Am I lying, did you say? Not I, little mouse. I haven't visited Aeolus because he doesn't like visitors, least of all Cyclopes. But I've stood on the hilltops up there,' he gestured to the cave roof, 'and seen his bronze walls in the distance, many a time, gleaming in the morning light.'

He dropped his elbows onto his knees and let his head fall into his hands. Odysseus looked round knowingly at Eperitus, so pleased his plan was working that he seemed to have momentarily forgotten his grief at Antiphus's death.

'Any time now,' he said in a low voice.

'What's that, mouse?' asked the herdsman, raising his head. His hair had fallen forward to cover much of his eye. 'Mouse isn't your name, though, is it. You must have a name, mouse.'

'My name is my own.'

'A guest must always state his name.'

'But we aren't playing by those rules, are we. I might give my name to a worthy host, but not to a savage who eats my men.'

The Cyclops sat up.

'Savage, you say, am I? Then let's follow the rules. Give me your name and I'll give you the gift I promised.'

Eperitus watched Odysseus shake his head and felt a stab of annoyance. A warrior's name was his greatest possession. For Odysseus to refuse to state his identity – to deny who he was – was a dishonour to himself and his family. Eperitus stepped forward and looked defiantly at the Cyclops.

'If he won't tell you then I will. He is –'

A large, hot hand closed over his mouth and pulled him back.

'Nobody,' Odysseus said. 'I'm nobody.'

'Nobody?' the Cyclops asked. 'What sort of name is Nobody?'

Eperitus, his mouth still covered by Odysseus's hand, stared at his friend. Odysseus frowned back momentarily, then a familiar light entered his eyes.

'Nobody is the name my father gave me,' he said, 'and it's the name my mother and my friends call me by. Now, you promised me a gift.'

The Cyclops's face was now ashen beneath his wild beard, and he held his hand gingerly to his stomach. After a moment he let out a belch that reverberated around the cave.

'Your gift is this, Nobody,' he answered scornfully, 'that of all your party, I shall eat you last.'

And with that he toppled backwards into the carpet of soft dung, scattering the sheep and goats that had gathered in his shadow. With a mighty groan, he turned his head and vomited a thick slurry of wine and human flesh that spread in a dark pool over the floor. Then his head dropped back and at once he began snoring.

Eurylochus was dreaming of the lotus when he felt a hand on his shoulder. He brushed it away. If he could not have the lotus, then to dream of it was better than nothing.

The hand returned, this time accompanied by a voice.

'Eurylochus.'

It belonged to a woman. Perhaps this was part of his dream.

'Yes?'

The hand squeezed his shoulder gently.

'Eurylochus, wake up.'

'Who is it?' he snapped.

'Quiet, we don't want the others to hear.'

He looked up. The act of opening his eyes increased the pounding in his head, but after a moment of sharp pain he began to see a tall figure dressed in white. The moon was behind her, creating a silver halo of her hair and silhouetting her body through the thin material of her chiton. It was Astynome.

He felt a sudden sense of panic. Why was she here? Had Odysseus and Eperitus returned? Did they know of his plan to take Astynome by force? He propped himself up on one elbow and blinked at the stars. Midnight was still some way off.

'What do you want?' he asked.

She knelt down beside him and placed her hand on his crotch, squeezing his genitals through the cloth.

'I want you.'

He caught her face in the darkness, her large eyes pale and serious. She stood and – more by instinct than design – he reached up to touch her between her legs. She stepped away, laughing gently. Teasing him.

'Not here,' she whispered. 'If Eperitus ever returns I don't want the others to see and tell him. He'd kill us both.'

'Then where?'

'Follow me.'

She ran up the sloping shingle to the top of the beach, a silver figure in the moonlight. Eurylochus tossed aside his blanket, thought briefly about whether he should find Selagos and tell him, then ran after her.

She was not at the top of the ridge when he reached it. He listened for her, but there was nothing but the hiss of breakers and the gently snoring crew behind him. He ran on, clambering over the fallen rocks at the foot of the headland and avoiding the little pools that lay hidden between them. When he reached the other side of the promontory she was nowhere to be seen.

'Go back, you fool,' he told himself.

But his manhood disagreed. He looked again and saw something pale further along the beach.

'What are you waiting for?' she called.

'Be quiet,' he hissed back.

He felt suddenly uneasy, standing in the darkness on a strange coastline. Odysseus and the others had gone this way and not come back, he reminded himself. And yet his need for Astynome conquered all fear. He ran on, following the phantom figure and wondering when she would think they were far enough away from the rest of the crew to be safe. He was soon out of breath, but she kept stopping and silently beckoning for him to follow. Perhaps she, too, had sensed the change in atmosphere. As if they were not alone. Eventually she disappeared into the shadows beneath a neck of woodland that ran down from the hills above.

It was then he realised she had no intention of sleeping with him, but was leading him away from the camp. Perhaps she had guessed what he would do to her if Eperitus did not return and intended to murder him out of sight of any witnesses. He felt for the dagger in his belt and gripped it tightly. He could go back for Selagos, of course, but by the time they returned there was no certainty they would find Astynome again. Besides, she was just a woman. If she wanted to kill him then he would pay her in kind. But first he would take what he had wanted from the first moment he had set eyes on her.

He ran to the wood and found a broad path through the trees. Something about the place warned him to turn back, but his anger and lust spurred him on. The path was steep and soon had him breathing hard. He began to wonder whether he might have missed Astynome going back the other way in the darkness. Then the night was split by a dreadful, unearthly scream. That it had not erupted from the lungs of an animal was clear. But neither had it come from a man or woman. Within moments, answering shouts came from the hills above and were followed by a heavy thudding that shook the ground beneath his feet. Eurylochus ran into the undergrowth at the side of the path and leapt behind the trunk of a fallen tree.

Eperitus fixed his eyes on the vomit puddled around the Cyclops's head. Among the morsels of flesh was a hand with the middle and forefingers missing. The horrible reminder of Antiphus's death drained Eperitus of his energy. He slumped onto all fours in the dung and hung his head, letting his dark emotions slip over him like a shadow. For a while he was aware of nothing but the black hole that his friend's loss had left behind. Then he felt a hand on his back.

'Now isn't the time to succumb to our grief, Eperitus,' Odysseus said. 'Not yet. First we must deal with the monster and make sure he can't kill again. Do you understand?'

Eperitus inhaled deeply and sat up.

'You're right.'

He looked about him. Polites was kneeling with his face in his hands; Omeros stood beside him, his arm about the huge warrior's shoulders. Elpenor was further back, pale-faced and silent, staring fixedly at the sleeping Cyclops. The other two were half-hidden in the shadows. Epistor had been with the army from the first and was openly sobbing; Perimedes, a Taphian replacement, was quiet but visibly shaken.

'Omeros, you'll take Antiphus's place,' Odysseus told him. 'Go tell Perimedes he's to replace Drakios. Do it now.'

'Let me stand in for Drakios,' Elpenor said.

Odysseus eyed him warily.

'I need a man who can control his fear.'

'I'm not afraid.'

'Then you're a fool,' Eperitus said. 'This job needs courage, not recklessness.'

'Elpenor will be alright,' Omeros defended him. 'We'll fetch the pole now.'

Odysseus nodded and they slipped away into the shadows.

'A moment's nervousness from him and we'll all be killed,' Eperitus said.

'I know.'

'Then let me take the front.'

'Because you want to avenge Antiphus's death? Or because you'd rather the Cyclops eats you than me if he wakes?'

'I promised Athena I would protect you with my life,' Eperitus reminded him, 'and a king is more important than a warrior.'

'Sometimes a king needs to take risks to prove he's worthy of the title. Now is one of those times, my friend. I'll take the head.'

As Omeros and Elpenor reappeared from the shadows, struggling beneath the weight of the pole, Odysseus sent Epistor and Perimedes to pull willow branches from the Cyclops's bed at the back of the cave, which they were to weave into lengths of twine. Taking the head of the pole, and with the help of the others, he held the sharpened end over the fire. The wood was still green and quickly began to smoke. Eperitus glanced through the vapour at the sleeping monster and felt a pang of terror. He forced his eyes back to the tip of the stake, which by now was glowing red and threatening to catch fire.

'That'll do,' Odysseus said, pulling it from the flames. He turned to the others and Eperitus could see his expression was edged with fear. 'The time has come. Be brave, friends.'

They raised the head of the shaft and angled the white-hot tip at the Cyclops's lidded eye. The dread weakened their limbs and seemed to double the weight of the stake, so that the five men struggled to lift it. Then someone's hold slipped and the wooden beam dropped to the floor with a clatter that echoed off the cave walls. Eperitus looked round and saw Omeros standing back, while Polites and Elpenor were bending down and struggling to lift the pole back up.

'He's waking,' Odysseus warned. 'Quickly!'

The great lid of the Cyclops's eye quivered like a sail in the wind, then rolled up to reveal the hateful orb beneath. The four Ithacans, joined after a moment by Omeros, lifted the pole high under their arms. The eye was now staring directly at them, and in that moment Odysseus led his men forward, sinking the tip into its black pupil. The aqueous fluid hissed and bubbled around the scorching wood, followed by jets of blood as Odysseus twisted the point deeper into the wound. Then the Cyclops let out a terrible scream and jerked upwards, tearing the impaled stake from the hands of his attackers and scattering them across the floor. He leapt to his feet and, with a bellow that warped the air about Eperitus's ears, plucked the shaft from his eye and hurled it across the cave.

Everything was now in uproar. The sheep and goats scattered in bleating panic and the Ithacans ran with them into the furthest corners of the Cyclops's lair. Above them the monster whirled like a giant oak in a tempest, shrieking with pain and crushing his beloved animals underfoot as he stumbled blindly from one wall of the cave to another. For long, terrifying moments his fingers tore at the rock in a futile attempt to pull himself out of his suffering, all the time his shouts echoing wildly about the cowering Ithacans. After a while Eperitus heard another sound through the noise of the monster's distress. It came from outside the cave and at first was like the roaring of the sea. Then he felt the thud of heavy footsteps and heard horrible voices calling out a name.

'Polyphemus! Polyphemus!'

'Do you hear that?' Elpenor asked. 'There are voices in the wind. The others have come to save us.'

'Those aren't the voices of men,' Polites said.

'They're Cyclopes,' Odysseus said, 'come down from the hilltops to see what's happening to their friend – if these creatures can be said to have friends.'

'Then you've killed us all,' Elpenor exclaimed. 'Your plan to set us free has doomed the lot of us.'

'Be quiet, boy,' Eperitus admonished him with a scowl. 'We were dead anyway.'

'Polyphemus!' a voice boomed, directly outside the cave entrance.

The Cyclops's wailing – now as much the result of self-pity as his pain – stopped, and he turned to face the sound of the voice.

'What's all this shouting about?' asked another. 'Are you being attacked, Polyphemus? Only a Cyclops could cause another Cyclops to cry out so.'

'It's Nobody!' Polyphemus bellowed. 'Nobody attacked me.'

He fell to his knees, threw both hands over his destroyed eye and began to sob loudly. Eperitus could hear the voices mumbling beyond the rock slab that sealed the cave.

'Who's in there with you?'

'Nobody! Don't leave me here with him.'

'What are you talking about? You drag us from our women's sides with your shouting and screaming, only to tell us you're alone! You're sick, that's what –'

The voice paused and a tense silence fell over the Cyclopes beyond the cave entrance, as if they were listening to something. Then they began to speak hurriedly, and Eperitus could hear their footsteps as they ran off.

'Go to bed, Polyphemus,' one of them called over his shoulder. 'You'll feel better in the morning.'

'Come back,' he shouted.

Seizing hold of the stone slab, he heaved it aside with a grunt and called after them again.

But they were gone.

Astynome was watching Eurylochus from behind the bole of a tree when the still night air was torn open by a scream. Long and horrible it was, like the cry of an animal in terrible pain. But there was something monstrous about it, too, that stiffened her flesh and filled her with dread. Booming shouts arose in response from the ridge above, and moments later the trees began to shake as if Poseidon's anger was stirring the ground beneath their roots. It took all her courage to turn and run away from the path into the undergrowth. More tortured screams came from the beach below, though muffled as if the lost souls of Hades had found a single voice for their agony. They were answered by more yells, closer this time, and as Astynome glanced over her shoulder she glimpsed giant figures running down the sloping path, their heads lost in the foliage.

She caught her foot on an upraised root and fell into a pile of leaves. Her fingers dug into the damp soil, imagining that at any moment a huge hand would reach down and pluck her up. She wanted to bury herself beneath the leaves and pray that some god would conceal her from the eyes of the creatures she had seen through the trees. But she knew it was a false hope. Quickly, before the temptation to hide became too much, she pushed herself up and ran on.

'Astynome!'

She turned and saw Eurylochus, barely discernable in the thin moonlight that filtered down through the trees. He was some way off, at the edge of the path, but she caught the gleam of the blade in his hand.

'Astynome, where are you going?'

She looked back up the slope, through the trees to the crest of the ridge where she had seen the fires the evening before. After overhearing Eurylochus's plot to rape her, she had planned to lead him up to the fires in the hope he would be captured or killed by the figures she had seen silhouetted by the flames. Knowing now that the giant shadows they had cast into the night air had not been exaggerated, she hesitated at the thought of going any further. Briefly she wondered whether Eperitus had stumbled on the fires and been killed by the creatures that had made them. Then Eurylochus began jogging towards her and she knew she had no choice. She turned and ran up the slope.

'Astynome!'

His voice was a hissed whisper but carried sharply through the night air. Reaching the eaves of the wood she saw wooden pens at the brow of the ridge, filled with sheep. They bleated gently, still unsettled by the earlier disturbance. In the cliff face behind were the dark mouths of caves. Some were giant fissures that leaned to the left or right, others were holes delved deep into the rock behind. There was no sign of movement so she stumbled on over the slippery grass. Reaching the ridge she saw that a narrow plateau separated her from the caves. It was dotted with more animal pens and the remains of several large fires, but there was no sign of the shepherds. A path led from the caves into the treeline to her left. Knowing it would take her back down to the beach, she began running towards it, cursing the long dress that hampered her movements.

Then she saw Eurylochus sprinting up the slope to intercept her, the dagger still in his hand. She tried to turn and run back to the trees but lost her footing on the wet grass. He was on her in a moment, seizing her arm and pulling her back to her feet.

'So you thought you would lure me up here did you?' he gasped, still trying to catch his breath. 'To be murdered by whoever lives in these caves.'

'You saw the size of them. If they find us here they'll kill us both.'

'I saw nothing, though I heard them. And I'll hear them coming back, too. But before they do you're going to give me what you promised.'

'Eperitus will kill you.'

'If he does there'll be a full-blown mutiny. Is that what you want?'

'You overestimate your own importance,' she said.

'The men are sick of Odysseus and you know it. I'm the only one keeping them in check, so if you want to keep the peace then give me what I want.'

'I'd die before I'd let you have your way with me.'

She tried to strike him, but her anger lacked conviction and he laughed at her, knowing his words had planted seeds of doubt in her mind. She had seen the discontent among the Ithacans and guessed at the thin veneer of Odysseus's power. Perhaps Eurylochus really was the only barrier between the king's authority and rebellion. Or perhaps Odysseus and Eperitus were dead and none of this mattered anyway.

Then a figure emerged from the cave behind Eurylochus. It was larger than Polites and had the silhouette of a man, though Astynome sensed it was not human. As the moon emerged from the cloud that had been hiding it, she saw the features of its face and threw her hand over her mouth to stop herself from screaming.

Eurylochus spun round in panic and saw the young Cyclops. He let out a cry of terror as it stumbled towards him, and he lashed out with his dagger, severing three fingers from its lumpish hand.

Astynome was already running down the slope when the Cyclops's high-pitched shriek pierced the air. That the noise transformed into a pitiful wailing told her Eurylochus had not finished the monster off. By its size she knew the creature was only a child, and that its cries would soon bring the adults running back to their caves. As she rushed between the trees, the undergrowth tearing at her dress and skin, she only hoped that they would find Eurylochus still waiting for them.

Chapter Twenty-Two

POLYPHEMUS

Odysseus sat with his remaining companions at the back of the cave, as far away as possible from both the stench of Polyphemus's bed and from the creature himself, who was still sitting across the cave entrance. The king had barely spoken since they had blinded the Cyclops, preferring to sit with his back to a rock and watch the miserable features of the monster in the dying light of the fire. Eperitus was beside him, his presence a comfort as he tried to think through the next part of his plan. But Odysseus's thoughts were disturbed by his grief for Antiphus and did not follow their usual logical path towards an understanding of what he had to do. The Cyclops's sorrow for his lost eye and the animals he had crushed underfoot was also a distraction. It expressed itself between helpless sobbing and moments of vengeful wrath, cursing Nobody and the gods and threatening the most terrible deaths to the men hiding in the cave. Sometimes one of his men would let his fear show in impatience, asking the king what he intended to do or when he was going to act. A quick look or a sharp word from Eperitus soon quietened them, but the interruption would often send the fragile train of his thought tumbling back to the basic problem: how to get past the Cyclops unnoticed.

He had a solution, of course. He had thought of one the moment he had seen the pole and decided to blind their gaoler. But the perfection of his plan – the detail that he usually found so satisfying to think through – was evasive. It was as if his own inner eye had been blinded.

'Dawn is approaching,' Eperitus said beside him.

They were the first words the two men had shared since the other Cyclopes had disappeared into the night. Odysseus could detect no change but trusted his friend's instincts. He looked over at Polyphemus, who sat with a dead sheep in his lap, groaning to himself as he stroked its black wool. Then, almost as if he had heard a distant sound, the monster sat up and looked outside. He, also, had sensed the coming of the new day.

'Pass me the ropes.'

Perimedes handed him several coils of twine and Odysseus tested each one for strength. The flocks huddled together on the cave floor began to stir, occasional bleats echoing from the misshapen walls. And, at last, Odysseus sensed a faint lessening of the darkness beyond the cave's mouth and thought he could smell a new freshness in the smoky air.

He turned to his men and waved them closer.

'Listen to me. Spread out in pairs and bring back the largest rams from the flock.'

'What will we do? Ride them out?' Eperitus asked, a wry smile touching the corners of his mouth.

'Exactly that,' Odysseus replied. 'Omeros, come with me. Elpenor, you can go with Eperitus.'

Polites had already set off alone towards the nearest ram, followed by Epistor and Perimedes. Odysseus watched Eperitus rebuke Elpenor for some lapse of attention – he had not taken favourably to the young Ithacan after he had accused Odysseus of leading them to their doom – then point out a large ram close to the hearth. Odysseus turned to Omeros. The young bard had dropped the stake at the moment they were about to blind the Cyclops, and Odysseus wondered whether he was losing his nerve.

'Ever done any shepherding, Omeros?'

He shook his head. 'Antiphus was the one for that, my lord.'

'Then do exactly as I tell you. See that one there? Move round in front of him, not too close, and keep his attention.'

Omeros did as he was ordered, and a moment later Odysseus rushed up behind the ram and seized its horns. He dragged the oversized beast forcibly to the back of the cave, where the others were returning with their own captives.

'Ah, my children, you can smell the dawn,' said Polyphemus, turning towards the sound of their bleating. His voice was tremulous and filled with self-pity and his fingertips hovered over his blackened and swollen eyelid. 'You want me to take you up to the hillsides where the sweetest grass grows. Not yet, though. First I must count you out and then I will eat. Six well-fed men and then Nobody himself. Do you hear me, Nobody? I'm going to roll the stone shut and hunt you down one by one. And when I've eaten your men I'll give you the guest-gift I promised.'

As he talked of his revenge his tone hardened to savagery. The Ithacans listened with growing terror, almost forgetting the animals they had captured.

'Lash these three together,' Odysseus ordered. 'Perimedes, you're to cling beneath the middle one.'

'I'm to *what*?'

There were murmurs of disbelief as Odysseus's plan suddenly became clear to them.

'Cling to its wool while we tie you in place with the twine. Quickly, man!'

'But that's madness,' Perimedes protested in his thick Taphian accent.

'I'll go,' Omeros said. 'Better to be first than last, when there's nobody else to lash you in place'

'Alright, alright, I'll do it,' Perimedes said, seeing Omeros's logic and pushing him aside.

He crawled beneath the biggest ram and pulled himself up by its black wool. The animal tried to wrest itself free, but the Ithacans lashed Perimedes securely beneath it and tied the other two rams on either side. The darkness beyond the cave had turned to a pale grey, encouraging the Ithacans to work faster. Polites gathered the rams while the others bound them together into threes and secured their comrades beneath each trio. When only Polites, Eperitus and Odysseus remained, Polyphemus stood and planted his feet in the corners of the entrance.

'Come now, my children,' he boomed. 'The sun is rising in the east and the dew on the hilltops will soon evaporate. Pass beneath me into the outer courtyard so that I can deal with our guests.'

The largest ram mounted the boulder by the hearth and watched as the herds of goats and sheep answered their master's call. Odysseus slapped the backsides of the animals that carried the Ithacans, urging them to follow the others, then ordered Polites and Eperitus to lash more of the captured rams together. As the flock passed beneath Polyphemus's legs, he passed his fingertips over their backs to ensure none of the prisoners were among them. Then the three rams that held Perimedes approached the mouth of the cave. Odysseus could make out the Taphian beneath them, dagger in hand to cut his bonds should he be discovered. The animals were bleating in protest at his weight and it seemed Polyphemus must discover something was wrong. If he did, not only would Perimedes be devoured but the Cyclops would realise Odysseus's scheme and search the rest of the herd. Epistor, Omeros and Elpenor would be killed and he would be the author of their doom, all because he had not been able to think through all the possibilities and account for them. The three rams passed beneath Polyphemus. His fingers brushed their horned heads. And then they were gone, jogging through to the courtyard beyond.

Odysseus released the breath he had been holding and saw Polites and Eperitus approaching with three more rams between them. The animals complained loudly as Polites's heavy bulk was strapped to their bellies, but their abnormal size and strength enabled them to take his weight. Soon they had joined the back of the crowd that was still pressing towards the cave entrance.

Epistor and Omeros must have already passed through, Odysseus realised, as he studied the great flock in the dawn light and only saw Elpenor. The lad's face was red with exertion.

'What's up with him?' Odysseus asked.

'One of the cords has come undone,' Eperitus answered, pointing at the length of twine trailing from between the middle animal's legs. 'He's hanging on with all his strength.'

As the Cyclops's fingers brushed the tops of the rams' heads, one of them pulled aside and trotted out into the courtyard. Elpenor gripped harder at the flanks of the remaining animals, and to Odysseus's relief passed through undiscovered. Then he saw Polyphemus rise to his full height, a length of willow rope held between his fingers. He sniffed at it and after a moment let it fall to the ground.

'Does he suspect?' Eperitus asked.

'That's a risk we have to take. Come on, there aren't many rams left and we need to get you bound.'

'You know as well as I do the last man left won't be able to lash three rams and himself beneath them. You go. You're the king, so it's my duty to stay and take my chances with the monster.'

'How long have you known me, Eperitus? Do you think I haven't worked out another way for me to escape? And the longer you hold things up, the harder it'll be for either of us to get out.'

Eperitus looked him in the eye and Odysseus could read his doubt, but in the end he realised time was running out. He nodded his consent and together they found three more rams and lashed them together, with Eperitus underneath. Odysseus sent them to join the back of the rapidly diminishing flock, then paused to watch Polites pass beneath the Cyclops. He heard the shepherd talking to the rams as he touched their woolly backs, asking them why they were bleating so loudly He did not hinder them any more, but there was doubt in his voice. Polyphemus suspected.

Odysseus could not afford to wait and watch Eperitus pass through. Barely two dozen animals remained in the cave, other than the lambs and kids. And as Odysseus had hoped, the head of the flock was still standing on the boulder. He saw the man approaching, leapt from the rock and charged. Odysseus had made a sliding loop with the last of the twine, which he hooked over the ram's head as he jumped aside from its attack. The loop drew tight and pulled the animal back with a jerk so that it collapsed on its side. Odysseus leapt on top of it and twisted his fingers into its thick brown wool, before rolling onto his back and dragging the beast up onto all fours. It continued to fight, but Odysseus's will was stronger and eventually the ram gave up resisting his hold.

'Where are you, my old friend?' the Cyclops called out, his voice echoing in the now empty and almost silent cave. 'Only you are missing, you and the three I crushed in my pain last night. Nobody will pay for them, too. Come now, my sweet ram, let me feel your fleece beneath my fingers before I roll back the stone and plunge Nobody and his comrades into darkness. Then we will all be blind. *Do you hear me, Nobody?*'

His sudden anger shook the air, but the ram did not fear his master and jogged towards the cave entrance, carrying Odysseus beneath him. Odysseus's fingers were slipping through the greasy wool, forcing him to grab more in a desperate effort to hang on. He had reached the mouth of the cave and could see the courtyard beyond it, shrouded in a luminous mist. He could smell the fresh air and hear the sound of waves breaking on the pebble shore. And then Polyphemus's giant feet were either side of him and he could sense the monster's bulk overhead as his hand brushed along the ram's back.

'My friend, why are you last?' he said. 'You're always the one to lead out the flock. Is it Nobody? Does his presence disturb you? Is he plotting a new scheme to destroy me? Tell me what he is doing, my friend.'

Then, as if sensing that all was not right, the Cyclops let his hand fall to the animal's flank and the tip of his finger run across Odysseus's clenched fist. At that moment something fell with a clatter inside the cave and the kids and lambs began to bleat loudly.

'I hear you, Nobody!' the Cyclops roared, moving his hand to the ram's behind and pushing it out into the courtyard. 'I'm going to tear the flesh from your bones for what you've done to me.'

Odysseus let go of the ram's sides and rolled away, just in time to see Polyphemus enter the cave and pull the stone behind him. He jumped to his feet, terrified that the sound he had heard was Eperitus still trapped inside. Then the crunch of footsteps on the pebbles made him turn.

'So you lied to me,' Eperitus said, his fists on his hips. 'Your only plan was to cling on to the biggest ram and hope the gods were with you. If I hadn't thrown that rock over the Cyclops's shoulder you'd be dead by now.'

Odysseus had rarely been happier to see his friend and embraced him tightly.

'Let's find the others and get back to the ship before the Cyclops discovers we've fooled him. We'll take some of these animals with us.'

'Never one to leave a situation empty-handed,' Eperitus said.

Odysseus glanced ruefully at the cave. 'A poor price for the six men I lost.'

'That wasn't all you lost,' Eperitus added, before turning and shepherding a few of the animals into the mist.

Odysseus followed, driving the ram he had hidden beneath before him. They found the others waiting anxiously by the entrance to the compound. To their surprise Astynome was among them. She ran straight into Eperitus's arms and buried her face in his shoulder.

'What are you doing here?' he asked with a mixture of surprise, pleasure and anger. 'I gave Eurybates orders to keep his eye on you.'

'It's not his fault. I came looking for you.'

'Alone? Where are the others?'

Odysseus thought he saw something in Astynome's expression, something quickly hidden.

'At the ship, stubbornly following Odysseus's orders to stay put. They're just as certainly preparing to sail back as we speak.'

'Ironic they should start obeying me so faithfully now, don't you think?' Odysseus said, embracing Astynome. 'That'll be Eurylochus's influence.'

A phantom of guilt flitted across her dark features and disappeared again.

'More like Selagos's, my lord.'

'How did you find us?'

'I heard a scream last night, something inhuman, and knew you had to be inside the cave. So I waited, fearing the worst and praying to every god I could think of. I'm only happy they listened.'

'They haven't entirely abandoned me,' Odysseus agreed. 'But if we don't leave now, my own crew will.'

Hurried on by fear of the Cyclops, they soon reached the headland that hid the galley. They found the ship fully manned, with its mast, cross spar and sail fitted and the oars out. On the beach, two groups of around a dozen men each were facing each other, some leaning warily on their spears, others with their hands resting on the pommels of their swords. Selagos and Eurylochus were at the head of one group and Eurybates the other, so engrossed in their debate that it took them a few moments to register the bleating of sheep and goats and realise they were not alone. As they turned, Odysseus noted the sudden joy on Eurybates's face, while Selagos gave an angry scowl. Eurylochus stared not at his cousin but at Astynome, his face blanching as he surreptitiously hid behind Selagos's bulk. Astynome seemed no less surprised to see Eurylochus.

'What's this?' Odysseus asked as Eurybates ran to greet them.

'They were going to leave without you; I and a few others wanted to stay.'

'Well, we're here now, just as I said we'd be. Get these animals aboard and lift the anchor stones, as quick as you can.'

Before long, the galley was slipping out of the bay and rounding the headland. The sun had topped the distant cliffs and only a thin veil of mist now clung to the shoreline. Then someone gave a shocked cry. Heads turned towards the beach, and more dismayed voices called out until Odysseus ordered silence. Standing up to his thighs in the surf was Polyphemus, stock still as he trained his ears on the shouts that had been carried to him by the sea breeze.

'What did you mean in the Cyclops's compound when you said I had lost more than my men?' Odysseus asked.

Eperitus was standing beside him in the stern, looking out at the monster.

'You took the Cyclops's goats and sheep because a warrior's reputation is built on what he brings out of battle. You did it to humiliate him. But whose name is he going to attribute his shame to? Whose name will he live in fear of and blame his woes on? Nobody's, Odysseus. *Nobody's*. And a man is truly nobody if he loses his name.'

Eperitus looked him in the eye and then went to join Astynome, who was staring tight-lipped at the giant figure standing in the surf. Odysseus followed her gaze and felt his cheeks burn as he looked at the great monster he had blinded. Without his cunning and courage he and all his men would have perished. He had defeated the Cyclops where many greater men would have failed. And yet Eperitus was right. Where was his credit for what he had done? Where was *his* glory? Was he a king, or was he Nobody?

As he watched, the Cyclops raised his head and sniffed the air.

'I can smell you, Nobody, you and your vile companions with the animals you stole from me. But your name isn't Nobody, is it?'

'Don't answer him, my lord,' Eurybates warned from his position at the twin rudders. 'He wants to know where we are, that's all, and the sea isn't so deep yet that he couldn't wade out and smash the ship with his bare fists.'

But Odysseus paid him no attention. He was intrigued that the Cyclops had seen through the false name. But how, he wondered.

'What's my name to a savage like you, who ignores the decrees of the gods and treats his guests with contempt? In your arrogance you thought I was nothing more than a bit of sport to be played with, until I put out your precious eye and repaid you for murdering my men! Who am I? A servant of Zeus, meting out justice on the ungodly.'

The Cyclops gave a bellow of rage and strode back up the beach. Tearing up a boulder, he hurled it towards the sound of Odysseus's voice. The crew shouted out in terror as the black rock spun through the air towards them. Odysseus stood fast, his fingers gripping the bow rail. He felt the wind of it pass over the top of the mast before hitting the sea three or four oars' length from the stern of the ship. The impact threw up a wall of water that caught the galley and drove it forward, tossing its occupants across the crowded deck. Odysseus locked his arms about the mast to steady himself, but to his horror realised the wave was propelling them towards the beach. Grabbing a long pole, he signalled to Eperitus and Polites to do the same. They thrust them down into the sand and only by the greatest effort prevented the ship's prow from embedding itself in the shingle.

'Row!' Eurybates shouted.

The crew took up their oars and hauled the galley back out to sea. They were barely a dozen lengths from the shore when Polyphemus found another boulder and – looking directly at the struggling Ithacans as if he could see them – heaved it above his head. Odysseus threw down the pole and fought his way to the stern.

'Cyclops, you ask for the name of the one who put out your eye. Then listen to me. My name is Odysseus, son of Laertes, king of Ithaca and sacker of cities. When men ask who could have blinded one as powerful as you – a son of Poseidon – then tell them *my* name.'

The Cyclops dropped his boulder and fell to his knees.

'Then the prophecy I was given in my youth has come true. Telemus told me that a warrior called Odysseus would take away my sight, and in my pride I had imagined an enemy at least my own size and strength. But as the years passed I found no-one to match me, even among the race of the Cyclopes, and my fear of Telemus's words faded until I forgot them altogether. Now *you* come, a mere man, addling my senses with your wine and fooling me with a trick. Damn you! But I am not defeated, not yet. Poseidon is still my father.' Raising his maimed face to the sky, he stretched out his arms and spoke in a loud voice. 'Lord Poseidon, Earthshaker, God of the Seas, hear your son. Grant that Odysseus, son of Laertes, will never see his home again. But if it is the will of Zeus that he should do so, then let him come late, a friendless outcast in a ship not his own. And let him find strife on Ithaca when he returns.'

His booming voice rolled across the waves, the words terrible in Odysseus's ears. Then, as the king watched in taut silence, the Cyclops picked up the rock and hurled it at the galley. It landed with a great splash astern, in the exact place the ship had been moments before. Water drenched the Ithacans, but to their relief the ensuing wave carried them swiftly away from the shore and the monster's wrath.

Chapter Twenty-Three

THE RULER OF THE WINDS

Odysseus's first action on their return to the wide bay where the rest of the fleet lay at anchor was to sacrifice the ram that had brought him safely out of the cave. He offered its life to Poseidon, asking the god for safe passage to Aeolus's island. Eperitus felt the sacrifice was more an appeasement than an appeal and doubted the Earthshaker would be mollified.

The next day they awoke before dawn and were pulling at the oars by the time the sun rimmed the eastern horizon. Having tricked Polyphemus into telling him that Aeolus's island was within sight of the cliffs above his cave, and that the morning sun reflected on the bronze walls of the palace, Odysseus had deduced that the island could only be a short distance to the west. Sure enough they soon spotted a small island to the north with a flattened peak on its western side. A metallic glint from the top of the hill had to be the battlements of Aeolus's palace. Taking heart from the sight, the steersmen ordered the sails to be raised to the full and pointed their prows to the north-west.

It did not take long before Eperitus could see high cliffs sheering up from the waves that frothed at their base. On the south side two stone spurs reached out to form a natural anchorage large enough to protect the whole fleet. And yet there were no vessels of any size in the bay or on the sandy beach that rimmed it, and no houses on the clifftops above. Only a single path winding up the face of the cliff suggested habitation, and that might just as easily have been trodden out by the wild sheep visible on the plateau above.

He reported what he had seen to Odysseus and returned to the bench where Astynome sat with her gaggle of orphans. Catching her eye, he noted the evasive look she had been trying to conquer since the morning before. Something was wrong, but so far she had avoided his questions. She would tell him in her own time, he thought, slipping his arm about her waist and pulling her close. After the horror of the cave and his grief for Antiphus, he had found a new comfort in being with her. And as she laid her head on his shoulder and her pleasant, familiar scent filled his nostrils, he hoped that everything Odysseus had drawn out of Polyphemus was true: that the island's ruler could tell them the way back to Ithaca and that the years in the wilderness would soon be over. Then, for the first time since his youth, he would know the pleasure of having a family again.

The air was strangely still as the twelve galleys rowed into the bay and dropped their anchors. Eperitus joined Odysseus, Polites, Omeros and half a dozen others in the shore boat. The king had also ordered Eurylochus to join them, preferring to have him close at hand than leave him on the galley where he could foment trouble. They beached the boat and approached a pool at the foot of the cliff, where Odysseus splashed cold water over his face. He raised a handful to his lips and drank deeply, letting it run down his beard and neck.

'We are not in the habit of receiving visitors,' called a voice above them.

A grey-haired man with a beard that was long enough to rest on his protruding stomach stood at the top of the looping path. He wore a blue robe and a simple woollen tunic, but had the bearing of a king. Six young men surrounded him, each carrying a spear and a shield.

'Who are you and what is your purpose on Aeolia?'

Odysseus contemplated the figure standing high above him, then wiped his beard and proceeded to climb the narrow path. Eperitus followed with the others at intervals behind him. When they reached the final bend, Odysseus bowed low before the grey-haired man.

'I am Odysseus, son of Laertes, and these are my companions. We are seeking the way back to our home, Ithaca, and had heard that a man named Aeolus might be able to help us.'

'Who told you that?'

'The Cyclops, Polyphemus.'

'A Cyclops?' asked the grey-haired man, eyeing him sceptically. 'Then I wonder you are even alive. But perhaps you aren't telling us everything about your meeting with this Polyphemus. As for Aeolus, son of Hippotas, you are talking to him, and these others are his sons.'

Odysseus bowed low again.

'You guess rightly, my lord. Our meeting with the Cyclops was not a genial one and it cost the lives of six of my men. Indeed, we have faced many trials on our voyage so far and would be grateful for a place to shelter and rest a little before we move on again. Perhaps –'

'As I said, we are not in the habit of receiving visitors, especially so many at once. You ask too much of our hospitality.'

Eurylochus snorted and Eperitus shot him a silencing stare.

'But you can help us find our home,' Odysseus persisted. 'Polyphemus may have been a monster, but he believed in your reputation. Can you tell us the way to Ithaca or not?'

Aeolus leaned in to one of his sons and spoke in a low whisper. Eurylochus kicked impatiently at a stone and spat.

'Six spears against six hundred and they think they can keep us begging at their doors like a pack of hounds,' he said, none too quietly. 'Anyone else might look down at a bay full of galleys and take a more welcoming approach.'

'You think I should fear you?' Aeolus asked, his narrowed eyes boring into Eurylochus. 'You think I don't have power of my own, power enough to defeat a band of marauding pirates and send them all to the bottom of the sea? Then you think wrong.'

He raised his hand, and immediately the warm, flat air was split by a blast of howling wind. It caught the cloaks of the Ithacans and pushed them almost to the edge of the path, before passing down the cliff face and driving a channel across the surface of the harbour. At a flick of Aeolus's finger, a sail was torn from one of the galleys and sent whirling up into the sky, only falling back into the sea when the old man lowered his hand again. Eperitus looked open-mouthed at Odysseus, whose own expression was one of controlled alarm.

'I know the way to Ithaca, lord Odysseus,' Aeolus announced. 'But why would I tell you and have you lead the outside world back here? This is a happy place. We don't suffer the troubles that plague mankind and we do not welcome having them brought to our doorstep. So when you leave here you will find yourself in a thick fog, and when you emerge from it, Aeolia will be nowhere in sight and far beyond your ability to find it again. You will be left to your own devices and the mercy of the gods.'

'You speak of the gods and in the same breath send us away like beggars,' Odysseus said, his voice soft and reasonable. 'But we are not beggars. We are suppliants and we call upon you to honour the gods. As Zeus is my witness I implore you to treat us as your guests and respect the laws of *xenia*.'

Aeolus looked at him and then shook his head slowly as he turned to leave.

'A pirate is not worthy of being treated with honour.'

'We are not pirates, Aeolus, as one look at us will tell you. We are Greek soldiers returning from the siege of Troy, where for ten hard years we suffered and died. And I am no common warrior, but a king who was considered an equal by Agamemnon, Achilles, Ajax and a host of others. Would you turn away a man of noble blood?'

'Yes, if he was a threat to the peace of this island,' Aeolus responded. 'But I am not so isolated here that I have not heard of this war between Greece and Troy – though the last I knew the fighting still raged. Is that no longer the case?'

He stood with his back to the Ithacans, but even Eperitus could sense the change in his attitude. Whereas before he had been eager to see the newcomers gone, now he hesitated. Odysseus took two paces forward.

'The siege is over, my lord. I could tell you a little of how it ended, but such an account cannot be hurriedly blurted out under a mid-morning sun. Like all great stories, it needs wine and an open fire beneath the stars – or better still, between the echoing walls of a hall where men gather to hear songs of death and glory. However, I agree there are too many of us for such a small island and respect your wish for us to go. We will depart as soon as we have replaced the sail on the galley you –'

'There *are* too many of you, Odysseus,' Aeolus said, 'but you are right: to turn you away would dishonour the gods. I will permit you and two of your companions to come to my palace tonight, and in return you will tell me the outcome of the war. Your men have enough supplies to feed themselves here for one night, I hope?'

'For several nights.'

'One night will be enough,' Aeolus told him. 'I will send a slave this evening to show you and your companions the way. Be ready.'

Eperitus brushed Astynome's cheek with the backs of his fingers. Her bronzed skin was soft and appealing, but the dark eyes that he loved so much were still hiding their secret from him.

'You'll be safe with Polites,' he reassured her.

'But will you be safe? I don't trust this Aeolus. He's no Cyclops, but it's clear he doesn't want us here either.'

'Would you welcome an army of six hundred men into your home? Besides, what choice do we have? We're lost in a place where even the stars betray us. Aeolus is our only hope of ever finding Ithaca again so we have to win his favour. If anyone can do that, it's Odysseus.'

Astynome looked sceptical.

'You forget he's been leading us from one near disaster to another. A king who has lost the patronage of the gods is… is a liability.'

Eperitus kissed her fingers.

'I still have faith in him.'

He took the path to the plateau above where Odysseus and Omeros were waiting with Aeolus's guide. They set off through a land that was flat and lightly wooded with hundreds of sheep moving through the scrub in loose, unshepherded flocks. The high roofs of their host's palace were soon visible on a flat-topped hill at the western end of the plain, where the circuit of bronze walls gleamed in the evening sunlight. Before long they climbed the hill and passed through unguarded gates into a wide courtyard. Up to that point there had been no hint of a breeze – something that struck Eperitus as strange on a sea-girt island – but once inside the walls a strong wind rushed across the courtyard and slammed the gates shut behind them. Eperitus caught Omeros's eye and saw the poet was as perplexed as he was, but before either could comment their guide was leading them across the open space towards the palace. Lights shone from the windows of both storeys, but otherwise it was quiet and unwelcoming.

'Through here,' he said, ushering them between large wooden doors into a gloomy antechamber where torches sputtered on the walls and more doors were visible in the shadows at the back of the room.

'I don't like this,' Eperitus said in a low voice.

'We're safe enough,' Odysseus replied, 'as long as you let *me* do the talking.'

The slave pointed to the swords strapped to their sides.

'Your weapons, please.'

Odysseus surrendered his without hesitation, followed by Omeros and – with reluctance – Eperitus. The doors swung open to reveal a columned hall with a circular hearth burning at its centre. Behind the hearth was a long table where Aeolus and his six sons were seated in silence, their features distorted by the rising heat. The Ithacans were led to another table opposite them and directed to sit. Ever conscious for Odysseus's safety, Eperitus scanned the shadows for concealed figures and noticed rich murals half-hidden in the darkness. On the back wall boldly coloured waves rose up to consume a fleet of galleys with shredded sails and snapped masts, while to his right was a lifelike fresco of armoured warriors fighting each other before the lofty ramparts of a great city. His attention was momentarily caught by the dismembered bodies lying about the battlefield, portrayed with a careless glee that was unconcerned with the horrible reality of war. Then a side door opened and two female slaves brought baskets of flatbread and cold meat, which they deposited on the empty table before the Ithacans. Another followed and poured each man a krater of wine.

'Eat,' Aeolus commanded, indicating the plain food before them. There was nothing on his own table.

The guests poured libations into the flames and returned to their table. Odysseus rolled together a piece of bread and a slice of mutton and took a large bite. Eperitus and Omeros followed his lead, washing down each dry mouthful with wine that was clearly not their host's best. Aeolus watched them for a while with disdainful eyes, then with a discreet gesture dismissed the slaves.

'You claim to have participated in the war against Troy,' he said, 'and indeed I have heard that a man named Odysseus was a lesser king in Agamemnon's army. But how do I know that you are he? After all, unscrupulous men will claim to be what they are not if it will earn them a scrap of bread and a swallow of wine.'

Odysseus laid down his half-eaten food on the table and looked Aeolus in the eye.

'Why would any man claim he was Odysseus? Achilles perhaps, or Great Ajax, but not Odysseus, the least of the least. Who would profess to be the king of Ithaca when he could pretend to rule Sparta, Athens or Corinth? Unless he *was* Odysseus, of course.'

'We shall see,' Aeolus replied with an amused smile. 'Perhaps the test will be in the truth of your tale. The gods made me ruler of the winds, and is there anywhere on earth that the winds do not visit? Does anything happen under the sun that they do not know about? Will I not then know if you are a warrior returned from Troy or a mere beggar dressing himself in the robes of better men?'

'You'll find I'm no beggar, my lord, and I doubt you'll have heard the things I have to tell. For one thing, these winds you command must lack a voice. For if they'd spoken to you of things far and wide then surely you would've known the war at Troy had ended. Wouldn't you also have questioned my ability to pretend I was Achilles or Ajax, since both men are dead? No, the truth is that *you* are the charlatan, not I! You rule over a lonely rock in the middle of an uncharted sea with just your sons and slaves for company. And you're hungry for news of the outside world because you sit here in ignorance, gleaning morsels of information from lost sailors whom you treat with open contempt before sending them on their way again –'

'Silence!' shouted one of the young men, jumping to his feet. 'If you weren't a guest in my father's house I'd strike your worthless head from its shoulders and –'

'Sit *down* please, Androcles,' Aeolus commanded. 'Our guest may be a little brash in the presence of his betters, but he has at least shown himself to be intelligent and discerning. And you are right, Odysseus: the winds see much but say little. I live in happy ignorance on this rock, as you call it, where visitors are few and far between. For that reason I hope you will forgive me if I forget some of my obligations as host. But if life here is peaceful and idyllic by the standards of mankind, it can also be dull. A little news of the outside world would therefore be welcome. You say the war is over, but you failed to say who won. You also tell us that Achilles and Ajax are dead, but not how they fell. Clearly you have a tale to tell and I would be glad to hear it.'

Odysseus lifted his wine to his lips and gave a little grimace.

'A man's tongue functions better when greased with a higher quality of wine.'

Androcles frowned and balled up his fists on the table, but Aeolus clapped his hands and called for his slaves. Women appeared with cups for Aeolus and his sons, which a steward filled with dark wine. Another slave approached the Ithacans with the same wine as before, but Aeolus waved her away and ordered his steward to fill Odysseus's cup. Odysseus took a long draft and nodded contentedly, before indicating the empty vessels of his comrades. The steward glanced at Aeolus, who gave him a sharp look in return. Eperitus took a mouthful. The difference in quality was notable.

After the slaves had left, Odysseus told Omeros to remove his tortoiseshell lyre from his bag and play a tune. Then, when everyone's moods had been eased by the mixture of wine and music, he stood.

'My lord Aeolus, you've asked for news about the end of the war and I can easily give you it. After all, any man can state the outcome of an event; perhaps he can list a few names, too, before sitting back down and leaving his hosts feeling unsatisfied and only a little wiser than they were before. Reports of that kind might be fit for a commander's tent in the middle of a battle, but not for a ruler's palace. What, after all, is the purpose of a great hall, where men sit down to feast before a blazing hearth, surrounded by the deeds of men and gods?' He indicated the walls with a sweep of his hand, lingering on the mural of the fortified city and the battle before its gates. 'A place like this exists for one reason: glory. To give glory to the master of the hall by showing his wealth and power; to give glory to the gods when men honour them with sacrifices and libations; and to give glory to men whose feats are depicted in paint on the walls – and in words. So no story worth its bread or wine should start at the end. It should start at the beginning.

'Questions have also been raised about me. Am I who I say I am: a king, trying to find his way home after ten years of war, or a wandering beggar desperate to find a generous host? Perhaps I'm both. But a great tale must have a worthy teller, so before I speak of the war, I will speak of myself. I am Odysseus, and without me there would have been no war with Troy.'

His voice was soft and melodious, audible over the crackle of the flames and the gentle notes of Omeros's lyre – almost blending with them – but not so clear that his listeners were not forced to bend forward a little, careful not to make any other sound that might cause them to miss a word or disrupt the rhythm of his narrative. Even Eperitus, who was familiar with the magic in his friend's voice, was rapt as Odysseus retold the story of when Laertes had been king of Ithaca and his throne threatened by the traitor Eupeithes and his Taphian mercenaries. Eperitus knew that, under Odysseus's spell,

Aeolus and his sons were seeing the Pythoness in their minds' eyes as she riddled Odysseus's future in her cave below Mount Parnassus; and that they were imagining themselves fighting alongside the Ithacans as they were ambushed on the way to Sparta, and again as they encountered the great serpent in the temple of Athena – though he made no mention of the appearances of the goddess herself. Nor did he confine the story to his own trials, telling how Eperitus had saved his life by claiming to have entered Penelope's quarters when it was Odysseus himself who had risked death to see her. He described the greatest of Helen's suitors in detail, embellishing each attribute or defect as he saw fit. He made clear the dilemma Tyndareus had created for himself: that to offer his daughter and her inheritance to one man would enrage the others and invite a bloodbath; then, after a pause in which he drained the last of his wine, he revealed his own resourcefulness in suggesting the oath that bound every suitor to the protection of Helen and her father's choice of husband.

'And though the scheme won me Tyndareus's gratitude and with it the hand of Penelope, it also sealed my doom.'

With those words, Odysseus lowered himself onto his chair and slumped forward over the table, his head in his hands. Omeros's lyre stuttered to a halt and Eperitus felt himself emerging from the enchantment of Odysseus's words. He glanced up at the hole in the roof where the stars were visible through the wisp of smoke feeding up from the flames. He guessed that midnight had already passed, and suddenly, released from the world of twenty years before and returned untimely to the present, he realised how tired he felt.

'What's wrong?' Aeolus demanded, half-indignant and half-imploring. 'Odysseus, my friend, you must continue. Why did this oath seal your doom? What do you mean? And what about your father's kingdom? Did you return? Of course you did – but what happened when you found your way back to Ithaca?'

'My lord Aeolus,' Odysseus replied, raising his head wearily, 'I'm afraid the exhaustion of our voyage has left me drained and unable to continue. You will forgive me, I'm sure, if I beg your leave to return to my ship. I intend to sail at first light.'

'Nonsense! Nonsense, you will stay here under my roof, you *and* your friends. I will send a slave to tell your men that you will sleep in the palace. And there's no need for you to hurry off, is there? Stay another night. Let us hear the end of your story.'

Odysseus shook his head and held up a hand.

'I can't. My family awaits me –'

'I insist.'

Reluctantly, Odysseus gave a nod. He stood and thanked his host with a bow, then turned and followed a waiting slave from the hall.

'He played the old man like a lyre,' Omeros whispered to Eperitus as they followed.

'But to what purpose?' Eperitus replied.

Odysseus simply smiled.

Chapter Twenty-Four

AEOLUS'S DAUGHTERS

Eperitus rolled onto his side and lazily reached out a hand, but Astynome was not there. Opening his eyes he saw a white-washed wall and a heavy curtain, the edges of which were grey with pre-dawn light. He could hear Omeros snoring in one of the neighbouring rooms and the sounds of slaves going about their business as Aeolus's palace roused from its slumber. At least he had not been murdered in the night, he thought to himself, before returning to a half-sleep that was only broken some time later with the arrival of Odysseus.

'You've missed breakfast,' he announced cheerfully. 'So has Omeros, though I've asked Aeolus's slaves to bring you both a little something to start the day on.'

Eperitus sat up and scruffed his hair into some semblance of its usual mess.

'Seen anything of the old man?'

'Aeolus? Not a thing. Nor his sons. But that's good. I intend to use their absence to do a bit of exploring. You're welcome to stay in bed, of course –'

Eperitus gave a dismissive snort and looked for his sword, before remembering their weapons had been taken from them the night before. He felt uncomfortably naked without it as he pulled on his sandals and unrolled his cloak, which he had used for a pillow. Throwing it over his shoulders, he followed Odysseus into the next room to wake Omeros, just as a slave arrived with freshly baked bread and a skin of water. They finished the bread quickly and, with Odysseus shouldering the water, began their exploration of the palace.

It was a plain and homely dwelling, sparsely populated with slaves and with no sign of Aeolus or his sons. Odysseus used their freedom to explore the passageways and rooms of various functions, while Eperitus instinctively gained his bearings and made note of the best escape routes, should their hosts become less than welcoming at any point. He also found himself sizing up the vantage points for any defence from within the palace and the walls without. Not that gates and battlements could withstand any attack for long without defenders to man them – and there were no fighting men other than Aeolus and his sons. They visited the stables where a dozen fine horses and two chariots were housed, then proceeded out from the open gates and down to the plain beyond. This was as empty as the evening before. A few score sheep and goats lazed about in the early morning sun, watched over by two elderly shepherds who gave surly nods in reply to Odysseus's greetings, before moving away from the Ithacans.

They completed a half-circuit of the clifftops and reached the harbour where the fleet lay at anchor. The bay was full of men, laughing and shouting as if they were safe in their home waters. Odysseus smiled at the sight, then led his companions down the path to the beach. While the king was greeted by Eurybates and Polites, and Omeros stripped off to join Elpenor in the harbour, Eperitus sought out Astynome. He found her on the galley teaching Greek to a group of children. She brought her lesson to an early end and told her students to go and enjoy the water.

'It's what they wanted to do anyway,' she explained as he told her she did not need to stop for his sake. 'They were more interested in the sounds coming from overboard than anything I had to teach them.'

A little later they climbed the path to the cliff above and made love in a secluded hollow, under the shadow of a lopsided oak tree. In the afternoon, as they sat on the cliff edge talking about what had happened in the Cyclops's cave, Eperitus heard the crunch of approaching sandals and turned to see the same slave who had led them to Aeolus's palace. He disappeared from view down the path that led to the harbour, reappearing a short time later with Odysseus and Omeros. Eperitus kissed Astynome goodbye and joined his companions as they followed the slave back to the palace.

The hearth burned low as they entered the great hall, scoring black shadows into the faces of Aeolus and his sons. But this evening there were torches in the iron brackets on the walls and columns, illuminating patches of the muralled walls and making the room feel larger. Slaves appeared with baskets of flatbread, fruit, bowls of olives and haunches of freshly cooked meat. The wine that was placed before them was sweet and warmed Eperitus's throat as he took his first swallow.

'Welcome, Odysseus,' Aeolus said, reclining in his fur-draped throne and watching the Ithacan carefully from beneath his heavy eyebrows. 'You slept well?'

'As well as any man can sleep when he is anxious to return home and see his family.'

'A home is something to be cherished, as are a wife and children. How many children did you say you have, Odysseus?'

'I didn't. The subject of my family was barely raised.'

'You have a wife, as I recall. Penelope?'

'And she bore me one son, Telemachus. A babe in his mother's arms when I sailed to war, but now in his tenth year and with no memory of his father.'

'Doubtless you will be reunited soon,' Aeolus said. 'A man of your resourcefulness can find the way back to Ithaca, I am certain of it. And when you are reunited with your boy the years you lost will be made up for by the tales you have to tell him. War makes a man, Odysseus, it tests his character, *sifts* him. We are refined by the heat of battle, are we not? And when our impurities have been purged, what is left is a man of *true* character.'

Or a husk, Eperitus thought to himself. It was obvious Aeolus had never fought in anything more than a skirmish, let alone had his impurities cleansed by prolonged war.

'You are right,' Odysseus replied. 'I will have tales to tell that will excite and terrify him, though perhaps he will also learn there is more to a man than the ability to kill the fathers of other children.

But the chariot is outpacing the team, I think, with this talk of war. When weariness overtook me last night, I'd only reached the oath that the kings of Greece took to protect Helen and her future husband. The war with Troy was another ten years away, and far from inevitable. As you will see.'

And so the story continued. Long into the night, as Omeros played on his lyre and the rest of his audience drank wine and ate, Odysseus's voice filled the hall with stories of love and war, treachery and courage, gods and men. With his eyes fixed on Aeolus he explained how he won back Ithaca from the usurper Eupeithes and how his father gave him his throne. Knowing that his host was a man fascinated by the glory of combat, he breezed over ten years of peaceful rule and resumed with the arrival of a band of mercenaries on Kefalonia on the day his son was born. He detailed the wrestling match between Eperitus and Polites and how the giant Thessalian had agreed to join Odysseus's royal guard.

'Indeed, you saw the man yesterday,' Odysseus said. 'He was with me when you spoke to us from the clifftop.'

'The colossus with the barrel chest and fists like boulders?' Aeolus asked in surprise, turning his gaze on Eperitus. 'Then you were either enormously brave or incredibly stupid to fight him, my friend. And tomorrow this man must accompany you here to the feast.'

'Tomorrow, my lord?' Odysseus asked. 'But we sail in the morning.'

'By all means, raise your sails if you wish. But without a favourable wind to fill them you will find it very hard going.'

'Then if we stay one more day you will provide us with a favourable wind?'

Aeolus ran his fingers through his beard.

'I won't send a hindering one. Now, please, the story –'

Odysseus continued, painting Helen in a particularly harsh light for betraying Menelaus and running away with Paris. It was the act that required the fulfilment of the oath Odysseus had unwittingly proposed in Sparta ten years before, and which brought the independent kings of Greece together under Agamemnon. Only Achilles had failed to come, and when Odysseus described his mission to find the greatest warrior in Greece and persuade him to join Agamemnon's army, Aeolus's attitude changed from one of satisfied engagement to one of close attention. Even Androcles, who until that point had insisted on making the Ithacans aware of his displeasure at their presence, sat up and listened. But Achilles faded from the story again as Odysseus described the sacrifice of Iphigenia to appease the gods and win the Greeks passage to Troy. The memory provoked painful emotions in Eperitus, who finished his wine and held up his cup for more. Odysseus continued until the beaching of the first galley on the shores of Ilium, then sat down and, with a yawn, begged his hosts' forgiveness as he was too tired to continue.

The next night Polites joined the group. Odysseus related the events of the early years of the war, and when his tiredness forced him to stop at a key point in his story, Aeolus again asked him to stay on for one more day. Once more Odysseus agreed, but only if Aeolus would promise not to hinder their passage from the island when they left. The ruler of the winds had been so pleased with Odysseus's tale that he even offered to provide them with a favourable west wind for the first day of their voyage. And so it continued night after night, with the Ithacan king spinning out the story and growing ever larger in the estimation of his host. The feasts became richer and longer and always ended with the same ritual: Aeolus would ask Odysseus to stay another day, and the Ithacan – after a show of reluctance in his eagerness to return home – would concede in return for another favour. Sometimes the requests were small, such as asking for Eurybates to join the following night's feast; but mostly they were more daring, such as sailing directions or a clue to the next landfall. Aeolus's desire to hear more of Odysseus's tale tamed his natural hostility, but Eperitus could see that Androcles grew more suspicious with each new indulgence his father gave. He had inherited Aeolus's natural suspicion of outsiders, but this quality had not been tempered by age. Indeed, his youth sharpened it so much that there had been times when Eperitus had expected him to speak out and challenge Odysseus's story. That he had kept his silence must have been thanks to the beguiling effect of the king's voice.

On the night Elpenor was permitted – at Odysseus's request – to join the ever more elaborate feasts, Eperitus was surprised to see he was not the only new guest. Seated beside Aeolus was his wife, Telepora, a plump, large-chested woman with a loud laugh. She also had an eye for the visitors, caring little that her husband was beside her as she let her gaze linger on their battle-hardened bodies. Aeolus's six sons had also been joined by their wives, whom Aeolus explained were also their sisters. The incestuous marriages were not the only sign of their isolation on Aeolia, though. Apart from the ageing male slaves in the palace, the young women had clearly not seen other men before. If Telepora perused the Ithacans with the idle desire of a woman recalling her youth, her daughters stared at them with a lust that sought satisfaction. Eperitus was almost embarrassed by the looks he was receiving, and Polites – fearless in a battle against armed warriors – turned a deep red as Aeolus's daughters did little to hide their admiration for his great bulk. Their husbands seemed unconcerned, making Eperitus suspect the marriages between the siblings were not monogamous, and Aeolus himself seemed to take amusement from the discomfiture of his guests. Not that some of the Ithacans seemed to care what their hosts thought: Omeros and Elpenor often returned the looks they received with smiles and winks.

Eperitus reached for a basket of bread and Odysseus leaned forward with him.

'We need to be careful,' Odysseus whispered. 'I suspect Aeolus's daughters aren't here at their father's request.'

'Then whose?'

'Their husbands', led by Androcles. He hasn't wanted us here from the start. He believes I'm stringing the old man along –'

'You are.'

'...and he wants us gone. He'd prefer us dead, but won't dare kill us while we have six hundred men waiting in the harbour. So what better way to get rid of us than if his father's guests raped his daughters? Aeolus will throw us out if there's even the slightest indiscretion.'

'Shouldn't we be looking to leave soon anyway? We've been here three weeks and I'm starting to wonder whether the old man is ever going to let us go.'

'We're only prisoners as long as I'm telling him about the war. The moment my story ends he'll send us on our way, but before that time comes I want him to have given us the exact route home and to have promised us a favourable wind all the way back to Ithaca.'

'And what if everything he's told us has been a lie? I doubt he's ever been off this island, so how can he tell us the way home?'

'If you hadn't fallen asleep the other night you might have heard me ask him about his own life. He wasn't always trapped here, you know. He comes from a land far to the west, near to where the sun sets, and spent his youth travelling from one island to another. I believe he's telling us the truth and that he knows the way back to Ithaca. I *have* to believe that if I'm ever to see my home again! The problem is that warriors are warriors, and if any of us touches one of his daughters he won't just send us away without help, he'll pursue us with a gale that will rip the sails from our masts and have us drowning beneath colossal waves. Which is exactly why Androcles brought his sisters here tonight: to seduce us and destroy any hope we have of reaching Ithaca alive. We can't let them.'

He stuffed a piece of bread in his mouth, washed it down with a swallow of wine and stood. In an instant, the great hall fell silent but for the crackle of the hearth and the hiss of rain on the roof. Then he began his tale, recalling the night in the temple of Thymbrean Apollo when Helenus revealed the three oracles that had to be fulfilled before the walls of Troy could fall. Even Aeolus's daughters listened as the king's voice transported them to Pelops's tomb. But for once the story did not end at the moment of greatest tension, with Odysseus claiming tiredness. As he described the chamber in which Pelops's tomb lay, Dia – Androcles's wife and the most beautiful of Aeolus's daughters – stood and threw her arms wide in a yawn.

'My lords, I am not used to such a late night. I hope you will forgive me and my sisters if we retire to our beds.'

Odysseus, the spell of his voice broken, bowed and waited for the six women to stand. As they were about to leave, Androcles also stood and begged his guests' forgiveness. He was followed by his brothers, leaving just Aeolus, Telepora and the Ithacans behind. Despite his disappointment and barely disguised anger, Aeolus insisted that Odysseus stay another day, and then, accompanied by his wife, left the hall.

A robed and hooded figure stood in the passageway, the clay lamp in her hand casting a sphere of orange light that fought against the encroaching shadows. The hiss of the wick and the drumming of the rain beyond the windows were loud in the otherwise silent corridor, so the figure waited a few moments longer before raising the lamp and advancing. She stopped by a door that was slightly ajar, opened it enough to put her head through, then quickly withdrew it again and waved the lamp from side to side. The signal was followed by the patter of bare feet and the whisper of robes approaching from the end of the corridor. Dia snuffed out the flame and placed the lamp carefully on the floor.

'You're sure this is the room?' asked a voice from the darkness, barely able to contain a whisper.

'Shush! Of course I am. Six men under six blankets, all of them asleep.'

'I want the giant!' said one of the sisters, suppressing a giggle.

'There's enough of him for the two of us,' said another.

'Be quiet,' Dia ordered. 'And keep it down when you're in there, unless you want your brothers to find out.'

'They'd enjoy it,' one of her sisters declared.

Dia slapped her across the face and stared down the younger girl's shocked glare until she looked angrily away. Then she pushed open the door and entered the room where the Ithacans were sleeping. For some reason the curtains had been removed, revealing a sky filled with sheet rain. The six men were barely visible in the faint light that seeped into the room. Dia shrugged off her heavy robe and stood naked in the darkness. Her sisters did the same, their skin a pale grey in the gloom.

Eperitus felt miserable. Soaked through by the incessant rain and freezing cold – his double cloak rolled up under a blanket in the warm, dry room Odysseus had made them abandon – he wiped the wet hair from his eyes and looked up at the empty window.

There had been a noise – only faint, like the clapping of a hand, but his ears had picked it out clearly.

'Something's happening.'

'What do you hear?' Odysseus asked, standing beside him in the thick mud of the courtyard.

At that moment a scream pierced the damp night air. It came from the window that all six Ithacans had been despondently watching as the night wore on. A second scream was followed by cries of dismay.

'I think they've discovered we're not there.'

'So you were right,' Eurybates said.

'Then I wish I had been there,' Elpenor muttered, wrapping his arms about himself and looking up with a dejected expression.

Eperitus scruffed his sodden hair.

'You'd have paid a high price if you had. We all would. There are much easier ways to find a woman than sacrificing your own life.'

Another shout came from the upper window, this time from a man. An orange light drove back the darkness and the room was suddenly filled with a squabble of voices, male and female.

'Come on,' Odysseus said. 'Let's get out of this damned rain.'

They ran across the courtyard and up the stairs to their room, which was strewn with blankets and the cloaks and torn curtains they had filled them with. Aeolus was there with Androcles, the younger man holding a flaming torch over his head. Its light revealed Aeolus's daughters huddled together in a corner of the room. Three held cloaks across their bodies, while the others were naked, covering themselves as best they could with arms and hands. As the Ithacans entered, Aeolus turned to them, his face fierce with rage. At the sight of Odysseus his anger receded a little.

'I'm glad you weren't here, my friend,' he told Odysseus. 'But then you knew this would happen, didn't you?'

With a last glance at his daughters, he left the room. Androcles tried to follow, but Odysseus stopped him with a hand on his shoulder.

'It'll take more than that to trap me, lad,' he hissed, taking the torch from his hand. 'And now, perhaps, you'll send us up a few towels. You wouldn't want us to catch cold, would you?'

Androcles scowled at him and moved to the door.

'Get out of here,' he commanded his sisters. 'Now!'

To Eperitus's surprise, a slave brought warm towels a short while after.

The next night, Aeolus's daughters were present at the feast, though this time their eyes were downcast with only one or two daring an occasional glance at the guests. Neither did anyone interrupt Odysseus's narrative, that night or any other, until he reached the story of his escape from the Cyclops's cave.

'And so we set sail again, leaving the blind Polyphemus behind and steering for this island, filled with hope at the monster's words and believing we would find help from the wise Aeolus, ruler of the winds and favourite of the gods. For without help how can I ever hope to find my way back home to my beloved Ithaca and the family I have not seen for ten years? Every battle I have fought, every obstacle I have overcome, has been for their sake, to hold Penelope in my arms again and look upon Telemachus, the son I haven't seen since he was a baby. And yet my prayers have been answered. You,

Lord Aeolus, have shown me and my comrades mercy, taking us under your roof, feeding us and even describing to us each leg of the journey home. Tomorrow we can sail in confidence, knowing that Ithaca is but a few days away. Thank you, my lord.'

He sat, and for a while there was silence as the two men stared at each other across the heat haze. The silence continued to the point of embarrassment before Aeolus pushed himself up from his chair and looked across at his guests.

'I am grateful to you, Odysseus, for sharing your adventures with us. This hall has not heard the like since its foundations were laid. I also owe you an apology. From the day you arrived, Androcles has shown you nothing but hostility. For that my son offers you his apologies.'

At a gesture from his father, Androcles stood and bowed to Odysseus, though his eyes remained downcast and did not meet the king's. Odysseus returned the bow.

'But you must not blame him,' Aeolus continued. 'You see, he simply thought he was trying to defend me from my own folly. He believed that in telling you how to chart a course back to Ithaca I was also giving away the means for outsiders to find our island, something I had sworn never to do.'

'Sworn?'

'With Zeus's name on my lips. And why not? This is a peaceful island where I live happily with my wife and children. A blessing that I know, you, Odysseus, will appreciate the value of. We have no need for contact with the outside world and we do not seek it.'

'But –?'

'No, my friend, I did not break my oath. As much as you thought you were leading me blindfold down a path of your choosing, it was in fact *I* who was leading *you*. After the first couple of days you would have realised the courses and landmarks I revealed to you each night, at such pains to yourself, had been false. Not even for a story like the one you have told with such skill would I provide any man with a map to return to this blessed isle.'

Eperitus looked across at Odysseus, whose face was empty of expression. Empty of hope. He had used all his wit to fool Aeolus into telling him the way home, but for once he had misjudged his opponent. And now he was as lost as he had been when they had arrived thirty days before. On the other side of the hearth, Androcles's sullen look was replaced by a triumphant smile. He reached across and took Dia's hand in his.

'And yet you should not consider your efforts fruitless, Odysseus,' Aeolus continued. 'Though I had my doubts when you arrived, I have not invited you to remain night after night because I enjoyed your attempts to fool me. Even from the first I sensed there was something about you and some of your comrades,' here he bowed slightly towards Eperitus, who in his surprise forgot to bow back, 'that deserved a little patience on my part. Had I really suspected you of being a pirate or some other miscreant, I would have driven you back into the sea and sent a hurricane to wreck your fleet without hesitation. But it was clear you were not, and when you mentioned the war I decided you might be worth listening to. And you have been. Not only for the stories that you told with such skill, filling this hall with the sound and smell of battle and intriguing us with the politics of kings, but because, through your ordeals, you have shown me that you are a man of quality. You are more worthy of the title of king than many others who bear it. Yes, you are clearly capable with spear or sword and you know how to command men in war, as well as balance favour with allies more powerful than you are. But kingship is more than that. You have convinced me that your heart does not lust for glory alone. Your concern is for the land over which you rule and for its people, not for the wars and ambitions of other men. Greater still, your heart's desire is for your family. Though the wars of men fascinate me, I do not understand them. But the love of one's family – for all their faults – that I *can* understand. So I will not keep you from yours any longer. If I cannot tell you the way home, there are other ways I can help you. When we part as friends tomorrow morning and I give you my guest-gift, you will see I am not so mean a host as I might at first have seemed. But for now, King Odysseus,' he said, rising from his seat, 'I will bid you goodnight.'

Odysseus said nothing as they returned to their quarters, and Eperitus knew better than to disturb him. Besides, he had thoughts of his own to keep himself occupied: about whether the gods were still with his friend, despite Athena's curse, or whether it was his quality, as Aeolus had termed it, that saw him through. He believed it was the latter.

Chapter Twenty-Five

THE RETURN TO ITHACA

T he Ithacans were woken by a male slave who invited them to breakfast with Aeolus. He led them down to the courtyard, which was half-covered by the shadow of the palace walls. A number of tables and benches had been arranged in a semicircle in a bright patch of sunlight by the open gates. At its apex were two high chairs in which sat Aeolus and Telepora. Their sons and daughters were sitting on either side of them with a dozen slaves in attendance. The tables were laden with food and several drinking cups glinted gold in the sunshine. At the centre of the semicircle was a large leather sack the size of a bull's torso.

At a gesture from Aeolus, the slave led the Ithacans to the tables where they were seated in pairs. Eperitus and Odysseus were placed between Aeolus and Telepora on their left and Dia and Androcles on their right. Aeolus began the feast by pouring a libation to Zeus in the sand. The others followed, and for a while the only sounds were of hungers being satisfied, punctuated by the cawing of seagulls overhead as they awaited the opportunity to swoop on any discarded scraps. Eperitus sat peeling the shell from a boiled egg and wondering what was in the leather bag. If it contained Aeolus's guest-gift for Odysseus, then rather than holding the sorts of treasures one ruler might usually give to another it looked as if it had been filled entirely with air.

Aeolus stood and raised his hand for silence. After a few words honouring Odysseus and his visit to Aeolia, and beseeching the protection of the gods upon his journey home, he faced the king.

'My friend, you have a long voyage ahead of you and I do not wish to delay you any more than I already have. It is customary for a host to provide his guest with a gift, something befitting his status and which brings him honour. But I doubt there is anything I can give you that will increase the honour you have already won for your name. Instead I present you with something more valuable than glory. If I cannot tell you the way back to Ithaca, I will at least give you a favourable wind to guide you home to your family.' He raised his hands to the skies and closed his eyes, muttering words under his breath. At once a strong breeze blew across the courtyard, raising straw and dust from the floor. 'Keep this wind full in your sail and it will bring you home in nine days. What's more, I have imprisoned the other winds in this bag so that they will not hinder your progress. All I ask is that you untie the silver cord and release them again when you are safely on the shores of Ithaca – *and not a moment before*. I'll know when you have freed them and will call them back again.'

Because of its size they tied the leather bag to a pole, which Eurybates and Polites carried on their shoulders back to the fleet. The bored Ithacans greeted the news they would be leaving with a cheer and set about readying the galleys. The bag aroused much interest as it was stowed in the hold of Odysseus's ship, but the king had sworn his comrades to secrecy and neither kindness nor bribes could persuade them to reveal its contents to the others. Eperitus found Astynome under the watchful eyes of the two soldiers whom Polites had assigned to guard her while he was in Aeolus's palace.

'Thank the gods we're leaving,' she said, greeting him with a tight embrace. 'I'm tired of being treated like a prisoner. At least I *like* being guarded by you.'

One by one the fleet rowed out of the cove and with the wind at their backs made good progress into open waters. At a signal from Odysseus the sails dropped and were stiffened by the breeze, driving the galleys across the waves. There was no sign of any other landmass west of Aeolia and Eperitus felt uneasy about sailing over an unknown sea with no idea of where or when they would encounter the next landfall. Odysseus, though, seemed unfazed as he stood at the prow watching the distant horizon. Then, when the afternoon was growing old, he called over to Eperitus over his shoulder.

'Look out there and tell me what you see.'

Eperitus shielded his eyes from the lowering sun. The farthest point of the horizon was topped by a layer of white.

'It looks like fog.'

The chariot of the sun had ridden over the horizon by the time the fleet reached the bank of mist. The wind that Aeolus had promised would take them all the way home now dropped away and the twelve galleys were met by vaporous arms that drew them into a half-lit world of thick fog. Ghostly tentacles crept over the bow rails and quickly shrouded everything in white. The ships on either side became grey phantoms that soon disappeared altogether. Eurybates, his voice deadened in the still, damp air, called for the oars to be lowered into the becalmed waters, an order that was echoed by the invisible galleys around them.

'We're in trouble if there's land out there,' Odysseus said.

'I can't smell anything,' Eperitus replied. 'As far as I can tell we're still in the middle of an empty ocean. Do you think Aeolus has betrayed us?'

'The wind has gone, but he can't have sent this fog. I don't like it, though. It's getting dark, and even if we don't get smashed to pieces on rocks we could emerge on the other side with the fleet scattered and lost.'

The dense mist persisted until night had fallen, then began to break up and thin out until a few stars became visible overhead. The westerly breeze returned, chasing away the last tattered banners of fog and half-filling the sail so that it rumpled and flapped back into life. Eurybates ordered the oars to be withdrawn, and the weary crew cheered, only to be silenced by an order from Odysseus.

'Do you hear or see anything, Eperitus?' he asked.

They were clear of the fog now, which was receding rapidly behind them, and though there was no moon, the stars were bright enough for him to see the outline of a sail away to their right. The voices of the crew came to him across the waves.

'There's at least one other ship,' he said, pointing, 'and I think there's another ahead of us to the left.'

'Polites,' Odysseus called, 'go aft and light a torch. We need the others to know we're here.'

'There's another thing,' Eperitus said. 'Look at the stars. They're how they used to be before the land of the lotus eaters.'

A slow smile crept over Odysseus's face.

'We're on our way home, Eperitus. We're on our way home!'

The doors of the great hall were open and bright daylight reached into the centre of the open space, cramming the shadows into the corners so that the darkness there seemed thicker and more impenetrable. A breeze wafted in and encouraged the flames on the hearth to dance higher. The smell of bread from the palace ovens mingled with woodsmoke and Penelope's perfume, an interesting and not unpleasant mix that distracted Eupeithes momentarily from his thoughts. His son's angry voice brought him back again.

'Ten years is too long,' Antinous said. 'Ithaca needs a king now, and you, my lady, should recognise that. If you agree to remarry then the people will accept your decision.'

'But will my husband when he returns,' the queen replied, smiling affably.

Antinous waved his hand dismissively.

'Those rumours your son spread were lies, even if they had a few simpler minds believing them for a while.' He looked at Melantho waiting in the shadows with a pitcher of wine, but she refused to meet his eye. 'The war will probably continue for another ten years. The Trojans show no sign of weakening, and with the Greek kings bound by Odysseus's oath they're stuck there until the matter is decided one way or another.'

'Are you already trying to overturn the agreement made by this Kerosia only a few months ago?' said one of the others sitting in the circle of seven high-backed chairs.

He was a handsome middle-aged man with a blue cloak that flowed down from his broad shoulders to lap about his ankles. The stump of his right hand, encased in a leather cup, rested on his thigh.

'I am mindful of what is best for our island, Mentor,' Antinous replied. 'You've all heard about these tribes of wanderers filtering down from the north. They're settling wherever they feel like because there are no fighting men – and no kings – left to stop them. Soon they'll want more than parcels of abandoned land: they're going to establish their own towns, set up temples to their own gods, and protect themselves with armies. There's going to be war, Mentor, in every part of Greece. Ithaca may be an island, but we won't be immune to it. Our time's coming and we need a king to govern the defence. We can't simply wait ten more years for Odysseus to return!'

'Very impassioned, my son,' said Eupeithes, shifting slightly in the uncomfortable chair and smiling at Antinous. 'And yet we made an agreement and we must honour it, especially as it was made by this Kerosia.'

If Eupeithes smiled it was not because he felt at ease. No, his sense of discomfort came from more than just the chair. As for the terrifying news of the northern tribes that had unsettled not just the Kerosia but every farmer and fisherman across the islands of Ithaca, Kefalonia, Samos and Dulichium, that did not concern him. After all, he had encouraged the rumours for his own purposes, to quell ominous rumblings from among the people after Penelope was persuaded to sell her son's birthright. And it had worked handsomely. Rather he was unsettled by certain reports he had received from his own contacts on the mainland. Fellow merchants had heard from other merchants who supplied the Greek camp, saying that the gods had sent a great horse to kick down the walls of Troy and give Agamemnon the victory he had sought for so long. Not that Eupeithes gave much credence to the gods, and even less to their inconvenient oracles that so easily swayed the minds of the simple. But experience had taught him not to dismiss tales out of hand, even fantastic ones. If men were suddenly saying Troy had fallen when no such gossip had passed their lips before, then he was worried.

Antinous's complexion darkened. He brought his fist down on the arm of the chair.

'Great men know when to honour an agreement and when to overlook it! Odysseus would have served his country better if he'd turned his back on that oath. Instead he let himself and all the fighting men of these islands be dragged off to another man's war.'

'And if he had ignored his duty he would have been a king without honour, weaker by his presence here than his absence when all others had answered the call,' Penelope said.

'Yet I hear he tried to feign madness so that he wouldn't have to go,' Antinous said, rising to his feet and standing before her. 'He at least understood that a king's place is defending his own country, not fighting on the shores of a foreign land. If he was prepared to deny the oath he had taken – though by trickery rather than manly defiance – shouldn't you, my queen? Show your loyalty to Ithaca and give her a new king.'

'Penelope's loyalty is also to her husband,' said the large man next to Mentor. 'Sit down, Antinous, and keep your foolish notions to yourself.'

'For once I agree with Halitherses. Sit down and let your youthful impetuosity be ruled by the wisdom of our greater years.'

Antinous turned and glared at his father. Then, laying the speaker's staff on the floor, which he had clung on to since almost the start of the debate, he returned to his seat. It irked Eupeithes to humiliate his son so, especially as he understood his fears. Antinous saw his chance of power slipping away from him and wanted to pull it back as loudly and forcefully as he could. But to compel Penelope to choose a new husband now would destroy everything his father had worked for. All they had to do was wait. The Pythoness herself had foretold Odysseus would not return for another ten years, and Penelope had agreed to remarry if her husband did not return within that time. So they must be patient, even though Eupeithes knew the assassins he had planted among Odysseus's men would ensure the king was dead long before then.

'The Kerosia can deal with any threat from these northerners,' he continued. 'We can raise a militia –'

'You're wrong, Eupeithes.'

Had the opposition come from Mentor, Halitherses or Penelope, he would not have been surprised. But it had come from Oenops, the grey-haired old fool he had placed on the Kerosia to be an echo of his own voice.

'You're wrong because the Kerosia is ineffectual,' Oenops continued, barely able to look Eupeithes in the eye as he spoke. 'The people know we're divided and so they neither trust us nor respect our authority. If these barbarians decide to make Ithaca their home, do you think the Kerosia could organise any kind of defence?'

'It would be every man for himself,' added Polyctor, the final member of the council and another of Eupeithes's cronies. 'Before we could draw them together into a unified force our enemies would have overrun the island and taken it for themselves. What we need is a king, a single leader to help us prepare.'

Eupeithes now saw that Antinous had persuaded Polyctor and Oenops to support his own bid for power, in the hope his father would join them. Halitherses and Mentor added their own voices to the argument, refusing to accept that the previous agreement should be overturned. Penelope, who was only there to represent her husband and had no vote, stood and held out her hands in a plea for silence.

'Antinous, you cannot force me to marry against my will, not when my husband still lives.'

'You will obey the will of the Kerosia,' he answered.

Mentor stood and looked angrily at Eupeithes's son. But before he could speak, silence descended suddenly on the hall and every eye was turned to the open doorway. A man stood silhouetted against the sunlight, the horsehair plume on his helmet almost touching the upper beam. A shield was on his back, but he carried no spear and his scabbard was empty, his weapons doubtless having been confiscated by the guard at the outer wall. The man peered into the gloom of the hall and dropped to one knee as he saw the circle of chairs.

'My lords,' he called out in an accent that Eupeithes did not recognise, 'I have a message for Queen Penelope.'

'Come forward and speak.'

The man crossed the dirt floor and passed between the chairs of Oenops and Halitherses, where he removed his helmet and bowed before Penelope. His leather cuirass was well made but battle-worn. As Eupeithes surveyed his suntanned face with its hardened expression, he thought he knew what the man was going to say. He glanced at Antinous, who by the despairing look in his eyes seemed to have come to the same conclusion.

'My lady, I bring a message from King Nestor of Pylos, the first of the kings to return from the war. Troy has fallen! Your husband lives and is even now sailing back to Ithaca.'

Odysseus and Eperitus stayed awake all night, watching one torch after another flicker into life on the pitch-black sea. The last three ships did not come into sight until dawn, and with the fleet now huddled together in a pack, Odysseus let the wind take them westward. As the sun approached its zenith, Eperitus suddenly called out that he could see land. The announcement was greeted with wild enthusiasm by the crew.

Astynome wondered if it was Greece and felt a sudden apprehension at the thought of reaching their long hoped-for destination. Her eagerness to set up home with Eperitus and start a family was dulled by the thought that Eurylochus would never be far away. After she realised he had avoided capture by the Cyclopes and returned to the ship, she had considered telling Eperitus that he had tried to attack her. That would have been an end to all her fears, for Eperitus would have killed him without hesitation. But she had not forgotten Eurylochus's words: that if Eperitus killed him there would be a mutiny, and that he was the only one preventing the crews from murdering Odysseus. And she did not dare to risk that he might be right. Even on Ithaca she doubted whether Eperitus could kill

Eurylochus without consequences. So she decided that she would never speak of it to anyone. And hoped Eurylochus had the sense not to try the same thing again.

The island they had spotted was uninhabited and not known to any of the experienced sailors in the crew. Against their advice Odysseus insisted on sailing on through the night, perhaps fearing that the west wind would abandon them before time and return home to its master. It did not. Instead it continued to blow day after day and night after night, and all the time Odysseus stood on the same spot, refusing to give control of the sail to anyone else. He was there when Astynome closed her eyes and he was there still when she opened them again in the morning, his bloodshot gaze fixed fervently on the horizon. Eperitus was usually beside him, determined to support the king in his vigil. But after the fourth night at sea he joined Astynome for breakfast and was asleep within moments. Odysseus spared his friend a glance and then gave Astynome a nodding smile as she cradled Eperitus's head in her lap, before setting his eyes back on the distant horizon. Eperitus did not stir until the last light of day was fading. He admonished Astynome gently for letting him sleep so long, then rejoined his friend on the deck. He slept twice more over the next few days, both times from exhaustion rather than choice, but Odysseus – if he slept at all – must have napped standing. His face had become ashen and his eyes were dark-ringed, but his stoic determination to see Ithaca again held him fast to the spot, controlling the sail to take full advantage of the wind and drive them ever westward.

On the eighth day there was a great clamour on deck as a familiar coastline was spotted. Now every man seemed to know where he was and the realisation that they were nearing home gripped them and the air was filled with excited chatter. By now Odysseus was swaying on his stocky legs, and Eperitus and Polites took it in turns to support him. But he refused to close his eyes or sit down, possessed by a superstitious fear that Ithaca might slip away from him if he rested for a moment.

Neither would he take the fleet into one of the many harbours or bays they saw along the rugged coastline. This caused some grumbling among the crew, especially in the portion of the benches where Eurylochus and Selagos held court. Despite the knowledge they would soon be home again, there were some who wanted fresh provisions and the chance to sleep on firm land by a warm fire. Astynome watched the scowling faces with concern and voiced her fears to Eperitus, who simply nodded and told her that everything would be alright as soon as they reached Ithaca. But the crew's discontent was not only down to Odysseus's determination to reach Ithaca without stopping. There were rumours about the contents of the leather bag that was in the ship's hold. Aeolus's gift had fired the men's imagination so much that it was soon held to contain untold treasures, which Odysseus had no intention of sharing with his men. This above all seemed to anger them, but when Astynome asked Eperitus what was in the bag, he said he had sworn to keep the contents a secret until they reached Ithaca.

When the tenth morning since they had set sail from Aeolia arrived, the skies were grey and the air had turned cold and damp. Odysseus stood like a corpse, his knuckles white as they gripped the ropes controlling the sail, and his eyelids so heavy that he struggled to keep them open. Eperitus, standing beside him, was also showing signs of fatigue, for he had not slept for the last three nights, worried as he was by the rumours that had been spread about the leather bag. The crew, with little else to do, were pointing out hills and rocks and fishing villages on the familiar coastline to the east, talking excitedly among themselves about home. Only Eurylochus and Selagos looked unhappy to be returning and sat talking together in whispers. Omeros and Elpenor also seemed distracted as they watched Odysseus, perhaps worried the king was pushing himself too far. Not long now, though, Astynome thought to herself. Not long now.

Eperitus was the first to succumb. For some time Astynome had watched him battling to stay awake, so she moved quickly to support him when his eyes closed and refused to open again. He slumped into her arms and it was only with Elpenor's help that she shifted his bulk to one of the benches, where Polites was already sleeping off two nights at Odysseus's side. There Eperitus remained fast asleep, his head in Astynome's lap, so that even the cry of 'Zacynthos! It's Zacynthos!' and the resulting uproar did not rouse him.

Odysseus's head had begun to drop and his body was swaying with neither Eperitus nor Polites to support him, but at the name of the southernmost island of his kingdom his whole body stiffened and he lifted his eyes to the large island forming on the northern horizon. Signalling to Elpenor to take the ropes from his hands, he staggered to the prow and forced his way through the men who were crowded there. Even those who had previously voiced hostility to him stepped aside and returned to the benches, leaving the king to regard his realm in peace. And so, as the galley slipped past Zacynthos and the islands of Kefalonia and Ithaca came into sight, Odysseus stood alone at the prow looking at that which he had longed to see for ten years.

'So that's Ithaca?' Astynome asked Elpenor.

'Mostly it's Kefalonia. It looks like one island from here because you can't see the channel between them, but Ithaca is the small spur to the right.'

After a while the strait that divided the islands became clear. Ithaca seemed tiny to Astynome's eyes, but she nevertheless felt a sense of relief that after everything they had been through they had finally reached the end of their voyage – even if the threat of Eurylochus remained. Smoke trails were rising from the hilltops and the glow of small fires could be seen where farmers and shepherds were cooking their dinners. Farmsteads and orchards were visible on the hillsides and there were boats in the water around the rocky skirts of the island, the crews of which must have been looking at the fleet of galleys with trepidation. Soon their fear would turn to jubilation, she thought, and a smile crossed her face at the knowledge that her dream of a life with Eperitus was about to begin. She looked at him fast asleep on the bench and wondered whether to wake him. Then she glanced at Odysseus and saw that he was slumped over the prow.

She ran to his side. Taking his bulk in her arms, she struggled to lift him from the bow rail. She stared at the nearest crew members as they sat watching her from the benches.

'Help me.'

'Let him rest,' an old greybeard replied. 'He'll be home soon enough.'

'Back in his palace with all his plunder,' said another.

'And very little for us,' added the greybeard.

He was answered by a few disgruntled murmurs, though some shook their heads and one man at least told him to be quiet.

'He has always promised to share everything fairly, you know that,' Astynome protested.

She was acutely aware of her Trojan accent as hostile eyes stared at her from the benches.

'What about the bag Aeolus gave him?' This voice was also foreign, though the words had a thick Taphian burr. Selagos stood up and looked at the men around him. 'He never told us what was in the bag, did he?'

'Gold is what I heard.'

'Keep your gold, man. That bag's filled with diamonds and rubies or I'm a satyr.'

'Its contents are the king's business and nobody else's,' Astynome said.

'What's it to do with you, you Trojan whore,' Eurylochus spat. 'Elpenor, tell us what's in the bag or it'll go hard with you when we get back.'

'He's sworn to silence,' Eurybates called from the stern where he was leaning on the twin rudders.

'Tell us, Elpenor,' Eurylochus insisted, his small eyes fixed on the youth. 'Tell us and we'll make it worth your while.'

Elpenor – hanging on to the sail ropes as if tied in place – looked Eurylochus square in the eye.

'If you want to find out you'll have to look for yourself. I won't tell you.'

'Then that's what we'll do,' Selagos said.

Eurylochus looked at him in surprise.

'B–but we can't! What if Odysseus wakes up?'

Selagos looked at the unconscious king with a sneer.

'I hope he does. There's enough treasure in that bag to make every man here rich. Do we want to return to Ithaca as poor men ruled by a rich schemer, or do we open it up and take our share now?'

'You wouldn't dare,' Astynome shouted, pulling as hard as she could at Odysseus's inert body until he slumped to the deck.

'Let's not do anything rash!' Eurylochus warned. 'Selagos speaks in jest, of course. But Odysseus did say he would share all plunder fairly, and that includes gifts. I say we look inside the bag and list everything in it so that he can't exclude us from our split.'

There were loud words of agreement from the crew, whose outrage at being denied a share of the treasure was growing. Astynome looked in desperation at Eperitus and Polites – who were still in a deep sleep on the benches – then down at Odysseus. Taking hold of his tunic she began shaking him as hard as she could.

'Wake up, Odysseus! Wake up!'

'You're all fools,' Omeros warned the others.

He had been sitting on a sack of grain beside Eurybates, watching the course of the debate with concern. Now he got to his feet and stood over the hatch that accessed the hold. Selagos approached him with a mocking grin on his face.

'Out of my way.'

Omeros drew his sword. Selagos leapt at him, grabbing hold of his wrist and twisting the weapon from his grip. Omeros cried out in pain and was thrown into the scuppers by the powerful Taphian. Leaving the twin rudders, Eurybates leapt forward and swung at Selagos. His fist caught him in the jaw, almost knocking him back into the men on the benches. But Selagos rocked back with a counterpunch that caught Eurybates square in the face. He fell back against the sacks of grain and was silent.

With no-one at the rudder the galley lurched suddenly to starboard, rolling both Eperitus and Polites from their benches. They did not wake, and to Astynome's continued dismay she could not shake Odysseus from his exhausted slumber. As Omeros ran to take control of the rudder, Selagos tore open the hatch and dropped into the hold. A moment later he clambered back out, dragging the leather sack behind him. There was a look of confusion on his face as he lifted it lightly in his arms and threw it onto the deck.

'It hardly weighs anything,' he told the others.

'Open it anyway,' said the greybeard.

'Yes, open it, Eurylochus,' said another. 'Let's see what he's been keeping from us.'

'Stop, you fools, before it's too late.'

But Omeros's pleas were in vain. Eurylochus had already unpicked the knot in the silver cord and was pulling it loose. A terrific blast blew the bag apart and threw Eurylochus across the deck. The escaping gale rushed out in every direction, hurling crew, slaves and livestock against the bow rails and crushing Astynome into the prow. She watched, wide-eyed with terror, as the winds spiralled several times around the galley then drew together into a towering whirlwind that twisted upwards, past the mast and into the sky above. It hovered briefly over the ship, tottering like a great tree in a storm, then with a howl of fury tore itself into three and swooped down over the surface of the sea. Water that had been almost flat moments before was churned into a maelstrom of swirling waves that spun the galley about like a small log. Two children were picked up by the winds and blown across the deck. Astynome caught one by the forearm, but the other was sucked over the bow rail and was gone in a moment, her screams swallowed by the deafening roar. A wave swept over the deck. Astynome grabbed the bow rail with her free hand and tried to steady herself, but felt the other child's arm slip from her weakening grip.

'Take my arm with your other hand,' she cried out in her native tongue.

But the child could not hear her or was too terrified to react. Her pleading eyes looked into Astynome's and then a second wave washed her away. Astynome reached after her and fell across the bow rail. The sea raged below her, hungry for another victim. And then a new wave broke over the deck and took her legs from under her.

At the same moment something caught her and pulled her back.

'I've got you,' Odysseus shouted. 'I've got you both.'

He pushed her down under the shelter of the bow rail and gave the frightened child into her arms. Astynome clutched the girl tightly and looked up at the drenched and wind-blown figure of the king. The mast was behind him, the sail flapping loose and twisting in the ferocious gale. Then she remembered Eperitus.

'Where's Eperitus?' she shouted.

He knelt beside her.

'I don't know. Can you tell me what happened?'

The wind almost stripped his voice from him, but she understood what he was asking her.

'They opened the bag.'

The confirmation of what he must have known took the fight out of him and he collapsed beside her, hiding his face in his hands.

'What have they done? *What have they done!*'

The galley pitched again and another wave crashed over the decks. Odysseus struggled to his knees and clutched the bow rail, staring into the storm with tears streaming down his face and a desperate look in his eyes. Then he threw off his cloak and sword and climbed onto the prow.

'What are you doing?' Astynome shouted, seizing a handful of his tunic.

'I can swim to her.'

'You'll never make it. The sea's too rough.'

'Then let the sea take me!' he snapped. 'A few moments of pain and then the gods can't torment me any more. Don't you see, Astynome? They're never going to let us be together again.'

She tried to pull him back, but he prised her hands away and looked down at the snapping jaws of the waiting sea.

'Do it! Jump and save us all from the curse the gods have put on you!'

It was Selagos. But if his words were meant to encourage Odysseus's madness, then they failed. As the king stared out at the raging waters, Astynome could see the flames of self-destruction slowly fade from his eyes.

'Come back down, Odysseus,' she said, taking his hand. 'The gods won't keep you from her forever, but death will. Come back down.'

He lowered his face in a final indulgence of his hopeless sorrow, then dropped back down to the deck. He turned his gaze on the Taphian.

'Damn you, Selagos. Now grab hold of those ropes and get that sail under control. If we ever needed your strength, it's now.'

Chapter Twenty-Six

THE LAESTRYGONIANS

C'ursed by the gods.'

'What's that?' Eperitus asked.

Odysseus turned, surprised to see his friend standing behind him.

'Don't pretend you didn't hear me.'

'Of course I heard you,' Eperitus replied, leaning on the bow rail beside the king and watching the dolphins racing alongside the galley. 'But what do you mean?'

'They were Aeolus's last words before he sent me away. He refused to give further help to a man who was cursed by the gods.'

After the winds had been released from the bag, Aeolus had recalled them to Aeolia. But he had not expected the Ithacan fleet to return with them, and his reception on their second visit had been curt and hostile. That had been a week ago, and with the ships still needing proper repairs, Odysseus was anxious to find a protected harbour with plenty of wood close to hand.

'We can find our way back without the gods,' Eperitus said with a shrug.

'Can we? We're back in this strange other-world, where the stars are confused and we've no idea of the way home. And we were so close, Eperitus. Damn Eurylochus.'

'Damn him? You should have killed him, cousin or not. And that Taphian henchman of his. They're at the heart of the discontent in this fleet.'

'I'm not a tyrant, Eperitus, and I can't lead the army by strict discipline and summary execution. Besides, I've dealt with the matter.'

'By splitting them up and transferring them to different galleys, where they can just spread mutiny to more of the fleet.'

Odysseus shook his head and Eperitus regretted pushing the point.

'I'm sorry. I know it's not an easy matter to deal with. If it's any solace, I'm glad you're king and not me. I'd make a horrid mess of everything.'

'You'd get on with the job, Eperitus, and that isn't such a bad approach. Sometimes I wonder whether I don't think too deeply about things. It didn't work with Aeolus – I should have seen that an honest appeal would have served us better. In truth, we wouldn't even be in this mess if I'd followed my instincts and obeyed Athena in the first place. Sometimes intelligence is more a curse than a blessing.'

'Maybe. But it was intelligence – *your* intelligence – that conquered Troy, not the brute strength of Achilles, Ajax and the rest of us.'

'*Land!*'

Both men looked to the stern where Eurybates was standing on tiptoes and shading his eyes. Eperitus followed the direction of his gaze and saw a bar of land low to the horizon on their starboard side. He wondered what challenges it would hold, but for the crew struggling at the oars for their seventh day – Aeolus had refused them any assisting wind after turning them away from his island – any landfall would be a welcome relief from their labours. Several moved to the bow rail for a better view, causing the galley to list and forcing Eperitus to order them back to their benches. He followed Odysseus to the stern, where Eurybates was already steering a course towards the distant coastline. The rest of the fleet followed, the oars of each vessel dipping and rising in the still waters with renewed vigour as the landmass began to take shape. By now everyone could see they were approaching an island. A handful of low mountains rose from its centre, but only Eperitus's eyes could see the jagged rocks that encircled its high grey cliffs, waiting to chew holes in any wooden hull that dared come near. He was also the first to see the only break in the barrier: a gap between two steep headlands that opened into a large cove.

'There,' he announced, pointing. 'A harbour. It's the only safe place on the whole coast.'

Odysseus nodded to Eurybates, who altered course towards the cove. Soon, the jutting promontories that overlooked the entrance were visible to all. Each was skirted by a shingle beach, while on the headland on the left a series of irregularities formed a stair to the clifftop above.

'Make for that beach, Eurybates,' Odysseus said. 'Eperitus and I will climb to the top and see what we can see of the rest of the island.'

The beak of the galley bumped against the black shingle and Odysseus jumped down into the water with a cable that he tied fast about a shoulder of rock. One by one, the rest of the fleet passed between the stone sentinels into the calm waters of the cove. Here, in the shadow of the high ring of cliffs, they would be safe from any change in the weather for as long as it took the Ithacans to make their repairs. The splash of anchors being tossed into the water and the shouts of the crews echoed loudly in the enclosed space.

Eperitus jumped down and joined Odysseus.

'They're making enough noise in there to bring every enemy within earshot down on us,' he complained. 'Let's pray there's nothing more than a few goats in this place.'

'I doubt that,' Odysseus replied. He was studying the steps that led up the side of the headland. 'Look at these. There's little craftsmanship to them, but there's no mistaking they've been carved by men.'

'These weren't made by men. The steps are much too high. Perhaps we've found our way back to the land of the Cyclopes.'

'By all the gods, I hope not,' Odysseus said, tugging at his red beard. 'No, that's impossible. We've maintained a true north-easterly course, *away* from the Cyclopes. But it's worth having a look around before we settle down for the night.' He turned back to the ship and signalled to two men who were watching them from the bow rail. 'Perimedes, Oicles, get down here. And bring your weapons.'

The steps were roughly hewn and steep, but at the top they were rewarded with a clear view of the harbour below – half-filled by the Ithacan fleet – and the country beyond. The island was covered with dense woodland that crept down from the sides of the mountains to fill the undulating contours of the land. A thin trail of smoke was rising from a fold in the hills to the west.

'At least that confirms the island's populated,' Eperitus commented.

'Yes, but by whom?' Odysseus replied. He paused in thought, his arms folded. 'Take Oicles and Perimedes and head for the smoke. If you find who made it and they're friendly, send Oicles back with a message for the rest of us to join you. If they're hostile, get back here as quick as you can. We'll not do anything else until you return.'

Eperitus nodded and, with Oicles and Perimedes trailing behind, set off along a dirt track that led into the woods. Inside, the trees were tall and their trunks thick with age. The late season had turned the canopy a variety of browns, reds and deep oranges, while dusty spokes of sunlight penetrated the gaps in the canopy to illuminate the gloom. The ground was thick with fallen leaves, but the path remained clear as it led them twisting and turning to the north-west.

'Someone maintains this path,' Perimedes said as they walked, his spear resting casually over his shoulder. 'Someone tall enough to reach all the way up there and strip off new branches.'

Eperitus saw where whole boughs had been torn away high above them.

'Why would anyone bother to pull down branches?' Oicles asked, dismissively.

'To keep them out of their faces.'

'That high up? Don't be a fool, Perimedes.'

'He's right though,' Eperitus said. 'You saw the size of those steps we had to climb. Whoever made them – whoever made this path – is twice our size. You remember the Cyclops.'

'You're saying there're more of those things?' Oicles said. 'Then why in the name of Hades are we looking for them? Shouldn't we just go back to Odysseus and tell him the island is full of monsters?'

'Not until I've seen them with my own eyes,' Eperitus replied and continued walking.

Perimedes followed without objection and, after a nervous glance into the murky depths on either side, Oicles joined them. The path continued upwards and then began descending again. After a while the woods started to thin out and they saw open land through the trees ahead of them. Eperitus signalled for his companions to slow down and spread out. Clutching his spear in both hands, he approached the eaves at a crouch and hid behind a tree. Peering cautiously from behind it he saw he was at the edge of a sunlit meadow that lay between two arms of a low mountain. Before him the ground sloped away over a ridge before rising up again on the other side. Hearing the trickle of water, he advanced to the edge of the ridge and saw a stunted tree growing from a rocky outcrop below. Its branches overhung a pool of bubbling water from which a small stream trickled away down the hillside. A figure was moving at the edge of the pool and Eperitus instinctively dropped to his stomach. Hearing Oicles and Perimedes approaching behind him, he motioned for them to get down.

'What is it?' Perimedes whispered as he crawled up beside him.

'A woman, I think.'

'She's *big*!' Oicles said.

The figure was indeed tall and broad-shouldered, though with narrow hips. She was dressed in a long blue tunic of coarse wool and was filling a clay jar from the spring. Eperitus knew at once she was not a Cyclops, and the fact she was dressed in homespun clothing suggested civilisation. As he watched she began to sing. It was not a language that he recognised, but her voice was clear and melodious and dispelled the last of his caution. Giving his spear to Perimedes, he stood up and walked down the slope.

'Please, my lady,' he began.

At the sound of his voice the figure turned sharply and dropped the clay jar on the grass. She had a lumpish, oversized body and a heavy-jawed face, but the eyes belonged to a child of no more than perhaps five or six years old. Eperitus was as shocked as she was and stepped back in momentary horror before collecting himself and holding up his hands.

'Don't be afraid. I won't hurt you. I just want to speak with you.'

The girl turned to run, but Perimedes and Oicles had skirted round behind her and blocked her escape with levelled spears. She stumbled back, her face filled with desperate fear.

'Where is your father?' Eperitus asked.

Whether she understood was not clear, but she pointed up the slope to where an arm of the mountain formed a low cliff. In its shadow were several large wooden dwellings, unprotected by a ditch or stockade. At the centre of the village stood a tall building with a high roof, from which a twist of dark smoke was rising. It was the same one that Eperitus and Odysseus had spotted from the headland.

'Antiphates,' the girl said, pointing harder. 'Antiphates.'

Eperitus caught a glimpse of her teeth as she spoke and felt a shudder of revulsion. His hand automatically clutched at the pommel of his sword and he had to consciously pull it away. Then, mastering his unease, he retrieved the jar the girl had dropped and placed it in the grass at her feet. She did not touch it, but simply stared at him as he backed away up the slope to join his comrades.

'Surely you're not going *up* there?' Oicles protested. 'That thing's just a child; imagine the size of the adults!'

'We have our orders.'

'But you saw her teeth.'

'Of course I saw them!' Eperitus snapped.

He strode towards the village. Perimedes caught up with him and handed him his spear.

'Oicles is right, Eperitus.'

'Odysseus told us to find out who lives here and make contact with them. And that's exactly what we'll do.'

'He wasn't asking us to throw our lives away!' Perimedes persisted. 'Whatever lives up there is dangerous. I can feel it in my blood. I think we should go back and report what we've seen.'

Eperitus did not reply because he had the same feeling. But if the fleet was to lie up and lick its wounds from the storm then they had to know what sort of people inhabited the island and whether they posed a threat.

Deep, rumbling voices came from behind the closed doors of the first house they passed, though Eperitus did not understand the words that were spoken. He had an overwhelming sense, despite the girl's clay jar, her woven dress and the carefully constructed dwellings of the village – all signs of a civilised and functioning society – that they were walking into a nest of unspeakable savagery. He wondered whether the villagers were aware of their presence and whether hostile eyes were already watching them. But as they walked quietly between the large wooden huts, they did not hear a door open or the sound of a single footstep. Not until they reached the threshold of the largest building. Its towering doors swung open before him to reveal a woman of almost twice his own height. She wore a plain dress and cloak and her weathered face was brutal and ugly, with a heavy jaw that reminded him of the child at the spring. Her eyes were almost entirely black and stared at him from beneath a single eyebrow, as surprised to see Eperitus as he was to see her. Clutching at the door jamb, she leaned back into the palace and shouted.

'Antiphates,' her voice boomed, following the name with a flow of unintelligible words.

Eperitus stepped back hurriedly to stand between Perimedes and Oicles, whose spears were at the ready.

'Put them down,' he instructed. 'We don't want to provoke them. They could be friendly.'

Perimedes gave him a look that told him exactly what he thought of that. Another giant stepped from the gloom of the open doorway. He wore a scarlet cloak and a woollen tunic that reached down to his knees, and across his brow was a silver diadem. He glowered at the men with dark, bloodshot eyes.

'I am Antiphates, lord of the Laestrygonians,' he announced in a voice that struggled to form the words. 'Who gave you permission to come to my island?'

'Our ships were damaged in –' Eperitus began.

'I asked who gave you permission.'

'My lord, nobody gave us permission.'

'Then you are trespassers.'

'Not by choice. But if you would be willing to –'

'How many ships?'

'Enough to defend ourselves,' Eperitus retorted, instantly regretting his tone. Odysseus would not have made that mistake. 'Twelve ships, my lord. My king has sent me to –'

'There are no kings on this island but me.'

'A diadem doesn't make you a king,' Oicles challenged, succumbing to his temper.

Eperitus glared at his companion but noticed that the doors of the other dwellings in the village were beginning to open and more giant figures were emerging into the daylight. He turned quickly to Antiphates.

'My king has sent me to plead for your mercy, King Antiphates. In the name of Zeus, the protector of strangers, we offer ourselves before you as suppliants and ask for your protection. Will you obey the will of the gods?'

'Who or what is Zeus? I rule here, not Zeus,' Antiphates said. He extended a long-nailed finger towards Oicles. 'You! Come here, I have a message for this king of yours.'

Oicles looked at Eperitus, who accepted his spear from him and gave him a nod. The Ithacan walked towards the Laestrygonian king and stopped several paces from him. Suddenly Antiphates gave a roar and leapt down from the threshold. He seized Oicles by the throat and sank his teeth into his arm, tearing out a huge chunk of flesh that exposed the bone beneath. Oicles screamed horribly, but only for a moment, before Antiphates's jaws closed about his face and silenced him forever.

Eperitus had been rooted to the ground with shock but quickly shook himself into action and hurled Oicles's spear at Antiphates. The woman threw herself in front of the king and the point of the spear passed through her throat. She fell dead in an instant, crashing heavily to the ground at her master's feet. Eperitus turned to Perimedes.

'We have to tell the others. Run!'

Side by side, they dashed at the loose ring of over twenty Laestrygonians that had formed behind them. One rushed towards Perimedes with his jaws wide open and his arms outstretched. The Taphian threw his spear at the monster, piercing him below the left nipple and felling him at once. He drew his sword and ran on, yelling at the top of his voice. Two more Laestrygonians ran to block their escape. Eperitus thrust his spear into the first creature's shoulder and it rolled away, bellowing with pain. There was no time to draw his sword before the second was upon him, grabbing his arm as he tried to twist aside. The strength in the monster's fingers was unbearable and as it squeezed his upper arm he knew the bone was moments from breaking. Then Perimedes's sword cleaved through the Laestrygonian's wrist and the terrible pressure receded, though the severed hand still clung grimly on to Eperitus's arm. He threw it back over his shoulder at the others.

They slipped through the last of the creatures and ran out of the village. The sound of pursuit was close behind, but for all the length and power of their limbs, the Laestrygonians lacked speed. As they neared the eaves of the forest, a figure appeared from the edge of the dell where the spring was hidden. It was the girl they had found drawing water. But now she was running to intercept them, her mouth opened wide to reveal the rows of hideous fangs that had first struck such fear into Eperitus. He drew his sword as she lumbered towards him and with a single swipe lopped off her head. A roar of dismay boomed out behind them, filling the whole meadow with its grief and anguish.

Eperitus reached the opening to the forest path and plunged into the gloom. He could hear Perimedes's panting behind him, but no sound of pursuit. He did not stop to see if the Laestrygonians had given up.

'Keep going, Perimedes,' he shouted.

'I'm not likely to stop now,' came the gasped reply.

With reckless disregard for the twists and turns in the path and the roots the trees had pushed out across it, they ran until they reached the top of the last ridge that would lead them back down to the ships. With lungs bursting, Eperitus stopped to catch his breath. Then he heard the thunder of heavy footsteps accompanied by the snapping of branches and the hollering of angry voices. The sound was not behind him, though, but to his left.

Perimedes had caught up and was leaning against a tree trunk.

'What is it?'

'The Laestrygonians,' Eperitus replied, suddenly realising their danger. 'They're cutting through the woods to intercept us before we reach the cliffs. Come on!'

They ran on, using the slope to increase their speed as they spotted the colossal shapes crashing through the trees beside and now slightly ahead of them. The path levelled again and became lighter as the canopy thinned. Eperitus saw an arch of daylight ahead, but as he threw his remaining energy into a final sprint, the black shape of a Laestrygonian stepped from the trees to block their escape. It was Antiphates, his jaws still red with Oicles's blood. In his right hand was a club the size of a man's leg, set about with crude iron studs. He swung it at Eperitus's head, but the Ithacan anticipated the attack and ducked. The club smacked into a tree trunk with a hollow thud that brought down a shower of leaves. Eperitus recovered his poise first and unsheathed his sword. He slashed at Antiphates's arm, but the Laestrygonian jumped back from the blow with surprising agility. Perimedes rushed his other flank and Antiphates batted him aside with a backwards swipe of his free hand, sending him crashing against a tree. Perimedes fell and lay still. Other Laestrygonians – scores of them as it seemed to Eperitus's tired senses – were now stomping through the woods towards them. Casting aside caution, he dashed at Antiphates. The giant swung the club down at his head, but Eperitus sidestepped the blow and lunged with the point of his blade. It pierced the monster's thigh and with a bellow of agony he dropped his weapon and collapsed against a tree. An answering roar came from the other Laestrygonians, who came sprinting to their king's aid, heedless of the obstacles in their path. Eperitus hooked his fingers into the neck of Perimedes's leather breastplate and hauled him out of the pile of leaves where he lay. Putting his arm around his shoulder, he dragged him as quickly as his tired legs would allow to the edge of the wood. The bright sunlight brought him back to his senses and together they stumbled to the clifftops above the cove where the Ithacan fleet lay at anchor.

'Get out!' Eperitus shouted down to them as hundreds of Laestrygonians emerged from the eaves of the wood. 'Cut your anchor cables and get out to sea. *Now!*'

Chapter Twenty-Seven

THE DESTRUCTION OF THE FLEET

The galley crews looked up at Eperitus in confusion. Many had already taken smaller boats to the shingle beach at the foot of the cliffs and were making campfires or filling skins from a small waterfall that zigzagged down to the bay.

'Get out! *Get out!*' Eperitus repeated himself, his voice echoing from the rock walls.

Most just stared up at him, unable to see what he could see. A few sensed his urgency and jumped into the boats and began rowing back to the ships. But it was too late. The first Laestrygonians had reached the clifftops and were staring down at the helpless fleet. Yet more were streaming out from the woods behind them, several carrying long iron spears attached to ropes that were coiled over the giants' shoulders. Others carried tall wicker baskets, the purpose of which Eperitus could not even guess at. The whole village must have been emptied, for there were women and children among them, every member of the tribe howling with fury. The Ithacans below looked up in horror at the monsters lining the cliffs around them.

'Eperitus?'

Odysseus pushed himself up from the trunk of a small tree where he had been sleeping. His eyes widened at the grotesque figures on the other side of the cove, then he leapt to his feet and ran to Eperitus and Perimedes.

'What in the name of Zeus are *they*?'

'They killed Oicles,' Perimedes began, his hands shaking as he took hold of the king's shoulders. 'They bit his face off.'

Odysseus eased him aside and joined Eperitus at the cliff's edge. The screams of the Trojan women and the terrified cries of their children mingled with the urgent shouts of the Ithacans as they slashed the hawsers that tied them to the anchors and scrambled onto the rowing benches. Oars were sliding out into the still waters, but the galleys were so closely packed that they clattered against each other or snapped against the hulls of neighbouring vessels. The men trapped on shore were leaping into the water and swimming back to their ships. Several were caught in the frenzy of oars and screamed briefly before they were forced under. Then something large and grey fell from the cliffs. A helmsman looked up from the rudders as its shadow fell over him but was dead before he could cry out. The boulder crashed through the deck where he had stood, lifting the fore of the ship clean out of the water.

All along the cliff the Laestrygonians were tearing up rocks and hurling them at the hapless ships below. The shouts of terror and the screams of pain and death were almost lost beneath the crash of splintering wood and the rush of exploding water. Eperitus turned to Odysseus, whose face was pale as he watched the destruction of his fleet.

'We have to do something,' he said.

'Do what? What can three men do against *those*?'

'Look!'

Perimedes pushed his way between them and pointed at the Laestrygonians. The purpose of the iron spears and the wicker baskets had become horribly clear. The first galley to have been struck was already sinking, and as the survivors swam towards the other ships the Laestrygonians threw their spears at them. It seemed that every one found a target, and as the Laestrygonians pulled on the ropes, both weapon and prey were hauled back up to the clifftops. Here the giants would pull the struggling victims from the barbed tips and toss them to the women and children waiting behind. The dead and dying were devoured in a frenzy, but those that might survive were thrown alive into the wicker baskets. Two in every three were women.

'Why are they targeting the women?' Perimedes asked. 'Why would they do that?'

Eperitus thought he understood, but it took Odysseus to voice the awful answer.

'Because they're going to breed them.'

'Then we must stop them,' Eperitus said, reaching for his sword.

'No,' Odysseus replied. 'It's too late for them now. We have to get back to the ship.'

Eperitus stared at the ranks of Laestrygonians, some of whom were descending the cliffs on rough-hewn steps similar to those he and Odysseus had climbed earlier. Two more galleys had been holed and were sinking, while the decks of all the others were strewn with dead. Many had lost the majority of their oars to the falling rocks, though the remaining crews still struggled to row their way out of the carnage. Eperitus feared their efforts would be in vain unless the one remaining ship – Odysseus's own galley – could come to their rescue. What they could do to help he did not know, but Odysseus would think of a way to save them. He had to.

'Let's go before the Laestrygonians notice us,' he said.

They descended the cliff to where their galley was safely moored outside the entrance to the cove. Fear and confusion were evident on the faces of the whole crew.

'What's happening?' Eurybates asked. 'It's all I could do to stop the crew cutting us free and rowing into the harbour.'

'That's exactly what we're going to do,' Eperitus answered him. 'The fleet's being attacked. Any man with a bow and arrow, make your weapons ready and get into the prow. I need a dozen more with ropes: there are a lot of men in the water and we might even get a cable to one of the other ships and tow it free.'

Odysseus drew his sword and cut the rope that tied the ship to the shore.

'Get back to the oars,' he shouted as men left the benches to fetch ropes and weapons. 'Eurybates, take us out to sea as quickly as you can.'

An uproar of voices greeted the order.

'If you want to live, *do as I command*!'

'Get to your oars,' Eurybates called, and reluctantly the crew returned to the benches.

As the galley was eased free of the shingle, Eperitus forced his way through the confusion towards the prow. Astynome appeared before him, her face full of concern, but in his anger he barely heard what she was asking him. He moved past her and found Odysseus clutching the bow rail.

'What in Zeus's name are you doing?' he said, grabbing him by the arm.

Odysseus shook him free.

'I'm doing what's necessary.'

'*Necessary*? Your whole army is being massacred inside that harbour! What's *necessary* is that we save as many of them as we can.'

'Damn it, what do you think I'm doing?'

Eperitus seized hold of Odysseus's cloak.

'Those men fought loyally for you for ten years. They're your countrymen, your friends, and you're going to *abandon* them?'

The spark of anger passed to Odysseus, who knocked Eperitus's hand aside and pushed him away.

'They're already dead. Can't you see that? They're dead, Eperitus, and if we row into that cauldron we'll be dead too. But right now we're alive and I'm going to keep us that way.'

'Then save your own skin. It's what you're best at.'

Slowly the galley began to pull away from the shore. Eurybates turned her across the entrance to the cove, though the high cliffs on either side prevented the crew from seeing what was happening within, making the constant screams and smashing of wood even more horrific in their imaginations. As Eperitus watched, seething with fury, he saw men swimming from the mouth of the bay. Without thinking, he cast off his sword and cloak and dived into the sea.

The cold water closed about him, muffling his hearing and darkening his vision. As he broke the surface again he saw the splashing of the men ahead of him and swam directly towards them. He gave no thought to what he would do when he reached the mouth of the bay, or how he might rescue any survivors escaping the slaughter within. All he knew was that he had to do something. Just as clearly as Odysseus believed the best thing he could do was save the men on his own ship, Eperitus knew he could not leave the others to be massacred. It seemed a long time before the cliffs were towering above him, time in which many more of his countrymen would have been crushed by rocks or harpooned by the Laestrygonians' iron spears. He almost collided with the first man, but when he took his arm he realised he was already dead. He pushed him aside and swam on. Another man called to him for help. As Eperitus reached him he saw that he was barely able to keep his head above water. He fumbled to undo the clasp of his cloak and realised he was wearing a leather breastplate. Drawing his dagger, Eperitus cut the laces on one side and prised the armour away.

'Swim for the galley,' he gasped, pointing towards the mast still visible over the waves.

He swam on, not knowing whether the man had enough strength left to make it to the ship. He passed more men, all of them powerful swimmers, and pointed them to the galley. One called for him to turn back, but he ignored him. Now the cliffs were towering up on either side of him and he could see the destruction inside the harbour. A ship had crashed into the foot of one of the cliffs and was blocking the escape of two others behind it. Of the other eight vessels in the fleet he could see nothing but sunken hulls and here and there a mast protruding from the surface of the water. Even as he reached out and grabbed a piece of wood – the wreckage of a rowing bench – he witnessed a hail of boulders fall onto the remaining ships. The screams of the dying were almost unendurable, but he knew he had to go on. He had to do something.

A body bumped into him. He was about to push it away, then realised the man was still alive. His face was covered with blood and he was groaning with pain.

'Here, take hold of this,' Eperitus told him, guiding his hands to the piece of bench. 'Can you move your legs? Then kick out to sea. Odysseus's galley is there if you can reach it.'

Or at least he hoped it was. The man wrapped his arms about the wreckage and Eperitus swam on towards the nearest galley. The vessel had been holed by a rock and was settling against the bottom of the harbour. Grabbing one of the rudders, Eperitus pulled himself half out of the water and looked at the terrible scene before him. The surface of the water was covered with broken wood, shattered oars, sails, rigging, dead animals and the bodies of men, women and children. Many, though, were still alive, some swimming for the harbour entrance and others crying out for help as the harpoons of the Laestrygonians plucked them from the water.

A few Ithacans were still leaping from the sides of the shattered hulls as they sank. In the stern of the nearest was Selagos, with an unconscious Eurylochus in his arms. The Taphian jumped into the water, disappeared momentarily below the surface, then reappeared shaking the water from his eyes. Eurylochus bobbed up beside him, still unconscious, and Selagos threw an arm about him and swam with his free arm towards the mouth of the harbour. Behind them, on the narrow stretch of shingle at the foot of the cliffs, several Laestrygonians were wading into the water and pulling out the living. Some they tossed onto the beach to be eaten later or kept for breeding, others they sank their rows of sharp teeth into and drained their blood before devouring them. A few Ithacans tried to fight them off with swords or broken oars, but it was impossible to swim and wield a weapon at the same time. The Laestrygonians snapped their necks or crushed their skulls with heavy clubs.

As Eperitus watched, one of the monsters set his gaze on Selagos. With a roar, he waded out into the water towards him. Another followed, hoping for more easy prey. Eperitus felt for his sword and remembered he had left it on the deck of the galley. Then he saw a corpse in the water, its cold fist closed tight around the shaft of a spear. He reached across and pulled the weapon free.

The first Laestrygonian had reached Selagos, who released his hold on Eurylochus and turned to look up as it reached into the water and pulled him out. Despite his hatred for the Taphian, Eperitus could not stand by and watch him murdered. He tried to pull himself further up the side of the sunken ship he was holding onto, gripping the rudder with one hand and setting one foot against the submerged hull, while with his other hand he pulled back the spear and took aim. At the last instant he lost his grip and slipped back down into the water. Then he saw the gleam of metal in Selagos's hand. As the monster's long jaw opened to reveal gore-flecked rows of teeth, Selagos plunged the point of his sword into the roof of its mouth and out through the top of its head. It fell dead into the water on top of Selagos, who emerged a moment later wiping his eyes and choking. Immediately, he reached across and took hold of the neck of Eurylochus's tunic, pulling him back into a half-embrace as he continued towards the mouth of the cove, unaware the second Laestrygonian was wading through the flotsam behind him. Only when the giant's shadow fell across him did the Taphian realise his danger. He turned to face his pursuer – this time without his sword, which remained in the skull of the first Laestrygonian – and at the same moment Eperitus threw his spear. It found the base of the creature's throat and passed through his spine, killing it instantly. Selagos turned once more and began swimming.

'I'll help you,' Eperitus called to him.

'Help someone who needs it,' Selagos growled, and carried on alone.

Seeing another man struggling in the water, Eperitus swam to his side and hooked his arm around his neck. Behind him the cove still rang to the screams of the dying, but he accepted there was nothing more he could do. He only hoped Odysseus had not sailed beyond the reach of his remaining strength.

But rather than sailing away, the king had brought his galley almost to the edge of the harbour's mouth. Eperitus felt a surge of relief as he saw its hull and the rows of oars resting in the water, knowing that he would see Astynome again and that the gods had permitted them both a little more time together. Then a pair of strong arms grabbed at his tunic and started pulling him from the water.

'Not me. Take him first,' he protested, wafting a hand towards the man he had brought with him.

'He's dead,' said a voice he knew. It took his exhausted mind a moment to recognise that it belonged to Polites.

He slumped down beside a sack of grain and someone placed a cloak around his body. He fought the tiredness a moment longer and opened his eyes to see Astynome. Someone was shouting at the crew to row and he was aware of the creak of the oars in their leather slings beating an almost frantic pace. Water exploded behind the galley and cascaded down across the deck. More urgent shouts came from the men on the oars.

'Selagos?'

'Yes, we picked him up,' Astynome answered. 'And Eurylochus. And another ten at least. Men who would have perished if it hadn't been for you.'

'He shouldn't have abandoned them. We could have saved more.'

'He did the right thing, Eperitus. He came back and he stayed as long as he dared.' Another loud splash was followed by more water. 'But some of them have seen us and are throwing rocks from the clifftops. Odysseus couldn't have waited any longer.'

'No. We could have saved more,' Eperitus replied, his words slurred as he slipped into unconsciousness.

book
THREE

Chapter Twenty-Eight

SWINES OF MEN

Eperitus woke, his heart pounding in his chest and his breathing tight. A hand was on his shoulder and he felt the heat of a naked body beside his.

'Be still, my love. It's just a nightmare. Just another nightmare.'

It was Astynome. He raised his hand from beneath the blanket they shared and took her wrist, lifting the palm of her hand to his lips. It was warm and soft, a reassurance that the horrors of his dream were over. She raised herself on one elbow and looked at him, her black tresses spilling down over his chest and shoulder. It was still dark, blurring her features but not her beauty.

'I love you,' she said.

He smiled and ran his hand up her arm. He was conscious of the breakers lapping at the sand and the smell of the tall grass on the dunes that surrounded them. They had made their bed here after landing on the island two days ago, desperate for a place away from the others where they would not be disturbed. A place to find sanctuary in the intimacy of each other's bodies, to forget for a while the horrors they had faced. And as he looked at her he knew – as he had known when he had rescued her during the sack of Lyrnessus – she was the answer to his life's quest. What could glory and honour give him that a single glance from her eyes could not? What was a line in a song compared to a place in her heart? For years he had faced his enemies without fear, because there was little to lose and everything to gain in a courageous death. But she had given his life sweetness; made it worth living again.

He laid his hand on her ribs, his thumb stroking the underside of her breast. Lazily, still half-asleep, she straddled him and lowered her lips to his, her hair falling about his face like a curtain. Then she guided him inside her and they made love again.

The sun was already up when Eperitus woke to the sound of Odysseus's voice calling his name. He turned and looked at Astynome.

'Go,' she said, 'and not because he is your king. Go because he is your friend.'

She had a wisdom that his own pride denied him. Where he had felt nothing but anger at Odysseus's decision to abandon the rest of the fleet, Astynome had done all she could to persuade him he had taken the only option available to him. She had not witnessed the destruction and slaughter within the enclosed harbour, he had told her. He had not seen the bitter anguish on Odysseus's face, she had replied. When he had insisted that Odysseus only cared about returning home to Penelope and Telemachus – and had sacrificed his men for his own selfish aims – she reminded him that if Odysseus had sailed into the harbour the Laestrygonians would have destroyed his galley and all its crew with it. And if Odysseus cared for his family, did not Eperitus care what happened to her? How would he have felt if she had perished, or worse still if the Laestrygonians had taken her alive? Was Odysseus worthy of contempt because he had understood the futility of helping his countrymen, rather than allowing his heart to command his head? Indeed, the king had not abandoned hundreds of men to their fate; rather, he had saved a few dozen to make it back to Ithaca and preserve the memories of those that had died. And Eperitus had known she was right.

Odysseus called his name again. He dressed quickly and put on his weapons, then kissed Astynome on the cheek and trudged up the nearest dune. The Ithacan camp was some distance away, a dreary mess of despondent men and their captive women and children, many still sleeping off their exhaustion. The galley lay at anchor in the shallow cove, silhouetted black against the rising sun. Odysseus was on the beach below. His shield was slung across his back and he was leaning on his spear.

'Good morning! You know, you should sleep closer to the camp for safety. We don't know who or what lives on this island yet.'

'I don't want to know. The sooner we set sail for Ithaca, the better.'

'I agree, except we don't know where Ithaca is. And you and I are going to find out if there's anyone here to tell us.'

Up to that point only cursory patrols had been sent out to ensure there was no imminent danger of attack, but with the men's strength starting to recover the king had decided it was time to carry out a deeper exploration of the island. His spear over his shoulder, he walked off towards the wall of trees that hemmed the crescent-shaped beach. Eperitus looked at the mountain rising up out of the heart of the forest, its long arms stretching out in different directions to form undulating, tree-covered ridges. Here and there a spine of rock protruded from the trees like a watchtower, glowing orange in the morning sun. After wondering what new horrors the place would hold, he sloped his spear across his shoulder and followed Odysseus into the shade of the wood.

It took them much of the morning to walk to the top of the nearest ridge and climb one of the rocky heights. From there they could see they were on an isolated island with no other land for as far as the eye could see. Until that point they had found no paths nor come across any other signs of habitation, but as they looked down into the valley beyond – formed between the ridge they had ascended and another arm of the mountain – they saw a thin column of smoke rising from a circular clearing. It twisted its way innocently upwards, unaware and unconcerned that it was being observed from afar.

'I saw the same thing on the island of the Laestrygonians,' Eperitus said. 'What if there are more of those things here? We should go while we still can, Odysseus.'

'Go where? We can't spend the rest of our days sailing this other-world, from one danger to the next. For all we know, the makers of that fire could be civilised. People similar to ourselves who will help us find our way home. Are you willing to forego the chance? I'm not.'

He began the descent to the forest. Eperitus followed, though the going down was more treacherous than the coming up, especially with a shield on his back and a spear in his hand. But Odysseus's footing was as sure as a mountain goat, and Eperitus nearly fell twice in his haste to keep up.

'To march in on the makers of that fire will be folly,' he said as he caught up with Odysseus. 'You act as if you still have Athena's protection, but you don't. Everything that's happened to us since we left Troy has proved it.'

'Especially the massacre by the Laestrygonians? So you're beginning to think like the rest of the crew. Well, if you're afraid to come with me then run off back to the camp. I'll go alone if I have to.'

'Being reckless won't help. If you insist on investigating the smoke, then at least wait until we have a few more men with us. A couple of dozen should be enough; the rest can stay back and guard the camp.'

'No. Two of us can approach without being... Wait. What's that?'

He dropped to one knee, his spear at the ready, and pointed into the undergrowth. Eperitus adopted the same pose and stared hard at the area in the trees indicated by Odysseus. He saw it almost immediately: a stag moving slowly through the scrub, barely visible in the dappled sunlight except for the outlandish shape of its great antlers. It paused and turned towards the two men, and then with a kick of its back legs leapt away in the opposite direction. Odysseus sprang up and hurled his spear. The point hit the creature in the back and with a bark of pain it twisted and fell. The two men ran to where it lay, staring down at the magnificent beast as it kicked out the last of its life.

'By all the gods,' Eperitus exclaimed. 'Artemis herself couldn't have thrown better than that.'

'Perhaps she guided my hand,' Odysseus said. He knelt beside the stag and stroked its motionless flank as if it were merely sleeping.

'And you say the gods have forsaken me? I think they sent this animal to prevent us going to that clearing alone. Which means you're
right. We'll go back to the beach and choose a party of men to come
with us.'

The death of the stag seemed to have cheered him. He pulled his
spear free of the carcass and began stripping creepers from around the
trunk of a tree, weaving them together and using them to bind up the
ankles of the animal. With a grunt, he hauled it up onto his shoulders
and set off through the brush, using his spear as a staff. The journey
back was long, but he refused all Eperitus's offers to share the burden –
though even his strength was flagging beneath it – until they stumbled
out of the trees and found their way back to the camp.

Throwing the dead stag down in the sand, he looked around
at the pitiful faces of his men as they huddled together around their
fires, some of them returning his stare with resentment.

'The gods haven't abandoned us yet, my friends. Even though
our comrades are dead and have gone down to the Halls of Hades,
are we not alive? And as long as we live, then they live in us – in our
songs and the stories we will tell of them when we return home. Yes,
home. Or have you forgotten Ithaca in the depths of your pity? Have
you forgotten those we left behind, our fathers and mothers, our
wives and children?'

'I have,' said a man to Eperitus's left. 'Their faces, at least. And
the sounds of their voices. They might as well be dead.'

Odysseus looked at him for a lingering moment.

'But they're not, and neither are you. And as long as we still have
the blood of life inside us then we should make it our goal to return
home. There isn't a day – barely even a moment – that I don't think
of seeing my family again. Like you, I can barely remember what
Penelope looks like; and as for Telemachus, what chance would I
have of telling him apart from any other ten-year-old? They're like
spirits to me that flit about at the back of my memory, without face
or form or voice. But I know this: without them I am incomplete.
And when I succeed in returning to Ithaca, those spirits will take on
flesh and fill in the gaps that have existed in my life since we sailed

for Troy. Whatever you feel now, whatever emptiness is inside you, I tell you your self-pity and all the wine you can drink will not cure you of it. Only returning to our families and homes can do that. So put your mourning for your friends at an end and make Ithaca your goal, or die in the process. Now, fetch what wine we have left from the ship and use whatever grain has been spared us to make bread. The gods have given us meat. I suggest we eat it instead of dying here of starvation.'

The stag was large enough to feed all the crew and the Trojan slaves. Though they had finished the last of their provisions, there would be plenty of fruit and game on the island to keep them from going hungry as long as they remained. It also lifted their spirits to eat well, and the last of the Cicone wine – watered down with four parts water – was sufficient to have them singing and dancing around their fires until the light waned and evening dispelled any possibility of scouting out the source of the smoke that day. Again Odysseus had shown wisdom, for the Ithacans were still too broken to face danger again. But if he expected them to be in a much better mood the next morning, he was wrong. After a frugal breakfast of porridge on a beach wreathed in fog, he called his men about him and told them of the smoke he and Eperitus had spied. The very thought that the island was occupied provoked cries of dismay and even tears from some.

'Don't the gods ever tire of punishing us?' shouted Perimedes. 'What will it be this time? More man-eating giants? Another Cyclops? Yet another city of foes to ride us down in chariots bristling with spears?'

Voices were raised in agreement, especially by the group seated around Eurylochus.

'Listen to me,' Odysseus commanded. 'The truth is we're lost. We have no choice but to find out who lives on this island and whether they know a way back to Greece. But we won't make the same mistake as last time; we'll make sure there're enough of us to deal with whoever or whatever made the smoke, if they turn out to be unfriendly. We'll split into two groups. One can come with me into the forest to find out who lives there, while the other can remain here to guard the ship.'

'There are some who would have a problem following you, my lord,' Selagos said, rising to his feet. 'They say you're a curse on this voyage, that you bring doom to everyone around you.'

'It's true,' Eurylochus agreed, staring down at his sandals and refusing to meet his cousin's fierce gaze. 'The men are becoming wary of your leadership. Every decision you've made since we left Troy has been wrong.'

Voices were raised in agreement and some of those who remained silent nodded. Eperitus gripped the pommel of his sword, sensing that the crew had reached their breaking point.

'Really?' Astynome asked. The sound of a female voice among an assembly of men shocked them into silence. 'Is that what you really think, after he saved you from the Cyclops? After he won over Aeolus and persuaded him to give you a friendly wind home, only for you to let the other winds out of the bag and drive us all the way back?'

'Quiet, woman!' Eurylochus shouted.

'Astynome's right,' Eperitus said. 'And if Odysseus hadn't taken the hard decision to leave the rest of the fleet to perish beneath the rocks and harpoons of the Laestrygonians, we'd all have died with them.'

He glanced at Odysseus who gave a faint nod.

'Let Eurylochus lead us,' said Perimedes, his voice tentative and low.

'Aye,' said another.

'I'm with Eurylochus,' Selagos said, his usually hard face betraying the satisfaction he felt.

And to Eperitus's shock, Odysseus agreed.

'As you wish. We will split in two, as I said. One group will be led by me, the other by Eurylochus; one will stay and guard the camp, the other will go find the source of the smoke. Are we agreed?'

'This isn't a council of equals,' Eperitus hissed, leaning in towards Odysseus's ear.

'It is for now,' Odysseus whispered back. 'It *has* to be.'

Eurylochus, seeing the chance to establish his authority, nodded. 'Agreed.'

'Then somebody give me a helmet.'

A soldier removed his bronze cap and passed it to Odysseus. Picking up two stones from the sand, one dark grey, the other white, the king dropped them into the helmet and shook it gently from side to side.

'Choose a stone, Eurylochus. Whoever's comes out of the helmet first will lead their group to find the source of the smoke.'

'Grey.'

The stones rattled and one fell out into the sand. It was grey.

'Eurylochus will take half the ship's crew to the clearing in the forest and find out what sort of man lives there. The remainder will stay here with me.'

'This is insanity,' Eperitus protested, keeping his voice low despite his frustration. 'The man's an idiot! He'll either get everyone killed and we'll be none the wiser about who rules this island, or Selagos will convince him this is his chance to become king and overthrow you!'

'No he won't, because I'm going to insist that Selagos stays here with me. What's more, you and Polites are going with Eurylochus to keep an eye on him. After all, it's likely only a single dwelling. What can go wrong?'

Eurylochus was out of his depth. Though he insisted on leading the men Odysseus had given him, it was only Eperitus's guidance that brought them to the pinnacle of rock that he and the king had visited the day before. From its flat crown they could see the same column of smoke angling up from the clearing in the forest below. Eurylochus wiped his sweating brow and heavy jowls with the corner of his cloak.

'By Zeus, there could be a whole army of those man-eating monsters down there. We should return to the ship at once and tell Odysseus it's hopeless, or we risk being devoured.'

'Devoured by what?' Eperitus scoffed. 'You've seen nothing more than the smoke trail Odysseus and I reported yesterday. Whoever made it might welcome us.'

'Welcome us as food if our previous encounters are any measure. Carry on alone if you like, but I've seen enough.'

'We were ordered to find out who or what is making that smoke and that's what we'll do. Now, you can either lead us there like Odysseus entrusted you to, or I'll take command while you run back to the camp and show everyone what a coward you are.'

'So that's why you came along,' Eurylochus said. 'To humiliate me and take my place in command of these men, just like you usurped my rightful place as captain of Odysseus's guard all those years ago. No, *I'll* lead us to the source of the smoke and *I'll* bring us all safely back again, which is more than would happen with you in charge!'

Eperitus stared hard into his small, close-set eyes and felt the heat of his temper stiffen his sinews. But as quick as it came he mastered it again. He knew Eurylochus too well to fall into such a simple trap. One day he would go too far, but Eperitus would not let that day come sooner than it had to. For now he was content to bow to Eurylochus's temporary authority – and hopefully watch him make a mess of it.

The two men descended to rejoin the others waiting below and, with Eurylochus leading, set out in the direction of the smoke. It was downhill and all they needed to do was keep the sun behind them and follow their own shadows. Nevertheless, Eperitus allowed Eurylochus to lose his way two or three times – just enough for his sympathisers to get a taste of what life under his leadership would be like – before quietly steering him back onto the right path. Eurylochus resented the hints, but took them anyway, and eventually, with the sun climbing to its zenith, the dappled gloom of the forest was relieved by a growing lightness ahead of them. They had reached the clearing.

For some time, Eperitus had discerned the distinctive smells of herbs and garden flowers amid the savoury tang of smoke and the natural aromas of the forest. He also became aware of a droning sound pervading the birdsong and the wind in the trees. More concerning were the growls of unknown creatures, which became louder the closer they came to the clearing. Squinting through the trees at the open space ahead, he saw a two-storeyed house set in the middle of a wide lawn. Its walls were of polished stone that gleamed in the sunlight and a trail of smoke tapered up from an unseen hole in its flat roof. The porch was supported by four whitewashed columns entwined with ivy. Beds of wild flowers surrounded the building, some tiny and numerous, others tall and nodding. Together they formed a skirt of colour around the house that was only interrupted by the pigsties and other outbuildings that leaned in ramshackle disorder against its walls. There were several windows with white curtains blowing in the breeze and the air was filled with the humming of bees. After all Eperitus had been through it looked like paradise. And yet his instincts refused to lower their guard.

'It's just a house,' Eurylochus exclaimed, shielding his eyes as they left the shade of the trees. 'Though like none I've ever seen before. There are no battlements, no gates. Whoever lives here *must* be peaceful.'

'The Laestrygonians had no battlements or gates,' Eperitus said. 'They didn't *need* any.'

'Stay here and gibber about Laestrygonians if you want. This house was made for men, not monsters, and I'm going to see who lives here.'

He crossed the lawn towards the porch. Sensing all was not as it seemed, Eperitus set off after him, determined to reach the house before he did. The rest of the party followed.

'We're being watched,' Polites said, catching up with him.

'We've been watched for some time now, and not by men.'

As he spoke, a roar shook the air and a lion sprang out from behind one of the thick shrubs that dotted the lawn. Eurylochus gave a yelp of terror and stumbled backwards, tripping over himself in an effort to flee. The roar seemed to have been a command, for from behind the house and the other shrubs came more animals, with yet more leaping out from the eaves of the surrounding forest. There were lions with thick manes that trailed down to their huge paws and long-legged mountain wolves with open jaws and hanging tongues.

'To me!' Eperitus shouted.

He and Polites unslipped their shields and lowered their spear points as the other Ithacans ran to join them, forming a defensive knot amid the circling animals. Eurylochus struggled to his feet, but the first lion jumped and knocked him back to the ground, pinning his shoulders with its paws and lowering its face towards his. Eperitus's spear was poised to be thrown, but before he could launch it the lion opened its jaws and passed its tongue over Eurylochus's cheek. Eurylochus screamed, but was cut short by another sweep of the beast's tongue. Then, spluttering and spitting, he turned onto his stomach and dragged himself away by his elbows, scrambling hurriedly back to his comrades. Eperitus saw the dark patch spreading over his groin and realised with a smile that he had wet himself.

To the amazement of the Ithacans, some of the other animals rose up on their hind legs and began walking towards them. A wolf approached Eperitus, who raised his shield against it. It scratched the leather with its claws and there was the strangest look of sadness in its brown eyes. It seemed to shake its head, as if warning him away. Indeed, as it leaned its weight against his shield, Eperitus felt it was trying to push him back towards the forest.

'Lower your weapons!' he warned the others. 'Don't strike them, whatever you do. It's like they're –'

He fell short of what he intended to say, realising the thought was absurd.

'Listen,' Polites said. 'I can hear a voice in the house.'

Eperitus heard it at the same time. A woman was singing, the words high and clear and so beautiful that he forgot the beasts and turned to look at the polished double doors in the shadow of the porch.

'We have to get back and warn the others,' Eurylochus said. 'Whoever that is, these animals are under her control. Listen to me, we *must* leave before they attack us again.'

'Not until we find out who that voice belongs to,' Eperitus replied.

The rest of the party looked uncertain. Some gazed at the pack of wolves and lions, others turned to listen to the song floating out from the open windows.

'I'm in charge here,' Eurylochus insisted. 'Come with me now, you fools, or you'll be torn to shreds!'

'Torn to shreds?' Perimedes sneered. 'What are you talking about? They're more like dogs than wild animals. Look at them.'

'Eperitus is right,' Polites said. 'The lot fell to us to find out who's making the smoke. I say we finish what we were sent here to do.'

The rest of the party nodded, though some looked down at their feet and refused to meet Eurylochus's accusing eye.

'So be it,' he said. The animals were grouped between the Ithacans and the porch, leaving the way back to the trees clear. 'And may the gods give you what your insolence deserves.'

He ran to the eaves of the wood, where Eperitus noticed him slip behind the bole of an oak.

'Let's go.'

He led the men towards the house. The lions and wolves growled fiercely now and bore their teeth, but as he had suspected, it was more a warning than a threat. As the Ithacans fell beneath the shadow of the building, the brutes parted and scattered to hide behind the shrubs. Mounting the porch, Eperitus hammered his fist against the double doors.

'Come out! We mean you no harm.'

The doors swung inward at once, almost pitching him forward into the house.

'Indeed, you could not harm me if you wanted to.'

He looked up to see a wide, airy hall filled with sunlight that poured in through high windows. A long table stretched before him with high-backed chairs on either side. It was set with wooden bowls full of fruit and plates stacked with flatbread. Kraters of wine were waiting on the table and there were wheels of cheese and pots of honey placed at intervals up the centre. All the feast lacked was the smell of roast meat, but for some reason Eperitus was glad of its absence.

'Enter, my friends. You have faced many trials on your travels, but here you can rest. Be seated. Help yourselves to food and drink.'

It was as if a barrier had been lifted. Eperitus stepped into the hall and for the first time noticed the owner of the voice standing at one side of the table. She was as tall as he was, with white skin and full red lips. More striking still were her green eyes: large with dark lashes, it felt as if they were looking into rather than at him. Flowers were woven into her long red hair and she wore a green chiton fastened at her right shoulder with a brooch. It swept down below her left breast and gathered around her waist, but the material was so thin that her naked form was clearly visible beneath it. There were four other women around the table, all of them young and attractive, though clearly servants by their rough-spun garments and simple cloaks. Aware of the silence of the men behind him, he remembered himself and bowed low before her.

'Thank you, mistress. My men and I are in need of –'

'*Your* men? These men are no more yours than they are mine, though judging by the look in their eyes I would say they are more mine than yours. And we both know that you and they answer to the commands of another, do we not? Now, sit – all of you; I have prepared food for your arrival.'

All but Eperitus now crowded around the table and took their seats, some reaching straight for the wine while others served their hunger first with mouthfuls of bread and cheese. And all stared with a different kind of hunger at their hostess. She looked at Eperitus, still standing by the open doors.

'I see you are a lord among pigs. Do you refuse to sit because you are stubborn or because you distrust me?'

'I will let my men eat first.'

'They are not your men. Neither do they belong to the one who skulks behind that oak yonder. But, nonetheless, you are a lord. Perhaps you don't sit with your comrades because they disgust you.'

'Not all of them, my lady. Can I ask –?'

'When you have eaten you can ask anything you like, and any question you can put to me will be answered. But first you must eat.'

She walked to the far end of the hall where a small hearth was ablaze, sending a trail of smoke up into the rafters where it escaped through a square hole. A large copper pot was balanced on a tripod over the flames, and as she stirred the contents with a wooden ladle her maids brought her bowls of honey and cheese and a krater of wine. These she added to the mixture one by one, and after stirring the mixture again, she began scooping it into wooden bowls held out to her by the servants. These were carried back to the Ithacans who took long draughts accompanied by exclamations of approval and demands for more. But they each only received one bowl, and last of all one of the maids brought a bowl for Eperitus.

'Drink, my lord,' she encouraged him. 'It will make you feel yourself again.'

The bowl was warm in his hands and the smell of the broth was irresistible. He raised it to his lips and swallowed. It tasted wonderful, and yet as his acute senses appreciated the mixed flavours of the honey, wine, barley meal and goat's cheese in a way that none of the other Ithacans were able to do, so they could also discern a discordant tang. Something else had been added to the broth, something subtle, barely determinable. Something he knew should not be there. He looked at the servant girl and saw the wry smile on her lips. Immediately he spat what was left of the mouthful back into the bowl.

'Too late,' she whispered.

'Yes, too late,' her mistress said.

She was standing at the head of the table behind the shoulder of Polites. A gnarled stick, no longer than a dagger, was in her hand. Lightly, she tapped the knobbed end on Polites's shoulder. Then, passing from one man to the next – each looking round at her with a glance that drank in her barely concealed nakedness – she touched each one in turn with the stick. By the time she had reached the end of one side of the table and was passing back up the other, Polites was staring at the back of his hand in confusion. Long hairs were sprouting from the skin, and slowly, impossibly, his fingers seemed to be fusing together in pairs. At the same time, to Eperitus's astonishment, his arms seemed to be shortening. He slumped forward onto the table, knocking over his wine and scattering some bowls.

'What's...?' he cried.

But his voice was not his own. It was thicker, more nasal and, as Eperitus watched, his face began to change. His nose was turning up and at the same time growing larger, while the flesh of his face was thickening and his eyes receding back into the folds. By now the other Ithacans were undergoing similar transformations, some quicker than others. Many fell from their chairs under the table, where they began making strange squealing sounds. Like pigs.

'By all the gods, what have you done to them?' Eperitus shouted.

He leapt forward and caught hold of Perimedes as he kicked his chair back from the table and fell crashing to the floor. And immediately he released him again, crying out in disgust at the disfigured features and lumpish body before him. Looking up in confusion, he saw the woman staring at him in amusement, her arms crossed, with the curious stick in one hand.

'Stop this! Turn them back!'

'I shall not.'

'Why are you doing this? What have we done to you?'

'Done? Nothing, of course. You are simply men, and men like to fight and rut and dominate their packs. Just like animals. So animals you must become.'

'Give me that!' he cried.

He lunged at her, reaching for the stick in her hand. In the same moment a pig ran squealing from beneath the table and knocked him off his feet. His head hit the floor hard and he felt his vision momentarily blacken. Forcing his eyes open, he looked up to see the woman standing over him, the stick raised in her hand.

Then she struck him.

Chapter Twenty-Nine

CIRCE

Odysseus slapped his cousin hard across the cheek. The shock of the blow brought Eurylochus to his senses and he blinked at the king with tear-filled eyes.

'You're not making any sense. Tell me where the rest of your party are, at once.'

Odysseus felt sick at heart. Ever since the moment Eurylochus had come stumbling through the trees to the head of the beach he had barely been able to put more than two or three words together, and what he had said was all a nonsense about lions and wolves. But the fact that he was terrified of something and that he had returned alone of the twenty-three men who had left that morning filled Odysseus with misgiving for the fate of half his crew. After his experience at the hands of the Cyclops and the Laestrygonians, the single-minded self-belief that had brought him this far was beginning to crumble. And the thought that Eperitus might not be there at his side for the rest of the voyage home – if the gods ever allowed him to return to Ithaca – seemed suddenly unbearable.

He slapped Eurylochus again.

'We found the house, the house where the smoke came from.'

'Where?'

'In a clearing –'

Eurylochus pointed vaguely behind himself.

'And the others?'

'There was a woman. I didn't see her. I heard her though, singing to herself inside the house. And there were lions and wolves in the clearing –'

'*Together?*'

'Yes, but they fawned on us like dogs –'

'Lions grovelled to you?'

Odysseus looked around at the circle of faces. Eurybates swivelled his eyes and tapped his forehead, while Omeros just continued to rub his chin thoughtfully. Astynome, who was barely able to hide her concern, frowned at the mention of fawning lions.

'So they didn't attack you? Then what happened?'

'Eperitus wanted to find out who was singing. I knew there was something wrong and pleaded with them not to go into the house. But they wouldn't listen. Eperitus knocked on the doors and they swung open to reveal a woman and her maids – a goddess, I think. And that was the last I saw of any of them.'

'You mean you ran away,' Eurybates said.

'Of course not! I waited, but when the doors opened again – it was the strangest thing – out came a herd of pigs! She drove them into a sty at the side of the house, threw them some food and went back inside. I didn't see anything else after that, not a sign of our own men. And I stayed behind that tree a long time, though the thought of those lions and wolves terrified me.'

'Here,' Odysseus said, pouring him a cup of wine. 'You did your best, Eurylochus, but now you must be brave once more. Omeros, pass me my sword and bow.'

'Once more? What do you mean once more?'

'I'm going to the house and you're coming with me to show the way.'

'*With* you?' Eurylochus dropped the cup in the sand and threw himself at Odysseus's feet, wrapping his arms about his legs in supplication. 'Please, no,' he sobbed. 'I've had enough. Can't you see I've had enough? And you'll not escape their fate. Whatever happened to the rest of them will happen to you – you'll not bring any of them back again. We should leave this place at once and sail on –'

'Go if you must,' Selagos said, peeling Eurylochus's arms from around Odysseus's legs, 'but leave Eurylochus here. He'll be no good to you anyway.'

'Very well, then, I'll go alone.'

'Take me,' said Elpenor, who until that point had sat quietly at Omeros's side. 'I'll go with you.'

Odysseus shook his head.

'Stay here, lad. I wanted Eurylochus to show me the way, but I can just as easily follow the smoke. Other than that, this is a job for one man.'

'You're being reckless, Odysseus,' Eurybates chided him. 'It's late afternoon already. Wait until the morning and a few of us will come with you.'

'The morning might be too late. Take charge of the camp, my friend, and if I'm not back by midday tomorrow then sail without me. Those are my orders.'

'You say that every time.'

'And every time I come back, don't I?'

Dusty beams of sunlight angled down through the trees and lit up the patches of small white flowers that carpeted the woodland floor. The smell of smoke was growing stronger and, though there was no path that he could find through the undergrowth, he knew he was nearing his goal. He became aware of a distant humming, which aroused his curiosity for a while before his thoughts returned to the fate of his men, and in particular Eperitus. Without half his crew the return home would be more difficult, but still possible; without Eperitus, it would be possible but incomplete. He was more than just a comrade in arms; he was a part of Odysseus's identity. Eperitus had been there with him through all the triumphs and tragedies of his life. He was a living link to all he had ever done, a part of his past that was with him every day. And he was just as essential to his future. With the daily dangers of the war behind them and home – possibly – just over the next horizon, he was suddenly conscious of how much he needed his friend. Eperitus was not just his right hand, but his conscience; like a polished brass mirror that reflected his virtues and his vices. Eperitus kept the excesses of his character in check and reinforced his qualities, and without him he knew he was lost.

'Are you lost, my lord?'

Odysseus jerked his sword from its scabbard and turned. A man stood a short distance away, silhouetted by a shaft of golden sunlight.

'Who are you?'

'A friend.'

'Elpenor?'

Odysseus shielded his eyes against the light and saw that it was, indeed, the young Ithacan, though he had exchanged his usual brown cloak for a black one – a garment so black that no light seemed able to rest on it; as if a hole had been torn in the living world to reveal the darkness of Hades beneath – and his naïve expression had been replaced with one of weariness with the world.

'I've come to help you, my lord.'

'If I'd wanted your help I wouldn't have ordered you to remain with the others.'

Elpenor allowed the allusion of a smile to touch his sad face.

'But you do need my help. The woman you seek is called Circe, a sorceress whose power you cannot begin to imagine.'

'How can you know that?'

'And Athena told me you were intelligent.'

Odysseus's eyes narrowed at the mention of the goddess's name. Then he looked at the young man walking in a slow circle around him, his cloak like night as it flowed around his ankles, and saw that his sandals were flanked on both sides with wings – not fastened on to satisfy some strange quirk of the wearer's character, but living wings that flexed as if restless for flight. Immediately he fell to his knees and covered his head with his hands.

'My lord Hermes.'

For the first time in as long as he could remember, Odysseus felt fear; as far as most mortals were concerned, Hermes had but one purpose.

'Don't be afraid, King Odysseus. I have not come to guide your soul to the Underworld. Your life is still yours – at least for now. If you want matters to remain that way, you'd do well to regain your feet and listen to what I have to tell you.'

Odysseus had seen gods in their full glory before and had little desire to do so again. Cautiously he tilted his head upwards and opened an eye. Hermes, though, had retained his disguise as Elpenor. He rose to his feet.

'What has happened to my men?'

'They live, though you would not recognise them. This island is full of creatures that were once men, but whom Circe has transformed into representations of their true selves. Some were foolish enough to threaten her.'

'And the rest?'

'It amused her, I think, to keep them as her pets. Pirates became wolves, proud sailors of Phaeacia she turned into lions, others became donkeys or stags as befitted their characters. And what, I wonder, might you have become, Odysseus? A king among the lions – or a prince among snakes?'

Odysseus gave him a sharp look.

'Were *all* the animals on this island once men?'

'Perhaps you are thinking of the stag you shot yesterday?' Hermes answered with a slight grin. 'All I can tell you is that not all are, and those that drank of Circe's potion tend to stay close to her house. Like dogs faithful to their mistress.'

'And what of my crew?'

'Pigs, I'm afraid. The sorceress has a way of understanding men.'

'But there must be a way to release them from the spell.'

Hermes nodded.

'It will not be easy. Only Circe can undo her own magic and she will not do it under threat. You must win her over, Odysseus, and *not* by trickery. First she will try to add you to her menagerie, so you must protect yourself.'

'How?'

'With these.'

He indicated the carpet of white flowers that pushed up through the dirt, grass and fallen leaves of the forest floor. Odysseus stooped to pick one.

'Stop!' Hermes warned, placing his hand on Odysseus's shoulder. 'It is not safe for mortals to pluck moly. Aphrodite and Circe detest each other, so the goddess placed these flowers here as antidotes against Circe's magic for anyone who eats them. As soon as Circe realised this, she knew she could not remove them against Aphrodite's will so she enchanted them instead. Any mortal who pulls up the moly flower will forget who he is at once.'

Hermes bent down and grasped the stem of one of the plants, tugging it out of the soil with a gentle flick of his wrist. He held it out before Odysseus, who looked at its spindly black roots with distrust.

'It's quite safe,' the god reassured him.

'Is there an alternative?'

'Of course. Circe's magic cannot transform those of pure intent. If you approach her with honesty and tell her you want your men back, keeping no other desires hidden in your heart, her potion will fail.'

'And if she refuses my request?'

'You will have to return to your galley and sail away with only half your crew.'

'Then give me the moly,' Odysseus said, holding his hand out.

Hermes laid the delicate plant on his extended palm and looked him in the eye.

'Once you have eaten the herb – the whole herb, mind you – you will be safe from her magic. But you still have to persuade her to turn your crew back to their normal selves. After you have drank her potion she will strike you with her wand. When you remain in your natural form, she will think you are a man of pure heart – the one she has been waiting for all these years on her lonely island. Then she will offer herself to you. Do *not* refuse to sleep with her. It is dangerous for any mortal to refuse the advances of a demigod, but if you want your men back you must give her what she wants. First make her swear an oath by all the Olympians that she will not try to turn you or any of your men into animals again, then it will be safe to lie with her.'

'And if I don't want to lie with her?'

'Then your crew will stay swine until the ends of their days,' Hermes replied, turning to leave. 'Odysseus, you must decide between restoring your men and remaining true to Penelope. Choose the former and they may help you find your way back to Ithaca and the woman your heart truly desires; choose the latter and your return may not happen at all. What's more, only Circe can tell you how to get back home. She will not share that information with you if you deny yourself to her. Good luck, Odysseus.'

Odysseus watched him wander off through the trees until his black cloak had blended completely with the deepening shadows. Then he looked down at the moly in his hand. More than most he knew the help of the gods came at a price, but this time they were asking too much. For a moment he was tempted to toss the little herb away. And yet if Hermes himself had chosen to intervene it was unlikely there was another way to defend himself from Circe's magic. As for his men, his cunning had helped him through worse trials before and would serve him again now, without the need to betray his wife.

Quickly he put the herb in his mouth and chewed. The taste was bitter and he had to close his eyes and force it down. When he opened them again he caught a flash of white through the trees. A little further on was a clearing with a stone house. Smoke was rising from the roof, and at once Odysseus knew it was the house Eurylochus had described. He ran to the edge of the glade, where lions and wolves were lying on the grass before the portico. Several sties stood at the side of the house. In one he could see a crowd of pink backs jostling against each other. The sound of grunting and snuffling cut to his heart and brought tears to the corners of his eyes. Grim-faced with determination, he strode across the lawn towards the house. The lions and wolves sprang up at his approach and some walked towards him on their hind legs, just as Eurylochus had described. They reminded him of trained bears, evoking nothing, but as they tried to crowd him away from the house, he pushed through them and took the steps up to the covered porch.

Two large doors of polished wood stood before him. Somewhere inside, a woman was singing. He hesitated a moment, then beat the heel of his fist three times against the doors. The singing stopped at once and for while he wondered if he had scared the occupant into hiding. Then the doors swung open to reveal a woman with pale skin and long red hair. She wore a green chiton that left one breast exposed and through which her naked body was clearly visible. Her beauty – like all who had been touched with the blood of the immortals – was flawless and striking, and her large green eyes were entirely without fear as they regarded him.

'Welcome stranger,' she said, turning and moving to a long table set for one. 'Come in and eat with me.'

Her words seemed to compel him, and as he walked forward she pulled round a chair and invited him to sit. He fought against the desire to obey her and remained standing.

'I've come to find my men,' he began, clumsily. Something about the presence of the woman fogged his thoughts and it was as much as he could do to blurt out the first words that came into his head. 'I sent half my crew to investigate a pillar of smoke I had seen rising from the forest. We are lost and our voyage has been long and arduous to the point of despair, so I had hoped they would find a ready welcome and a place for us all to seek respite. But only one returned.'

'What did he say?'

'That his comrades entered this house and never came out again.'

'And yet you have come alone. Are you not afraid of succumbing to the same fate as the others?'

'Of course, but that doesn't mean I should abandon them to it. Are they here?'

'They are my guests.'

'Then bring me to them at once,' Odysseus asserted.

Circe smiled.

'You will be reunited with them soon enough. But first, sit down and rest from your troubles while my maids prepare you a broth. Though I am but a woman,' she demurred, 'I will not have it said I am a poor host. When you have eaten we can talk more about these men of yours.'

She pointed at the silver-studded chair and this time he sat. A young woman brought a footstool and lifted his feet onto it, while Circe went to the hearth and spooned a steaming liquid from a cauldron into a golden bowl. She carried it to him and placed it in his cupped hands.

'Drink, stranger, and put your burdens aside while you can. Then I will bring you to your comrades.'

As she spoke, her hand reached out and found a gnarled stick that had been lying on the seat of a chair. Odysseus felt the warmth of the bowl against the palms of his hands and smelled the rich aromas wafting up from the broth, powerfully alluring despite the dangerous drug that he knew it contained. Not wishing to arouse Circe's suspicions, he pushed aside his hesitation and raised the bowl to his lips. It was hot but drinkable and the taste and feel of it as he swallowed soothed away the tiredness that had hung about his limbs like leaden weights for weeks. He took another mouthful, then placed the bowl on the table and looked up at Circe. She was smiling, but there was no warmth in her expression. Instead her beautiful features were hard and cold as she raised her stick and struck him on the shoulder.

'Your wish is granted, stranger. Go join your friends in the pigsty.'

Odysseus hesitated, half expecting to feel the first pains of the unnatural transformation Circe had intended for him. But when no signs of change came, and when he saw Circe's look of triumph turn to doubt and confusion, he reached for his sword and drew it. Realising her magic had not worked, she looked down at his blade and stumbled backwards.

'What kind of man are you that you can drink my potion and be touched by my wand but retain your human form?'

'Not the kind you can turn into a lion or a wolf, or indeed a pig!' he answered, stepping towards her.

'But I have the power to turn *any* man into a reflection of his true self,' she insisted. 'Unless... unless you are the one I was told to expect: a man whose noble character would be able to resist my enchantments.'

Odysseus's mouth was touched by a sneer. 'All men are animals at heart, even if their souls struggle against the yearnings of their inner nature. Now, take me to my men and release them from your spell.'

Despite her shock at the failure of her magic, she looked at him and laughed.

'They are what they were meant to be, and the threat of your sword won't save them from that.'

He lunged forward and seized her by the hair, forcing her down onto the table and pressing the edge of his weapon against her soft white throat.

'Do as I tell you!'

She glowered up at him, half in pain, half in anger. He could feel the soft warmth of her body beneath him as she struggled against his greater bulk. One hand gripped his wrist while the other still clung to the gnarled wand.

'You seem to forget I am not a mortal. If you harm me, all you will do is invoke my anger Not that you *can* harm me!'

She struck his sword with her wand. He felt the pommel go soft and pliant in his hand and, looking down, saw that he was holding a blood-red snake. It hissed loudly as it curled round to face him, its long fangs and flickering tongue hideous and threatening. He reeled back in shock and threw the serpent onto the table. It clattered loudly across the surface, a sword once more.

'What is your name?' Circe asked, pushing herself up from the table with her elbows.

Her hair had come loose and lay tangled across her chest, while the skin of her neck was marked red where Odysseus had pressed his sword against it. He watched her chest rising and falling rapidly and saw that the blood had risen to her white cheeks, but if anything she looked more beautiful in her vulnerability than she had with all the self-confidence of her powers. He offered her his hand and pulled her to her feet.

'I am King Odysseus of Ithaca, son of Laertes. My men and I mean no harm to you. We simply want to return home.'

She drew close and took his hand, entwining her fingers with his.

'Many men have come to my shores over the years, but none like you. In all that time I have slept alone, waiting and suffering, surrounded by those who failed the test. You did not fail.'

Odysseus drew back and shook his hand from hers.

'My lady, I too have spent years sleeping alone, keeping myself for the one whom destiny has chosen for me. But I am not the one you are waiting for.'

'You *are* the one, Odysseus, and has not your destiny brought you here? Come to bed with me and end this emptiness we both feel.'

'You ask me to treat you with the tenderness of a lover, and yet you have acted with nothing but contempt towards me. First you use your magic on my men, then you try the same with me. But by the will of the gods you have failed. Now, restore my men to me and tell us how to return to Ithaca and we will honour you with half the treasures we've brought back with us from Troy.'

Circe smiled and drew close again, taking his hand and holding it against her hip.

'What need do I have for gold, or copper cauldrons, or slaves? Everything I require is on this island, and I have my nymphs to serve me. No, there is but one thing you can offer me, Odysseus. Sleep with me and your men will be freed. Deny me,' she added, taking his hand again and leading him towards a door at the far end of the room, 'and they will remain swine forever.'

Odysseus followed her like an animal being led to water. The intelligence that had always offered him a solution to every challenge now seemed lost in an impenetrable fog. In twenty years he had never once betrayed Penelope's trust in him, though as a king he could have taken any woman he wanted and she would have been powerless to stop him. Their marriage, though, had not been founded on a need for wealth or alliances, or to establish power; indeed, he had spurned Helen and her father's kingdom of Sparta with her, just to be with Penelope. And while he had not seen her for half of their married years, the love that had bound him to her had never waned or been displaced by desire for another. But the choice now was not between one love and another, or between love and lust; it was between faithfulness to Penelope and the lives of his men; between struggling on with half a crew through a nether-world that offered no escape, or having a full complement of sail-ors and the help of a sorceress who, Hermes had said, could tell him how to return to Ithaca; between an ever diminishing hope of seeing his family again, and the near certainty of it. Even if he could bring himself to abandon twenty men who had proved their disloyalty again and again since leaving Troy, what of Eperitus and Polites? In particular, how could he abandon his one true friend: the man who had stood by him in everything, saving his life on countless occasions, not to mention his honour, sanity and sense of humanity? He could not. If he wanted Eperitus back, if he ever wanted to see Penelope and Telemachus and Ithaca again, what choice did he have?

The nymphs who served Circe looked on in silence as their mistress opened the door and led him from the hall. Odysseus now found himself in a long corridor lit by a series of tall windows on one side. She led him without pausing to a flight of stone steps that led to another passageway on the floor above. Soon they were standing before a door, which she pushed open to reveal a large, airy bedroom. White curtains floated inwards on the back of a faint breeze, grop-ing, it seemed, for the fur-covered bed in the centre of the room. Pots of flowers of every colour were set on the furniture and on the floor against the walls, filling the chamber with heady scents that were as potent as Circe's magic. Shutting the door behind them, she began to pluck at the laces along the sides of his breastplate, her fingers as nervous and clumsy as a virgin's. Giving up halfway down, she took her wand from the cloth sash about her waist and ran it down the sides of his armour. It fell to the floor with a clatter and was followed by her wand and sash.

She fumbled now with the brooch that held his cloak, the same brooch that Penelope had fastened with such ease the day he had parted for Troy. It depicted a dog killing a faun. If Circe's magic had worked on him, would he have been turned into a dog, he wondered? Placing his hand on hers, he loosened the pin that had become so bent and awkward after ten years of war. He pulled off his cloak and folded it gently before placing it on the floor by her feet.

'She gave you that, didn't she?' Circe said. 'The one you've been waiting for.'

He answered with a nod.

'You will soon forget her,' she added.

With a touch of her fingertips her chiton fell away to form a pool around her ankles. She stepped free and kicked it aside so that it covered Odysseus's cloak and its golden brooch. When he refused to look at her nakedness and instead gazed past her shoulder to the window, she lifted her hands to his head and pulled it downward.

'Look at me, Odysseus. Am I not more beautiful than her?'

'I have no memory of what she looks like,' he whispered.

She draped her arms about his shoulders and placed her lips upon his. They were warm and moist and he could feel the soft swell of her breasts as she pressed her body against his. He began to feel the first stirrings of lust and hated himself for his disloyalty. She reached down and tugged his tunic up over his head and arms, before tossing the garment aside and wrapping her arms about his naked body. Now he could feel his skin against hers, that intimate heat that he had not experienced for so long.

'Make love to me now,' she insisted, her voice nervous with anticipation. 'Give me what I want.'

'You must promise to give me back my men.'

'I promise,' she said, pressing her lips against his again, more urgently this time.

He pulled away. The passion in her eyes was now tinged with anger.

'Swear that you will not try to turn me or any of my men back into animals? And that you will help us to find our way back to Ithaca.'

'Yes! Yes, of course,' she assured him. 'You will be my guests, all of you. You will stay here for as long as you need, until you recover your strength and have a mind to resume your voyage. But first you must earn my hospitality, Odysseus. I am ready.'

She pulled him towards the bed.

'Swear it by the Olympians, Circe.'

'I swear it,' she said, pulling him down onto the furs.

Chapter Thirty

PENELOPE AND ANTINOUS

The news that the war was over and Odysseus was coming home had fallen on Penelope like a hammer blow. Her mind and heart had prepared for a long siege, believing her husband would not return to Ithaca for another ten years. So to learn that he was at that very moment sailing back from Troy was a shock she had not been ready to withstand. She remembered rising to her feet with her hand over her mouth, then everything going black. The next thing she knew, she was in her bed with a breeze blowing the curtains into the room and the scent of lilies filling the air. It had only taken her a moment to recall the news, and then she had leapt to her feet and gone running through the corridors of the palace shouting for joy.

That had been weeks ago and still Odysseus had not returned. Elation had turned to jubilant expectation, which in turn had become patient anticipation, but now was stagnating into desperate hope. Two and sometime three times a day she would climb Mount Neriton and look south to the sea that would one day bear his sail. Once she had even seen the broad canvas of a fighting ship in the distant haze, followed by glimpses of several more. When she saw what looked like a dolphin motif on their sails, she broke down in tears, sinking to her knees and sobbing uncontrollably into her hands. But when she had finally wiped the tears from her eyes and looked out again, the phantom fleet was gone. Unperturbed, she had rushed down to the harbour, waiting until long after sunset for the ships to arrive. They never did.

She had said nothing of it to anyone, not even Telemachus. But she had faithfully maintained her visits to the lookout on Mount Neriton every day since, longing for another glimpse of a dolphin sail. Though many merchantmen came and went, and two brought further messages of victory – one from Diomedes and the other from Menelaus and Helen – her husband did not follow.

Fortunately Telemachus was not disheartened. Ever since his fight with Eurymachus and Antinous he had been more confident. She was quietly pleased to see he had also made a new friend, Peiraeus of Kefalonia, and together they roamed the island with impunity, afraid of no-one. For a while even Eurymachus and Antinous had avoided them, fearful of what would happen when the king returned. But as the weeks passed with no sign of him, their old arrogance began to return. Behind her back, Penelope knew the women in the marketplace were talking about terrible storms sinking whole fleets, and that Odysseus and his men were among them. Indeed, the wives of those who had sailed with him now looked at her with animosity. Their own renewed hopes were fading and they turned their blame on her, as the wife of the man who had failed to bring them back.

She hid from their accusing eyes on Mount Neriton, where she sat now. The thatched canopy of the lookout post afforded her some shelter from the sun, but none from the biting wind that found every gap in her double cloak. She held it close about her and stared out at the surrounding ocean. It was early, so a few fishing vessels were still returning with their catches. To the south a small merchantman was beating its way up the coast. At the first sight of its sail – a dash of white against the beige coastline – her heart had beat faster. But long before her eyes could tell the shape of the canvas or the size of its hull, her instincts told her it was not him. And with the disappointment had come the usual bitterness. Where was he? Why was he absent when so many had returned? And all too often she asked herself whether he even intended to come back. In all the ten years they had been apart, would he have resisted the temptation of other women? It was a long time for anyone to go without the intimacy of sex, and every other man of power she knew of had their mistresses. Her father and her uncle – both kings – had not bothered to conceal the fact they slept with other women. Odysseus had always been different, but wars changed men. If he had found another woman, why would he come back?

'All alone?'

Penelope brushed the tears from her eyes as discreetly as she could. The voice did not belong to the old lookout, whom she had relieved of his duties and told not to return until midday. Turning, she saw Antinous.

'What do you want?'

'You shouldn't be here by yourself.'

'I've nothing to fear, Antinous. If you climbed all the way up here to protect me from the sun and the wind, I'm afraid you've had a wasted journey.'

'And has your journey been worthwhile, my queen? Is there a fleet on the southern horizon? Do you see his sail at their head? I imagine your disappointment is far greater than mine.'

'Don't mock me,' she snapped.

'It's the truth. He isn't coming. If he was, he'd have been here by now.'

He approached the open-sided shelter and she saw the dagger in his belt. He always wore it, she suspected, but she had never noticed it until now. She stepped back so that the thick posts that supported the canopy were between them.

'You should be looking to the east, not the south. If there's going to be a fleet that's the direction it'll come from, but it won't be Ithacan.'

'Still worried about your phantom invaders?'

'More than your phantom saviour. And when they do come Ithaca will be unprepared.'

'The Kerosia agreed to increase the militia –'

'The *Kerosia*! A bunch of old men with nothing better to do than play politics while foreign eyes watch our rich farms and fat livestock from the mainland, just waiting for the day when they can make it theirs.'

'You exaggerate, Antinous.'

'And you procrastinate, Penelope.'

'You will call me "my lady" or nothing at all.'

'Stop this dangerous game you're playing. Odysseus is not coming back. He's at the bottom of the ocean with the rest of the fleet, or he's in the arms of another woman –'

She crossed the space between them and slapped him hard across the cheek. His eyes flashed with anger so she struck again. This time he caught her wrist, crushing it between his fingers so that the pain made her want to cry out. Only her pride prevented her.

'Let me go!'

He eased his grip.

'You will marry me, Penelope. Whether ten years from now or ten days, you're going to be mine.'

'You overestimate your charm, boy.'

'I'm not a boy. You'll find that out one day. Maybe today.'

'How dare you? How *dare you*? I'd rather die than let you so much as touch me.'

'Really?' he asked, reaching up and brushing her shoulder where the cloak had slipped.

Again she tried to slap him and again he caught her wrist, forcing her arm downward and at the same time pressing her back against the post.

'The watchman will return any moment.'

'I hope not, for his sake. Marry me, Penelope. Make me king so I can give this island the ruler it needs.'

'It has a ruler.'

'You will give me what I want,' he snarled.

He grabbed her breast clumsily and tried to press his mouth to hers. She turned her face away and fought the hands that were on her body, but the power in his arms was too much. She felt his hardness against her groin, urgent and threatening with the strength of his desire. And then the force that drove it stopped suddenly. His body tensed and the lust in his eyes turned to quiet fear. The point of his own dagger was pressed against his crotch.

'You will not touch me again, Antinous. If my husband has not returned in ten year's time you will have your opportunity to marry me then, but not before. And if he comes back before the ten years have expired I will make sure he kills you for this. Do you understand?'

Antinous's eyes narrowed.

'Then you should understand this: Odysseus is never coming back. He's already dead.'

'What do you mean?'

Antinous stepped away and walked back to the edge of the steep hillside that led down to the town.

'Tell me what you mean,' Penelope insisted.

'I've heard that two assassins hide among his men. Neither knows the other and both have just one task: to slit the king's throat in the dead of the night. How's your faith in his return now, my lady?'

With a mock bow, he turned and jogged slowly down the slope. Penelope let out a scream and thumped the blade into one of the posts. Then she slid to the ground in a heap, sobbing quietly.

Odysseus had been dreaming of Ithaca when he awoke. He turned and laid his arm across the empty furs beside him, expecting to find Penelope there. He opened his eyes to the bright light of mid-morning streaming in through the windows. Then he saw the pots of flowers and the mural on the wall opposite – of golden men and silver women feasting on a long table – and he remembered that Ithaca and Penelope had been just a dream, a dream that his decision of the day before had turned bitter. He buried his face in the furs and wept.

Before long, the bedroom door opened. His body stiffened at the sound of bare feet padding across the wooden floor.

'Master, your bath is ready.'

He looked up and saw Clonia, one of Circe's maids.

'Will you come with me?'

He rose naked and followed her to a door further down the corridor. Gouts of steam wafted out as she opened it and inside he found a burning hearth with a bronze cauldron hanging over the flames. There were no windows in the room and it was hot and humid. A bath was in the corner, which Clonia had already filled with water from the cauldron and let cool to the right heat. At her invite, Odysseus tested the water and stepped in. Wearily he leaned forward over his knees and let the nymph pour warm water over his head and shoulders. A pungent mix of herbs had been added to the cauldron, and after a while he felt himself reviving a little, though not even Circe's skill with herbs could drive away the lethargy that had consumed his spirit. As he closed his eyes and tried not to think about what he had done, Clonia knelt down behind him and began to massage his tired muscles. When the bath was over she rubbed him with olive oil and dressed him in a tunic and cloak that she told him she had made herself. Then she led him back through to the hall where the long table was set for two. He sat down at Clonia's bidding, but there was no sign of Circe.

Another maid set a silver basin before him and filled it with water. As he washed his hands, a large, middle-aged woman he had not seen before brought him a selection of foods. She spoke roughly to him in a language he did not recognise, but when he showed no interest in her offerings she helped him to a generous portion of each before shuffling off to a corner of the room. Odysseus looked at the food before him, as fine as anything he had been presented with at Aeolus's palace, and pushed the plate away.

'Not hungry, my dear?' Circe asked, emerging from the door behind him. 'Not even after last night's exertions?'

She sat down opposite him and leaned her chin on her hands, gazing at him until he eventually returned her stare. Her normally white cheeks were flushed pink and there was a light in her eyes that had been absent when she had welcomed him yesterday. She smiled as he looked at her, an easy smile that recognised the intimacy they had shared, but which also sprang up from a newly tapped well of contentment. Circe, it seemed, was happy.

'Come now,' she continued, 'have the gods struck you dumb? Isn't the food and wine to your liking? Or do you suspect a trap, Odysseus? Surely last night has shown you my intentions towards you are honest and good?'

'Perhaps your guest would prefer some pork?' suggested the housekeeper, filling Circe's plate with the same delicacies she had offered Odysseus.

Circe laughed aloud at the suggestion, before waving the woman away.

'She's joking, of course. Your men are perfectly well.'

'Apart from the fact they are pigs,' Odysseus retorted. 'How do you expect me to sit here and eat good food when my friends are wallowing in mud and snuffling at acorns?'

'Wouldn't you prefer to eat alone with me, rather than surrounded by a mob of rough-mannered sailors? Right now they're happy eating nuts and cornel berries; let them stay that way a little longer and you and I can enjoy breakfast together in peace.'

'I can't eat a crumb until I see my friends again. Nor can I take pleasure in your company until you have honoured your promise to me.'

'Very well then,' she said sternly, rising to her feet. 'You will have your wish. But don't think I will tolerate being ignored when your countrymen are with you again.'

She sat again and took his hand in both of hers. They were soft and warm and he was reminded of their touch on his body the night before.

'You won't ignore me, Odysseus, will you? I have waited so long for... company. Promise me you'll stay here on Aeaea with me, for a few days at least. It will give you and your friends time to recover – put your ordeals behind you and look to the future with renewed courage and hope. And it will gladden my heart to hear these lifeless walls echo with the sounds of human voices and the ring of laughter, and to have you here with me a little longer.'

Odysseus thought of Penelope waiting for him on Ithaca while he wasted time feasting with the woman he had betrayed her for. The bitterness of his treachery – necessary though it may have been – touched his heart and filled him with black thoughts. He had sold his honour many times over the past ten years to bring the day of their reunion closer, but he had never been unfaithful. And now that single remaining strand by which his humanity hung had been severed. He felt as if he was made of stone, and it was only by an act of pure will that he took her hand and lifted it to his lips.

'It will be my pleasure.'

Circe leaned across and kissed him on the mouth. Then, snatching her wand from her belt she ran lightly to the double doors and threw them open. She was gone before his eyes could adjust to the morning sunlight that came flooding in, though he heard her singing to herself on the lawn outside. It was a song from the heart, as joyful as he was sad, but it was soon lost beneath the loud grunting of a herd of pigs. The animals charged up the porch steps and into the hall, knocking over chairs and sending the servants scuttling into corners for safety. The din of frightened squeals filled the room and Odysseus looked on in dismay as the creatures that had once been his men rushed beneath the table and overturned furniture in their madness. For some reason he had expected them to retain some human qualities: perhaps a sense of misery at their condition, or a restrained dignity in defiance of their brute form. But they were just swine, as much beast as they had once been man. In a moment of horror he wondered whether anything of their old selves would remain when Circe transformed them again.

Bringing up the rear was a great boar, its skin and bristles as black as the others were pink, its tusks long and fearsome. Remembering the creature that had gored him in the leg as a boy, he stood in alarm, almost tripping backwards over the hairy bodies that crowded around him. But the boar did not succumb to the hateful nature of its kind and spring into a headlong charge. Instead it stood in the doorway, fierce, proud and noble as it watched the panicked chaos of its sty-mates. Circe appeared behind the boar, a clay jar in the crook of her elbow.

'You might prefer to look away,' she warned Odysseus. 'There is no dignity in the metamorphosis of an animal to a man.'

'Can it be as undignified as changing a man into an animal? I will watch.'

He sat and reached for the cup of wine, though he felt his hand tremble as he grasped it. Circe scooped a honey-like ointment from the mouth of the jar and knelt beside the boar, smearing it along the top of its head and spine. She repeated the action on the nearest pigs and then touched each animal with her wand. At first nothing happened. Odysseus looked questioningly at Circe, but she merely smiled back at him. Then the boar gave a strangled grunt and fell heavily on its side. Continuing to emit a deep-throated squeal, it kicked at the air with its legs and twisted its head sideways as if trying to get back to its feet. Odysseus held his cup tighter and forced it to his mouth. As the liquid touched his lips the boar gave a terrified grunt and almost rolled onto its back, making Odysseus spill some of his wine. Then it happened. The coarse hair began to grow and curl and drop to the floor. Its forelegs jerked forward, thickening dramatically as the trotters became fingers, twisting and grasping at nothing. The boar's back arched and its chest broadened. All the time its black hide paled rapidly to sunburnt white. Its back legs stretched out, writhing with pain as bone, skin and muscle grew rapidly to form human legs and feet. The squeals had become shouts now and all about it the pigs that Circe had smeared with her lotion were going through similar transformations. Odysseus looked on with horror, repulsed by the sight before him and yet transfixed by it; wanting to run to the aid of his men, but too appalled to leave his chair. All the time Circe had been moving among the remaining swine, smearing them with the balm and touching them with the tip of her wand until the floor of the hall was a living mass of contorting flesh.

The figure in the doorway – once the boar but now recognisably a man – lay curled up in a ball. His hands were over his head and his muscles were strained so that the veins stood out in thick lines beneath the skin. His bare flesh was still smeared with the dirt of the pigsty, and though naked, Odysseus recognised Eperitus at once. He kicked back his chair and picked his way through the half-formed bodies of the other Ithacans.

'Eperitus! Eperitus! Answer me.'

Eperitus turned and looked at him with dazed eyes. He recognised his name but seemed insensible to all else. Then, as Odysseus approached, he rose to his full height. For a moment it was as if a god had entered the hall. He seemed taller than he had been before. His skin was taut and the many scars that had marked limb and torso were gone. Even his face, which had endured the rigours of countless battles and many years beneath a merciless sun, looked as it had done when Odysseus had first met him, shining with the naïve zeal of youth. Then a shadow passed over him and he collapsed against the door jamb. He would have fallen back onto the porch had Odysseus not leapt forward to catch him.

'Eperitus, it's me.'

'Odysseus?'

The sound of his voice – the knowledge that his friend still recognised him – drove the despair of his infidelity out of him in a blast of sudden joy. He wrapped his arms about his friend and held him tightly, tears of relief filling his eyes. Then he stood back and looked at him again. The godlike aura had gone. The scars and the lines of experience had returned; the light of new life that seemed to have filled him had faded once more; but his friend was back.

'Odysseus,' he said, forcing a groggy smile. 'What are you doing here?'

A glance around the room followed. Then he beheld Circe and his memory returned with a jolt.

'You!' he said, tearing himself from the king's embrace. 'Where are the others? What have you –?'

'Look about yourself, my friend,' she said.

Slowly, the other Ithacans, the last vestiges of their porcine features gone, were struggling to their feet and staring blearily around at their surroundings. Some saw Circe and fell back, while others recognised Odysseus and came towards him with relief and joy on their faces. Before they could throw their arms about him, Eperitus pushed himself between them.

'Odysseus, we are in danger. That woman is a witch. Where is your sword?'

'His weapons are of no use against me,' Circe responded. 'Neither does he need them. None of you do. Odysseus has proved himself to me, and at his request I have made men of you again. You have nothing to fear now.'

Eperitus turned to Odysseus, who nodded.

'Indeed, you are now my guests,' she continued. 'If I was hasty in my treatment of you before, then forgive a woman acting in fear for the safety of herself and her household. Your master has convinced me that you mean no harm, so if you will forgive me then my maids will wash away the mud of the pigsty and dress you in new tunics. Then, after Odysseus has returned to your ship and fetched the rest of your comrades, we will eat together and hear stories of your adventures.'

She looked at Odysseus, who avoided her eye and turned instead to his men. Their faces were filled with doubt and fear at the thought of remaining in the sorceress's house while he returned to their crewmates. He raised his hands to calm their anxiety.

'Circe has sworn before all the gods of Olympus that she will not turn you back into swine, or anything else unnatural. She has also asked us to remain here on Aeaea while we recover from our tribulations. A few days ago not a man among you would have refused such an offer.'

'That was before she turned us into pigs!' Perimedes said. 'Besides, what value is there in the oath of a woman? She'll have us back in that sty the moment you're gone.'

'Then why doesn't she turn us *all* into pigs?' Odysseus asked. 'Why let me go?'

'Because she wants you to bring the rest of the crew back here and put them under her spell, too,' Eperitus said.

It was a thought that had occurred to Odysseus, but his instincts told him Circe would not break a promise made before the gods, despite what his men thought. He placed a reassuring hand on Eperitus's shoulder.

'I trust her, and you should trust me. Stay here and rest; I'll be back with the others before sundown.'

But his men were so afraid it took all his authority to make them stay with Circe while he returned to the galley. Even then, Eperitus refused to remain without him. If only to reassure Astynome – whom he knew would be torn with anxiety because he had not returned from the first expedition – Odysseus agreed to let Eperitus come, and together they set off through the woods, leaving their frightened shipmates behind.

On their return to the galley they were greeted with elation. Eurylochus had been busy spreading the tale of his narrow escape, so the sight of Odysseus and Eperitus walking across the beach caused an outpouring of emotion as tensions were released. Odysseus had insisted Eperitus say nothing about what had happened, and when the others were told their countrymen were being bathed and oiled by nymphs in preparation for a feast – to which they were all invited – they were easily persuaded to return with them to Circe's house. Only Eurylochus refused to believe Odysseus's story that the rest of the crew had received food and shelter for the night and that his earlier concerns had been unfounded.

'Don't listen to him,' he shouted as the others hauled the ship up the beach into the mouth of a cave. 'He may be king, but that didn't give him foresight to avoid the Cyclops's cave or the harbour of the Laestrygonians. Follow him again now and you'll be walking into another trap. I saw those lions and wolves with my own eyes, as tame as dogs and walking on their hind legs like men. Because they once *were* men! The woman in that house enchanted them and she turned our friends into pigs, too – though Odysseus must have given her something in ransom for his favourite henchman. This is a fool's errand and I can't be held responsible for what happens to you!'

'Are you calling me a fool?' Odysseus asked, drawing his sword.

Eperitus placed a hand on his chest and turned to the crew, who had stopped hauling the ship up the sand and were listening to Eurylochus.

'Who would you rather believe?' he asked them. 'Your king? Or a coward who ran away when he saw lions walking like men and wolves rolling on their backs like dogs?'

The crew laughed out loud and returned to their work. Later, when the galley was inside the cave and everything safely stowed, they followed Odysseus and Eperitus into the woods. Eurylochus sat on the sand and watched them go, until Selagos hauled him to his feet and forced him to join the exodus.

They found their crewmates on the lawn before Circe's house. Their limbs were clean and their hair and skin had been oiled. True to her promise, the sorceress had dressed them in new tunics and cloaks, and as they sat at a long table laden with food and drink it was clear they were all happily drunk. They gave a great cheer as Odysseus and the rest of the crew emerged from the edge of the forest. The memory of their metamorphoses had succumbed to many golden cups of wine, and as the Ithacans approached, several left their chairs and came dancing and singing towards them. The newcomers, though, with the exception of Odysseus and Eperitus, withdrew in fear at the lions and wolves that lay on the grass around them.

'Look,' Astynome said, hooking her arm through Eperitus's in surprise. 'Some of them are lapping at bowls of wine and chewing cooked meat like they were men.'

'They are men,' Odysseus said, overhearing her words. 'Or at least they were before the Fates brought them to Aeaea.'

Astynome was horrified.

'And you want us to remain here? This Circe – how do you know she isn't trying to lure us all into a trap? My lord, you say she has invited us to stay in her home until we've recovered our strength, but maybe she just wants to fatten us up before turning us all into a herd of pigs.'

'She won't do that. I have her word and I know she'll keep it.'

'How do you know?' Eperitus asked. 'What reason do you have to trust her? And if she agreed so easily to turn us back, couldn't you have pleaded with her for the rest of these poor souls?'

He gestured towards the wolves and lions that surrounded them.

'For one thing, Circe was not so *easily* persuaded. For another, these animals weren't part of the bargain.'

'But they were men, my lord,' Astynome said, 'just like you and Eperitus. They could think for themselves; perhaps somewhere they have wives and children who are awaiting their return. Isn't it your duty to speak with Circe about them?'

'Astynome, my duty is to *my* wife and son and to the men under my command. Even if I didn't have enough troubles of my own to worry about, the price for their freedom is more than I am willing to pay.'

His words were calm and controlled – as much out of respect for Eperitus as Astynome – but Eperitus could see he was angry. Astynome knew it too and with an apologetic bow she went to the rear of the group to comfort the Trojan orphans, several of whom were crying at the sight of the lions and wolves. Eperitus glanced at Odysseus and wondered what the bargain was he had struck with Circe. What had he given to free his men that he would not offer for the other wretches living under her curse?

Circe now appeared, dressed in a yellow chiton that trailed over the grass as she walked. Seeing the newcomers were afraid of the lions and wolves, she sent the animals yelping into the trees with a wave of her hand. Then she beckoned her guests – sailors and slaves alike – to the empty seats at the table. Eperitus hung back, but when Odysseus took an empty chair and made a show of biting into a leg of goat, he decided his place was at the king's side, come what may. He took the empty seat beside Odysseus and took a slice of bread from one of the many baskets. Sensing a presence behind, he looked up to see Circe standing there.

'There is a place for you on the other side of the table, Eperitus, son of Apheidas.'

She smiled as she spoke, but there was no warmth in it. Instead there was a strange compulsion in her voice that convinced him to surrender his place to her without so much as a frown. If he protested at all, it was to take a seat beside Astynome rather than the one Circe had indicated. Soon all the Ithacans were eating as heartily as if they had not seen food for a week. Circe's nymphs, led by her house-keeper, attended them with baskets of fresh food and skins of wine, refreshing the feast so that it carried on until the light faded and twilight shrouded them with shadows. Candles made from beeswax were brought so that the faces of the revellers were lit with a yellow pall, while behind them clouds of fireflies appeared in such numbers that Eperitus fancied they had been summoned by Circe. Then the moon rose over the treetops and bathed the glade in silver light. The Ithacans became steadily drunker, forgetting their hardships and the deaths of their comrades and filling the air with raucous songs. Even Eurylochus forgot his suspicions and eventually fell back from his seat unconscious. Only two men remained sober. From his place at a corner of the table, Eperitus refused the wine that was pressed upon him and drank only water from a skin he had brought from the galley, while all the time his watchful eyes were on Odysseus and Circe. It interested him that Odysseus, too, refused to lower his guard. He barely drank any wine, preferring to close his lips and let it spill down over his beard than let his senses be dulled by its effects. As the evening progressed he acted more and more drunk, singing along with the others and laughing out loud as he slammed his fists on the table. But if Circe was fooled, Eperitus, who knew him better, was not. He also watched the sorceress slowly submit to the wine. And with each golden goblet her guard fell lower and lower. Perhaps she thought everyone else was too drunk to notice, or perhaps she did not care, but what had begun with the occasional hand laid on Odysseus's arm soon progressed to a wrist draped over his shoulder until eventually she was leaning drunkenly against him for support, with her head against his and her hand in his lap. All this Eperitus watched with concern. Then, shortly after Astynome laid her head on the table and fell into the deep sleep of utter exhaustion, Circe cupped her hand to Odysseus's ear and whispered something that even Eperitus's hearing could not discern over the songs and laughter around the table. He observed Odysseus's reaction closely, but though the king had paused at Circe's words and his fool's mask had slipped for a moment, he said nothing in return. A little later, to Eperitus's satisfaction, he let his head fall to the table with a loud bang and began snoring at once. This elicited great amusement from those Ithacans still awake, but Circe's irritation was obvious. She shook his shoulders to no effect, then stood and bid her guests goodnight before walking – with the occasional stagger – back to her house. Eperitus suddenly felt very tired after his long watch. Content that Odysseus was safe, he picked Astynome up in his arms and carried her to the porch. The doors to the hall were open and he could feel the warmth of the fire that burned in the hearth. Piles of furs covered the floor, enough for every Ithacan and slave, and laying Astynome down in a corner he stretched out beside her and covered them both with one of the pelts. He had barely closed his eyes before he was asleep.

Chapter Thirty-One

CIRCE'S DECEIT

The feasts continued night after night, mostly in the hall where the Ithacans could easily find their furs when they had drunk too much. Eperitus noted no adverse effects on them, unless it was an over-hasty desire to remain on Aeaea and shun talk of resuming the journey home. At least no-one's features were turning pig-like, he thought, other than Eurylochus's, who had no need of Circe's wand for that. Indeed, the crew were losing the exhausted, haggard expressions that had haunted them after the disasters of the preceding weeks. The colour had returned to their faces and a fullness to their flesh, clear signs they had put their woes behind them and were returning to full mental and physical health. A few were beginning to look the way they had before the war, with the plumpness of well-fed farmers rather than the hardened physiques of soldiers.

But if his men were beginning to forget their ordeals, the island was having the opposite effect on Odysseus. Though he remained healthy and powerfully built and retained his warm, attentive and intelligent character, something had changed. When he spoke to Astynome and Omeros about it, neither could see it. But he could. A certain light no longer burned in Odysseus's eyes. His broad shoulders, too, seemed a little lower, as if they carried an unseen burden that had not been there before. There was an emptiness about him that worried Eperitus. But whenever he asked his friend what was wrong – as they explored the island together during the bright, cold days of approaching winter – Odysseus would say he was imagining things and quickly change the subject. Eperitus also noted that Odysseus no longer spoke of Penelope, Telemachus or Ithaca.

After the first week, Eperitus decided it was safe to drink the wine brought to him by the nymphs. It was not as good as the wine Maron the priest had given them, but it had a reviving quality that explained the rapid improvement in the crew's morale. Odysseus, too, soon gave up his abstinence, choosing to get drunk every night to avoid Circe's increasingly obvious attentions. He never snubbed her, Eperitus noted, and was always careful to show her the closest consideration. But when her attraction for him revealed itself, he would whisper in her ear and she would restrain herself again. Then, one evening, Elpenor, who had a weakness for wine and was always the first to get roaringly drunk, watched the sorceress run her hand across Odysseus's chest and down to his thigh. Leaning across the table, he pointed a finger at Circe and told her it was plain to everyone that Odysseus was not going to sleep with her. Silence fell, but Elpenor went further and offered to fulfil her needs himself. Circe leapt to her feet and pulled out her wand. In the same instant Odysseus's hand shot up and snatched it from her fingers. Whatever fate he had saved Elpenor from, no-one ever found out, for their hostess turned on her heel and marched out of the hall. Odysseus was equally incensed.

'Take him out and throw him in the pigsty for the night,' he ordered Polites. 'Maybe that'll remind him what will happen if he dares insult our hostess again.'

He left through the same door Circe had taken. Eperitus did not see him again until the next morning, when he awoke to find Odysseus on his usual pile of furs near the hearth. While the rest were still asleep, Eperitus put some bread in a leather pouch and woke Astynome. They left in silence and walked out into the forest. As the sun climbed higher, thick shafts of sunlight broke through the canopy, heating the air until it became unseasonably warm and they were obliged to remove their cloaks.

'Have you thought about leaving yet?' he asked as they strolled hand in hand through the dappled undergrowth.

'Leaving? But we haven't been here more than… I don't know – a couple of weeks?'

'I don't know either. That's the odd thing about this place. I know the stars are strange here, familiar and unfamiliar at the same time, but that's been the same since Malea. Here, though, I seem to have lost all track of the days.'

'That's part of the charm of this place. For the first time since we left Troy – no, since before then – I feel relaxed. We're safe. We have more than enough to eat and drink. Circe asks nothing of us, though I've offered to help. Her nymphs seem to manage everything by themselves. It's… magical!'

'That's what worries me,' Eperitus replied with a sigh. 'It's too good. The thought of setting sail again barely enters my head; it's easier to stay on Aeaea. Everybody's happy: Omeros plays his lyre; Elpenor gets drunk; Polites sleeps; and I just want to be with you. The idea of going back to sea and facing whatever else is out there… it doesn't even occur to me any more.'

'That's good, isn't it?' Astynome said with a smile. 'We're together in a place where the burdens of the world can't touch us. I've never seen you this relaxed before. And I like it, Eperitus. I *like* it.'

'I don't. I don't trust Circe and I'm worried about Odysseus.'

'I know you are. But you always have been! Perhaps the soldier in you can't relax his guard. You have to have something to worry about, so you fall back into old habits and worry about Odysseus when he's just fine.'

'Then why hasn't he mentioned Penelope or Telemachus since the night of the first feast? In all the days we've been on Aeaea he hasn't mentioned home once.'

'Where *is* home, Eperitus?'

He looked at her. She shrugged her shoulders and turned away, as if her comment meant nothing. Then she frowned a little and pointed.

'The forest is coming to an end. Come on, let's go a little further.'

She ran off, a white figure flitting from one shaft of light to the next. By the time he caught up with her the trees had ended and they were looking down at a grassy slope. It led down to a gently curving beach between two headlands. From where they stood they could see the shelf of yellow sand stretching out beneath the blue waves until it disappeared into darker water. Astynome looked at him and raised an eyebrow. At that moment, with the sun on her brown skin and her face framed by her long black hair, he felt she had never looked so beautiful. Then, with an easy movement of her fingers she unclasped her brooch and stepped out of her dress to stand naked on the thick grass.

'Come on,' she said, and ran down the slope towards the beach.

Eperitus grinned to himself and chased after her.

The journey back from the beach seemed longer. Whether it was the humid air of the forest or the fact he felt relaxed after their lovemaking, he could not tell. But as he held her hand in his and told himself he should be feeling happy, he knew he was not.

'What do you think of her?'

'Who? Circe? How am I supposed to answer that?'

'Just... tell me what you think of her.'

'Well, she's not like us. She's some sort of nymph herself, or a witch. I think she's one of the immortals.'

'And she wants Odysseus to sleep with her. I'm concerned that the longer we stay here, the harder it will be for him to resist her advances.'

'What do you mean?' she asked.

'Isn't it obvious to you that she's trying to seduce him?'

'Isn't it obvious to you she already has?'

Eperitus looked at her incredulously. 'Don't be foolish. Of course she hasn't. He would never betray Penelope.'

Astynome faced him and took both his hands in hers. The look of lazy contentment that she had worn since the beach was replaced with concern.

'Can't you tell? She may be a demigod or an enchantress, but she's still a woman and she shows all the signs of having –'

'That's ridiculous! What *signs*?'

'The signs all women show when they are with a lover. The way she can't stop touching him; that familiar light in her eyes when she looks at him; the fact he's the one man she doesn't regard with that remote pride she shows to everyone else. Perhaps it takes another woman to see it, I don't know, but he *has* shared her bed.'

'But why would he? I know him. Everything he's done in the past ten years has been to bring about the day he can go home to Penelope.'

'Maybe he's still trying to –'

'Why didn't you tell me this before?'

'I thought you knew.'

'You thought I knew and yet you didn't think I wouldn't have said something to him? And that's what I *will* do, Astynome, the moment we get back. I'll ask him to his face and prove you wrong.'

'Don't, Eperitus. Think about it. Why did he sleep with her? It's like you say: why after all this time would he betray Penelope?'

'He wouldn't.'

'He would for your sake. Why else did Circe turn you and the others back into men? Why not leave you as a herd of swine, to join the packs of lions and wolves and the gods know what else that live around that house? He did it to save you, because he loves you and without your help he knows he'll never see Penelope again.'

At last Eperitus understood. He understood the bargain Odysseus had talked about. He understood the price that had been paid and why he would not pay it again for the sakes of the other animals under Circe's spell. But he could not accept it. And he would not believe it until he heard the words from Odysseus's own lips.

The lions and wolves barely stirred when they reached the glade, content to bask in the early afternoon sun and whisk away the flies with their tails. Several Ithacans were lazing on the thick grass, listening to Omeros as he thumbed his tortoiseshell lyre and pieced together verses for the song he was working on. Polites, as ever, was at the young bard's side, along with Eurybates and Elpenor.

'Eperitus!' the giant warrior called. 'Come over here and listen to this.'

'Where's Odysseus?'

'Haven't seen him since breakfast. Sing that part again, Omeros, and see what Eperitus thinks.'

Omeros saw the urgency in Eperitus's expression.

'Odysseus is inside. Said he wanted to look at the tapestry Circe was working on.'

'Stay here,' Eperitus said, turning aside to Astynome. 'I'm going to speak to him.'

She slipped her hand behind his elbow and led him out of earshot of the others.

'Don't be hasty, my love. You judge everyone by your standards, but, remember, Odysseus isn't you. He has his own ways and his own version of honour, and whatever he may have done he did it for what he believes to be the best.'

'Treachery is treachery, Astynome, whether it's between a man and a man or a man and a woman. And if he has betrayed Penelope –'

'Betrayed? If he has betrayed her in body, he hasn't in his heart. What is he but a man swept along by the tide of events? Maybe he did fail Penelope, but only because he had no other choice. And before you condemn him, look first to yourself. Have you never failed anyone? You, the most honour-bound man I know. You know you have, because nobody can live up to your mark, not even yourself. There's no battlefield code to be adhered to here, Eperitus, only the code of friendship. And if your friendship is to survive, you *must* forgive him his weaknesses.'

She looked at him imploringly and as he ingested her words he knew she was right. For a moment, and he did not know why, she reminded him of Iphigenia. Her talk of failure made him think of how he had failed his daughter. He had failed to save her, failed to avenge her. But he knew he could not have done more than he had, not without giving up life itself. Was not Odysseus doing the same? Failing Penelope so that everything else could go on, so that one day he could be with her again?

Or had there been another way? Had he simply succumbed to lust? Was he any better than Eurylochus, Selagos, Little Ajax or even Agamemnon himself? Perhaps only one thing lay at the heart of all great men: themselves.

'Stay here,' he told Astynome, and he strode towards the house.

He found Odysseus exactly where Omeros had said he was. Circe's house was not large, overpowering and austere. It did not have stuccoed walls brightly painted with panoramas of warfare or scenes from the stories of the gods. Instead the walls were hung with tapestries depicting mountains and lakes, or woodland temples populated by animals. Rather than echoing with the booming voices of great men, the walls in Circe's house absorbed sound so that the feasts they enjoyed night after night felt more intimate, more like family meals than the formal interaction of host and guest. And each tapestry had been woven by Circe herself on the large loom before which Eperitus found Odysseus standing now.

The king did not appear to notice Eperitus's entrance. He stood alone, his hands clasped tightly behind his back as he looked down at the loom. On it was a new tapestry, almost complete, depicting a wooded island with a large house at its centre. A woman stood at the porch, tall and dark haired. At her feet were several animals that may have been wolves or swine, but the design had not been completed so Eperitus could not be certain. The woman's hand was raised as if refusing the creatures entrance – or as if casting a spell.

'It's beautiful,' he said.

Odysseus started. In that brief instant, with his guard down, Eperitus could see the burden that he carried clearly written on his features. He seemed to have aged, and even his slowly forced smile could not remove the years.

'Does she weave them all herself?'

'Yes, I believe so,' Odysseus replied. 'I've only ever seen her at the loom.'

'That doesn't surprise me. You just have to look at the tapestry: it's just Circe, alone –'

'Circe?' Odysseus seemed genuinely surprised and turned to look at the picture again. 'Strange, but I never thought of the figure as her. From the first moment I saw it I could only think of my wife.'

'Penelope? I thought you'd forgotten about her.'

'*Forgotten?*'

'How many weeks have we lingered here?'

'I haven't forgotten Penelope or Ithaca, though it seems the rest of you have.'

'Then what's keeping you from setting sail again? All you have to do is give the order and we'll obey.'

'I… I don't know the way. And the men still need to rest.'

Eperitus closed the fingers of his right hand into a fist.

'Or is it something else, Odysseus? Why not go now? Why do I see Circe in that tapestry and you see Penelope?'

'I don't know what –'

'Is it guilt?'

'Guilt?'

'Yes, guilt. Guilt! You've murdered, deceived and even denied the gods to get yourself this far home. And now you're an adulterer too.'

'*How dare you!*'

Anger flashed into Odysseus's face and every muscle in his hulking chest and arms grew taut. Eperitus met the king's rage with his own. All it needed was one word. One word to release his fury and end their friendship forever.

'Did you sleep with her? Did you sleep with Circe?'

Odysseus's eyes narrowed and he set his teeth in a grim snarl. Then, as suddenly as it had appeared, the fire that filled him went out. He took a step back, reaching for the loom to steady himself. His eyes were downcast as he answered in a weak voice.

'Yes. Yes I slept with her.'

There was no attempt to defend his action. No excuse that what he had done he had done for Eperitus's sake, or the sake of the crew, or even that he had had no choice if he wanted to return to Penelope. Neither did he declare his regret for what he had done. He had admitted his crime and there was nothing more to be said.

Eperitus's fists remained clenched, but his anger, too, had faded. No fire burned in Odysseus's eyes now, only the tears that had quenched it. Part of him wanted to strike Odysseus hard across the face, as if that would see justice done; as if Penelope's honour – like all honour in a hard world – could be restored by violence. But honour had nothing to do with it. Odysseus was a man, not a god. He had failed because the gods had abandoned him, and the gods themselves must take the blame. Who else was there?

He laid a hand on his friend's shoulder and Odysseus embraced him silently. Eperitus could feel him shaking with the strength of his tears as, at last, he was able to express something of his grief for what he had killed.

Astynome lay on her side, her hand on Eperitus's chest as it rose and fell in its slow, contented rhythm. She could feel the warmth of his flesh and the beating of his heart, and it made her feel safe. Safe from the world beyond the furs that covered them. Safe from what lay beyond the shores of Aeaea.

Her other hand was on her stomach, her fingertips pressing the flesh gently as she wondered how long they had been on the island. It was almost impossible to judge the passing of time. Spring seemed to have arrived early – or they had been there longer than any of them had guessed – for the woodland flowers had sprung up and the trees were starting to bud again, filling the Ithacans with new heart if not new vigour. For she was not the only one who had found her ease. All talk of resuming the voyage had died off. Perhaps it was for fear of the dangers they would face moving from one hostile landfall to another. Or perhaps it was because, like her, the others were happy where they were. Not even Odysseus seemed eager to return to Ithaca any more. He and his men would still reminisce as they sat around the feasting table each night, drinking good wine and eating richer food than they could ever have hoped for at home. As the merriment faded and sentimentality set in, they would talk of the people and places they had left behind. But they were looking backwards now, not forwards as they had done before they reached Aeaea. Eperitus had fallen into the same stupor as the others. He no longer mentioned the plans he and Astynome had made to start a farm on their return to Ithaca. More worrying to her mind, he had stopped talking of the children they had dreamed of having together.

The thought that he might no longer want a family bit into her drowsiness and pulled her back from the edge of sleep. For some nights now she had struggled to sleep. Raising her head from Eperitus's shoulder, she propped herself up on one elbow and looked about the room. The ashes in the hearth had died to a dull crimson and one of the tall wooden shutters that the nymphs were so careful to close every night had come loose and swung inwards, letting the bold light of the full moon spill into the hall. Then, as her senses were lulled again by the snores of the sleeping men and women around her, she saw a shadow cross the open window. It was only a fleeting glimpse, but it startled her to full wakefulness.

'Eperitus,' she whispered. 'Are you awake?'

He did not stir, a sure sign he was fast asleep. The same deep sleep that had taken him every night since they had become guests in Circe's house.

She thought for a moment, then lifted aside the furs and stood. The night air chilled her naked skin. Slipping hurriedly into her chiton and sandals, she pulled her cloak about her shoulders and moved to the doors. She opened them a crack and peered out at the brilliantly lit glade. Trees and shrubs cast long shadows across the silvered grass, but there was no sign of the lions and wolves that usually slept together in their packs on the sward. As she looked for them among the trees she caught a movement by the outhouses at the far end of the clearing. A hooded figure crept with a slow, halting gait to one of the doors, opened it and slipped inside.

Astynome's instincts told her that she should return to her bed, pull the furs back over herself and go to sleep. But instincts were natural cowards and she refused to listen to them, succumbing instead to the nagging voice of her curiosity. After a last glance over her shoulder, she stepped out onto the porch and crossed the lawn. The harsh moonlight left her exposed and a sudden fear she might be seen forced her to run to the nearest outhouse. It was the same windowless, single-storey building she had spotted the figure disappearing into. As she pressed her back against one of its walls she cursed herself for not having brought a dagger for protection. Nevertheless, she moved quietly to the door and saw that it had been left ajar. After listening carefully for a few moments, she looked in.

At first all was dark. She could see nothing and began to fear the figure was watching her from the shadows, perhaps moving its way invisibly towards her as her eyes struggled to penetrate the gloom. Then she heard mumbled words and a light flickered into life. It pulsed against the darkness, slowly expanding until Astynome was able to glimpse a hooded face and a pair of hands cupped around the base of a candle. Placing it down on a table, the figure opened a leather satchel hanging from its hip and removed what looked like a small wooden vial. Behind it, just visible at the edge of the circle of candlelight, Astynome could see the clay pithoi where Circe kept her wine. The figure pulled the stopper from the vial and poured the contents into the nearest vessel.

'Forget and be happy,' the figure declared.

The voice belonged to Circe. She returned the empty vial to her satchel and turned towards the door. Astynome moved quickly, slipping out of sight round the corner as the sorceress emerged from the outhouse and moved across the glade to the house. Astynome waited a while, then returned to the hall and the furs she shared with Eperitus.

Odysseus looked up at the night sky. The moon was out and great banks of silver-edged cloud scudded across the open expanse, sometimes obscuring the stars and sometimes opening up to reveal them in their thousands. At first glance they were the same constellations Odysseus had observed for years from the hilltops of Ithaca and the plains of Troy. But since being blown off course rounding the Cape of Malea they had changed subtly: a star brighter here and another dimmer there; one or two appearing where they had no business appearing, and others disappearing altogether; while some had shifted slightly, as if gently nudged out of place. To a sailor used to manning a rudder late at night the constellations were faithful companions that knew their place and their time. But not here. In this strange other-world, nothing could be relied on, not even the stars. And yet, as he waited for the last of the voices in the hall behind him to fall silent, he seemed certain of one thing. The stars were almost back to the same positions he had observed them in when they had first arrived on Aeaea. Could a year have passed already? The realisation left him cold. A year lost to Circe's potions, which had made it seem as if they had only been on the island a couple of months. Had it not been for Astynome following the enchantress to the outhouses and seeing her drug the wine, they might have remained on Aeaea forever.

He shuddered at the thought of not seeing Ithaca again; of not setting eyes on his wife and son, or ever returning to the happy life Agamemnon's summons had torn him away from ten – no, eleven – years ago. For a month now he had refused to let a drop of Circe's mellow wine pass his lips, resorting to his trick of letting it spill down his beard while feigning the descent into drunkenness. And gradually the memories of home had returned, reviving in him the passion to seek once more his kingdom and his family.

Voices rose in laughter from the house behind him. Three or four of his men at least were awake, prolonging the moment when he would be able to do the thing he had committed to do. He recalled how, at the feast earlier, Circe had taken his hand and discreetly placed it between her open thighs, below the table while the others had been busy with their wine and songs. He had resisted the instinct to pull it away again. Indeed, for a whole year he had denied the urge to spurn her advances, resenting the fact she was not Penelope and had no claim on his passions. Though he had lied to Eperitus, deceived Astynome's intuitions and given the rest of his crew the impression he drank himself into a stupor every night, he had shared Circe's bed on several occasions. The first time had been out of necessity, to save his men from spending the rest of their existence as pigs. But surrendering the final part of his honour that remained intact – his fidelity to Penelope – had broken something in his spirit. After that his resistance had crumbled. Sometimes he had succeeded in getting himself too drunk to respond to her advances, which now seemed ironic as her drugged wine had made Ithaca slip further from his heart. But too often her frustrated passion had turned to threats to break her oath, and all the time he was conscious of Hermes's warning that without her favour he would never see his home again. And so he had accepted the invites to her bedroom, promising to come to her when the last of his men was asleep. Tonight, though, would be the final time.

Again he heard voices from the house, but louder and clearer. He turned and saw a figure on the porch, closing the door behind him. It was Perimedes. Odysseus watched him approach across the lawn, weaving a wary path between the groups of sleeping lions and wolves.

'Here you are, my lord,' he said.

'Evening, Perimedes. Has our hostess run out of food and wine?'

'Has she ever? No, I'm hot and sweaty and need some fresh air. Not that it's much better out here. Feels muggy, more like a summer's night than early spring.'

'That's because it is summer, and late in the season, too,' Odysseus replied. He pointed up at the stars. 'Look at the position of Perseus and Andromeda.'

'The constellations here are different to the ones we used to know.'

'They move the same, though, and when we arrived on Aeaea, Perseus and Andromeda were almost in the same place they are now. A year has passed, Perimedes, and we've barely noticed it.'

Perimedes stared at the stars with a doubtful look in his eyes. Like the handful of other Taphians who had joined Ithaca's army, he was rough and simple, good material for a fighting man. Selagos, too, was an excellent warrior and would have been highly valued were it not for the look in his eyes. Odysseus had seen it too many times: a darkness in his expression that spoke of hatred; a hatred that was too deep to be born out of any loyalty he might feel for

Eurylochus. Not that Odysseus trusted any Taphian after they had helped Eupeithes usurp his father's throne.

Perimedes was standing beside him now, still looking up at the stars. Odysseus gave him a sidelong glance and caught him doing the same. Perimedes looked away again and as Odysseus's gaze dropped to the Taphian's side he saw the sword hanging from his hip. Suddenly he felt the absence of his own weapon, which he had not worn since the first few days of their stay at Circe's house.

'Since when have you felt the need to wear your sword here, Perimedes?'

'It's these beasts, my lord,' he said, hooking a thumb at the lions and wolves behind them. He settled his hand over the pommel of his weapon. 'The others say they were men before Circe turned them, but not me. I don't trust them, and you shouldn't either, or one morning we'll find you torn to shreds on the lawn.'

At that moment the door of the house swung open again, spilling a dull orange glow over the porch. A man staggered across the porch and leaned against one of the pillars, then after a long look at the two men on the lawn dropped to his knees and retched loudly on the grass.

'Elpenor,' Perimedes said. 'The boy's no good, no good at all.'

'He can pull an oar, and that's all I need him for now. Go see to him, Perimedes. Put him to bed and then get some sleep yourself. We'll soon be glad of all the rest we can get.'

Perimedes lingered a moment, looked once more at the stars, then nodded and strode towards the kneeling figure. Odysseus watched him take Elpenor inside and close the door behind him. After a while, satisfied that there were no more voices coming from the house, Odysseus made his way round the side of the building and entered by a back door.

The passageway was dark but for a single torch at the far end. He followed its light until he found the stairs that led up to Circe's bedroom. Another torch burned red in a bracket on a wall, casting its light over the two nymphs asleep on a single pile of furs beside the door. Odysseus nudged it open, slipped inside and shut it behind him. The solitary flame of a candle formed a small circle of light that throbbed feebly against the encroaching darkness. It filled the room with the odour of beeswax, through which he could detect the scent of Circe's perfume. As he entered, she rose from her bed and entered the circle of light. Her breasts were large and firm and the triangle of her pubic hair was black.

'You were a long time,' she said, laying an arm across her nipples and a hand between her legs in false modesty.

'I was thinking.'

'Of me?'

'Of home.'

'Home?' There was a hint of surprise in her voice. 'I thought you were happy here.'

'I know you've been drugging our wine, Circe.'

'I –'

'That's why I haven't drunk a drop for four weeks. And now it seems all I can think about is getting back to Ithaca again.'

She moved towards him.

'Why? What does Ithaca have that I can't give you here?'

'You know the answer to that.'

'And if I don't want you to go?' she replied, her voice stern and hard now.

He fell to his knees before her and wrapped his arms about her legs.

'You made me a promise, Circe, that the moment I was ready to leave you would help me find my way home.'

She struggled against his hold, but he refused to let her go. Fighting back his revulsion, he kissed her thigh – the soft flesh was still warm from her bed – slowly moving his mouth higher, kiss by kiss, until his lips pressed against her pubic hair.

'Don't leave, my love,' she whispered.

'You invited me to stay for a few days, but a whole year has passed. Circe, I *must* go home. You promised to help me.'

She placed her hands either side of his head and kissed his hair.

'I can't. For your own sake I can't. You don't understand –'

'You *swore* before all the gods you would tell me the way home. Do you, an immortal yourself, dare to break such a promise?'

She pulled his arms from her legs and knelt down to face him. Tears were streaming down her cheeks and there was a softness in her eyes he had never seen before. Then she kissed him, first on the forehead, then the lips.

'Son of Laertes, I cannot keep you here against your will. But I cannot tell you the way home. For that you must consult with the prophet Teiresias.'

She said the name with a shudder and turned her eyes away.

'I only know of one prophet by that name,' he answered. 'Teiresias of Thebes, but he died before the Trojan War. Who is this man you speak about? Where do I find him?'

'He is the one you know of, who died after drinking from the well of Tilphossa. He resides now with the spirits of the dead, though he alone among them retains wisdom and the ability to speak.'

Odysseus heard Circe's words, but it was as if she was talking to someone else. Then her meaning became clear and he felt the hairs on his arms stand up and his flesh go cold.

'If he's dead, how can I speak with him?'

'I tried to tell you, my love, to warn you that the path home is a dark one. If you insist on returning to Ithaca, you must first go down to the Halls of Hades.'

Chapter Thirty-Two

ELPENOR

Odysseus pushed aside the heavy furs and sat up. The little sleep he had managed had been fitful and disturbing and as he shrugged off the nightmares he recalled the horror that had induced them. The memory of Circe's words settled on him like a weighted net, constraining and inescapable. If he was to find his way home he must first visit the Underworld. The thought filled him with panic. Now more than ever he wished he had not rebelled against Athena at Troy and thrown away her protection. But he was no Teiresias. He could not have known the dark path he had chosen would lead him to this point. And the oracles had demanded the Palladium be taken from her temple if the war was to be won. The alternative was to have remained encamped on the Trojan plain until death took him, doomed never to see his wife and son again. Perhaps that *was* his doom, despite the Pythoness's promise he would return to Ithaca, for how could a man enter Hell with any hope of coming out again?

He looked behind him at the sleeping form of Circe. Last night as he entered her she had begged him to stay on Aeaea, to forget his old life and start a new one with her. It was the easy path. He and his men would have everything they needed. They could settle on the island and make wives of the Trojan slaves. They could create a new Ithaca with Odysseus as king and Circe as queen, living a life of peace and plenty. *Let Aeaea be your home and I will make you immortal*, she promised as she wrapped herself about him and pulled him deeper into her. And in his confusion, undone by his terror at the thought of the Underworld and his lust for the divine beauty before him, he almost succumbed. But his heart was stubborn. It would not abandon his love for Penelope and the son he had barely known. The paradise of Circe's island would become a living Hell in which a single day would be more torturous than the eleven years he had spent away from his family. Better to face the realm of the dead than surrender all hope of seeing his family again.

He pushed himself up from the bed and returned to the hall, which was filled with the familiar snores of his men. Finding his own furs, he pulled them over himself and waited until the birds in the trees outside began heralding the approach of the new day. As the air grew lighter a few of the men rose and slipped outside to empty their bladders before returning to the warmth of their beds. He wondered how he would tell them of what lay ahead, and what their reaction might be. To visit the land beyond the ocean's edge was terrifying enough, even if he was the only one who would descend to the Underworld.

'Good morning,' he said as Eperitus stirred and raised his head.

'Morning, Odysseus. You look terrible. Didn't you sleep well?'

'Barely a wink,' Odysseus replied, yawning. 'Listen, I think it's time to resume the journey home. I'm going to speak with Circe, and I want you to be armed and ready when I return.'

'When are we leaving?'

Odysseus lowered his voice.

'We set sail today, but not for Ithaca.'

'Then where?'

'You'll find out soon enough,' Odysseus replied. 'Wake the men before I return, will you?'

He found Circe in her bedroom, sitting on a golden chair by the window. She wore a cloak around her shoulders, but beneath it she was still naked. The dawn breeze teased her red hair as she gazed out the window at the forest beyond. The eaves were still dark and filled with shadows in the thin morning light.

'Must you go?' she asked without looking at him.

'I must. Do I have to find Teiresias?'

'If you want to return to Ithaca, yes.'

'And how do the living find the dead?'

'At great cost to themselves,' she answered, meeting his gaze.

'The spirits of the departed don't scare me,' he said.

'Yes they do. I can see it in your face. And you *should* be afraid. A ghost cannot kill a man, but when you witness their suffering and understand that the same fate awaits you, it will not leave you unchanged. It will haunt you, Odysseus, until the very day you go down to become one of them. It will make you value every moment of your short, mortal life.'

'My life only has value if I am with Penelope.'

Circe's white brow furrowed slightly and she returned to looking out the window.

'You left early again. Still trying to keep up the pretence you're not sharing my bed? Well, you're becoming sloppy: you forgot your cloak.'

She rose from the chair and picked up a square of folded cloth from the bed. She hung it around his shoulders and clasped it together with Penelope's brooch. Then she crossed the room, removed her own cloak and lifted a dress from her dressing table. The material shone like silver as she slipped it over her head and fastened it about her waist with a golden belt. Finally she fitted a veil in her fiery hair and pulled it down over her face, though the thin material barely hid her beauty.

'Again I ask you, how do the living find the dead? Where do I find the entrance to Hades?'

'No pilot can show you the way, neither can you set a course towards it by the sun or any star. Rather you must sail with the north wind behind you, and if you are resolved to visit the dead, then the entrance to the Underworld will find you. And if it hasn't revealed itself to you by nightfall of the day you set sail, then it never will. One last time: do you insist on going?'

'I do.'

'Then I won't keep you any longer,' she said, her eyes filling with tears. 'I will tell my maids to prepare your breakfast.'

'You'll join us, of course?'

'Don't pretend you enjoy my company, Odysseus. I know I've been nothing more than a convenient sanctuary on your voyage home, someone to use and perhaps be used by. Why else would I need to drug your wine to make you forget your home? So no, go eat with your men and think of Penelope. I will fetch the animals you need for the sacrifices I spoke of last night.'

She turned her back on him with all the pride of an immortal and left the room, slamming the door behind her. Her footsteps receded along the corridor and down the stairs, leaving him to his thoughts. Then the silence was broken by a thud. Looking up at the ceiling, he heard more thuds and a scuffing sound. Someone was on the roof.

'What's happening?' Astynome asked.

'We're leaving,' Eperitus answered, kicking a sleeping figure beneath a pile of furs. 'Wake up, Eurybates. The day'll be half gone before you show your ugly face.'

'Go away,' came the muffled reply.

Eperitus moved to the next bed and gave another figure a shove with the sole of his sandal.

'Leaving? When?' Astynome persisted.

She laid a hand on her stomach, a recent habit Eperitus had noticed when she was concerned about something.

'Do we know the way?'

'Gods, I hope so. Circe will, I'm sure of it. Get up, Omeros.'

'Eperitus, there's something I need to tell you.'

He offered a hand to his squire and pulled him up from the heap of pelts, where he stood and yawned loudly. Eperitus turned to Astynome and caught the particular look in her dark eyes. Whatever she wanted to share, he knew it was important. He reached out and took her fingers in his.

'Will it wait? Just until I've got these laggards out of their beds ready for Odysseus?'

She paused, then gave a nod.

'I'll get the women and children up.'

The crew had become lazy and ill-disciplined during their long sojourn on Aeaea, and it took a lot of kicking and shouting to rouse them all. His task was not helped by the appearance of Circe's nymphs and the housekeeper bringing freshly baked bread and pots of hot porridge for breakfast. Fortunately Odysseus was slow to return, enabling Eperitus to get the men out of their beds and eating. He was just pondering how fit they were for an immediate voyage, when he noticed an empty space beside Omeros.

'Where's Elpenor?' he asked.

'He was feeling sick from last night's wine – too much, as usual – so he went up to the roof to sleep it off in the fresh air. What's going on, Eperitus? What's with all this kicking and rolling us out of our beds?'

'Ask Odysseus when he returns. First you can get up to the roof and bring that good-for-nothing friend of yours down here.'

Omeros looked down disappointedly at his steaming hot porridge, then gave a sigh and made to rise. Eperitus took pity on him and restrained him with a hand on his shoulder.

'Don't worry, lad. Sit and eat your breakfast. I'll fetch him.'

Elpenor lay on the thick fur and listened to the voices below. He had often come up to the roof to sleep after a night's feasting and had learned much from it. Many of the crew had guessed the price Odysseus had paid for turning them back from swine to men, but to a man they also believed he had kept his own company at night ever since. His faithfulness to Penelope had been a topic of debate since Elpenor had arrived at Troy with the other replacements. No other fighting man from the highest king down to the lowliest spearman had given much thought to the women they had left at home, but Odysseus's fidelity was renowned. Some even admired him for it, though only Elpenor knew the truth. Several times as he had lain quietly on the roof looking up at the oddly misaligned stars he had heard Odysseus and Circe's voices coming from her bedroom window, always followed by the sound of their lovemaking. And yet Elpenor had said nothing to the rest of the crew. They all thought him a drunk of little intelligence, so rarely questioned his habit of sleeping on the roof. The last thing he wanted was for any of them to join him there so they could hear the evidence for themselves.

Let them keep their illusions that Odysseus was a good king, he thought. Even those that despised him at least respected him, including Eurylochus and his Taphian henchman. But not Elpenor. From an early age, his father, Melaneus – an ally of Eupeithes – had taught his sons to hate the king of Ithaca. Elpenor's eldest brother, Amphimedon, had even vowed that one day he would kill Odysseus. That was a lot of old bluster, of course, for everyone knew Amphimedon was a coward. But Eupeithes, the one-time usurper and now member of the Kerosia, would always encourage Amphimedon's ambitions. Doubtless he had few hopes that the young braggart would ever pluck up the courage to carry out his promise, but if he did – and actually succeeded in killing Odysseus – it would serve the old traitor's purposes to perfection. And there was nothing Eupeithes would not contemplate that offered the possibility of relieving Ithaca of its rightful king. Elpenor knew that well enough.

Not that Eupeithes intended to take the throne himself. The man had even less courage than Amphimedon and knew the people would never follow him. But he was rich enough, ambitious enough and ruthless enough to make his son, Antinous, king and rule Ithaca through him. If he succeeded, the old hierarchy would collapse and a new one would rise up in its place. And with such changes came opportunities. Eupeithes also had a daughter, and for someone of Elpenor's lowly rank – the youngest of four brothers with very little expectation of inheriting either money or power – marrying into the family of the future king was his best hope of joining the new hierarchy. So when Eupeithes had offered him his only daughter's hand if he would volunteer to join the replacements being sent to Troy, he had accepted the proposal without hesitation.

'Again I ask you, how do the living find the dead?' he heard Odysseus say. 'Where do I find the entrance to Hades?'

Elpenor turned from his own thoughts and listened.

'No pilot can show you the way, neither can you set a course towards it by the sun or any star. Rather you must sail with the north wind behind you, and if you are resolved to visit the dead, then the entrance to the Underworld will find you. And if it hasn't revealed itself to you by nightfall of the day you set sail, then it never will. One last time: do you insist on going?'

'I do.'

So the strange discussion he had heard the night before, after the grunts and squeals of their copulation were over, had been genuine. Circe had spoken of a dead seer and sacrificing a ram and a black ewe at the meeting point of the River of Lamentation and the River of Flaming Fire, but the conversation had often drifted out of earshot and left him with only a fragmentary grasp of what they were talking about. Now, though, he understood. Odysseus was going to sail to the Halls of Hades and consult the dead.

A door slammed in the room below. Elpenor stood and tried to buckle his sword about his waist, but he was distracted and it fell from his fingers to land with a thump on the floor. He picked it up again, secured the belt and began gathering up his sleeping furs. The thought of the Underworld had sent a shudder down his spine. It also woke him from the slumber he had fallen into during the months on Aeaea. He had gone to Troy with a specific purpose, one which he had barely thought through when he had taken it on but which had proved almost impossible to fulfil since. It was not that he was afraid to kill Odysseus. Unlike his brother, he was not a coward. But neither was he a fool. If he was to murder the king, he would not do it at the expense of his own life. There would be no open assassination attempt that would give Odysseus the chance to defend himself, nor would he risk a knife in the dark if there was any chance he would be caught or implicated in the crime. What would he gain by killing the king if he could not return to Ithaca and claim the reward Eupeithes had promised him?

Yet the chances were fewer than he had hoped for. Odysseus had never been unguarded during the last months of the war, and though Elpenor had considered stabbing him in the back during the confusion of battle, the risks had been too high for his liking. During the voyage the confines of life on a galley had restricted the opportunities for him to carry out his mission unseen. Only in the Cyclops's cave had a chance arisen: at the point Odysseus was about to blind Polyphemus, Elpenor had dropped the sharpened stake in the hope the monster would awake and seize hold of Odysseus, but his feeble plan had failed. With determination, he should have been able to fulfil his mission during their long sojourn on Aeaea. But something about the island had weakened his resolve. In the first few days he had been too traumatised by the terrible things they had suffered on the voyage and needed to recover his courage and strength. After that, the nightly feasts had pushed all thoughts of assassination to the back of his mind. Though he had continued to feign drunkenness while drinking no more than a cup or two of wine each night – adopting the persona of a drunkard was an essential part of his plan if he was to deflect suspicion from himself – he had become distanced from his mission. The thought had occurred to him, while he lay on the roof looking up at the stars and listening to Odysseus's gentle snores, that he could easily slip down in the darkness and plunge a knife into his chest. The thought of disrupting the peace of the island, though, and the consequences that followed – including their inevitable resumption of the voyage home – had dissuaded him from acting.

But suddenly everything had changed. They were to set sail once more, and their journey would take them to the last place on earth any sane man would want to venture: the Underworld. The name alone struck dread into Elpenor's heart. His soul would be led there one day, where it would drift without memory of either sorrow or happiness and exist without sense or consciousness; but to go to such a place in a living body, able to understand and experience the horror, was too much. He had put his mission off for far too long. He must fulfil it before Odysseus could lead them to Hades.

'Elpenor? What are you doing up here?'

Elpenor turned to see Odysseus at the top of the ladder that led up to the roof from the floor below. He felt a sudden twinge of nerves. The gods, it seemed, were bringing matters to a head.

'Sleeping,' he answered, holding up the roll of furs in his hands.

Odysseus frowned. 'Who said you could sleep up here?'

'Nobody, my lord. I came here last night to look at the stars and get some fresh air.' He rubbed his forehead with the flat of his hand and squinted at Odysseus. 'Circe's wine is powerful. I'm sure her maids don't water it down enough.'

Odysseus stepped onto the flat roof.

'It's strong, that's for certain. I'm surprised you didn't fall off and break your neck.'

'I've got a good head for heights.'

'And too much of a head for wine,' Odysseus added, giving him a look before walking to the edge and surveying the view. It was mostly forest, but to the north the land sloped away to reveal a stretch of sea between two green peaks. 'It's odd, but in all our months on Aeaea I haven't once been up here. I didn't know you could see the ocean.'

His back was turned as he spoke, staring out at the blue waters and the sun glinting on the waves. Elpenor could feel his heart beating fast now, as if it were lodged in his throat. He took a step closer to the king and laid a hand on the pommel of his sword.

No, he thought. Be patient.

'Have you slept up here before?' Odysseus asked, turning to face him.

Elpenor's hand shot up from his sword to his forehead, kneading the flesh with his thumb and forefinger.

'Sorry? My head's pounding, I didn't catch –'

'I asked if you've slept on the roof before.'

Odysseus was eyeing him suspiciously now.

'Have I…? Erm, yes. A few times, I suppose.'

'Circe's bedroom is directly below us. Did you know that?'

'No, my lord.'

'Her window is just below here,' Odysseus continued, moving along the edge and pointing down. 'Have you been eavesdropping? Answer me! What have you heard?'

'Nothing. I only come up when I've had a little too much wine, and I'm in no state to listen to… whatever Circe might have to say to her maids. When I wake up in the morning I can't even remember how I got here. Usually I just go straight back down to the great hall before anyone else wakes and wait for breakfast to be served.'

'But not this morning, Elpenor. You're still here, I notice. Why?'

'I… I –'

'What? Overslept? Or were you too busy listening to my conversation with Circe?'

'No. I heard voices, but nothing clear and besides –'

'Besides what?'

'I was watching a sail approaching from the north.'

'A sail?' Odysseus's expression changed instantly from distrust to concern. 'Can you still see it? Did it approach the island?'

Elpenor's nervousness left him. As Odysseus turned northward to look at the expanse of ocean, he slid his sword slowly and silently from its scabbard. The moment had come and his only hesitation was in deciding the manner of the king's death. Too many of the crew knew that Elpenor had a habit of sleeping on the roof, so to run Odysseus through would point to him as the murderer. But if the king was to fall from the roof and break his neck it would be nothing more than a tragic accident – an accident that would earn Elpenor the power and wealth he had always craved. Odysseus was only a few steps away from the roof: a simple run and a push would do it. And yet a fall of two storeys might only result in a broken leg, a gamble he was not prepared to take.

'It was still there when you came up,' he replied. 'Close to the shore on the right. Yes, there it is, I can still see it.'

'Are you sure?' Odysseus asked, standing on his tiptoes and shielding his eyes from the low sun. 'I can't see anything.'

There was only one way to be sure: Elpenor had to break the king's neck before he pushed him from the roof. But even if he

attacked him from behind, Odysseus's greater bulk would surely prevail. With quick, light steps he ran up with his sword raised over his
shoulder and brought the pommel down hard on Odysseus's head.

Eperitus reached the top of the ladder in time to see Odysseus collapse beneath the blow from Elpenor's sword. With a shout, he
sprang up the last few rungs and drew his own weapon. Elpenor
turned in surprise, threw a glance around the edges of the broad roof
and realised he was trapped. He bent his knees and with a furious
expression launched himself at the newcomer.

Eperitus raised his sword to meet the blow aimed at his head.
The blades clashed loudly in the cool morning air before parting
with a slither of metal and clashing again. In the last few weeks of
the war Elpenor had earned himself a reputation as a poor fighter,
too ready to hang back in a battle and let others do the fighting for
him. He had also proved himself a weak-willed drunkard with a
passion for wine and little else, so their fight would be short-lived.
But before Eperitus killed him he would find out why he had struck
Odysseus.

Their blades locked again. Eperitus used his superior strength to
push Elpenor backwards, then followed up with a lunge that should
have taken him in the upper arm and ended the fight. To his amazement, Elpenor ducked deftly aside and swept his weapon in an arc
at Eperitus's stomach. Eperitus leapt back but the bronze tip slashed
through the tunic and across his skin. He felt the searing pain of
the cut but had no time to glance at how serious it was. Elpenor
reversed the blade, jumped forward and swung again, this time from
right to left. Again Eperitus had to jump back to avoid the worst of
the attack, though the point of Elpenor's weapon nicked a rib and
sent another wave of stinging pain through his body. Only at the
last moment did he remember the drop behind him. Realising this
had been Elpenor's tactic all along – to drive him over the edge to
the first-storey roof below – he brought his sword down with all the

speed and strength he possessed and met the youth's blade as it came at him a third time. Drawing the blow aside, he threw a punch with his left hand and caught Elpenor squarely in the jaw, sending him sprawling across the roof. In the moment it took him to get back to his feet, Eperitus glanced down at his chest and saw his tunic was torn and bloodied, though his wounds were more painful than they were life-threatening.

Elpenor threw himself into the attack again. His expression was fierce, but each thrust was controlled and purposeful, testing Eperitus's defences and skills as the blows were parried or beaten aside. Whatever Eperitus had thought of the lad before, he knew now he had been wrong.

'You've more skill than you've been letting on, Elpenor,' he said.

'There's a lot about me you don't know.'

'Indeed. Such as why you would attack your own king.'

'Because Ithaca deserves a better one, of course,' Elpenor grunted, deflecting a thrust from Eperitus's sword and following up with a failed attack of his own. 'And if you hadn't appeared I would have broken his neck and tossed him over the edge, an excuse for us all to go home and find ourselves a new ruler.'

'Yourself perhaps?'

'In time. Why not?'

'Because the throne passes to Telemachus. If the lad has grown up with even a scrap of his father's courage and intelligence, he'd make a far greater king than you or whoever it was that sent you. That's the truth, isn't it, Elpenor? You're nothing more than a hired assassin.'

Elpenor leapt forward, launching a series of attacks that tested Eperitus's skill to the limit. And with each counterblow he felt the raw edges of his wounds moving against each other, soaking his tunic in yet more blood until he felt his head growing light. There was no question of taking the young Ithacan alive. Though he wanted to know who had sent him to kill Odysseus, he knew that if he did not kill him soon he would grow too weak from blood loss and Elpenor would finish him off. Elpenor could see it too. What he could not see was that Odysseus was beginning to stir on the floor behind him.

'Give up, lad. Even if you kill me, do you think you'll cover your crime from the rest of the crew? You might have got away with making Odysseus's murder look like an accident, but how will you explain two deaths?'

'Simple. I'll make it look like you killed each other. After all, do you think the crew haven't noticed the tensions between you? You didn't like it when he abandoned the rest of the fleet to the Laestrygonians, did you? Or, I think, when you found out he had betrayed Penelope.'

Elpenor parried a sudden lunge from Eperitus's sword and responded with a thrust of his own. The movement was quick, the tip of his blade aimed at the groin, but Eperitus saw it coming and struck down hard. Using his greater strength, he drove his opponent's weapon aside and brought the point of his own in to stab at Elpenor's exposed chest. With the speed of his youth and the skill of a seasoned swordsman, Elpenor spun round and turned the blow away.

'Who was it, Elpenor?' Eperitus grunted as the two men pushed against each other, their faces almost meeting. 'Is he worth dying for?'

Elpenor laughed.

'I'm not the one who's losing blood, Eperitus. Your strength is fading faster than mine, so perhaps you should ask yourself whether Odysseus is worth dying for.'

'He's my king.'

'And as perfidious a man as ever lived. You know, of course, he didn't sleep with Circe just the once, don't you?'

'Liar!'

'I'm not lying. I've been up on this roof enough times to hear their lovemaking. Seems like she managed to turn him into a pig after all.'

As he drew his sword back to strike, two large hands seized his wrist and twisted it with a snap. Elpenor cried out with pain and his sword fell from his fingers. Odysseus swung him round and drove his forehead hard into the young Ithacan's face. Elpenor collapsed unconscious on the roof, blood streaming from his nose.

'Zeus's beard, you're covered in blood!' Odysseus declared.

'I'll be alright,' Eperitus said, though the pain was making him feel nauseous and light-headed.

Odysseus tore a strip from the bottom of Elpenor's cloak.

'Raise your arms,' he said, and began winding the cloth about Eperitus's abdomen. 'I'll take you down to Circe and her maids; they have lotions that will heal your wounds quickly.'

'Is it true?' Eperitus asked. 'Did you sleep with Circe again?'

'Whatever I've done has been out of necessity. Let that be an end to it.'

'Do you ask me as my friend,' Eperitus asked, 'or command me as my king?'

'Whichever you will respect enough not to ask me that question again.'

Behind them, Elpenor stirred and let out a groan. Immediately, Odysseus seized his tunic and dragged him to the edge of the roof. Kneeling down beside him, he slapped him hard across the cheek.

'Who sent you to kill me?'

Elpenor smiled through the blood that had dried over his face.

'One who wants your throne.'

Odysseus tightened his grip on Elpenor's tunic and lifted him up so that they were almost nose to nose.

'Tell me and you'll live; refuse once more and I'll throw you from this roof, just as you intended to do to me.'

'He's unarmed, Odysseus,' Eperitus said. 'You can't murder him in cold blood. He should stand trial before the rest of the crew –'

'They're to know nothing of this. An open trial will just give Eurylochus an excuse to question my leadership, and I don't want him stirring up rebellion again or making Elpenor out to be a martyr. Now, tell me who sent you.'

'I'll answer you if you tell Eperitus where you're sailing to,' Elpenor answered, still grinning. 'Or don't you think his loyalty is up to the test?'

His mocking tone angered Odysseus, who raised his hand to strike him again. The boy winced, but when the blow did not come he opened his eyes and stared at the king in defiance.

'What's he talking about?' Eperitus asked. 'Where are you taking us?'

'To the Underworld,' Odysseus replied, his voice almost a whisper.

'To…?'

The words fell dead before they had formed in Eperitus's mind. The Underworld. He recalled the time twenty years before when his soul should have been ushered there. With Damastor's fatal knife wound in his chest, he had watched Hermes coming for him, knowing then that he would spend eternity in the Chambers of Decay. Athena's intervention had saved him, restoring his soul to his body and reviving him to life. But he had never forgotten that fear of Hades. It was a fear his subconscious had to conquer every time he faced battle, and it was a fear that touched his conscious mind now.

Odysseus's eyes lingered on him for a moment, then returned to Elpenor.

'Who sent you?'

'You'll let me live?'

'You have my word.'

'Eupeithes. It was Eupeithes. He wants your throne for his son, and in return for your life he offered me his daughter's hand and my father a position on the new Kerosia. I… I didn't care about marrying his daughter. I only did it out of obedience to my father. You understand that?'

Perhaps it was the hope his life would be spared that broke Elpenor, for the courage that he had shown in his fight with Eperitus had evaporated and all that remained in its place was an instinct for self-preservation. Eperitus could see him shaking.

'I understand loyalty to a father,' Odysseus answered. He gave Elpenor an inquisitive smile and laid his hands gently on either side of his head, stroking his hair. 'And I thought you were just a poor drunk.'

'You're not the only one who can spill wine down his beard, my lord.'

Elpenor gave a nervous laugh. In the same moment, Odysseus's grip tightened and with a sharp twist of his hands he snapped the assassin's neck. Eperitus stepped forward but saw the light had already left Elpenor's eyes. The king looked up at him, challenging him to speak, but Eperitus knew Odysseus was beyond listening to him.

'What do we tell the others?'

'Let them work it out for themselves,' Odysseus replied, and rolled the body over the edge of the roof to land with a thump on the lawn below. 'Now, let's get you down to Circe before anyone else can see your wounds. You'll keep them bandaged and hidden beneath your armour until they're healed. Astynome can change the bandages, but she's not to say a word to anyone.'

'And the Underworld? Is this something you're set on?'

'Yes, if we want to find our way home to Ithaca. We sail this afternoon.'

Chapter Thirty-Three

PERSEPHONE'S GROVE

The tears were rolling down Astynome's eyes as she sat facing Eperitus under the eaves of the forest. The noon sun was high and hot and it seemed the flowers in Circe's garden had never looked so beautiful, and yet Eperitus's heart was filled with cold, dark despair. Beneath his breastplate his heavily wrapped chest stung where Elpenor's sword had twice nearly taken his life. He had not yet told Astynome about the fight on the roof and Elpenor's treachery, though the body had already been found by one of Circe's maids.

'I don't want you to go,' Astynome said.

He reached out and took her hand. It was cold and he could feel it shaking even as he held it.

'I must. Circe has said it's the only way; that Teiresias alone can tell us how to get back to Ithaca.'

'I don't trust her. My father is a priest: he says the spirits of the dead cannot talk.'

'Then he's been to the Underworld too?' Eperitus smiled as he spoke – hoping to lighten the mood – but Astynome merely brushed away more tears. 'Odysseus says Persephone granted Teiresias's soul the ability to speak.'

He looked across the glade to Circe's house. Several Ithacans were sitting on the lawn or talking quietly in pairs. Most looked forlorn; many had their heads in their hands or stared vacantly into nothing. Omeros sat on the porch, his eyes red from his grief at Elpenor's death. Polites sat beside him with his giant arm across his shoulders.

'They say Heracles went to Hades, Orpheus too, and that both men came back alive.'

'And what sort of men were they when they returned, Eperitus? Do the stories tell us that? What does it do to a man to witness what the gods have devised for him when he dies? It will turn your mind, I know it.'

'I'm stronger than that, Astynome. And perhaps it will make me cherish the living world more. Even now I can look at you and know there's nothing more I want than to spend every remaining day of my life with you.'

He kissed her hand and she smiled, though the happy glimmer was short-lived.

'And Elpenor's death. It has to be an omen, Eperitus.'

'It isn't an omen, that's one thing I'm sure of.'

'Why won't Odysseus bury or cremate him? Is he in such a hurry to leave that he can't even give one of his shipmates his burial rites?'

'He doesn't want to waste any time,' Eperitus said. 'None of us knows the way to Hades, only that we should go with the north wind in our sail and look for a landing place marked by black poplars. That's as much as Circe can tell us. And when I return, you and I will be married. I know we said we would wait until we reached Ithaca, but can either of us say for certain whether that day will ever come? Maybe the thought of being joined with you will give me the courage I need to overcome this darkness.'

She took his hand in both of hers and kissed it. Then she looked at him, and despite her red eyes and the tracks of her tears on her brown cheeks, he could see again the youthful beauty he had fought for that day less than two years ago in Lyrnessus.

'You will overcome it,' she said. 'And when you return we will be married here in this glade before Circe's home, with wolves and lions for guests, and… and what if you don't return?'

Her brief smile disappeared and she covered her face with her hands and wept. He took her in his arms, concerned that the inner strength he so admired her for seemed to have deserted her. As he comforted her, he heard Odysseus's voice calling for him. He looked up and saw the king waving to him from the porch.

'Come on, Eperitus, it's time.'

The rest of the Ithacans were gathering on the lawn, silent and stern as they prepared themselves for the voyage ahead.

'I have to go now, Astynome,' Eperitus told her. 'Be strong. I'll be back soon, I promise.'

She met his gaze and he could see that her familiar resolve had returned.

'There's something I must tell you, Eperitus. I wasn't going to say anything until you came back, because I didn't want to put doubt in your mind. But now I think you have a right to know. If you are to go to that place – and if you don't return – I don't want you to go without knowing that you are going to be a father.'

They sailed all day under a sky as grey as wet slate. The sun's face showed just once, at sunset as it passed between the ceiling of cloud and the distant horizon; a momentary glimpse before it plunged into the ocean in a blaze of gold and was extinguished. Complete darkness followed rapidly, though Odysseus ordered they maintain their course with a full sail. After some time a fog appeared and Eperitus was called forward to the prow to join Odysseus. He leaned against the curved bow rail and looked out at the grey mist that shrouded the galley. It looked as if they were floating on a bed of white vapour.

'I'd hoped you would've joined me earlier,' Odysseus said. 'A bit of company might have made the voyage pass quicker. It doesn't help any of us to sit alone and dwell on what lies ahead. We have to go and so we might as well face up to it.'

'Aren't you afraid then?' Eperitus asked.

'More than any man on this ship. I'm in terror at the thought of what we will see, and even more so at what we might hear. It's one thing for Teiresias to tell us the way home, but what if he says the throne now belongs to Eupeithes, or that Penelope has remarried, or Telemachus is dead?'

Eperitus placed a calming hand on his shoulder.

'You're right, we shouldn't think about what lies ahead. As for Eupeithes, he's burned his fingers once already trying to take Ithaca for himself. You can be sure he won't dare do anything while there's a chance you could reappear any day with a fleet and an army under your command.'

'Some fleet,' Odysseus said, glancing back at the crew sitting silently on their benches.

'*He* doesn't know that. And if he's expecting Elpenor to have succeeded in his task then he'll be in for a shock when you turn up. As for Penelope and Telemachus, I'm sure they're safe and well.'

'Well that's good to know,' Odysseus mocked. 'Perhaps you can prophesy the way back to Ithaca, too, and save us the need to visit the Underworld.'

Eperitus smiled. 'Can any course I guess at take us anywhere worse than the Land of the Dead?'

He leaned his weight on the bow rail and looked at the milky layer of mist beneath the bows. He was as scared as Odysseus about the thought of entering the Underworld – if indeed they could find the entrance to a place of such dark legend – but he was less afraid of entering than he was of the thought he might not leave again. He did not possess the strength and determination of Heracles nor the magical lyre of Orpheus, and it seemed to him that no ordinary mortal could enter Hades's kingdom without first surrendering his life. And the thought that he might never return to Astynome or see their child filled him with dread. He could face the dead, but he could not face losing the living.

After a while he detected a new odour amid the familiar concoction of brine, livestock and stale sweat. He raised his nose and took a deep breath. Rotten eggs. The unpleasant smell made him wrinkle his nostrils, but he was soon able to detect wet stone, earth and vegetation – all signs of land. The sound of wind whistling through rocky crevasses and waves crashing against a sandy shore confirmed it.

'We're near now,' he told Odysseus.

The king shouted back instructions to lower the sail and man the oars. If they were approaching an unknown shore, it would be at as near to their own speed as possible. For the first time in the voyage the crew began to chatter, though the tone was one of apprehension rather than excitement. Odysseus shouted for silence. Before much longer Eperitus was able to hear the wind whispering through the branches of unseen trees. It sounded like the unintelligible muttering of distant voices.

'Stop rowing,' he ordered.

The splash of the oars ceased at once and was followed by the trickle of water dripping from the blades. He gave a nod to Odysseus, who called for the anchor stone to be tossed overboard and for the small boat to be made ready. The plop of the anchor was followed by the flap of bare feet and the clatter of the wooden rowing boat being dragged across the benches and lowered over the side. Odysseus turned and signalled to Eurylochus, Perimedes, Omeros and three others on the front bench. They had been chosen by lot to accompany Odysseus and Eperitus to the Underworld, and their ashen faces showed the strain of fear that was upon them. Eurylochus and Perimedes untied the ram and the black ewe that were to be sacrificed to the dead, while the others carried the offerings of honey, milk, wine, water and barley. Without any word of parting to their comrades, they clambered down into the boat and rowed slowly through the mist towards the unseen shore.

A line of high black cliffs loomed up out of the mist ahead of them. The one sound that had been absent to Eperitus's ears as they approached had been the cawing of seagulls, and none were to be seen anywhere, either nestled among the crags of the cliff walls or floating on the air currents above them. A long shoreline of black sand emerged from the fog and they guided the prow of the little boat towards it, pulling it up the beach as soon as it struck. They secured it beneath the curtain-like branches of one of the willow trees that lined the foot of the cliffs and, wrapping their cloaks about themselves against the numbing cold, lit a pair of torches. With the light of the flames gleaming back from the jagged cliffs, they trudged along the shoreline in search of the poplar trees that marked the entrance to Hades's kingdom. Eperitus saw them first, tall and black like giant gateposts rising up from the mist. Soon they were visible to the rest of the party and he heard Eurylochus break into hushed sobs behind him. For once he pitied the man. Odysseus, though, showed only the briefest hesitation before pressing on. They entered the crescent of trees one by one and stood staring up at the fissure in the cliff face before them. The torchlight extended but a short distance into the cave, shimmering back at them from the tumble of boulders within.

'Is this it?' Omeros asked. His voice fell dead and his breath clouded in the still, icy air. 'Is this the entrance?'

'This is it,' Odysseus replied.

He raised his torch above his head and entered. Eperitus followed, his hand ready on the pommel of his sword, though he knew no weapon could help him where they were going. The stench of sulphur was powerful enough now to be noticed by the others, who wrinkled their noses in disgust. Within a short distance the walls of the cave had narrowed so much that they were forced to walk in single file with Odysseus holding the torch ahead of him. Eperitus had also become aware of a distant rushing sound, like whispers in a shell held to the ear. Worse still, he felt a black despair creeping into him, weighing on his thoughts and turning his limbs leaden. It was as if he was wading neck deep through water, each step a conscious struggle, each breath strained and heavy. He tried to remember Astynome's face, to act as a torch against the darkness that was seeping into his mind, but he found he could not picture her at all. Instead he found his gloom deepening. He knew now he would never see her again. They would not marry in the glade on Aeaea, nor build a farm on Ithaca as they had planned. And he would never see their unborn child, for whoever enters the Underworld has no hope of returning to the land of the living.

Odysseus came to a sudden halt.

'What is it?'

'We've reached the back of the cave,' he said. 'There's nothing here.'

'What?' Eperitus said. 'That's impossible. Circe told you the entrance was behind Persephone's Grove. This has to be it.'

'What's that? There's no entrance?' Eurylochus asked behind them, his voice suddenly filled with hope. 'Then we can't enter?'

'Silence!' Odysseus ordered as the men began to talk in animated whispers. 'Here, look for yourself.'

He squeezed aside and handed Eperitus the torch. By its dim light he could see a wall of rock before them. His spirit leapt within him as he realised that it was a dead end. Then he saw it: a darker blackness at the base of the cave wall that the light of the torch could not penetrate. He slumped to his knees and held the torch into the gap. It was a tunnel, just large enough for a man to crawl through. He felt a weak current of air fanning his face, like the breath of a dying man, and it carried with it the nauseating odour of sulphur. The faint rustling sound he had noticed before was clearer, too. As he strained his ears against the hiss of the torch he thought he could hear words, thousands of words uttered by hushed voices.

He looked back up at Odysseus.

'It's a tunnel, and –'

'And?'

'I can hear the voices of the dead.'

'No! No more. I can't go on.'

Eurylochus turned on Perimedes behind him and tried to push him back, clawing at his face when he did not move quickly enough. Perimedes, too, began to panic, lashing out at Eurylochus with his fist and hitting the rock wall with a shout of pain. Odysseus pulled out his sword and struck Eurylochus over the back of the head, bringing him down to the cave floor in a heap.

'Take him outside and wait with him until we return,' he told Perimedes, who was clutching his bloody fist in his armpit. 'If the rest of you want to go back with them, I'll not stop you.'

'I can't do it, my lord,' said one of the others and lowered his bag of barley and skin of water to the cave floor. 'I can't go in there.'

He retreated back towards the cave opening, following the already diminishing light of Perimedes's torch. The other two, infected by Eurylochus's open display of cowardice, also turned and fled, leaving only Odysseus, Eperitus and Omeros. Between them they trussed up the animals and attached them to their ankles by ropes – along with the other offerings – which they would drag behind them as they crawled. Then, with heavy hearts, they entered the tunnel. Odysseus led, holding the torch at arm's length before him, followed by Eperitus and then Omeros at the rear. For a short while they were able to move along on their hands and knees. Then the ceiling became gradually lower and the sides narrower, forcing them to move onto their stomachs and pull themselves along the hard, cold floor by their elbows. The way forward was now so tight that Eperitus felt the walls scraping at his arms and legs and catching the top of his head and shoulders. There was barely room for him to reach forward and pull himself along. He began to wonder what would happen if the tunnel led to a dead end. How would they get back out? He could hear Omeros behind him groaning with the struggle, and the small, frightened bleating of the black ewe that was tied to his own ankle. What if Omeros became too weak to carry on? What if he collapsed? Could he crawl out again, pushing Omeros, the ewe, the wineskin and all the other sacrifices before him with just his legs? He felt his breathing grow tighter and knew it was not just because of his leather armour or the thinner, more sulphurous air. He was starting to panic.

'Be calm,' he muttered to himself. 'There's only one way out of here. Give up now and you're stuck.'

Then the torch that Odysseus was pushing along ahead of him went out, plunging them into total darkness. Eperitus balled his hands into fists and squeezed his eyes tight shut, fighting the terror that was beginning to tear at him. He took a deep breath and moved on, faster this time until his groping hands found the warm body of Odysseus's sheep filling the tunnel before him. He wanted to shout at Odysseus to move quicker. He clenched his fists again and paused. How much longer now? How long had he been in the tunnel? What if there was a rockfall? What if the tunnel was endless? Was this what it meant to be dead: to be entombed forever in rock, still living and breathing but unable to move, trapped for eternity? And all the time inflicted with the biting cold that was turning his fingers and face numb, his ears filled with the whispers of the dead? He wanted to cry out, to scream at his imprisonment, *anything* but remain in that place. But he fought it. He faced down his fear with every last thread of his willpower, telling himself over and over again that there would be an end to the tunnel, that soon they would be out on the other side – wherever that may be – and that he would be free. He thought about Astynome. He tried to recall the forest on Aeaea. The wind on his face on the plains of Troy. The smell of the sea and the taste of Maron's wine. But he could remember nothing, nothing to relieve the terrible sense that he was trapped forever in the tunnel between Odysseus and Omeros.

'I can't do it!'

He opened his eyes to blackness. What had he said?

'I can't go on!'

It was Omeros. The sound of the lad's terror should have broken him, too. But it did not. Somehow it strengthened him.

'Omeros, listen to me,' he called back. 'You can do it. This won't go on for much longer. We can't go back; we can only go forward, so be strong. Now's the time to prove yourself.'

'I can see something!' he heard Odysseus say somewhere ahead of him. 'I can see a light.'

'Did you hear that?' Eperitus shouted back to Omeros. 'Odysseus can see a light. We're nearly there.'

A glimmer of hope now reignited itself within him. He thought again of Astynome and this time he could see her face. Gritting his teeth, he hauled himself forward, only to find Odysseus's sheep before him again. He grasped at the wool and squeezed it hard, feeling the panic return.

'Omeros, are you there?'

'Yes. Yes, I'm here. I'm sorry for –'

'If you apologise to me, lad, I'll give you the worst beating you've ever suffered the moment we get out of here.'

How could he even tolerate an apology from a boy when the same terror was clawing at every fibre of his own sanity?

His body was stiff with tension. He wanted to kneel, stand, walk, run, anything but crawl on his stomach like a worm through the bowels of the earth. But he could not, so he could either keep on crawling or go out of his mind. He kept crawling: one elbow at a time, reaching and pulling, reaching and pulling. Astynome had deserted him again. All he saw was blackness; all he felt was cold; all he could smell was sulphur; all he heard was the moaning of the dead.

And then it was over. A desperate scrambling before him, followed by a shout – a cry of joy or terror, he could not tell – and a thin yellow light, so faint he did not know whether he was seeing it with his eyes or in his mind. Then, realising his eyelids were tight shut, he flicked them open and saw a hole in the blackness ahead of him. It was the end of the tunnel. A moment later he saw Odysseus crouching down and stretching a hand towards him. He dragged himself forward, reached out and felt his friend's strong fingers around his wrist, pulling him out.

Chapter Thirty-Four

THE LAND OF THE DEAD

Odysseus dragged Eperitus onto the black grass, where he lay on his back and covered his face with his hands. Untying the ropes attached to his ankle, he hauled out the black ewe and the small bag of barley and then looked into the mouth of the tunnel. He caught the pale gleam of Omeros's terrified eyes further back in the darkness.

'Come on, take my hand.'

The poet stayed where he was.

'What's it like out there?'

'Don't force me to come in and get you.'

After a moment's hesitation Omeros pulled himself forward on his elbows until he could take hold of the king's outstretched hand. Once out, he raised himself on his hands and knees and stared in silence at the world they had entered, until finally he could take no more. He rolled onto his side and, like Eperitus, threw his hands over his face.

Odysseus turned and looked at the strange and terrible landscape he had only dared to glimpse as he had tumbled out from the tunnel. He was standing beneath a tall cliff face on a sward of black grass, looking out over a barren, mist-shrouded plain that appeared to have no end. Grey clouds tinged with yellow rolled in agony overhead, promising the refreshing sustenance of rain in that dry place and yet never giving it. At some distance to his right a cataract of thick red liquid like living fire plunged noisily down from the clifftop into a large pool, where it formed a river that oozed down towards the plain. It threw up a curtain of crimson light that danced and flickered in the murky air, but if it was indeed a river of fire then it emitted no heat, for this was a place of life-sapping iciness. Leaching over the cliffs to Odysseus's left was another falls, silent and black. From the summit, globs of tar-like slime drooped and spattered onto the dead meadow below, forming a heap that eventually seeped down the slope to create another river. This, Circe had told him, was Cocytus, the River of Lamentation. It carried the sluggish, shapeless grief of the living for their loved ones who had entered the Land of the Dead. The other was Phlegethon, the River of Flaming Fire that flowed with the blood of the dead. Both slid forward to join together beyond a pinnacle of rock that rose up out of the fog a bow's shot from the foot of the cliff where Odysseus stood. Here, at the point of their mingling, they plunged over another cliff into a third, much larger river that wound its way through the sombre landscape like a yellow scar. This was the Acheron, the greatest of the five rivers that ran through the Underworld. Its bitter waters gave the Land of the Dead its pallid illumination, a corpse light that was devoid of life and hope.

Beyond the pinnacle of rock Odysseus could see other peaks rising from the restless mist on the plain below, some crowned with the twisted husks of dead trees, others with crumbling walls and broken towers. But of the doleful occupants of the Underworld there was no sign at all. For that, at least, he was glad. They would come when his sacrifice of blood was made, but at that moment it was as much as he could endure just to breathe the parching air and feel its life-stealing ice penetrate his bones. Looking out at the emptiness before him drained his desire for the things of the living world he had left behind. What was the use in sunlight or the feel of water on his skin; why the need to taste meat, or hear the sound of a human voice, or fill his nostrils with the smell of a forest when all life, ultimately, came to this? It all seemed strangely puerile now: all those journeys he had undertaken; the battles he had fought; the councils he had spoken at; and the great schemes he had devised, when in the end he would leave it all for this. Where was the good in fame and glory, even love, if it gave him no comfort when his flesh was cold and his spirit was doomed to eternity in Tartarus?

'What was the point of any of it?' he asked.

Eperitus, who was now standing and staring at the landscape before them, turned.

'What did you say?'

'He asked what the point of it was,' Omeros answered, sitting with his chin on his knees. 'A good question, though I don't know the answer, nor care.'

'The point is, we carry on and do what we came here to do,' Eperitus said wearily. He laid a hand on Odysseus's shoulder and shook it. 'What did we just drag ourselves through that tunnel for? You remember, don't you?'

'To find Teiresias and ask him the way home.'

Odysseus turned listlessly to the sheep and the black ewe. Untying the rope that bound their legs together, he led the subdued animals towards the rock where the two rivers met. When he reached the foot of the pinnacle – where broad steps cracked with age led up to the flat summit – he drew his sword and began digging the trench Circe had instructed him to make. As he knelt he noticed that the dry grass was carpeted with masses of small, pale flowers, every one of which was dead. Lifting his eyes, he saw through the mist the shapes of lifeless trees along the banks of the rivers. They stood root-deep in fallen leaves, which never stirred because there was not a breath of wind to move them. Their branches hung with the rotted remains of fruit that had neither been picked nor had fallen to create new saplings. Like all the withered vegetation of that place, they stood in mockery of life, a warning of what all life would eventually become. Even the stench of sulphur that filled Odysseus's nostrils seemed to scorn the wholesome air he had breathed every moment of his life in the world above, never then appreciating its sweetness.

He stabbed the blade into the soil again, scraping away the grass and flowers with their shrivelled roots and the thin, dry earth that held them. Then he noticed something else in the soil, something small and white. He plucked it out and saw that it was a bone, the rib of a small mammal. Flinging it aside, he scratched away more of the dirt and found another bone, and another. The first he was certain was part of a fish skull; the second was a human knuckle. He dug deeper, bringing up more bones, some animal, some human. Finding the lower part of a man's jawbone, he dropped his sword with a cry of despair and fell back from the shallow scrape.

At once he felt Eperitus's hands under his arms, lifting him back onto his haunches.

'Here,' he said, handing him his discarded sword. 'I'll help you.'

Drawing his own blade, Eperitus began to hack at the parched ground, tossing aside the bones as he found them. Odysseus joined him, scraping furiously one moment, tensing the next as he picked out each new bone and flung it away. When the trench was as wide and deep as was needed, he turned to Omeros and signalled for the milk, honey and wine to be brought to him. Mixing the honey and wine in a wooden bowl, he poured it from side to side into the trench. This was followed by the last skin of Maron's wine, which he emptied, then most of the water, saving enough to wet the dryness in his throat and to offer a mouthful to each of his comrades. Last of all, he sprinkled the barley into the trench, stopping when it was half full.

'The voices have changed,' Eperitus announced.

'You didn't tell me you could hear voices,' Odysseus said, looking up sharply at the mist that seemed to have closed about them.

Eperitus gave him a questioning look.

'Can't you? You neither, Omeros? But they're not distant; I can hear them as clearly as I hear you, though I can only catch words here and there. It's like listening to a thousand people speaking at once.'

'And can you *see* them?'

'Glimpses out of the corner of my eye. They're all around us.'

Odysseus felt a shudder. He did not fear the dead, but he was afraid to witness their fate. It was the fate that awaited all men, and he did not wish to know it before his own time came. Already he felt the despair of the place, like an iron weight in his chest that encased his spirit and made him forget all that was good. From the moment he had fallen out of the tunnel like a stillborn child from its mother's womb he had felt the lust for life draining from him. Words like hope, desire and love were meaningless here. Here there was nothing but himself. A terrible self-obsessed loneliness consumed him, so that Omeros and Eperitus were strangers of whom he knew little and for whom he cared nothing at all. Worse still, he knew that he was here to learn the way home to Penelope and Telemachus, but he could not think *why*. In the Underworld, they were simply names. Nothing seemed to matter here but his own misery.

'Odysseus? Odysseus? Weren't we supposed to do something?' Eperitus asked.

'Who cares?' Omeros said. 'Leave him alone, why don't you? In fact, why don't you leave us both alone?'

'I should have left you in that tunnel, crying like a baby.'

'I'd rather be stuck in there than out here!'

'Shut up, both of you!' Odysseus snapped, pointing his sword at them. 'I don't know why in Hades's name either of you came. You were supposed to help me, but I'm starting to wish the pair of you had fallen off that roof instead of Elpenor. At least if you were here with the dead you might have been able to tell me what to do now, rather than squabbling over nothing!'

He sighed and let the sword drop to his side, then fell to his knees and rested his chin on his chest. He wished the others were gone so that he could just lie down and sleep, though something told him that sleeping here would be as torturous as being awake. Then, through the dark despair that was clouding his mind and robbing him of his purpose, a thought emerged like a torch. Pray – he had to pray.

Don't forget why you are here, said a familiar voice. *You draw your strength from your love of Penelope and Telemachus, of your homeland Ithaca, and from the undying hope that you will return to them. But love and hope cannot exist here. That is why your resolve is failing. But I will not abandon you and Eperitus entirely, not in this place, though you turned your backs on me at Troy.*

'Athena!' he whispered.

Summon the dead, Odysseus, offer them sacrifices and give them the blood of life they so crave. Learn what you must from Teiresias and from the other wretches who inhabit this place, some of whom it will pain you to see. Witness the horror of their existence if you have to, but remember you belong in the world of the living. Do not let despair keep you here. Isn't it enough that one day you will leave your bodies behind and join the teeming ranks of the dead? But that time has not yet come. Think of me and live.

Odysseus opened his eyes and turned to Eperitus. His expression told him he had not been alone in hearing the voice of the goddess.

'We must complete what we came here to do,' Eperitus told him, 'even though all hope of ever leaving this place has gone. You must summon the dead.'

Odysseus held up the palms of his hands and began calling on the spirits of the Underworld, promising them a barren heifer on his return to Ithaca. Naming Teiresias, he pledged the seer a separate sacrifice of a black sheep if he would present himself and answer his questions. When his invocations were done, he grasped the ram's thick fleece and straddled it, holding it fast between his knees. The animal sensed its coming death and bleated loudly until Odysseus drew his blade across its throat. The blood gushed out into the trench below, steaming in the frigid air. Tossing the carcass towards Omeros, he beckoned for Eperitus to hand him the black ewe. The mist that had thus far clung to the far banks of the two rivers now began to writhe and roll towards the Ithacans. At the same time, Odysseus started to hear the voices Eperitus had spoken of, a maelstrom of whispers in which single words rose to the surface to touch upon his consciousness for an instant, before being forgotten again. And every word was a name, though whether it was the name of the speaker or a plea for a loved one he could not tell. Grabbing the black ewe, he held it over the trench and slashed open its throat with a quick movement. The blood flowed quickly and heavily, splashing into the shallow pit and on the dead vegetation around it. And wherever it touched the grass or the flowers he saw that the colour began to return to them.

Then a terrifying moan rose up into the stagnant air, and from the formless mist hundreds of translucent figures began to emerge, rushing towards the trench with open mouths and grasping hands. Defying the instinct to run back to the tunnel and claw his way back to the world of the living, Odysseus summoned the last of his courage and stepped across the trench, holding the point of his sword before him.

'Stay where you are!' he commanded. 'Only those I permit can drink of the blood.'

He looked now at the teeming mass of insubstantial forms, the sorrowful imprints of humanity still clinging to the shapes they had held in life. They crowded around him: rank upon rank, tier upon tier; men and women, greybeards and infants; a bride with withered summer flowers in her hair; a young girl with gashed wrists held towards him; a bruised, bloody child stumbling towards him on broken legs; and countless men in gore-spattered armour, their wounds gaping open and the stumps of severed limbs dripping with spectral blood. Their eyes were white orbs, and though terrible to look at, Odysseus instinctively knew it was a mercy, for to have seen the suffering in them would have been unbearable. As he fought back his horror at the sight of them, he realised they were uttering just one name now. His.

'In the name of Athena,' he called out behind him, his voice shaking, 'flay and burn those damned animals and pray to Hades and Persephone for protection.'

The black ewe was dragged away by Eperitus and he heard the slither of a dagger being drawn. Risking a glance behind him he saw his comrades' blood-drained faces as they skinned and dismembered the two animals. But in that moment of inattention one of the wraiths rushed forward and grasped his sword, running its vaporous tongue along the blade. Immediately it threw its head back and seemed to draw breath, while the faintest flush of colour seeped into its ghostly outline. Odysseus recognised him at once.

'Elpenor? How can you be here before us?'

Because my guide was Hermes and my soul is no longer weighed down by the flesh, though I yearn to wear my earthly form again.

Odysseus felt he heard Elpenor's voice in his head rather than with his ears. Traitor though he was, the king looked at the spectre before him and felt pity. That same morning the man had tried to murder him, and yet there was no joy in Odysseus's heart to see what he had become. It was punishment enough that he existed now only as a vapid image of his former self, perfectly recreated but without the ability to connect with the physical world. Even his blank eyes were fixed on a point slightly above Odysseus's head, like the empty gaze of a blind man. Perhaps in this place it was a blessing.

Why did you not give me my burial rites, my lord? he said. *Are you so devoid of mercy that you could not burn my remains and raise a mound for me?*

Odysseus turned and saw Omeros standing and staring at the ghost of his friend. The fleece of the black ewe hung limply from one hand, a bloodied dagger from the other.

Does he know how I died, Odysseus?

'Be silent, phantom. You suffered a fool's death, but now I see you I feel compassion for you. If I ever leave this place and return to Circe's island, I will do as you ask.'

Swear it! Swear it by the names of your wife, your son and your father. Swear it by the great men who died at Troy, whose spirits I feel pressing behind me. Swear you will leave me a barrow on the shores of Aeaea and plant my oar in its fresh earth. Don't let my memory perish from the world of men, even if I only serve to act as a warning to others not to sacrifice life's riches for the sake of poor ambition. Swear it or bring the curse of the gods down upon yourself.

'I swear it!'

Elpenor's ghost lowered its head and faded away to smoke. As the vapour cleared, Odysseus recognised another phantom among the crowd of dead. Beneath its hood was the face of an old woman, lined by grief and with a black toothless hole for a mouth. At the sight of her, Odysseus's eyes widened and he let out a groan.

'Mother,' he whispered. His vision was blurred with tears, but he knelt before her and bowed his head. 'Anticleia, great daughter of

Autolycus, what terrible fate has brought you here when you should be among the living on Ithaca?'

The phantom hung before him, silent and loathsome, a ghastly parody of woman who had brought him into the world and nurtured him.

'Then if you won't speak about yourself, tell me about Laertes, and your grandson Telemachus? Are they alive? Is the kingdom still mine, or has it been taken by force? And what of my beloved Penelope? Why won't you speak to me?'

She can't, Odysseus heard a voice saying in his head. *Not unless you let her drink the blood.*

He looked aside and saw the spectre of an old man leaning on a golden staff. His eyes were not white orbs like the other spirits, but stared with black pupils directly at Odysseus. Anticleia's ghost bowed before him, then drifted to one side so that the old man could move slowly forward.

'Then why can I hear you?' Odysseus asked.

'Because Persephone, Queen of the Underworld, has cursed me with the singular luxury of retaining my faculties. In all her wide realm – the greatest of *all* the kingdoms – there are but four souls that have use of their senses. And before you arrived, there was just me.'

'Teiresias.'

'That was my name, here by the misfortune of death. But what of you? What ill fate brings a man of flesh and blood to shun the warmth and light of the sun and seek out the shades of the dead?'

'I came here to find answers. Answers that only you can give.'

'Then I must taste blood. Withdraw your sword and let me drink.'

Odysseus raised the point of his weapon and stepped back. Teiresias fell forward onto his knees and lapped at the blood like a dog. His grey outline – much fainter than Elpenor's had been – sharpened and took on a momentary flicker of substance. Then, when he was satisfied, he sat back and raised his head, breathing deeply and savouring the taste of the blood.

'That was good,' he sighed. 'When I was alive every artery and vein in my body ran with life and I barely noticed it. I was too busy worrying about life to spend any time *living* it! You'll know what I mean one day, Odysseus, son of Laertes. Or perhaps you already do. War, it seems, does not attract you with its hollow glory, nor fame and riches. Instead you seek the way home, to rugged Ithaca that you love so much. And to the humble palace where your wife and son await you. Your heart lies with them. Though you have forgotten Penelope's embrace and have not seen Telemachus since he was a babe in arms, they have left an imprint on you that time and pain and even the will of the gods cannot wipe away. That makes you greater than all the gory heroes of Tartarus, Odysseus. Their bleeding wounds stand as tokens of their foolishness for all eternity; their acts of bravery ring out from empty poems that entice hot-blooded young men to follow in their wake. But you don't relish the laurels that only the dead can wear. Rather you have the wisdom to seek love and savour it. You are a true hero, my lord.'

Odysseus did not feel worthy of the old seer's praise. Here his heart was not filled with love, only black despair that stole the desires of his heart and left him empty. Who was Penelope, after all? Who was Teiresias? What did it matter if he clawed his way back to Ithaca or not? It would be easier to lie down on the black grass and wait for his physical body to expire so that his spirit could wander down to the banks of the River Lethe and drink forgetfulness. And yet Teiresias was right. Though he could not recall Penelope's face or hear her voice, though he could not even remember the colour of her hair, there was barely a moment that he was not conscious of her absence or in which he did not yearn for her. Even in this place of utter hopelessness he was aware of his need for her.

'The way back is not easy, Odysseus. You blinded Polyphemus, Poseidon's son, and in your pride you gave him your name when you could have remained a mere Nobody. Now Poseidon is determined to avenge what you did to his son. He will not harm you himself, because Athena has made him swear not to raise a finger against you. So he will command the seas to imprison you on the island of Thrinacie, where

Hyperion keeps his beloved cattle. There you and your crew will be tested by hunger. But be warned: the flesh of the sun god's herds is not to be eaten. They roam the land from shore to shore, fattening themselves on the lush grass and afraid of nothing, for not even the most foolish of sailors would dare to kill them. Control your greed and you will return home safely, all of you. But if you fail – as Poseidon hopes you will – the gods will punish your sacrilege. Should you survive their wrath, Odysseus, your journey home will be prolonged by many years. When you do return it will be as a beggar in your own palace, where you will witness other men paying court to your wife with rich gifts while you yourself will become an item of mockery.'

'Then I will die a pauper, within sight of Penelope but only close enough to watch her give herself to another?'

Teiresias shook his head.

'I can speak about your death, if you have the courage to hear it.' He paused and looked at Eperitus and Omeros, who had flayed the sheep and were listening to the conversation. 'But I will speak only to you.'

Odysseus nodded and in his head he heard Teiresias speak of how he would die.

'Everything I have told you depends on the choices you make on Thrinacie.'

'But how do I reach the island of the sun god? And how do I find Ithaca from there?'

Teiresias smiled and shook his head.

'I do not have the sight for these things,' he said. 'But there is one who does know.'

'Who is he?' Odysseus pleaded. 'If he is one of the dead, send him here to speak to me.'

'Can't you guess who she is, my lord? She is the very one who sent you here.'

'*Circe*? But why send me here if she knew the way all along?'

'To test your resolve,' Eperitus answered.

'Your friend is right,' Teiresias said as his outline began to fade. 'She wanted to know whether you loved Penelope enough to come here. When you return she will have her answer and she will let you go. You have at least earned your freedom from her, something you would not have gained otherwise.

'Now I must return to my own misery. Thank you for making my existence a little more tolerable, Odysseus. If you wish to speak with the other spirits in this place, all you have to do is let them drink the blood.'

Teiresias faded away as Elpenor had done, and as he disappeared the other spirits pushed forward towards the trench, only to be driven back by a sweep of Odysseus's blade.

'Mother,' he said, turning to the ghost of Anticleia. 'Come forward and drink.'

She drifted forward and lay across the trench, lowering her face to the blood. Again, the spectral vision became clearer, its features more focussed and its pallor less grim. The white orbs blinked and vaporous arms reached out towards Odysseus.

My child? Oh my sweet child, why have you come here? Go back! Go back to the upper realms and savour what life remains to you.

Odysseus wiped the tears from his cheeks and reached for her outstretched arms, feeling nothing but icy vapour between his fingertips. But as his hands passed through hers she pulled away in shock, then raised her palms to her cheeks. He saw she was smiling.

It is good to be mourned, she said. *I feel your tears, my son, and they are like balm to me.*

'Then I will stay here and comfort you with my grief.'

No. It is no comfort to me that you have descended to Hades's Halls. It is with good reason the gods have made this place difficult for mortals to find. Why then are you here, instead of making your way to Ithaca, where Penelope awaits you with an aching heart?

'Then she hasn't given herself to another?' he asked, the sudden flash of joy he felt quickly stifled by the bitter memory of his own unfaithfulness. 'I would not be in this terrible place were it not for the desire to be with her again. Ever since Troy fell I have been a luckless wanderer, rejected and cursed by the gods and now led here to learn the way home from Teiresias. But now you must tell me how you… how it was you died. Is Father with you? And what about Telemachus? He must be a lad now. Is he strong? Is he bright? Will he grow up to inherit my throne, or has Eupeithes claimed the kingdom for his own son already? And tell me about my wife. If you have nothing else good to say, at least soothe my anguish and tell me she is happy.'

How can she be happy when you are absent? But you need not worry for her. She is strong and patient, and her wits were still a match for Eupeithes when I departed. Your kingdom is safe for now, but only if you hurry home. And hurry you must, my dear Odysseus. Each day Telemachus grows bigger and more handsome, with the heart of a lion and the wits of a fox. But the support he has from the people sleeps, and while they slumber Eupeithes's shadow creeps ever closer to the throne. Telemachus and Penelope alone will not be able to withstand his schemes for much longer. Neither can they look to your father. Laertes has retreated to his farm where he skulks like a beggar, dressed in rags and sleeping in drifts of leaves or in the ashes of a fire for warmth. His grief has robbed him of his senses, just as grief took my life. No arrow of Artemis slew me, Odysseus; I died of a heart that broke yearning for your return.

Odysseus's own grief welled up at her words. He stepped over the trench to fling his arms about her, but her flesh had long since perished in the fire. What remained slipped through his arms like smoke and fled wailing into the multitude of souls behind her.

Chapter Thirty-Five

THE SPIRITS OF THE FALLEN

Eperitus's relief at escaping the confines of the tunnel was short-lived. Immediately the whispering voices of the dead assailed his hearing, and at the edges of his vision he could see them in the mist, human shapes that writhed in the agony of their suffering. By comparison the tunnel seemed a place of sanctuary, a lifeline back to the physical world. Only his sense of duty to Odysseus kept him there.

He watched Odysseus collapse in tears on the grass as the ghost of his mother faded away. The spirits of many noble women had gathered in her wake and now surged towards the unguarded blood. Eperitus leapt forward with the point of his dagger and they fell back with a shriek, as if swept away by a gust of wind. Only one remained, a child in bloodstained sacrificial robes. The dagger fell from Eperitus's grip and he staggered backwards.

It was Iphigenia.

Again the dead rushed forward. Royal women who had never lifted a hand to serve themselves now clawed at each other's ethereal faces and arms in their desperation to taste the blood and feel their empty veins run with the memory of life once more. Only when Odysseus returned to his senses and drove them back with his sword did they stop, though those that had already slaked their thirst he permitted to remain and talk with him. But Eperitus was only vaguely aware of their whispers. For a long time all he was able to do was stand and stare at his daughter. He remembered how full of life she had been when they had first met in Mycenae. Now her white feet made no impression in the black grass, and her marbled eyes, which had once stared at him with love, now looked straight through him. As he watched, the dark stain on her robes where Agamemnon's blade had torn the life from her seemed to spread, as if the fatal wound had been struck only moments before. It was almost too much. His limbs shook so fiercely that he was barely able to stand, and though he wanted to turn to Odysseus and tell him to let her drink, he was afraid to. He was afraid that by taking his eyes from her she might disappear. He was more afraid that by giving her voice she might blame him for failing to save her, words that would crush what spirit remained to him in this place. So he stood and let the tears run in unending streams down his cheeks and into his beard. Then the rustle of empty, breathless voices beside him faded and the ghosts of the women who had spoken with Odysseus withdrew. Sensing Iphigenia would soon follow, Eperitus stepped forward and opened his arms to her. Only then did he see the tears in her eyes, empty though they were. At this evidence of her pain he fell to his knees and sobbed openly.

'Forgive me,' he pleaded.

She came to him with open arms. He saw the word 'Father' forming on her silent lips, but as he staggered to his feet and reached out to embrace her, she halted and glanced away to her left. Fear marred the features of her beautiful face, and then, like autumn leaves swept up by the wind, she turned and fled. Eperitus threw himself forward, as if his living arms could snatch up her spectral body and keep her there, but she was gone. He buried his face in the dead grass and beat the ground with his fist.

The agony of losing her again might have kept him there, but as black misery threatened to descend on him he heard a sound like the approach of a wave. The clamour grew and he recognised it at once: the shouts of men and the groans of the injured – the terrible cacophony of battle. Instinctively he raised his head and reached for the sword at his hip. A great crowd of warriors now pressed forward, struggling against each other like fish in a net. But as he watched he saw they were not fighting one another. Instead, each man seemed engaged in individual combat against an invisible enemy, all of them oblivious to the life-stealing wounds already imprinted on their wraithlike bodies. They hacked at the air with their weapons and screamed war cries as if they were still fighting for their lives, though they were already dead. They looked like an angry mob demanding the return of the lives they had thrown away. And as he watched he realised he could so easily have been one of them, protesting the theft of the only life he had to give. He saw then the real price of the glory he had sought for so much of his life; and he knew it would not have been worth it.

Odysseus lowered his sword and called to a man from a part of the crowd where there seemed to be no fighting. In answer to Odysseus's summons he detached himself from his comrades and walked naked across the grass. Water dripped from his muscular body onto the ground below. His face, head and shoulders had been cleaved in several places by a heavy blade and rivulets of blood ran down from the wounds to mingle with the water. The injuries were so terrible that for a moment Eperitus did not recognise him. When he did, he understood why his daughter's ghost had fled.

Agamemnon knelt and dipped his fingers in the blood. Raising them to his lips, he looked up and beheld his old ally standing before him. His empty expression changed and he tried to throw his arms around Odysseus, but his limbs passed through him. Reminded of his bodiless state, the king of Mycenae let out a mournful groan that silenced the clamour behind him.

Odysseus, great Laertes's son, do not look at me as if I shouldn't be here, he began. *This is my home now. Once I was the greatest of all the kings in the world of the living, but here among the dead I am poorer than the least of the beggars who sit before the mighty gates of Mycenae. If all my wealth and power could not keep me from this destiny, what use was any of it? I tell you now, Odysseus, I would not have sailed to Troy for all the oaths of men if I had known the real price of sacrificing my daughter to the gods. Only now do I see my folly.*

'But what tragedy has brought you here, my friend?' Odysseus asked. 'You led us to victory over the Trojans and should have lived to enjoy the spoils, and yet your spirit is here among the dead. What was it? A shipwreck? We saw Little Ajax's corpse on our voyage, floating among the wreckage of his galley, and now I see your body streaming with water. What did you do to anger Poseidon so much?'

Agamemnon shook his head.

It was no storm that killed me. I am almost too ashamed to speak of it, but if it will save you from a similar fate then I will put aside my humiliation. Odysseus, I returned safely home to my own palace, only to be murdered by my faithless wife. Clytaemnestra struck me down with an axe while I bathed.

Eperitus's fists clenched. Iphigenia had been avenged! If any joy was possible in that sombre land, he felt it then. Clytaemnestra had made him swear to protect Agamemnon's life so that she could make him pay for what he had done to their daughter, and just as Calchas had foreseen, she had succeeded. Then he remembered Iphigenia's forlorn ghost, weeping for the years that had been taken from her. Was she satisfied that her murderer had met a rightful end? Did the king of Mycenae's death lessen her suffering at all? Eperitus's momentary elation drained away as he realised Agamemnon's murder had solved nothing. All his presence in the Underworld had achieved was to cause Iphigenia to flee in terror from him, when she could have found a moment's solace in the company of her true father. Better Agamemnon had lived than have him cause Iphigenia's condemned soul more misery.

In her infamy the bitch slew Cassandra, too, Agamemnon continued. *What had the poor girl done to deserve such a fate, other than allowing herself to be captured alive in the ruins of Troy? When I first took her as my wife a few men dared to tell me Clytaemnestra was a witch, but I refused to listen. Oh that I had, Odysseus! Now you should take heed of my warning. Is Penelope the woman you believed her to be? Or is she even now in the arms of another man, selling Telemachus's inheritance because she could not wait for your return? Don't forget she's of the same unfaithful line as Helen and Clytaemnestra, so you can be sure she will be watching for your sail on the horizon and plotting to kill you the moment you return. Pray that if she succeeds she will at least permit you to set eyes on your son first, a privilege that was denied to me!*

As Agamemnon returned to the great army whose spirits he had condemned to Hades, Eperitus searched the faces of the dead warriors for Apheidas. It struck him as strange that he should seek out the man who had caused him such misery, but he could not see his father among the gory ranks. Then he saw Antiphus, his ethereal body showing the wounds where the Cyclops's teeth had mutilated his flesh. The archer's empty eyes glanced at him in momentary recognition before the multitude of the dead swallowed him up again. Arceisius appeared also, his mouth red with blood and a hole in his chest where Apheidas's sword had ended his life. Eperitus called to him, but he too was sucked back into the press of bodies. A moment later the ghost of Achilles forced his way through and stood on the empty sward before the phantom army. Paris's black-feathered arrow protruded from his ankle and he still wore the armour Hephaistos had made for him, though it had lost its lustre and the figures on the shield no longer moved. Despite this, of all the spirits Eperitus had seen, Achilles's was the only one that retained any of the pride it had carried in life.

Odysseus beckoned him forward and he knelt to drink the blood. His pallid outline became clearer and the carvings on his shield flickered momentarily into life, though by the time he had returned to his feet they were still again.

Odysseus, he said in a tired voice. *What trick did you pull to get into this place? And why in Hades would you want to come here anyway? Hoping to cheat me of my spectral armour, just like you cheated Ajax of the real thing? He hasn't forgotten that, even here where forgetfulness soothes the dead of all the burdens they carried in life. Many a time I've caught him eyeing my shield and helmet. Foolish cousin. Death should have made him realise the true worth of such things. But what have you done with them, Odysseus? Not lost them, I hope, especially after they cost what little honour remained to you?*

Odysseus looked down at his feet in shame.

'I had my reasons, Achilles. Perhaps you will think more highly of me when you learn I gave your armour to your son.'

Neoptolemus! Then you are forgiven, my friend. Twice forgiven if you will tell me about him. What sort of man is he? Is he worthy of the noble blood that runs through his veins?

'More than worthy,' Odysseus answered, and Achilles's grim face brightened a little as Odysseus described Neoptolemus's feats on the battlefield, his killing of Eurypylus and his part in the capture of Troy.

If only I could see him now. My mother warned me that if I went to Troy I would perish, even though my name would live on in glory. But I was young and foolish: I chose fame over life. If only I could be given the choice again.

'Do not regret your death, Achilles. All die, but few are honoured among the living as you are.'

And do not dismiss death so lightly, Odysseus, the wraith replied. *I would rather be a lowly farmer with the blood still in my veins than a king among the dead. Far better to feel the sweat on my brow and the strain of the plough against my muscles than to wear a ghost's crown in the company of the woeful departed. I would surrender my place in the hearts and minds of every man in Greece for a single moment back among the living! Cling on to life, Odysseus. Dig your fingers into it and never let go, for it's all you have.*

With those words he turned and strode away, the ranks of the dead opening to receive him. For as long as Eperitus could remember, he had hankered to be a warrior like his grandfather before him, risking his life again and again for the sake of honour. Only as the war had drawn towards its bloody climax – and Astynome had opened his mind to the possibilities of life – had he begun to comprehend its futility. But Achilles had shown him that glory had no value to the dead. Glory was a banquet without food.

'Ajax!' Odysseus called out. 'Come, drink the blood and speak with me.'

The great warrior now stood before the teeming dead, his arms crossed and his blank eyes staring at Odysseus. Blood still ran from the wound where, with his own sword, he had taken his life. But if

Achilles had come to realise the vanity of his lust for glory, which had driven him to his death, Ajax did not seem to understand the emptiness of the pride that had pursued him to his.

'What I did, I did with good reason,' Odysseus told him. 'Even so, I regret it with all my heart and all the more so because of what I did to you. You were the best of all the Greeks after Achilles's death; you should have taken his place and led us in the battles that remained. Instead the gods robbed you of your senses and fooled you into taking your own life. So why do you cling on to your hatred for me? Isn't there enough misery in this place without that, Ajax? Lay your burden down and let us talk like the friends we once were.'

But Ajax simply turned and pushed his way back into the crowd of spirits.

'Haven't you seen enough yet, Odysseus?'

Teiresias was standing on the steps that led up the pinnacle of rock. As he spoke, the dead began to drift away, leaving the meadow of black grass empty again. Odysseus stepped over the trench and crossed to the foot of the stone stairs.

'Odysseus,' Eperitus called after him. 'Let's go while we still have any will power left to us.'

'Listen to your friend,' Teiresias said.

But Odysseus was already climbing the steps, slowly and forcibly as if he was pushing against an invisible wall. Eperitus followed him, and after a long and wearisome climb they were at the top of the shoulder of rock, gazing down over the plain below. The falls where the Cocytus and the Phlegethon met was directly beneath them, its thick waters oozing down into the yellow Acheron. In the distance were two more rivers. One was as white as snow, which Eperitus guessed was the Lethe, the River of Forgetfulness. The other had to be the Styx, the River of Hatred, in which Achilles's mother, Thetis, had dipped her infant son by his heel to make him invulnerable. Both fed into the Acheron some distance away, helping it on its course towards a wall of peaks that rose up from the mist. Though even his eyes could not see it, Eperitus knew that that was where the souls of the dead entered the Underworld. Hermes would shepherd them past the Furies and Cerberus, the giant, three-headed hound, to the bank of the Acheron, where Charon would ferry them across to the Land of the Dead.

Though these horrors remained unseen, there were other spectacles in the barren planes below that were enough to fill both men with dread. Teiresias pointed his golden staff at an enormous figure lying across a distant hillside, his wrists and ankles shackled to boulders. His name, the seer told them, was Tityus, a giant who had attempted to rape Leto, the mother of Apollo and Artemis. Not satisfied with killing him for his crime, the twin gods had avenged their mother's honour by ensuring he kept his physical form in Hades and devising a particular punishment for him. As Teiresias spoke, Tityus's head was constantly looking up at the bleak sky, his eyes searching fearfully this way and that, until – with a piercing cry that forced Eperitus to cover his ears – two colossal vultures swooped down and settled either side of him. At once they plunged their hooked beaks into his flesh and began tearing at his liver.

'I'm told the pain is exquisite,' Teiresias added as the giant's screams shook the rock beneath their feet.

As Eperitus's eyes moved from the awful spectacle and passed with horror over the excruciating punishments of other men and women who had offended the gods, he caught a gleam like reflected light. Shunned by the misty hordes of the dead was a pool of clear water at the foot of a small cliff, from which hung the branches of a gnarled tree, heavy with fruit.

'Who's that?' he asked, pointing at a man who stood up to his neck in the middle of the pool.

'Tantalus,' Odysseus answered.

Teiresias nodded sadly and then shook his head.

'Agamemnon's great-grandfather?' Eperitus asked. 'The one who –'

'Who fed the gods a stew made from the body of his own son, Pelops,' Teiresias said. 'Yes, that is him. Like Tityus, the gods made sure he retained his body with all its physical needs. He stands in the only water in the whole of Hades, with the only living plant hanging just above him. His hands are shackled behind his back so that he can only take the fruit with his teeth or drink the water by lowering his mouth to it.'

'Then why doesn't he?'

'Watch.'

Tantalus had remained perfectly still all the time they had been discussing him. A bronze ring was fastened about his neck and attached by a chain to a metal plate on the cliff face behind him. Then, without warning, he leapt up with his mouth open at an overhanging cluster of grapes. But before his teeth could bite into them, a sudden wind blew the branches upward out of his reach. At the same time he reached the extent of his chain and was yanked back with a shout of pain. Immediately he threw himself down at the water, only for it to drain away too rapidly for him to reach it before the chain stopped him. He hung there for a while, choking violently and crying out his anguish in a hoarse voice. Eperitus looked away.

'And there is Sisyphus,' Teiresias announced, indicating with the tip of his staff a narrow shoulder of rock beside the banks of the Styx. 'He was once a king of Corinth and a man after your own heart, Odysseus, for he loved to deceive. Twice he cheated death, but when he boasted that he was cleverer than Zeus himself, that was the end of him. The Thunderer chained him to the bottom of the cliff below the peak of that rock, but he made the chain long enough for Sisyphus to climb the slope behind to the top. He also placed a round boulder at the foot of the slope that with enough force could break the chain and free him. The problem, of course, is getting enough force.'

Wearily, Eperitus stared down at the muscular figure of Sisyphus, whose bloodied shoulder was pressed against one side of the boulder. His face was screwed up with a mixture of pain and effort as he slowly edged the stone up the slope towards the peak. The path to the top had been worn smooth – ominously so – but Eperitus realised that if Sisyphus could get the huge rock to the top and send it crashing down onto the base of the chain below he would be free. Here was something as rare and strange in Hades as the water and fruit that existed to frustrate Tantalus: Sisyphus's determination was driven by hope. And as Eperitus watched the man's exertions, he felt hope too. He willed him on, knowing that if Sisyphus could reach the top and break the chain there was hope for anyone in that place. Slowly, the boulder came closer to the clifftop, one footfall after another until it seemed Sisyphus could go on no more. Then, when he was almost at the summit, he stopped. He had reached the point where the weight of the rock was too much for Sisyphus's strength, but his determination was just enough to stop it from rolling back down the slope. He stayed there for a long time, unable to move, and Eperitus realised there was still a way for Sisyphus to reach the peak only a short distance away. He took hold of Odysseus's arm.

'We have to help him.'

A similar thought must have occurred to Odysseus, who seemed ready to take the steps back down to the meadow and find a way across the rivers to the slope where Sisyphus was locked in his struggle with the boulder. Teiresias's voice broke their illusions.

'Even if you could cross the deadly rivers of the Underworld and climb the slope in time to help him, do you think it would do *you* any good to interfere with the punishments of the gods? Look.'

As he spoke, Sisyphus's foot slipped and he crashed to the ground. The boulder tumbled back down the slope to the plateau below in a tiny fraction of the time it had taken him to roll it up. For a moment Sisyphus pressed his face against the smooth rock and clawed at it with his hands. Then, slowly, he pulled himself back to his feet and trudged down the incline towards the waiting boulder.

'I can't watch any more,' Odysseus said. 'It's time to go back. Come on Eperitus, Omeros is waiting.'

book
FOUR

Chapter Thirty-Six

THE WAY HOME

Golden sunlight filled the glade. The warm air was thick with the scent of the myriad flowers that festooned Circe's porch, while from the surrounding trees the clamour of birdsong fought against the lazy hum of a thousand unseen insects. Eperitus ran a nervous hand through his freshly trimmed beard, conscious of the sweat prickling in his armpits beneath the pale green tunic the nymphs had made for the occasion. He glanced over his shoulder at the faces of his shipmates seated in rows on the lawn. Most were smiling, probably enjoying his discomfort. Only Omeros seemed sombre. For a moment Eperitus thought it was lingering grief from the burial of Elpenor only that morning. But when their eyes met he recognised immediately what troubled him. Even the brightest summer's day could not dispel the gloom of the ordeal they had suffered together. Indeed, Eperitus was afraid the shadow of Hades might never leave him, until the day his spirit returned to it forever.

He looked to his front again and stiffened himself, the same bracing of his body that he practised before a battle. At least the prelude to a battle was something he was familiar with, though. For all its horror and risk of death or dismemberment it was an environment he understood, a strictly male world in which he was confident of his abilities. This, though, *this* was alien to him. A wedding was complex, symbolic, feminine and spiritual; a ceremony over which the gods presided, but not the gods he knew. They were the domestic gods, the gods of life rather than death, of creation and nature rather than destruction and the force of a man's will. Yet the power of those gods ran deep. It was unfathomable and mysterious, fuelled by emotion and mocking of intellect. But nervous though he was, Eperitus was ready to surrender himself to them.

It would be a strange marriage. Unlike some of the other weddings he had attended, this would be no union of convenience in which the parents of the bride and groom had matched their children to tie the families together, bringing them status, wealth or power. Neither was it a matter of personal expediency in which the man was securing a suitable mate to continue his line, or the woman was seeking to become the legitimate head of a man's household. There would be no gifts to woo the bride, no parents to symbolically give a child away, and no home to which the groom would take his bride after the ceremony – and by living there with her and producing a child make their marriage binding. Astynome had not fulfilled the custom of holding a pre-marriage feast, nor had she made sacrifices to the gods. And rather than being young strangers with no carnal knowledge of each other, she and Eperitus had been lovers and friends from almost the moment they had met. Though many husbands and wives learned to love each other over the years of their relationship, the pre-existence of love between Eperitus and Astynome made theirs a very strange union indeed.

Not that Eperitus cared if their marriage was unconventional. Everything about it – the ritual and tradition, the symbolism, the pomposity and public spectacle – meant nothing to him. All he wanted was to be bound together with Astynome in the eyes of gods and men. She would not be disregarded as his slave or concubine but be honoured as his wife, coming under his protection and being respected as the future mother of his children.

The thought made him smile. Only that morning, as she had watched Elpenor's funeral pyre with him on the beach, they had spoken about the family they would make together. In the aftermath of death they prepared for new life. Whose looks would the child inherit? Whose temper and nature? Boy or girl, he told her he hoped it would be hers. She smiled and looked away; then she replied that the child would be a boy with his father's dark looks and surly temperament. Only when she added he would become a great warrior like him did he stop her.

'No, my love. If the child's to be a boy I'd rather he took up the ploughshare than the spear. Let him be a farmer, an honest man earning his living from the land. Let him produce a bounty in crops or livestock to benefit his family and those around him, rather than become a parasite like his father, sowing the land with blood to reap a harvest of hollow glory.'

Astynome had nodded and put her arm around his shoulders.

'Perhaps you're right. We've seen too much bloodshed in our lives. Let the time for warriors be over and the time for farmers begin. But now I must go back to Circe's maids. They'll have my bath ready and be laying out the wedding clothes on the bed.'

'Wait,' he commanded.

She turned and he caught her by the waist, pulling her into his arms and kissing her. She pulled away and tried to give him a chiding look.

'It's bad luck to kiss a bride before she's married! Wait until this evening and you can kiss me as much as you like – and wherever you like.'

As he watched her run back into the woods he thanked the gods that she was his. The Underworld still weighed heavily on his spirit and had left him haunted by dark thoughts. He had witnessed the emptiness of eternity and it had changed him. But she was the antidote to its slow poison. Without her, everything would be pointless.

A cough startled him from his thoughts. He heard the men shuffling on their chairs and the first notes as Omeros tested the strings of his lyre. Eperitus took a deep breath and straightened himself, staring directly at the doors in the portico before him. His stomach muscles tightened horribly. Then Omeros began to play, and for a moment the music cleansed him of all thoughts. Suddenly he felt the brightness of the sun again and smelled the sweet flowers. How a man who had experienced the despair of the Land of the Dead could find such beauty in his heart he did not know, but as Omeros's fingers stroked the strings, Eperitus felt his own burden lifted. He fought the tears – of joy? of relief? – and turned to see two figures behind him on the lawn. One was Odysseus, short, muscular and top-heavy. Circe's nymphs had dressed him in a blue tunic and patched and repaired the double cloak Penelope had given him so that it looked newly made. His red hair was tied back behind his neck and he appeared more kingly than Eperitus had seen him look in a long time. But he paid only brief attention to Odysseus. Hanging on his arm was a tall figure in a slim-fitting chiton with a red sash about her waist. Flowers had been threaded into her black hair and she held a bouquet of white lilies in her hand. Her eyes were looking down at the grass beneath her bare feet and for a moment she seemed frail and afraid. Then she looked up and the tears he had fought back at the sound of Omeros's playing now defeated him. Every eye was on Astynome, so none but she saw him dash them away.

She smiled and, with a glance at Odysseus, walked slowly towards him.

Odysseus looked at Eperitus and Astynome, sitting in the chairs that until then he and Circe had occupied. An outsider might easily have thought they had been married for years, not just a day. At one point he noticed Eperitus place a hand tellingly on Astynome's stomach. She brushed it away discreetly and looked around to see if anyone had noticed, forcing Odysseus to avert his eyes quickly. It was then he caught Eurylochus staring at Astynome, the gleam of hatred and desire in his eyes. The poor fool, he thought. Does he really think she would consider him, even now?

The notion jarred him back to the darkness of the Underworld and the sight of Agamemnon's apparition, dripping blood as it spoke of marital betrayal and murder. *Is Penelope the woman you believed her to be? Or is she even now in the arms of another man?* It was a question that had troubled him from the moment he had crawled back into the narrow tunnel that led back to the Grove of Persephone. And why not? He had betrayed her, he reminded himself, even if it had broken his heart to do so. Why should she sleep alone while he spent ten years fighting in a foreign land? Even if she had kept their bed pure for all that time, why should she continue when all the other kings had returned to Greece and he had not? *Don't forget she's of the same unfaithful line as Helen and Clytaemnestra*, he heard Agamemnon's voice repeating in his head.

Odysseus drank his wine through gritted teeth. He was angrier with himself for doubting her than he was at the idea she would have betrayed him. Had not the ghost of his own mother reassured him of Penelope's fidelity? If he was to worry about matters at home he should think of his poor father, grieving for his lost son, and Telemachus, still too young to stand up against the schemes of Eupeithes. Anticleia had warned him that the old snake was casting his gaze on the throne once more, an ambition that had been confirmed by Elpenor's confession before Odysseus had broken his neck. And if Eupeithes had dared send Elpenor to kill him while the war was still raging, how much closer to maturity would his plans be now?

Odysseus took a deep breath and began drumming his bitten nails on the table, cursing the fact his family and his kingdom were in peril while he wasted time on a feast in his lover's house. He wanted to leave now, but he knew he could not. Only Circe knew the way home, and though she was sitting beside him he could barely bring himself to speak to her. She had sent him to Hades's Halls on a false promise, just because she wanted to test his love for Penelope. Had he not made that clear enough already? Of course not, he heard Eperitus's voice answer him. He had slept with Circe when there had been no need; naturally she would question his love for another woman. If she had sent him to the place where no living man should go then he only had himself to blame.

'Eperitus is fortunate,' Circe said, breaking the silence that had fallen between them. 'Astynome will prove a good wife. And a good mother.'

He looked at her. 'Then you know.'

'I probably knew before he did. I'm happy for them. They were meant to be together, unlike us.'

'I'm sorry you thought we could ever –'

'Don't! I'd rather you didn't say it.'

Odysseus took another swallow of wine, keeping his eyes on Eperitus and Astynome.

'Did you really have to send me to Hades to prove I didn't love you?'

'Do you have to say it, Odysseus? Do you enjoy being cruel to me after all I've done for you?'

'This is not a *game*, Circe!' he retorted, managing to keep his voice low enough not to gain the attention of others. 'You sent me to the Underworld to prove something a real woman should have been able to work out for herself. But that's your problem. You're not a real woman, are you? You're immortal. The Underworld means nothing to you. But do you understand what going there has done to *me*?'

'I'm sorry, Odysseus. I didn't think.'

He laughed ironically. 'The gods and their kind never do. It's just a game to you, and mortals like me and Eperitus are the pawns.'

'That is our prerogative,' she answered sharply, 'and unless you think that by spurning my advances you are now my equal, I would not tempt my anger.' Her white skin had turned pink at the cheeks, but the hardness in her green eyes quickly softened again. 'We should not argue, not on our last evening together.'

Her words took him by surprise. They had not spoken about parting since his return and he had not known how to tell her that he intended to leave the next morning.

'Yes, I know. I may be immortal, but it doesn't mean I can't read a man's eyes. If I'm honest, I knew you wouldn't stay the first time you took me. Even though I drugged your wine to make you forget your home, I still hoped you would be mine of your own free will. And now I know that will never be the case. But I do not hate you for it, Odysseus. Indeed, I love you, and for that reason I will tell you how to find your way back to Ithaca.'

He reached out and took her hand. It was more than he had hoped for to have her reveal his homeward route, and he had not known how he might otherwise coax it from her. He had already promised himself he would not share her bed.

'Thank you, my lady. I'm glad we can part friends.'

'I wish it could be otherwise, but I'm not a fool. When you find Ithaca, maybe you will remember me when you're in Penelope's arms again. I don't mean as a lover, but as a benefactor. For if I had refused, you would have wandered through this netherworld – as you think of it – without ever finding your way home.'

'Then how do we get back?'

Circe glanced at the Ithacans around them then, still holding Odysseus's hand, pushed her chair back and stood.

'Not here.'

He followed her out onto the lawn, where several wolves and lions lay huddled together in their separate groups. The skies were clear but for a few skeins of cloud, silvered by the light of the half-moon that was rising over the treetops.

'The route is not easy, Odysseus. Only a man of your intelligence and single-mindedness can overcome the perils on the way. First, you must sail with the sun behind you until you pass an island to the north. You will know it when you see it by the broken hulls of the many ships that have come to grief on its shores. Though you will be drawn there long before you see it.'

'What do you mean?'

'It's the home of the Sirens,' Circe said. 'Terrible creatures to behold, but with voices so beautiful that no man can resist the sound of them. It is said the Sirens know all things that happen on the earth and in the sea and that they enchant passing sailors with news of the things closest to their hearts.'

'Would they speak to me of events on Ithaca? Can they tell me about Penelope and Telemachus?'

Circe frowned slightly at the mention of Odysseus's family.

'Don't be fooled, Odysseus. The Sirens are not prophets; they are monsters. They use their voices to bewitch sailors and draw their ships onto the merciless rocks that surround their island. Those that survive provide meat for the Sirens, who leave their gleaming bones strewn over the hillside where they have their nest.'

'Nest? What sort of creatures are they?'

'That you must learn for yourself, but only from afar unless you want to share the fate of their other victims. To avoid that I will give you beeswax from my hives to plug up your ears and the ears of your men, so you can sail past in safety. After the Sirens you will reach a mass of land that is impassable except for in two places. The most perilous of these lies to the south and takes you into a channel between high cliffs. It is broad and easily navigable until you reach halfway, when you will come to the Wandering Rocks. Here the strait narrows to a point only wide enough for a single galley, but as soon as it falls beneath the shadow of the Wandering Rocks the sea rushes in like a wall and smashes both galley and crew to nothing. Only one ship has ever survived the passage, and her captain was under the protection of a goddess – something you, Odysseus, can no longer count on.'

'And the other route?'

'To the north lies a narrow, meandering channel that passes between high cliffs on both sides. After a while you will reach a wider body of water. To your left is a straight cliff and halfway along it you will see a large fig tree growing from a crag. Do *not* go that way, Odysseus. Instead you must steer your ship to the right where another wall of rock rises sheer from the sea. It is much taller than the cliff where the fig tree grows, even though it is only a bowshot away. Its summit is always shrouded in cloud, but at some distance above the surface of the water you will see a cavern. If you are determined to reach Ithaca, you must sail close beneath it, as near to the rocks as you dare.'

'What's in the cavern?' Odysseus asked. 'And why can't I sail beneath the fig tree.'

'It's better that you don't know.'

But Odysseus was insistent. When Circe told him the answers to his question he stared at her horror-stricken.

'Is there no other way?' he asked.

'None.'

'And after that?'

'You will come to the island of Thrinacie. No monsters live there, but it is as perilous a place as any I have described to you so far.'

Odysseus recalled Teiresias's warning about the cattle of the sun god, but said nothing.

'Pass it by, Odysseus, and keep the prow of your ship towards the west. After some days you will come to Phaeacia, the happy island of King Alcinous that sits on the cusp between our world and yours. His people are great seafarers; if you can win his favour, he will order them to lead you back to your own home at last.'

As she finished speaking, the door of the great hall opened and spilled yellow light over the porch. Eurybates and Polites staggered out arm in arm, singing raucously.

'Odysseus!' Eurybates shouted, spotting his king on the lawn. 'So this is where you've disappeared to. Come back in and get drunk with the rest of us.'

Polites lifted the wineskin in his hand and threw it to him. His aim was so bad it landed in the middle of the slumbering lions, one of which struck it with its paw. The leather split and the dark liquid sank quickly into the grass, to laughter from the two men on the porch.

Odysseus turned to make his apologies to Circe, but she had gone.

Chapter Thirty-Seven

THE SIRENS

Eperitus shielded his eyes from the sun and looked again. At this distance the bird was nothing more than a dark blur against the blue, cloudless sky, but he could see that it was larger than any seabird he knew of.

'What is it?' Odysseus asked, joining him at the prow.

'An eagle, I think, but not like any I've seen before. And there's something else, something about its shape that looks wrong.'

Odysseus squinted beneath the cover of his own hand, but shook his head after a moment.

'Circe said these Sirens had a nest. Birds live in nests.'

'A monster bird?' Eperitus said, smiling wryly. 'We've faced worse. But I'll repeat what I said to you this morning: she lied to us when she sent us to see Teiresias. Perhaps these Sirens and Wandering Rocks she told you about are another trick to keep you in her clutches.'

'We'll know soon enough, I suppose.'

Eperitus!

Eperitus turned in surprise.

'What is it?' Odysseus asked.

Eperitus! Trust your instincts.

He gripped the bow rail and looked out at the green sea. The voice had been as clear and as pure as a note from Omeros's lyre, reaching deep into his heart so that the imprint of the words still lingered on in his mind.

'Did you hear that, Odysseus? A voice in the air that said my name.'

'All I can hear is the wind and the sound of the waves beating against the hull.'

Trust your instincts about Circe. She is a liar and Odysseus is under her spell. He is not himself.

'Do you still hear it?' Odysseus asked. 'The voice – can you still hear it?'

She lied to him, Eperitus. Both routes she told him about will lead to destruction. She knows she cannot have him for herself, so she would rather see him dead – and the rest of you with him.

'What did Circe tell you about the other passage, Odysseus? Not the Wandering Rocks, the other one.'

'Land!' Polites's voice boomed out over the rushing wind and the flap of the sail. 'Land to the north-west.'

Eperitus looked up at the top of the mast where Polites had lashed himself with rope. Following the direction he was pointing in, he was able to distinguish a low, flat hump on the horizon. The rest of the crew had seen it too and began talking in loud, excited voices.

'Omeros,' Odysseus called, 'bring me that lump of wax I gave you. Now! Polites, untie yourself and get down here at once.'

There is only one safe route, Eperitus, the ringing voice told him. Or was it more than one voice, speaking in absolute harmony? *Come to us if you want to live. Come to us and we will show you the way.*

Omeros presented Odysseus with the lump of beeswax, still wrapped in its cloth.

'Quickly now, take your knife and cut the wax into pieces,' the king ordered him. 'Give two pieces to each man and tell them to soften them and put them in their ears. Polites will help you. And make sure they wrap cloth around their ears to keep the wax from falling out.'

Omeros nodded and ran to where Polites was waiting. Odysseus turned and looked up at the sky.

'There are two of them now,' he said. 'They're the Sirens. I know it in my blood.'

Eperitus followed his gaze and saw the birds, still far off as they circled each other high above the island. He could see now that they were brown with small white heads. At that distance even his eyesight could not make out anything in detail, but the heads seemed blunt, rather than pointed like an eagle's.

'Can you hear them, Eperitus? What are they saying?'

'What is this passage Circe told you about?' Eperitus insisted. 'Is it dangerous? If it wasn't, why would she even mention the other way through the Wandering Rocks?'

The king hesitated just long enough for Eperitus to know he was preparing a lie.

'She said nothing about danger. It's narrow and there will be rocks beneath the surface, but little to worry about compared to the alternative. There *is* no alternative.'

'What about the Sirens? Surely they would know the way. Circe says they are monsters, but she's lied to you before –'

Odysseus placed a hand on his shoulder.

'She isn't lying this time, I know it. Why would she?'

'Because she can't have you for herself, so she'd rather see you dead. All we need to do is sail closer to the island and see them for ourselves.'

Odysseus looked over his shoulder.

'Omeros, bring the wax here.'

You see? said the voices. They were clearer now and the sound of them was as sweet as Hades had been bitter. *There's no reasoning with him. Circe has bewitched him. Only you can save the ship now, Eperitus. Only you can stop him leading you all to your deaths.*

He leaned against the bow rail again, staring hard at the island. The voices were at the edge of his hearing and still beyond the abilities of the others, but they were beautiful and powerful, filled with wisdom and the promise of salvation. The words touched his soul, unlocking feelings that had always been there but which years of self-discipline had suppressed. Emotions stirred inside him that freed his spirit from the shackles of the past: from the hateful memories of the death of Iphigenia, his father's betrayal and the horrors of the war; even from the shadow of despair that had fallen on him in the Underworld and which he had thought he would never be free of. The source of the freedom, he knew, lay on the island he could see on the distant horizon. And then he realised this was the safe route the voices had spoken of: to dwell forever on the island with the Sirens, where there was no sorrow or strife, only peace and rest.

Yes. Now you understand, Eperitus. You will be safe with us, You, Astynome, Odysseus, all of you.

A strong hand took his upper arm and turned him forcefully about. It was Odysseus.

'I know you can hear them, Eperitus,' he said. 'They're calling you to them, aren't they? Just as Circe said they would.'

'You'll hear them for yourself soon and then you'll understand.'

'I intend to listen, but you were never meant to. Here, put these in your ears before they have you jumping overboard.'

Eperitus looked at the balls of wax in the palm of Odysseus's hand, then at Omeros and Polites standing either side of him. He spun round and tried to climb onto the bow rail, but Polites seized hold of his arms and pulled him back. Against his great strength there was no escape. He pinned Eperitus's arms to his sides while Odysseus held his jaw with one hand and pressed the lumps of soft wax firmly into each ear. At the king's instruction, Omeros unknotted the filthy scarf from Eperitus's neck and wound it like a bandage around his head, covering his ears and keeping the wax in place. The voices stopped at once. The power of their music snapped like a bowstring and the beautiful emotions that had filled his eyes with tears crumbled away to leave him empty and sad once more. Then Polites released him and Astynome appeared, slipping her arms about him and pulling his head onto her shoulder.

The strong wind that had driven them forward from Aeaea now fell away, leaving the galley in a dead calm. Odysseus called to the crew to raise the sail and take down the cross spar, but with their ears blocked they looked at him dumbfounded, forcing him to signal his orders. Several rose from their benches to carry out his command before returning and sliding the oars out into the gently moving ocean.

Eperitus sent Astynome back to the stern with the Trojan women and their children – whose ears were also blocked with wax – then joined the rest of the crew at the oars. Odysseus now turned to Omeros and Polites, who were busy kneading the hard wax with their fingers to soften it.

'We're approaching the lair of the Sirens,' he told them. 'I warned everyone about them before we sailed and now we've seen the effect of their voices on Eperitus. Now, stop up your ears as closely as you can and take your places at the oars.'

Omeros offered two balls of wax to Odysseus, but the king shook his head.

'I want to hear their song.'

'So you can jump overboard like Eperitus tried to do?' Omeros asked.

'No. You're going to tie me to the mast as securely as you can. If I try to break free or order you to release me then you're to pull the bonds tighter. Do you understand?'

They nodded reluctantly and fetched a coil of rope. While Odysseus positioned himself against the mast, they wound the cord round his legs and body, pinning his arms to his sides until the only part of him that could move was his head. Then the two men joined their comrades at the benches and pulled the long oars that sped the galley across the becalmed sea.

The air was eerily still, broken only by the rhythmic swish of the blades hitting the water. There were no gulls to be heard or seen hovering over the waves, a sure sign to any sailor that something was not right. Odysseus noticed that the eagles he and Eperitus had observed earlier were nowhere in sight. The island was a hazy blue at that distance, but he could see the white surf that skirted it and also thought he could make out pale flowers gleaming on its grassy slopes. Then he heard the voices. His body tensed and he tilted his head towards the sound of the Sirens' song.

For as long as he could remember, Odysseus's consciousness had been dominated by thought. Every experience, every sentiment, every challenge and every pleasure had been analysed, interpreted and filtered through the sieve of his mind; but the beautiful music that now filled his ears spoke directly into his heart. The constant chattering of his thoughts was stilled and tears rolled down his cheeks as his emotions flowed unchecked: joy, sadness, love, anger, belief and fear, rolling together as one as if he were experiencing them for the first time. And perhaps he was, for he had never known such purity of feeling. He thought of his mother and the grief was all-consuming; he thought of Penelope and the depth of his love for her was overwhelming. So many passions, breaking through the crust that had formed around them over the years and leaving him as helpless as a child. It was both exhilarating and terrifying, and there was nothing his normally powerful mind could do to save him from it.

Then, when he was at his most vulnerable, the voice spoke.

We know what it is you fear.

The words were like a sword to his throat.

'I don't want to know,' he shouted, oblivious to the nervous looks from the men on the benches. 'I don't want to know.'

What is it to us what you want or don't want, Odysseus? You are just a mortal, but we are like the gods. And you will hear us.

The voices were as soothing as balm and beautiful beyond comprehension, and yet the words they spoke were like the teeth of a saw severing the taut strings of his emotions.

'Leave me alone! I'll do whatever you want.'

What followed was not more words but a vision, forming out of the music of the Sirens' voices. He was standing at the door of his own palace on Ithaca, unable to enter. The great hall was filled with handsome young men, all of them naked. They stood in a circle, shouting and punching the air with their fists like spectators at a cockfight. He moved his head from side to side, trying to see what they were watching but only able to snatch glimpses from between the crowd of legs. Then they parted, only briefly, while a sweating man was dragged from the floor and pushed out of the circle of on-lookers. In that short opening Odysseus saw a woman lying on her back, as naked as the men around her, while another man was al-ready pressing himself onto her. Before the circle closed again he saw the woman was Penelope, and that she was laughing as she pulled the man into her.

Odysseus screamed his anger and despair. He tried to rush into the great hall but realised the ropes that tied him to the mast were holding him back.

'Release me,' he shouted. 'Untie me now!'

The faces of Polites and Omeros appeared before him, their fin-gers pulling at the ropes. But instead of loosening his bonds, they pulled them tighter. Then, when the faces were gone, he heard the voices again.

We know what it is you fear.

'No,' he pleaded. 'Haven't I already said I'll do whatever you want?'

The voices began to sing again, lovely and terrifying beyond measure, conjuring up a new vision before his eyes. A young man in a ship with his comrades, his face hauntingly familiar.

'Telemachus,' Odysseus called, wanting to reach out but feeling again the tight cords that pinned his arms to his sides.

Another ship filled with armed men drew alongside, crunch-ing through the oars of Telemachus's galley. The crew of the second ship leapt aboard, striking down Telemachus's comrades with their swords. Odysseus strained against his ropes as Telemachus drew his own weapon before disappearing beneath a crowd of attackers.

'Stop this,' Odysseus begged, closing his eyes. 'Stop it.'

The image faded and was replaced by the voices of the Sirens.

You will find peace with us, Odysseus. Only with us. Steer for our island and we will relieve you of the burdens you have carried for so long. Are we not like the gods?

'I want to. I've had enough of all this. I want to rest.'

Then join us. Order your crew to row for our island.

'But I can't.'

Doesn't a king do as he pleases? the voice asked, more sternly now. *Tell your helmsman to turn aside. A great feast awaits you and your men.*

'But their ears are blocked with wax. They couldn't hear me even if I did as you command.'

There was a moment of silence. Then the air was rent with a terrifying scream, as hideous as the song had been beautiful. Odysseus's skin crept at the sound of it. As the scream died away it was followed by the beating of wings. He opened his eyes and saw a figure on the prow, a figure so repugnant it filled him with terror. It had the body of an eagle, but one the size of a donkey. Its talons grasped the bow rail as it swayed slightly with the motion of the ship, but its head was that of a girl, a mere child, so small and out of place on its feathered shoulders. And yet the head was more dreadful than the body, for its eyes were blood red and its mouth hung open to reveal long curving fangs that ran with drool. Even with their ears plugged and their backs turned, the crew sensed its shadow fall across them and looked around in horror. They cried out as one and, abandoning their oars, fought with each other to get away from the Siren. Many simply threw themselves to the deck in abject surrender to their fate. But the monster paid them no attention. Its eyes were fixed on Odysseus as it hopped down to the deck.

'We will have blood,' it declared.

There was no music in its voice now and the words were spoken rather than understood. Odysseus's mind was released from the chains that had bound it, but his body remained tied to the mast. Grinning, the Siren opened its jaws, spread its wings wide and with a single beat floated towards him.

Odysseus narrowed his eyes and tried to look away as death swooped upon him. Then, with a shout of anger, a giant figure leapt between him and the monster, landing a powerful blow on its jaw and sending it flapping into the benches. Polites now turned towards Odysseus, his face contorted with the fury of battle, and pulling a dagger from his belt he ran towards the king. As he sawed at the ropes, a handful of Ithacans – Omeros and Perimedes among them – drew their swords and formed a hesitant semicircle around the Siren. By now the creature had regained its balance and had retreated to the bow rail once more, hissing its hatred at the humans that dared to defy it. In the same moment a shadow fell across the deck and Odysseus felt the beat of great wings fanning the air. The second Siren swept in and seized Polites in its talons, lifting him from the deck and slowly into the air. He cried out for help but was already beyond the reach of his comrades and being carried out towards the nearby island. Odysseus looked on in despair and saw now that the white flowers he had seen littering the small hill that rose from the sea were the bones of men, many bleached white and more still with the desiccated skin still stretched across their ribcages.

Then he heard the sharp twang of a bow and saw the Siren jerk and twist in mid-air. Polites fell from its grip, his arms and legs flailing as he plunged into the waves. The monster dropped in his wake, flapping helplessly for a moment before beating down with its wings and forcing itself upward to make good its escape in the direction of the island. Its sister followed, crying out its anger but unwilling to continue the fight.

Eperitus, who had fired the shot, now threw aside his bow, mounted the bow rail and dived into the sea.

'Follow him,' Odysseus called.

Tearing at the partially severed ropes until one of his arms was free, he pointed at the small, dark figure of Eperitus in the becalmed waters. Many of the shocked crew saw his gesturing and returned to the oars. Others freed Odysseus from the ropes and, taking the twin rudders from Eurylochus, he quickly steered the galley towards the two stricken men. As they fell gasping onto the deck – hauled aboard by half a dozen of their comrades – Odysseus turned the ship westward and shouted at the crew to row. They did not need to hear him to throw their strength into pulling the oars, but no sooner was the dread island out of sight behind them than a long strip of coast appeared on the western horizon.

Eperitus joined Odysseus at the stern. His hair was still damp and he was shivering, despite the blanket around his shoulders.

'That shot would've made Antiphus proud.'

'It was a big target and I have sharp eyes,' Eperitus replied. 'Though when I saw Polites fall I thought I'd hit him instead.'

Odysseus smiled, the first happiness he had felt since the haunting visions the Siren song had put in his mind.

'What did they say to you?' Eperitus asked. 'I saw your pain, even if I couldn't hear it.'

Odysseus looked away.

'Nothing. Just lies. That's their power: not their song, but their false words.'

Eperitus nodded. 'I hope so.'

Astynome came with a cup of wine for each of them and a fresh blanket for Eperitus. Odysseus watched her affection as she wrapped her arms about him and closed her eyes in a moment of contentment. He wondered whether Penelope would be as loving to him on his return, or whether her heart had grown cold and unfaithful during their long separation. Partly it was the vision the Sirens had put in his mind that darkened his thoughts; partly it was the shadow of despair Hades had left on his heart. Would he ever be free from that darkness, he wondered? Astynome must have seen the sadness in his expression, for she released her hold on Eperitus and threw her arms about him.

'Have no fear, Odysseus,' she said. 'You'll see her again.'

The wounds from the Sirens' song were still fresh, and her words brought tears to his eyes. He blinked them away and put his hands on her shoulders.

'Astynome, listen to me. Soon we will pass through a narrow channel with tall cliffs on both sides. When you see a cave high up on one side, take those children you care so much about and hide beneath a tarpaulin or a piece of old sail. Do you hear me?'

Astynome nodded. 'Why?'

'Just do as I ask. Now, go back to the prow and remember what I told you.'

She looked at him questioningly, then nodded again and left.

'What's in the cave, Odysseus?' Eperitus asked.

'Death,' Odysseus answered, gripping the twin oars so hard that his knuckles turned white.

Chapter Thirty-Eight

SCYLLA AND CHARYBDIS

The entrance to the northern channel lay between two steep-sided cliffs. The galley slipped between them into a narrow gorge where tufts of vegetation clung to the craggy walls and the cries of seagulls echoed from one rock face to the other. These towering battlements had an oppressive effect on the crew, whose conversations trailed away to leave only the haunting voices of the birds and the swish of the oars over the water. A sense of anticipation hung in the cool evening air and after a while even the gulls were quiet in their nests as they watched the galley slip past.

Eperitus felt it more than most. He could not rid himself of the Sirens' warning that Circe was sending them to their destruction. Without the music of their voices the words alone felt hollow and could have been dismissed as the lies he hoped they were. But why had Odysseus told Astynome to hide beneath a tarpaulin, and why had he refused to answer any of Eperitus's questions? He had to trust that Odysseus knew what he was doing, yet the king's reticence to share the coming danger unnerved him.

The chariot of the sun had long since disappeared behind the clifftops, leaving the galley in deep shadow. The meandering gorge had narrowed, and with no sight of open water Eperitus was reminded of the tunnel he had followed into the Underworld. He glanced across at Astynome, huddled in the prow with the Trojan orphans. She smiled back at him and he felt comforted. Whatever surprises lay ahead, he would face them for her sake.

A subtle change in the air and in the compressed sound of the oars through the water told him the channel was widening. He could smell something foul, too, that reminded him of the Cyclops's cave. He rose from the bench where he had been sitting beside Polites and tried to filter out the sounds and smells around him, attuning his senses to whatever was waiting for them beyond the next bend. As he did so he heard a noise that seemed alien and strange in that barren place: the yelping of puppies. He frowned and tilted his head, but the loud caw of a gull overhead broke his concentration and after that he heard the sound no more.

He joined Odysseus and Eurybates in the stern. The king had wrapped his cloak about himself and Eperitus noticed his shield was uncovered and propped against the side of the ship with both his spears.

'What is it, Eperitus?' he asked.

'The gorge widens after the next bend.'

'Into the sea?'

'I don't think so.'

Odysseus looked disappointed but not surprised. Before long they were passing round the skirts of the next bend in the channel. Suddenly the steep walls that had enclosed them now warped apart to form a narrow body of restless water. At the far end the cliffs closed again to leave a gateway to the open sea, and in the blue distance Eperitus could see a low island on the horizon, its white bluffs caught by the dying rays of the sun. Was that Thrinacie, he wondered, the island Teiresias had warned them about? With the sun sinking fast it seemed unlikely they would pass it by without spending at least one night on its shores. A third of the way along the cliffs to the left was an old fig tree, its great, shaggy head hanging low towards the water despite its roots having nothing more than bare rock to cling to. A little further along on the right-hand side, high above the spume that crashed against the rocks below, was the mouth of a cave. The rank odour Eperitus had detected came from there, and the smell of the briny sea and the clean air above could do nothing to mask it. This had to be the cave Odysseus had warned Astynome about. He looked askance at the king and saw the doubt in his eyes. Odysseus licked his lips nervously and glanced across at the helmsman.

'Keep as far away from that fig tree as possible, Eurybates.'

Eurybates nodded and eased the galley gradually to starboard. Odysseus clasped his hands behind his back and began rocking anxiously on the balls of his feet.

'What is it?' Eperitus asked him. 'Listen, if that cave holds danger why not steer closer to the opposite bank?'

As he spoke a great jet of spume exploded from the water between the galley and the fig tree. It shot high into the air and came down again as a fine rain over the crew. Odysseus stopped trying to hide his concern and cupped his hands over his mouth.

'Man your positions and strike hard with the oars,' he called at the men on the benches. 'We're sailing into mortal danger, but we'll conquer it as we've conquered every other threat we've faced together. Do your duty, and Zeus will reward you with your lives. Now pull!'

Eperitus stared hard at the place from which the stream of water had erupted. The surface was now bubbling ferociously, the churning liquid moving in a wide circle while at its centre the water was sinking rapidly, opening like a mouth before his unbelieving eyes. A terrifying roar filled the air, causing several men to drop their oars in fright as they turned to watch what was happening. But as the crew's efforts faltered, the galley began to lean to one side and slip towards the growing vortex.

'Row, damn it!' Odysseus shouted, his cloak falling aside to reveal the breastplate beneath. 'If you want to see your wives and families again, put your backs into it.'

Eurylochus threw down his oar in alarm and cried out. Eperitus ran across the listing deck and – tossing Odysseus's cousin aside – took his place on the bench. He gripped the wet oar and pulled. Behind him, women and children were calling out in terror. He could see clouds of spray rising up into the air behind Eurybates and Odysseus as the ship was pulled inexorably towards the tumult.

'*Pull*,' the king hollered, his voice almost lost in the roar.

As one, the Ithacans heaved at the oars. Eperitus felt his blade bite the water then slip free with a sudden release that almost knocked him from his seat. He pushed it forward again, found the water and pulled with all his strength. Again he felt the pressure as the oar caught, but again the swell dropped away and released it. The sound of the approaching vortex was deafening now and cascades of spray crashed over the ship in waves. The men shouted as they pulled at the oars, some with the pain of their exertions, others in panic as they realised they were being sucked to their doom. Once again the oars bit into the water; once again the Ithacans hauled on the pine oars. And this time they held. Eperitus felt the galley's backwards momentum slow and stop. He gritted his teeth and thrust the oar forward and down again. The blade snagged, and with the pressure of the water straining at his muscles he dragged the oar backwards.

'That's it,' Odysseus shouted. He dared a glance over his shoulder, then leaned forward and shouted again. 'That's it. Pull harder!'

The banks of oars gained a purchase in the churning water and the galley edged forward. As it did so, Eperitus felt it lurch and turn. Squinting through the spray, he saw Eurybates struggling with the rudders as his feet slipped on the deck. More shouts of exertion from the oarsmen were mixed with cries of terror from the slaves. Eperitus glanced at Eurylochus cowering with his arms thrown about the base of the mast. He sprang up from his bench and seized the whimpering coward by the nape of his tunic.

'Get back on that oar and pull if you want to live,' he hollered over the thunder of the whirlpool.

He did not stay to see that his order had been obeyed, but sprang up and ran across the deck to the helm, sliding and almost falling in the ankle-deep water as he went. Reaching Eurybates's side, he seized one of the oars and – obeying a gesture from the helmsman – pushed it to the left. Looking over the bow rail he saw a yawning hole in the water less than a spear's cast away. All other sounds were drowned by the roar of the great vortex. Through the fine vapour that hung over it, Eperitus could see the blue-grey sand of the channel bed at the base of its gaping throat. White rocks gleamed like teeth, threatening to devour the stricken galley.

Eperitus felt the strain on the rudder, but it held and the ship straightened. Odysseus ordered his men to pull again and again, and with each hard-fought stroke of the oars the galley edged further away from danger. Here and there men were collapsing on the deck, but somehow the vessel clawed its way to freedom and the opposite side of the channel. With the pressure on the rudder easing, Eperitus handed control back to Eurybates and joined Odysseus.

'Was that the danger Circe warned you about?'

'It's one of them. She called it Charybdis, a sea monster that sucks ships and their crews down to a watery grave before vomiting them back up as driftwood and corpses. We were lucky.'

'And the other?'

'The other is Scylla.'

As Odysseus spoke, Eperitus heard the same yelping he had noticed before. They looked up at the sheer cliff now looming over the galley. High above them was a lip of rock, and as Eperitus stared through the mist that still filled the air from Charybdis, he thought he saw movement.

'What is it?' Astynome asked. 'The danger's over, isn't it? I hid beneath the tarpaulin like you ordered, Odysseus.'

Eperitus held out his hands towards her as she crossed the deck towards them, but before he could speak, the strange, puppy-like barking erupted from the cliffs above them.

'Get back, Astynome,' Odysseus shouted as he reached for his shield and spears, tossing one to Eperitus. 'Get back *now*.'

Eperitus sensed that something terrible was about to happen. The whole crew had heard the barking and now looked upward. Several shouted out in horror or threw themselves to the deck with their hands pressed over their heads. A handful reached for their swords. Gripping Odysseus's spear tightly, Eperitus stared up to see something large and black moving down the cliff face towards the galley. The sight of it turned his flesh cold.

It scrambled down the rock with the agility of a lizard, its six heads on their long, flailing necks darting this way and that as they identified their victims among the crowd of screaming men, women and children below. The monster was right above them now. One of its enormous heads darted forward and long scaly jaws closed about the head and shoulders of a man. His screams were muffled but audible as it plucked him from the deck. Two more heads dropped down towards the galley and seized two more men. One was bitten in half as Scylla's teeth snapped through flesh and bone, leaving the rest of his body from the waist down still standing on the deck as blood and intestines spilled from the monster's mouth. The other victim was Perimedes, who struck out at his attacker with his sword but only managed to drive the snarling head aside before it closed its teeth around his abdomen and pulled him shouting in pain and terror into the air. Odysseus cried out in anger and hurled his spear at the black body clinging to the side of the cliff, only to see it bounce harmlessly off its armoured scales into the water below. A moment later, two more heads had snatched up two more men, dropping severed limbs and a rain of blood onto the galley as they bit into their prey and swallowed them down. Before Eperitus could think to act, the sixth and final head shot down towards Astynome.

She threw herself onto the deck and covered her head. Eperitus ran forward to try and stop the hideous creature, but he already knew it was too late. Then, in the instant before it took her, Polites threw himself between them. His shield was on his arm and the monster's snout shattered it to pieces. It withdrew slightly then darted forward again. Polites seized hold of its jaws, trying desperately to hold them apart before they closed around him. But even his strength was not enough. The teeth closed about him and snatched him into the air.

As Polites cried out for help, Odysseus shouted to the remaining crew to take up their oars. The sudden lurch of the galley beneath his feet brought Eperitus back to his senses. He saw Astynome pushing herself up from the deck with one arm, her long, dishevelled hair hanging like a curtain over her face. Instinctively he moved towards her, only to hear again the pleas of Polites and Perimedes not to leave them to their fate. Scylla – seeing that the galley had already moved beyond the reach of her heads – retreated up the cliff face, there to devour her victims at her leisure. Eperitus turned to Odysseus.

'Order the crew to turn the ship around. We have to help them.'

'And lose six more men?' the king snapped. 'Are you mad or stupid?'

'You can't *leave* them. Polites has fought at your side for ten years! He's my friend and he sacrificed himself for Astynome.'

'And what will you do? Fly up the cliff face?'

'At least take us back within bowshot so I can put them out of their misery.'

'It's too late for that now,' Odysseus replied. 'Do you think I want them to suffer? Do you think I wouldn't turn back if I thought there was something I could do to save them from that monster?'

Eperitus's eyes flashed with anger.

'But you *knew* it was there, didn't you. Circe told you it would come down and take six of the crew; that's why you put on your armour and had your spears and shield at the ready – much good that it did any of us.'

'Of course I knew, but what choice did I have? Would you've rather I had risked the ship and the whole crew to the jaws of Charybdis?'

Eperitus stepped towards him, his fists clenched, but felt soft hands around his arms pulling him back. It was Astynome.

'Odysseus is right,' she said. 'What's more, he's your king and your friend.'

'No he's not, Astynome,' he growled. 'He's a murderer.'

Chapter Thirty-Nine

POSEIDON'S REVENGE

Selagos grinned to himself. The crew were distraught at the loss of their comrades, many openly weeping so that only fear of the six-headed beast and the great whirlpool kept them at their oars. But as soon as they had reached the safety of the open sea it was easy to see the rebellion in their eyes. During the long, easy sojourn on Aeaea they had forgotten their anger against Odysseus, so it was with satisfaction that Selagos saw the fleeting scowls they directed at their king and heard their whispers against him. Some muttered that Odysseus had knowingly led them into danger; others complained that he had abandoned six good men to the monster, suggesting they could have turned about and fired arrows at its eyes or climbed the cliffs to its lair. Brave sentiments, Selagos thought, and most meant them, though it would have only led to more deaths. They could not see that in their grief, though. The loss of their comrades – whose screams were heard for some time afterwards as they sailed away – had left a hole in them that could only be filled with anger. Anger against Odysseus.

It was a resentment he understood well. Not that he cared anything for the oaf Polites or the other Ithacans, nor even for Perimedes, his fellow Taphian. His reasons for hating Odysseus stretched much further back and struck far deeper than that. He had only been an infant when his father had joined Eupeithes's small army of Taphians, attracted by the Ithacan traitor's offer of land and livestock if they helped him usurp the throne from King Laertes. That was over twenty years ago, but he still remembered his father promising his family a farm of their own and all the food they could eat. While the revolt had succeeded in the absence of Odysseus – who had travelled to Sparta to compete for the hand of Helen – it was quickly defeated upon his return. And when the survivors came back to Taphos, Selagos's father was not among them.

Years of hardship followed. Selagos's mother was barely able to feed her seven children and resorted to the lowest means to put scraps of bread into their hungry mouths. Like all Taphians, Selagos had learned to fight, and as the bastard son of a prostitute mother he had become tougher and more brutal than the rest. Then Eupeithes arrived with gifts of food and clothing for the families of those who had died serving him. It was the first time Selagos had enjoyed a full stomach since his father's death. Eupeithes was no warrior, but the young Taphian respected that he had recognised and honoured his debt to those who had supported his rebellion. In his turn, Eupeithes had seen something in the tall, ferocious lad that brought him back year after year with more gifts of food for him and his family, nurturing his loyalty and ensuring that his potential for height and strength was fulfilled. And then, a year before the war against Troy had begun – when Selagos was fourteen and nearly as tall and broad as most Taphian men – Eupeithes came with different gifts: a sword, a shield and a long spear in the Taphian style. They were the weapons of his father, which Eupeithes had claimed from his dead body and kept for the day that Selagos would be old enough to wield them.

As the young man tested the weight of the shield on his arm and stabbed the blade into imaginary enemies, Eupeithes said he knew how his father had died. At once, Selagos forgot the weapons and sat down opposite the Ithacan noble. As he listened, Eupeithes told him the full story of the rebellion on Ithaca, of its initial success and ultimately of its defeat through the schemes of a young prince. And at last Selagos had a name on which to pin all his suffering and hatred. From that moment, he knew his purpose in life was to kill Odysseus.

Less than a year later, Odysseus visited Mentes, chieftain of the Taphians, to beg ships for the war. It was all Selagos could do not to walk into the welcoming feast and attack the Ithacan king. But Eupeithes had pre-warned him against rash acts, promising that one day the gods would give him the opportunity to avenge his father. And then, in the final year of the siege of Troy, the gods heard his prayers. Eupeithes appeared again, unexpectedly, after an absence of several years, and told him that Odysseus had sent back ships to gather replacements for the Ithacans who had died over the years of the siege of Troy. His own son, Antinous, had been called to arms, but the governing Kerosia had passed a law allowing men to send proxies in their place. If Selagos would take Antinous's place in one of the ships, Eupeithes would provide a farm and livestock for his brothers and mother. What was more, if Selagos could stop Odysseus from ever reaching Ithaca he would make him a rich man on his return. Selagos had agreed to take Antinous's place in exchange for a farm for his family, but he refused Eupeithes's offer of payment to assassinate Odysseus. That he would do for the sake of his father's honour and for revenge – even if it cost him his own life.

The light was failing rapidly as they approached Thrinacie, the island where Hyperion kept his herds and flocks. Odysseus listened to the lowing of cattle and the bleating of sheep and remembered the warnings Teiresias and Circe had given him not to land there. He listened also to the groaning and weeping of his men. The deprivations of the war had made them hardy, but the long, wearisome voyage had stretched them to the limit of their physical and mental endurance. Their eyes had witnessed things that the logical human mind was not equipped to understand and the latest horrors had brought them to the edge of an abyss. He felt it himself. He was exhausted. He needed to throw himself down on firm ground and grieve for the men who had been taken. But not at the price of losing Ithaca. It was so close now he could sense it, as if it lay just beyond the darkening horizon.

'I can see a cove,' Eurybates said. 'Beneath that high cliff. We'll be safe there, my lord, and with this wind rising it couldn't have come sooner.'

'Damn the wind. That island is a far greater danger to us. Turn the prow westward and keep going.'

'Into the night? Are you mad?'

The challenge came from Eurylochus. Odysseus watched his cousin rise up from the benches, Selagos's hand in the small of his back, urging him forward.

'You drive us too hard,' Eurylochus continued. 'Even if you don't feel the strain, *we* do. What we need is rest, and yet you insist on sailing in the darkness when there's a perfectly safe island just a bowshot away.'

Many of the crew openly voiced their agreement, and not just the same rabble that usually backed Eurylochus.

'We can't go on.'

'Listen to Eurylochus.'

'My friends,' Odysseus said, raising his hands for silence, 'I understand your tiredness and I share your grief, but you don't understand what you're asking for. We've overcome too many perils together to throw it all away now. Land on that island and it's not monsters you'll face but the gods themselves! Be patient. One more day's sailing to the west is another island, Phaeacia, where the people are great sailors and will lead us back to Ithaca –'

'Another hollow promise,' Eurylochus protested. 'Just like all the other phantoms you've been chasing ever since you failed us at Malea. Can't you see there's a storm brewing? *You* may be made of iron, but we're beaten. Why force us on into a gale that will tear the ship apart and drown us all when we can shelter in that cove for the night. It'll raise our spirits to have a hot meal and some wine, followed by a good night's sleep. You say we risk the anger of the immortals if we land there. Well, I'd rather face their anger on land than on sea, which is what we'll be doing if we carry on. Do as we ask and we can set sail in the morning to this island of Phaeacia or whatever other destination you pretend to know about.'

His words were greeted by a chorus of cheers that rang with rebellion. Odysseus felt his anger rising.

'Do as you ask, you say. Or do you mean *do as you tell me*? Am I king or are you, Eurylochus? Or perhaps we are all kings now? If that's where this is leading then we're all doomed. I'll concede this, though: every man will reveal his mind by a show of hands. If I have the support of the crew then you'll do as I tell you and sail to Phaeacia. If not, I'll give orders to lay up on Thrinacie for the night. But if we do that, you must all swear not to kill any of the sacred herds or flocks we find on the island. They belong to Hyperion and are not to be slaughtered by men. Circe has supplied us with enough food to last us a month, so be content with that. Do you agree?'

All but one of the crew voiced their agreement. Odysseus looked at Eperitus, who had listened to his speech with crossed arms and a cold expression. He knew the king had finally surrendered his authority and would pay the price for it, but in the end he answered Odysseus's question with a surly nod.

'Who will follow me to Phaeacia then?' Odysseus asked.

Omeros and Eurybates raised their arms followed by five or six more.

'And those for Thrinacie?'

Almost every other man lifted their hands into the air. Last of all, slowly, Eperitus added his vote to theirs. Then he turned and walked to the front of the ship where Astynome sat with the children. Odysseus knew he had lost more than his authority and any certainty of returning to Ithaca. He had lost his closest friend and ally.

They steered the galley into the narrow inlet and tossed the anchor stones overboard. Odysseus and Eurybates remained on the ship while the crew and slaves went ashore. His eyes heavy with impending sleep, Odysseus watched the men make hasty fires from the plentiful driftwood that had washed up at the top of the beach and then sit down to eat a simple supper of hot broth. A few returned to their grief for the men who had been lost, weeping openly as they allowed their sufferings to consume them. Others found consolation with the slave women. Most, though, threw themselves down on their blankets and fell asleep. After a while the only sounds Odysseus could hear were the moaning of the wind and the fateful sounds of livestock in the distance. He lay down on a sack of grain and drifted off into a deep sleep, dreaming he had returned to Hades to speak with the ghost of Eperitus; but every time Eperitus opened his mouth, all that came out were the pitiful cries of Polites, begging for an end to his pain.

It was in the last watch of the night that the storm arrived. Odysseus awoke to the feel of raindrops on his cheek. Before he could find a piece of tarpaulin to drag over himself, the night sky exploded with a flash of lightning closely followed by a loud crash of thunder. The wind screamed more fiercely and brought in heavy curtains of rain. He could hear shouts from the beach as men, women and children dashed for cover in a cave under the high cliffs. Odysseus crawled under a square of old sail and, despite the cacophony of the storm, soon fell asleep again.

He woke to grey light filtering through the walls of his tarpaulin. The wind was still howling outside and the galley was rocking on the choppy waters of the inlet, though the rain had stopped drumming against the canvas. Poking his head out, he saw a low ceiling of slate-coloured cloud that stretched across the sky for as far as he could see. Beyond the mouth of the cove the ocean was a tumult of high, white-capped waves that no galley would be able to survive for long. He recalled Teiresias's warning that Poseidon would avenge the blinding of Polyphemus by imprisoning them on Thrinacie. Had they sailed on to Phaeacia Poseidon would have been unable to harm them because of his promise to Athena. Now he and his men would have to sit out the storm until the god of the sea forgot about them or his men forgot their oath and ate Hyperion's cattle. And he would not allow the latter.

For the first two weeks the least of his worries was the food supply. Circe had given them livestock of their own and plenty of grain and wine, and there was a good supply of fresh water on the island. The sun god's herds and flocks would often venture to the top of the beach and gaze down at the Ithacans with a passing curiosity. For their part the Ithacans would stare back at the fat oxen and the well-fed sheep with temptation, but remained mindful of their oath not to touch any of the precious animals. Instead, their greatest challenge was boredom mixed with a rapid loss of discipline that led to frequent fights. At first these were over women, but, increasingly, food and the dwindling stocks of wine were the cause. Eperitus no longer cared for the men under his charge and had left them to the chaotic leadership of Eurylochus, while keeping his own company with Astynome and her orphans. Odysseus, too, had abandoned his countrymen to their own devices. As long as they did not go near the native herds and flocks or try to steal from the stores of food, he preferred to ignore them. Hyperion's livestock he left under the watchful eye of Omeros and two other men he could trust, who followed the docile animals from one part of the small island to another, counting them regularly to make sure none had been taken. Responsibility for the remaining food was given to Eurybates and another loyal soldier. They kept the stores on board the galley, which had been beached and dragged into the cover of the cave. From here they could keep a close watch on the dwindling provisions and dole out only what Odysseus permitted the rest of the crew to have. This caused more resentment and open voices of rebellion, especially when rations were halved in the third week and halved again in the fourth. But none were ready yet to openly challenge Odysseus's authority.

None, perhaps, except Selagos. Not that he had ever been foolish enough to speak out against the king, but if Odysseus feared any man in the crew it was the Taphian. On several occasions he had caught Selagos studying him through narrowed eyes. He was always quick to look away and carry on playing dice or pursuing whatever activity he was busying himself with, but Odysseus was not fooled. He had watched the man fight in the final battles of the war and knew he was a powerful warrior and a natural and cunning leader. That made him far more dangerous than Eurylochus. What was more, Odysseus suspected Selagos was using his fat fool of a cousin to stir up trouble with the crew. The only thing that eluded Odysseus's mind was why. What could a Taphian gain from challenging him?

Not that any challenge from Selagos, Eurylochus or the rest of his rebellious crew would have been any concern if Eperitus had still been at his side. The rift between them troubled him more than anything else. Without the loyal presence of his captain his authority as king was weakened, perhaps fatally. His chances of making it back to Ithaca were also reduced to the point that he now doubted he would see his home again. And he felt alone. The burden of leadership had always been a solitary one, but with Eperitus's friendship and loyalty it was bearable. Now it was crushing him. He had spoken to Eperitus of course – he made a point of doing so several times a day – but the replies were brief to the point of curtness. Something had snapped between them when Polites had been taken by Scylla. The oneness of spirit between himself and Eperitus was gone.

He wished he could undo what he had done. Looking back, he regretted not being open with Eperitus about the dangers that lay beyond the Sirens. It would have meant an argument about the best course of action, but at least they would have faced their decision together. Instead he had followed his own mind; trusted, as usual, to his own judgement rather than the counsel of others. Now he was paying the price with the loss of the greatest friendship he would ever know. And Eperitus was not the first friend he had driven away with his selfish schemes. Indeed, his duplicity in winning the armour of Achilles had caused Great Ajax – a man whom he loved and honoured – to take his own life. Worse still, he had betrayed Penelope. Before sharing Circe's bed he had felt certain he would one day return to his wife's arms, that it was fated to happen because he had remained true to her through all the hard years of the war. But now he had destroyed the one pure thing that remained in his life, and with it any right he had to return to her.

Then there was Athena. By refusing the goddess's command and trusting to his own plan for ending the war he had forced her to abandon him. Only an arrogant fool would be so reckless as to think he knew better than an immortal. And yet it was to the gods he was turning now. As the gales that imprisoned him on the island continued; as he saw his crew turning against him; as their food stocks dwindled; and as he had forced his only true friend away, he looked to the only source of hope left. Too long he had relied on himself rather than the power of the immortals, and it had led from one disaster to another. But if Athena could be persuaded to forget her anger – if somehow he could prove himself worthy of her love again – would his fortunes not change? And so every evening he would slip away to a part of the island where he would not be disturbed and offer his prayers to the gods, hoping that as the last of the food was eaten and as the storms continued, his promises of kingly sacrifices on his return to Ithaca would appease them.

Eurylochus's stomach growled loudly. He had spent some time staring down at his waist and wondering if it had shrunk again, and the more he looked the more he convinced himself it had. This was despite the fact he had been bribing Eurybates's assistant to give him twice the rations of anyone else in the crew. After all, the size of a noble's stomach was a sign of his wealth – and he had no intention of returning to Ithaca looking like a peasant farmer.

There were, of course, fine herds of fat oxen and flocks of plump sheep wandering about the island, oblivious to the ravenous eyes that followed their every move. Eurylochus had tried to persuade a few of his shipmates to push a cow off one of the cliffs, assuring them Odysseus would permit the eating of the animal if its death appeared natural. But none was prepared to risk the wrath of the sun god, let alone face Odysseus's sword. And the king had promised death to any man – which Eurylochus knew included himself – if just one of the creatures was slain.

He picked up a stick and poked the fire. A few sparks flew upwards followed by a wisp of grey smoke. The smell of it reminded him of cooked meat and made his stomach groan even louder.

'Damn it, there must be *something* to eat!'

'What about your rations?' Selagos asked in a tired voice.

The Taphian sat a little to his right, his arms folded across his knees and his chin rested on his forearms.

'A few oats and a strip of salted pork?' Eurylochus sneered. 'I ate those for breakfast. Do you have any of yours left?'

'Of course.' Selagos reached into the satchel at his side and pulled out a piece of dried meat. 'Here, you have it. I have no need of it.'

'Really?' Eurylochus asked, looking at him as if he were mad.

Fearing Selagos might change his mind, he snatched it from his fingers. The brown pork was as hard as wood and very salty, but after biting off a chunk and leaving it in his mouth to soften, it tasted as good as any other food he had ever eaten. His impatient stomach almost cried out in desperation, but Eurylochus wanted to suck all of the flavour out before he swallowed it.

'Starvation is the most miserable way to die,' he complained.

Selagos raised a knowing eyebrow. 'You are not nearly starving yet, my friend. When it comes you'll know.'

'I don't intend to wait that long. I have an idea for killing one of those stupid oxen.'

'You don't have the guts, and nobody else is going to do it for you.'

'Because they're afraid of Odysseus. But there's one man who isn't, the only one my cousin would never contemplate harming. Eperitus.'

The usually taciturn Selagos gave a dismissive snort.

'That man hates you almost as much as you hate him. Even if he has fallen out with the king, why would he slaughter one of those animals for your sake?'

'I... I don't know. Maybe a bribe or –'

'Forget such foolish ideas. Besides, tomorrow you can kill and eat as many cows as you like.'

'What do you mean?'

'Listen to me,' Selagos said in a low voice, staring hard at Eurylochus. 'You've told me many times you could do a better job of leading these men than Odysseus. Do you still mean it?'

'Of course.'

'And if the chance came, you would take it?'

'Is this what you've been brooding on all this time?'

'*Answer me.*'

'Yes,' Eurylochus replied, hesitantly. '*If* the chance came, but I don't see –'

Selagos gripped his arm.

'If? The chance is here, *now*. There is no food left. Other than Eurybates, Omeros and one or two others, the crew would turn against Odysseus in a moment. They've had enough of him leading them from one calamity to another, and since he's been spending every day away from the camp, the men have come to look upon you as their leader. All you need to do is give the word. Even Eperitus has come to see him for what he is.'

'Don't underestimate his loyalty to Odysseus, Selagos. Their friendship may have gone cold, but Eperitus will fight for his king if his authority is challenged.'

'I know that,' Selagos said, turning and looking through the flames to where Eperitus stood alone on the beach, staring out to sea. 'But he has a weakness. The woman.'

'Astynome?'

Even speaking her name stirred something inside Eurylochus. For almost two years in the confines of the galley, as they wandered aimlessly from one landfall to another, he had watched her with an ever increasing desire. Not only was she more beautiful than any woman he had ever set his heart upon, he wanted her simply because she belonged to Eperitus. To have her for himself would be doubly sweet because it would mean taking her from *him*. After all, Eurylochus had claimed her first during the sack of Lyrnessus, and that made her his by right.

'Yes, Astynome. Right now she's on the eastern side of the island where the lightning-struck tree overlooks the small inlet. I told her she could find some roots there to feed the Trojan children.'

'And are there?'

'Enough to keep her busy for a while. I promised her I'd tell Eperitus where she was, but of course I haven't. If you don't go after her soon, though, he'll go looking for her himself.'

'Go after her?' Eurylochus exclaimed. 'Why would I do that?'

'To take her hostage. We need to give Eperitus a compelling reason not to interfere when we make our move.'

'By all the gods, you *mean* this, don't you? You really mean to take control.'

'Do you think we've been playing a game all these months, Eurylochus? Every time you challenged Odysseus, did you think it was just harmless fun? Do you think Odysseus will just forget your insults when he's safely back home again? He won't. If you take on a king, you have to be prepared to pay the price. The least you can expect is exile; execution is more likely. Unless you deal with him first.'

'I can't kill the king, Selagos. My own cousin.'

'Who said anything about killing him? While you've been worrying about your hunger, I've been busy speaking to the others. Every man who voted to land here is ready to help us. When Odysseus returns this evening we'll disarm him and hold him prisoner, along with any of those fools who still support him. With fifty of us against less than ten of them, there won't be much resistance. Then we can eat as much beef and mutton as we want until this gale blows over. After that we'll maroon him and his followers and sail back to Ithaca, the only survivors from the war.'

By now Eurylochus had forgotten all about his hunger. All those times he had defied Odysseus, he had never really imagined it would come to this. But Selagos had moved without him. He had drawn up his plans, bided his time carefully and made sure that enough of the crew were on their side. Zeus's beard! Virtually every other Ithacan had been told about the plot. There was no going back now, even if he wanted to. His stomach was so knotted up he felt like he could vomit. And yet Selagos seemed as calm as if he were simply organising a boar hunt. The sight of his stolid, powerful face reassured him a little.

'Shouldn't I be here with you, rather than holding Astynome hostage? Can't one of the others kidnap her?'

'Two things:' Selagos began, 'if there *is* a fight, I don't want the others seeing you run off in a panic. It will unnerve them and undermine your authority. I also know how you feel about Eperitus's woman. While she's your prisoner, what's to stop you doing all those things you've been wanting to do to her all this time?'

'And what if I take her and come back to find your rebellion has failed, or the rest of the men have lost their nerve? Eperitus will murder me.'

'No-one's going to lose their nerve. But if you're scared then threaten her with something that'll keep her quiet. Don't forget she nearly got you killed by the Cyclopes. I think she owes you an apology, don't you?'

Eurylochus remembered how he had barely escaped the Cyclopes with his life. He also recalled the day they had spotted the land of the lotus eaters, when he had forced a kiss upon her and she had bitten his lip. Eperitus had almost killed him after that. The memory sparked anger but also revived his lust for Astynome. He reached for his sword and slipped the baldric over his shoulder.

'I'll do it. I'll take her to the cave facing the inlet. Send someone to me when Odysseus and Eperitus are your prisoners. And in Zeus's name, make sure you tie them up securely.'

'Don't worry about Eperitus. He's not a king; once he surrenders to us I'll cut his throat myself. Then Astynome's yours forever.'

Eurylochus threw a glance at Eperitus, still staring out to sea, then walked as quickly as he could to the grass bank at the top of the beach. Things were moving so fast now his mind could hardly comprehend the implications of what he was doing. And what if Selagos failed to capture Odysseus or kill Eperitus? But it was enough to know that Astynome would soon be his. Against her will, admittedly, but his all the same.

Chapter Forty

SELAGOS STRIKES

The chariot of the sun was descending towards the clifftops on the western side of the bay, nothing more than a white disc behind the ceiling of cloud. Out at sea the waves were as powerful and destructive as they had been every day for the past four weeks. Not a man among the Ithacans had known anything like it. A sure sign the gods were against them. But it seemed to Eperitus the gods had been against them from the moment the fleet had assembled at Aulis.

He listened to the howl of the wind and the laughter of the children playing on the beach. He had not seen Astynome since his visit to Omeros guarding the herds and flocks, checking on them as Odysseus had asked him to do before he departed to pray to the gods. On such a small island she could not be far, but even a short absence made him miss her. The shelter he had made from driftwood felt as good as any well-built home when she was in it, and the small amount of privacy it afforded them had helped them to rediscover their intimacy – something that had been impossible on the communal deck of the ship and in the crowded hall of Circe's house. Sometimes they would make love, but only at her instigation, because he was afraid he might harm the new life that was inside her. So mostly they talked as they lay together beneath the furs, about their child and the farm they would have, or about Odysseus and what would happen when they returned to Ithaca. Astynome would gently encourage him to turn aside from his anger and be reconciled with his friend, but he refused to forgive Odysseus for abandoning six of his men, even though reason told him it had been the right choice. He felt too bitter about too many things, from the death of

Polites back to the loss of Iphigenia and even his father's treachery when he had been a youth in Alybas. Those wounds had never fully healed, and Odysseus had become the target for the poison they left in him. But over time he knew Astynome would be the antidote. She had a good heart and a discerning mind that was already leading him out of his dark past to a future where his conscience could find rest.

A female voice calling to the children made him look up, but it was only one of the Trojan women telling them off for some misdemeanour. If Astynome was not back by dusk he would search for her. Odysseus usually returned before dark so it would be a good excuse to avoid any small talk he might try to make. Then he heard footsteps in the sand behind him and turned to see Selagos approaching. Instinctively Eperitus touched the hilt of his dagger, quickly lowering his hand again as soon as he became conscious of it.

'I have a message for you,' the Taphian said with his customary bluntness. 'From your wife.'

'Why would she leave a message with you?'

'Because she is not as angry or untrusting as her husband. But if you don't want to hear it –'

'Wait,' Eperitus said. 'Forgive me. Being imprisoned on this island can try a man's patience. You understand?'

'Yes, we have all become a little impatient with things.'

'What did she say?'

'To tell you that she had gone to the eastern cove where the burnt tree is. You know it? She's looking for roots to feed the children.'

'And when did she tell you this?'

'When you went to find Omeros, around midday, but other things drove it out of my head. She said she would be back before dusk, and that's what reminded me.'

He waved a hand at the twilight that was descending rapidly. Eperitus restrained his anger and gave the Taphian a curt nod.

'In that case I'll go find her. Thank you, Selagos.'

He watched the tall warrior return to the group of men with whom he had been playing dice, half expecting to see Eurylochus's mocking face looking back at him. But he was not there. A quick glance around the rest of the camp told him he was nowhere to be seen. Eperitus's stomach sank with the feeling that Astynome was in danger. He collected his sword from his shelter and passed out of sight of the camp before breaking into a run.

Of all the lands they had visited, with the unique horrors that each one held, none seemed so miserable to Astynome as the island of Thrinacie. Though they had suffered regular downpours since their arrival, the only vegetation that seemed to grow there was tough grass and gnarled trees. Everything else was rocks and sand, as if the sun god on his visits to his precious cattle had scorched the earth barren. Even the few flowers that clung to its dry soil looked pallid and drained of colour, unable to brighten the grey landscape. Apart from the wandering herds and flocks, the only creatures that scratched their living in that melancholy place were lizards, snakes and a multitude of creeping insects. These scuttled out from every boulder she overturned in her search for roots, making her flesh creep as they crawled over her fingers and up her wrists before she could brush them off. Had it not been for the few bulbs she found she would have gone back to the camp long ago.

Naturally she had questioned why Selagos – an ally of Eurylochus, who held no love for her – should tell her where she could find a few roots. He had excused himself by saying it was so she could feed her ever-hungry orphans and give him some peace from their constant wailing for food. Now she realised he had lied to her. But why?

She dropped the half-filled basket of bulbs and roots on the ground and sat on a rock. Beyond the cliff's edge and the little cove below it, the sea raged on with unabated anger. Eperitus said the gales were sent by Poseidon in vengeance for blinding the Cyclops who had eaten six of Odysseus's men. When she had asked if there was a way to appease the gods, he had answered there was not and fell silent. Only later did she remember that Agamemnon had sacrificed

Iphigenia, Eperitus's daughter, to lift a storm sent by Artemis. She laid a hand on her stomach, wondering what sacrifice the immortals would demand this time.

'Here you are.'

Startled, Astynome turned to see a man approaching over the brow of the hill. Somehow she had the impression he had been there some time.

'What do you want, Eurylochus?'

'No need to take such a tone,' he replied. 'I heard you were looking for roots and thought I might be able to help you.'

His overly friendly tone made her suspicious.

'If I'd been hunting for truffles I might have asked for your help. As I'm not, I'll thank you for your offer and request you go back to the camp.'

He ignored the insult and sat down on a boulder. His face was pink and he was breathing heavily.

'Not had much success, I see,' he said, picking up a thin, pointy root from her basket. 'I'm sure two pairs of hands would be better than one.'

She pushed herself to her feet. 'I was about to return to the camp.'

'Then I'll escort you back,' he said, standing.

'Escort me? Do you think I've forgotten Lyrnessus or what you tried to do on the galley, or on the island of the Cyclopes?'

He crossed the gap between them and took her wrist in his sweaty hand, pulling her down beside him on the rock where she had been sitting.

'But that's why I'm offering you my help, to make peace between us.' His breath stank and there was a dark hunger in his eyes. 'If we're to be neighbours on Ithaca then we should be friends and put the past behind us. I can be a useful ally to you – and Eperitus, of course. Better an ally than an enemy, don't you think?'

She saw the growing bulge in the crotch of his tunic and knew the danger she was in. Her heart was beating fast in her chest now. All she could think of was the safety of her unborn child.

'Take your hands off me, please.'

She tried to stand, but his hold on her wrist was horribly strong.

'What's the matter, Astynome? I'm just trying to be your friend.'

He placed his other hand on her thigh, pinning her to the boulder.

'I don't want your friendship.'

'Oh yes you do.'

Her fear turned to anger, strengthening her as she thought of her husband and of their child.

'I'll scream,' she warned him. 'Touch me once and I'll scream.'

'But who will hear you?'

'Omeros and the others are just over that hill there.'

'Funny, I can't hear the sheep or the cattle.'

His hand shot down to the hem of her chiton, pulling it up over her knees. At the same time he pushed his face against hers, his lips smearing wetness across her cheek as she turned her head away. They fell to the stony floor, his heavy weight upon her and the hardness of his erection pressing against her thigh. She threw her head back and screamed. Immediately his hot hand closed over her mouth, stifling the sound.

'Quiet!' he commanded.

He slipped his hand from her mouth down to her breast, squeezing it clumsily and painfully. She screamed again, and this time he slapped her so hard that for a moment she was stunned. As she blinked up at the grey sky she was aware his weight had lifted from her and his grip on her wrist had been released. For a moment she dared to think he had lost his nerve. Then she saw him, tugging his tunic over his head to reveal his naked body and the upward curve of his penis against his hairy, expansive stomach.

'Stop it, Eurylochus. Stop this now and I'll not say a word to Eperitus.'

She propped herself up onto her elbows and tried to pull herself away. He was on her in a moment, one hand on her forearm, the other fumbling at the sash that kept her chiton closed about her.

'You know you won't say anything anyway,' he grunted. 'Remember, if Eperitus attacks me it'll spark the rebellion that's been waiting to happen since the moment we left Troy. Is that what you want?'

The sash fell away and she felt the cold air on her bare skin. Then Eurylochus's body descended on hers, hot and clammy with his hardness trapped between his stomach and hers. She screamed again, this time with fury as she felt his bulk pressing down on the baby inside her. New strength rushed into her limbs and she punched him hard in the face, stunning him momentarily so that she was able to push him away with her hands and knees. Her fingernails tore at flesh and he shouted with pain, falling backwards on the ground like an upended pig. Long red claw marks were etched into his chest. Turning, she pulled herself across the stony floor, seized hold of a boulder and got to her feet. But before she could run up the hill, westward towards the camp where Eperitus would be waiting for her, a hand took hold of her ankle and pulled her to her knees. Another snatched her hair and with irresistible strength pulled her onto her back.

'I'm not afraid of your rebellion any more,' she hissed. 'And how long do you think you'll last once I tell my husband?'

She spat in his face. He slapped her hard, bringing tears of pain and frustration to her eyes.

'How do you think he'll react when you tell him you've been with me? He'll *reject* you, Astynome. I don't mean divorce – he wouldn't do anything as dishonourable as that. But do you think he'll be able to love you again? You'd be lucky if he even *looked* at you!'

'You're wrong!' she protested, struggling against his iron-like grip and the pressure of his great bulk against her. 'Eperitus isn't like that.'

But something inside her knew he was.

The waves crashed violently against the rocks below, sending up tall spumes of water that sprinkled Odysseus as he stood on the clifftop. He had finished his prayer with a promise of dozens of cattle, rams, black ewes and goats on his return to Ithaca, if only the storms would stop and permit him to set sail again. But Poseidon's rage seemed neither to lessen nor increase. The wind continued to howl and the seas to rage, as if he had not spoken a word.

He had never felt the rejection of the gods as much as he did then. Since boyhood he had known Athena's presence at his side, protecting and guiding him. But he had defied her and she had deserted him as punishment. All that existed now was Poseidon's implacable wrath shackling him to that cursed island. Were he to offer the lifeblood of every creature on Ithaca it would make no difference. Only the sacrifice of Hyperion's cattle would suffice, and with it would come the condemnation of all the gods. It was a riddle even Odysseus could not solve. Every way he looked at it he saw death.

He slumped forward onto his knees and lowered his forehead against the cold stone of the altar. He had built it in the first week on Thrinacie, though all he had been able to offer on it were vain promises and wishful thinking.

'Put aside your anger, Athena, if only for a day,' he whispered. 'You tested me and I failed. How can I deny it? But I'm just a man; one man lost in a world of monsters and gods. All I ask is to see my home again. Are my offences so great you'll deny me the chance to see my family one more time before I die? Has your love for me turned to such hatred?'

He pounded his fist on the rough stone and screwed his eyes shut against the tears of frustration. Then in the heat of his anger he heard a voice, quiet and calming as if it had come from the rock itself.

Look up, Odysseus. Look up now.

Suddenly he knew he was not alone. Raising his head he saw a tall silhouette striding towards him, the last of the sun glinting from its upraised sword. Odysseus threw himself aside, just as the blade came ringing down upon the altar where his head had been an instant before. Without hesitation, the figure raised its weapon again and leapt towards him. Odysseus rolled back onto his shoulders, lifted back his legs and kicked out with all his force. He caught his attacker full in the stomach and sent him crashing to the ground. Both men regained their feet at the same moment. Odysseus slipped the pathetically short dagger from his belt while his attacker slashed a cross in the air with his sword.

'What are you doing Selagos?'

'Killing you.'

He lunged at Odysseus's stomach, forcing him back towards the cliff's edge. The king felt the ground give beneath his ankle and heard the clatter of small stones falling down the rock face behind him. The terror of the sudden drop propelled him forward, lowering his head at Selagos's body as he raised his sword for the killing blow. He caught the Taphian full in the stomach and drove him back against the altar. It collapsed beneath their weight and the two men fell together in a heap among the stones. Odysseus brought his head up into Selagos's jaw and at the same time fumbled for his sword hand, grabbing his wrist and pinning it back against the ground. Gripping his dagger as hard as he could, he punched the blade into Selagos's ribs, only to feel it scrape over the hardened leather of his cuirass and into the soft earth below. With a fighter's instincts, Selagos rolled aside, trapping the knife and Odysseus's hand beneath his armoured body. As Odysseus tried to pull his hand free, the Taphian rammed his forehead hard into his face. Odysseus's nose broke and he felt the hot blood streaming out over his lips. Selagos pulled his wrist free and brought the pommel of his sword down into the side of his head. Everything went black. Odysseus was falling, his senses muffled as if he was underwater. It was strangely comforting, a transitory illusion as his consciousness retreated from the pain. Then his ears opened again to the crash of the waves below. He could see Selagos's brutal face close to his own, smell fresh sweat, leather and damp earth. The intense pain of the blow so filled his brain that it threatened to push out beyond the confines of his skull. And he knew he could submit to it then, if he chose; lay down the burdens he had carried for so long and let Selagos finish him. In Hades's kingdom he would be free from the anguish and frustration of the half-life he had led since leaving Ithaca. Then he remembered the last words of Achilles's ghost: *Cling on to life, Odysseus. Dig your fingers into it and never let go, for it's all you have.*

Grimacing against the pain, he brought his thigh up hard into his attacker's testicles and punched him in the side of the head. Selagos rolled aside with a moan and Odysseus dragged himself free, struggling to his feet and staggering away from the cliff's edge. He turned and saw Selagos pull himself up, breathing heavily and uncertain on his legs, but with his sword still in his hand. Glancing down at his feet, the Taphian snatched up Odysseus's dagger and tossed it over the cliff.

'You're going to die now, Odysseus,' he said. 'But not before I've told you why.'

'Murdering me won't make Eurylochus king. Even if he finds his way back to Ithaca, does he think the people will follow a fool like him?'

'They follow you, don't they? A poor king tied to an oath of his own making, leading away an army of six hundred and coming back with less than sixty. But if you think I'm stupid enough to follow the orders of any Ithacan – either you or that oaf cousin of yours – then that shows just how naïve you really are.'

Selagos moved towards Odysseus. The king backed away, keeping as much distance between them as he could. He could outpace Selagos, but there was a steep hill behind him and the ground was too stony and treacherous for him to flee with any hope of escape. And there were no weapons to hand other than the rocks. His only option was to keep Selagos talking until an opportunity presented itself.

'Every killer has a motive, Selagos: love, wealth, power, self-preservation... and as you attacked me, I know it's not the latter. I can't imagine it's over a woman either, or power: no Taphian thinks beyond the next whore or skin of wine. So is it wealth? Perhaps you think you can kill me and sail the galley and all the plunder back to Taphos.'

'You disappoint me, Odysseus. Where's this intelligence you've always boasted of? A clever man should be able to work out why someone wants to kill him, shouldn't he? I could tell you, of course, but I'm enjoying watching you squirm.'

'Every Taphian who came out with the replacements was a proxy, paid to take the place of some rich coward who wasn't ready to shed his blood for his homeland. Whose place did you take, Selagos?'

Selagos smiled.

'Do you really need to ask?'

'Eupeithes sent you to Troy instead of Antinous. And just like Elpenor, he gave you instructions to make sure I didn't come back.'

'He sent the boy too?' Selagos asked. 'So it was no accident he fell from Circe's roof.'

'Eupeithes must have offered to pay you well for such a dangerous mission,' Odysseus said, retreating to a boulder and sitting down. 'Whatever he promised, I can pay more. Much more. All you need do is put away your sword and I give you my oath you'll be safe until you get back to Taphos.'

'But I refused Eupeithes's gold, Odysseus. So why should I accept yours?'

'Refused?'

A wave crashed on the rocks below, sending a fine rain splashing over the clifftop.

'We Taphians may love to rut with whores and drink ourselves senseless, but we still have a sense of honour. Brutish and crude compared to yours, no doubt, but no less binding. And you forgot one of the greatest motivations for any killer: revenge. You see, Odysseus, Eupeithes told me my father's throat was cut while he slept in the courtyard of your palace. He said *you* killed him, that you didn't even give him the chance to die with his sword in his hand. But his sword is in *my* hand now, and with it I'll see that his honour is satisfied.'

Odysseus thought back to the night on Ithaca over twenty years before. He had tricked his way into the Taphian camp and ruthlessly set about slitting the throats of his enemies as they slept. Now the son of one of those men had followed him to the far edge of the world, fuelled by lust to avenge the blood of a dimly remembered father.

Selagos approached with his father's sword in both hands, ready to swing. Odysseus picked up a handful of grit by his foot and threw it at his face. As Selagos raised his arm before his eyes, Odysseus sprang up and ran at him. Selagos swung his sword blindly, but the aim was too high and Odysseus ducked under it. His shoulder caught the Taphian in the stomach, lifting him off his feet and carrying him at a sprint towards the cliff's edge. As another wave hurled seawater up into the air, Odysseus and Selagos plummeted through the spray and down to the rocks below.

Evening fell quickly on Thrinacie. Somewhere beyond the howl of the wind Eperitus could hear the cows lowing and the sheep bleating as they wandered aimlessly from one place to another. He could smell their damp hides amid the stink of seawater and wet rock, and in the semi-darkness he could make out the twisted silhouettes of the few trees that grew on the island. But of Astynome or Eurylochus there was no sign.

'Astynome!' he shouted, his voice stolen by the gale and carried out to sea. Cupping his hands around his mouth, he called again. 'Astynome!'

There was no reply, but a deeper instinct put his senses on edge. A noise, perhaps, or a movement caught out of the corner of his eye. He ran towards the cliff's edge, battling against the wind until he reached a rocky outcrop. An olive tree had somehow fought its way out of the thin soil and established itself on the peak so that it faced the sea with its branches curled like an upturned fist. There at its roots he found Eurylochus.

'What are you doing here?' he demanded in surprise.

'I'm sleeping!' he said, pointing at the blanket covering his body. 'Or I was until you woke me.'

'Sleeping?'

'It's the only way to keep my mind off the hunger, unless you want to go and kill some of those blasted cattle and save us all from starvation. And before you ask I came here to get away from the noise of those children.'

'Have you seen my wife? Selagos said she came this way looking for roots.'

'Why would I have seen her?' Eurylochus asked angrily, looking away. After a moment he threw off his blanket and rolled it up. 'And if I had I'd have turned about and gone in the opposite direction.'

He stood and glared at Eperitus.

'I'm going back to the camp. With any luck those slave children will be asleep by now. If I see her I'll tell her you're looking for her.'

Eperitus nodded. 'Do that. And make sure she stays there until I return – please.'

Eurylochus responded with a curt nod and then hastened off. Finding a rough path along the cliff's edge, Eperitus followed it until he topped a ridge that looked down over a small bay. Even in the dark he could see the white spray crashing against the rocks. Some way off he recognised the outline of an old tree that had been struck by lightning. On the ground nearby was a grey shape. At first he thought it was a flat rock, then he saw what could only be an out-stretched hand clutching at the grass.

Fear clutched at his chest and throat. He sprinted the short distance to Astynome's side and knelt beside her, gently rolling her onto her back and lowering his face to hers. The feel of her breath against his lips and the faint warmth of her cheeks beneath his fingertips filled him with sudden but momentary elation. Her eyes opened at his touch, and as she saw him tears welled up and rolled down her cheeks in thick streams. He raised her slowly in his arms and held her.

'What happened? Gods, there's blood on your forehead and your lips.'

The panic seized him again, but she raised a weak hand to his face and smiled.

'I fell in the darkness. The rocks –'

'And… and the child?'

Zeus protect our child, he implored, the words tumbling quickly through his head, drowning out his thoughts. *Athena protect them both. Artemis, goddess of unborn children, don't take this child like you took my other…*

'Safe, I'm sure of it.'

Even in the darkness Eperitus could tell Astynome had lost her colour. He picked her up and she leaned her head into his shoulder, covering her face with her hand. The journey back was agonisingly slow. A fine drizzle was falling, forcing him to step carefully over the wet rocks despite his need for haste. Tormenting thoughts that he might lose her filled his head, and his only solace was to feel the warmth of her body against his and the slight movements of her arm about his neck. When at last he saw the glow of the campfires and heard the conversation of the men – dulled by the lack of food and wine – he ran to the knot of Trojan women and laid Astynome on the sand between them.

'Help her,' he pleaded with the oldest, a woman whom Astynome had told him was a healer. 'Save her life and I promise you your freedom when we reach Ithaca.'

The woman spoke quickly to some of the others who ran to fetch the things she needed. The Ithacans watched in silence from their campfires while she bent over Astynome, staring into her eyes and feeling her temperature with the back of her hand. Eurylochus and Selagos were nowhere to be seen and Odysseus had not yet returned from his prayers. Eperitus noticed their absence as a distraction only, staring at his wife's pale face and feeling entirely helpless as he muttered prayers under his breath. After a while Eurybates appeared beside him.

'Eperitus, come with me.'

'No,' he snapped.

'You must. I wouldn't ask,' he said, nodding at Astynome, 'but it's Odysseus. He's injured.'

Eperitus looked at him sharply, then, after receiving a nod from the old woman, stood and followed Odysseus's squire.

'He's been in a fight.'

'Who with? There isn't another person on this island but us.'

Eurybates lowered his voice as they walked past the campfires.

'Selagos tried to kill him.'

'*Selagos*!'

Eurybates nodded and touched a finger to his lips.

'In here,' he said, pointing at Odysseus's makeshift hut.

Eperitus ducked through the low doorway, followed by Eurybates. Odysseus was seated on a chair in the far corner. A beeswax candle on a small table provided the only light, but it was enough to show the king's complexion was pale and both his eyes had started to blacken. Though he wore a fresh tunic and had wrapped a double cloak about his shoulders, his hair had been rubbed dry and there were cuts over his arms and legs.

'You… you look terrible,' Eperitus said.

'I'm lucky to be alive. What happened to Astynome?'

'She's being cared for.'

'I won't keep you –'

'I'm just a hindrance back there. It's probably best I stay out of the way for a little while.'

'But your heart's with her,' Odysseus said. 'Perhaps you'll let me come see her with you.'

'You should rest. Is there anything I can do?'

'I'd kill for some of Maron's wine now,' the king said with a slight laugh.

For the first time, Eperitus noticed that he looked thinner. On the subsistence rations they were eating – of which he gave half his own to Astynome – he imagined he must be looking gaunt himself. His stomach growled at the thought of food and he laid his hand flat over the hard muscles.

'And Selagos?'

'Dead. I ran him off a cliff and he broke my fall on the rocks below. It took most of my strength to stop myself being dragged out to sea, and what was left I used clawing myself back up to safety.'

'We have to find Eurylochus and put him in chains at once. His first move has failed, but –'

'I've just finished speaking to Eurylochus. I wanted to know if Selagos had been stirring more trouble with the crew, but Eurylochus says he hasn't.'

'But Eurylochus is the ringleader,' Eperitus protested. 'He's not going to admit his plans to you unless you force it out of him.'

'Eurylochus didn't put him up to this,' Odysseus said. 'It was Eupeithes, backed by a personal hatred for me. I killed his father, apparently.'

'Eupeithes!' Eurybates asked. They had not told him the truth about Elpenor. 'Then he's back to his tricks again.'

'Which is why we have to get off this island at the first sign of a break in the weather.'

'You know that won't happen,' Eperitus said. 'The gods are against us –'

Odysseus shook his head. There was a familiar light in his eyes, one Eperitus had not seen for many days.

'Not any more. I heard her voice, Eperitus. Athena warned me just before Selagos attacked. She's going to get us off this island, I know it. I just have to keep on praying. Now, take me to Astynome.'

Astynome gave birth the next day to a son. Eperitus built a pile of rocks over his tiny body on the highest point of the island, looking west towards Ithaca.

When he returned to the camp he found Astynome had been moved into Odysseus's hut, while the king had ordered his things taken to the deck of the galley. Odysseus himself had gone to the other side of the island to pray. The interior of the hut was dimly lit by grey daylight, seeping in through the gaps in the wood, and the wavering glow of a single candle. The aroma of the beeswax was strong but could not hide the foul air of illness. The Trojan nurse knelt at Astynome's bedside, wringing out a cloth over a bowl of water scented with a mix of herbs. She turned her gaze on him as he entered – the concern in her eyes clear – then dabbed the cloth across her patient's forehead. Astynome's face was paler than he had ever known it. She lay as still as a corpse, and the thought that she, too, might die struck him hard and sudden. Fear pierced his heart and left a bitter taste in the back of his throat. He wanted to fall to his knees and succumb again to the tears that had broken him once already that morning. He wanted to curse the gods and in the same breath plead with them for her life. But he did not. He would not give up on her. He would not so easily cast away what they had built together, and what they dreamed of building.

The nurse was watching him again, though this time her concern was for him rather than her charge. Standing, she laid her old but strong fingers on his arm in empathy and reassurance, then put the cloth in his hand and left. When he had buried their son, each stone he had placed over the linen-wrapped body had felt like a boulder. By the end he could barely see the cairn he had made for his tears. He had wept not just for the baby but for all the hardships he had known, so that he felt crushed of emotion. And yet as he sank to his knees beside her and laid his hand on her cold cheek, he felt the wounds open afresh and new tears force their way out.

When the weakness had passed he dried his eyes and looked down at Astynome.

'I've buried him,' he said. 'On a hill beneath an oak. I'll take you there in a day or two, when you're better.'

He touched her hair, which was still damp with sweat from her exertions that morning. With what little Greek they knew, the Trojan women had insisted he leave Astynome in their care, and so he had endured the screams of her pain alone, sitting on the sand with his head in his hands and feeling his world begin to fracture. He had begged the gods not to take her life, weakened as she was from hunger and her fall on the rocks, and for a while it seemed they had answered him. But as he looked down at her closed eyes he wondered whether they had heard him at all, or whether, like Odysseus hearing Athena's voice, it was all a cruel deception.

'You will live, Astynome,' he told her, wiping the fresh beads of sweat from her forehead. 'Whatever it takes to save you, I'll do it. The gods took Iphigenia and our son from me and I was powerless to stop them. But I won't let them take you.'

She did not open her eyes or make any movement throughout his long vigil, though her chest rose and fell in slight, regular movements. After a while Eperitus lay on the furs beside her and stroked her hair, hoping she would sense his presence and take comfort from it. Slowly his exhaustion began to lull him, but as he was about to succumb to sleep he heard a voice call his name. At first he thought it was his subconscious, a voice from the dream he was already slipping into. Then he heard it again, spoken more firmly this time. He sat up.

'Eperitus.'

He got up and pushed aside the flax curtain that acted as a door. By the quality of the thin daylight he reckoned it was still only mid-afternoon. The sight of Eurylochus standing a few paces from the hut irked him at once.

'Why do you call me from my wife's side? Don't you understand how ill she is?'

'Ill? She's dying.'

Eperitus seized his neck and pushed him hard against the bole of a tree. His fingers dug into the soft flesh, making Eurylochus choke as he struggled to prise them away.

'She is *not* going to die.'

'She is,' Eurylochus gasped, 'unless you act to save her.'

'I'm doing everything in my power.'

'Not everything. Not yet.'

Eperitus released him and he crumpled to the floor, drawing air with strangulated breaths as he massaged his neck.

'What do you mean?' Eperitus insisted. 'What does "not yet" mean?'

'Astynome will die,' Eurylochus croaked. 'She's weak, perilously weak, and you refuse to give her the strength she needs.'

Eperitus pulled him roughly to his feet and shook him by the shoulder.

'Don't you dare mock me. I'd give my own life to save her.'

'Of course you would. I've seen you risk death on the battlefield to save men you barely know. But what about your honour? What about your beloved sense of loyalty? Now *that* would be a sacrifice, if you could bring yourself to make it.'

'Honour and loyalty,' Eperitus said derisively. 'Cheap excuses for a man to turn his back on what really matters. If I could trade what little I have left of both for my wife's sake I'd do it. But honour and loyalty won't persuade the gods to lift this storm or give Astynome back her strength.'

'Of course they will. This… ordeal she's suffered might not kill her on its own, but she's already dying of starvation. Damn it, we all are. What she needs is food. What she needs even more is the favour of the gods. I know a way to give her both.'

Eperitus released his grip on Eurylochus's shoulder and stepped back.

'For days we've tried trapping birds and catching fish, but with no success. The gods deny us even the most meagre game because they hate us –'

'No, Eperitus, not us. Odysseus was the one who blinded the Cyclops and incurred Poseidon's wrath, that and all his other offences against the gods. But if we were to offer them a sacrifice, a few of Hyperion's cattle –'

'Don't be a fool!'

'A few cattle to placate Poseidon and give us the meat we desperately need… that Astynome needs.'

'No.'

'Not even for her sake? You've seen those herds. The best animals any of us have ever set eyes on. What god would refuse to accept such a sacrifice? Especially if you were to offer one in exchange for Astynome's life. They would listen to you, Eperitus, but your sense of honour and loyalty to Odysseus blinds you. Did you ever consider that the gods might want to break your pride and make you show some humility before them?'

'Get out of my sight!' Eperitus shouted, then turned on his heel and pushed through the curtain into the hut.

Astynome was looking at him as he entered.

'I didn't mean to wake you –'

'Don't do it, Eperitus,' she whispered. 'Don't do what he asks. Eurylochus is a liar.'

He knelt beside her and took her hand in his. The flesh was deathly cold. He smiled at her and looked into her eyes, then bent down to kiss her forehead.

'But he's right. You need food, and more than anything else you need the blessing of the gods. What choice do I have?'

She shook her head but had no more strength for words. He kissed her on the lips and then stood and left the hut. Eurylochus was waiting for him.

Chapter Forty-One

THE CATTLE OF THE SUN GOD

Odysseus woke with a start. He had been dreaming of Ithaca and for a moment believed he was there, waking on the shore where he had been left by the crew of an unknown galley. Then he recognised the stone altar he had rebuilt after the fight with Selagos and knew he was back on Thrinacie. He looked round, sensing something was wrong but seeing nothing other than the raging seas and the darkening skies of late evening.

When he was sure he was alone, he stood and began the walk back to camp. Every step of the way he felt on edge, sensing that something had happened at the camp while he had been away. He cursed himself for falling asleep, though he was not to blame. The gods themselves had put him into a deep slumber and he soon knew why. He saw the column of black smoke long before he smelled it, the sort of trail only a large fire could make. Then when the wind brought the aroma to his nostrils and it was mixed with the smell of roast flesh, his heart sank.

Topping the last ridge, he looked down at the beach and saw groups of Ithacans moving about, each man busy with his individual chores. For a moment he was relieved there were no cattle in sight. Then he saw men with their limbs covered in blood as they chopped and sawed at the carcasses of several animals. Others were skewering the meat and roasting it over small fires, while their comrades sat around eating and crying out for more. At the top of the beach were the flayed hides of six cows, stretched out over an old sail while several men scraped away the layers of flesh and fat. A seventh animal lay dead before a large, flat boulder. A man stood over it with a long dagger in his hand. Odysseus felt the fury rising within him as he recognised his cousin through the gore. Then he saw another figure, cloaked and hooded, standing before the fire with his back turned. In his hands was a parcel of meat wrapped in fat and topped with raw flesh. He threw the gods' portion into the flames, held his hands up in prayer and then bent to pick up a bowl of water by his feet. This he slopped onto the flames, using it as a libation in place of wine. Again he raised up his hands in a plea to the gods.

'You fools!' Odysseus shouted. 'You damned fools. You've brought doom on all of us.'

He ran down the hill towards Eurylochus, who dropped his knife in sudden fear. Odysseus grabbed his shoulder as he attempted to flee and spun him about.

'We had to do it,' Eurylochus squealed. 'We were starving –'

Odysseus silenced him with a single punch.

'You,' he said, pointing at one of the men carving the meat. 'Where's Eperitus? If only he'd been here –'

'I am here, my lord.'

The figure by the sacrificial fire tipped back his hood. Odysseus looked at him aghast.

'But why?' he asked. 'Why would you do this, Eperitus? Do you think Hyperion won't see what you've done because Poseidon has covered the island in cloud? Do you think he won't have heard his cattle crying out to him, or that he won't seek *vengeance* on every one of us?'

Eperitus's expression was hard and impenitent.

'Astynome is starving.'

'And now you've sealed her fate.'

'Her fate was sealed anyway. All our fates were sealed the moment you gave your name to the Cyclops and brought his curse down on us. But maybe the gods will taste these sacrifices we've offered and change their hearts. Perhaps they'll realise we've suffered enough and let us go home.'

'What gods are you talking about?' Odysseus said. 'The same gods who demanded your daughter's life to release the fleet at Aulis? The same gods who encouraged Greeks and Trojans to slaughter each other in their thousands? The same gods who've just denied you a son? You fool! They're going to kill us to a man.'

'*Then at least we'll face them with full stomachs*! And I'd rather take my chances with the gods than die of starvation. They'll listen; I promised to build Hyperion a temple when we return to Ithaca and fill it with offerings –'

'Not in my kingdom you won't. I'll take you back to Greece, but not to Ithaca. I'll set you down on the first mainland we can find and then you and I will never set eyes on each other again.'

As he spoke, a deep lowing broke out behind him. He looked round, but there were no cattle on the top of the ridge or anywhere else. Suddenly the men called out in alarm, some of them throwing down their knives and skewers of meat and running towards the sea. The panic spread quickly. Odysseus drew his sword, then let it fall from his fingers into the sand. The dead animal on the boulder was moving. Though its blood had coagulated in scarlet tributaries down the sides of the makeshift altar and added to the dark stain on the sand, its mouth was clearly moving as it emitted the guttural sounds it would have made in life. More terrifying still, a deep lowing was also emanating from the carcasses of the other dead animals as they lay abandoned on bloody sheets of canvas, though the heads had been removed and they possessed no lungs with which to produce the sound. If this dreadful omen was not enough, the flayed hides were moving. Odysseus's flesh turned cold and his primal instincts shrieked at him to turn and flee, but he did not move. He could not. As the pelts crept slowly across the sand, like wounded men crawling from a battle, his legs refused to obey the frantic orders of his mind. One by one, the six hides dragged themselves to the edge of the sacrificial fire and fed themselves to the flames, while all around the air was filled with lowing, as if the camp was surrounded by a thousand invisible cattle.

Despite the sacrifice, the storms did not abate. For a day the carcasses and the meat that had been cut from them lay where they had been left, in the sand or on spits over the ashes of the deserted fires. Though the lowing had faded away quickly, the superstitious Ithacans had been too afraid to touch the remains of the animals they had killed. Only when Eperitus rekindled one of the fires and cooked the meat for Astynome did the rest of the crew forget their fear and answer the need of their hunger.

Astynome barely had the strength left to eat, but she managed to take some of the broth Eperitus had made for her. He finished what she could not. Though his appetite was fading as Astynome faded, he knew he had to keep himself strong for her sake. For two more days she barely spoke. He stayed at her side every moment, holding her hand and silently imploring the gods to spare her life. The Trojan nurse came regularly with drinks she had brewed using what herbs there were on the island, but at the end of each visit Eperitus could see the concern in her eyes. When he asked her what was wrong she pretended not to have enough Greek to answer, but he had enough command of her own language to press for a response.

'She is dying,' she said, reluctantly. 'She should not be: she has food now and she is young – and was strong. But her heart is not in it. I believe she wants to die.'

Omeros, Eurybates and others had appeared from time to time, offering words of false comfort and hoping to help by their presence. Odysseus, too, had visited. At least, Eperitus had woken from an unwanted slumber to hear the curtain move behind him and sense that the king had been there. It had been a visit made out of love for Astynome, for Odysseus's anger with Eperitus remained too fresh and the two men had not set eyes on each other since the sacrifice of Hyperion's cattle.

On the second night Eperitus woke to find Polites in the tent. He was standing in a corner, a brown shadow on which the orange light of the small fire barely settled. Another time it was Astynome's father, Chryses, in his priestly robes. Eperitus had staggered up from his chair and drawn his sword, fearful that he had come to claim his daughter for the gods, but the figure had faded away. On a third occasion he had seen Hermes warming his hands over the flames and smiling at Eperitus. That had been a dream, though, for he woke with a start to find the nurse mopping Astynome's brow. When Eperitus had asked if she had seen Hermes, she only shook her head, though her look of concern deepened.

On the sixth morning since the sacrifice, Astynome's eyes opened and she reached out a hand.

'Where am I?' she asked, a faint smile touching her lips.

Eperitus slid from the chair to his knees and took her hand in his, touching the cold flesh with his lips.

'Odysseus's hut, on Thrinacie.'

'But that can't be. I was at the farm feeding the baby. You were outside, digging the stones from that patch of ground you've been meaning to plough. I could hear you singing, one of those old songs from the war. How can we be back on Thrinacie?'

Eperitus smiled to hear her voice again and to know that Astynome had been happily dreaming of their future home on Ithaca. Then he remembered their baby. The thought of reminding her that the child was dead stole away his joy.

'It was a dream, my love. You've been ill, but soon we'll set sail for Ithaca and build that farm for real.'

'A dream?' she echoed, disappointed. 'But what about the baby?'

He squeezed her hand gently.

'We'll have lots of babies. How do you feel?'

'Weak. Cold. But I'm glad you are with me. Have you been here long?'

He laughed and felt his spirits rise.

'A while. Are you hungry, my love? Someone's cooking a stew, I can smell it.'

She nodded. 'I can manage a little.'

He stroked her hair and kissed her forehead. Then, with a parting smile, he left the hut in search of the stew. A fine drizzle was falling but he barely noticed. Once he had claimed a bowlful of stew, he sought out the fire where the Trojan slaves were sitting with their cloaks over their heads. Seeing him, the nurse rose at once and raised an eyebrow.

'She's awake and she wants something to eat.'

The woman nodded and followed him to the hut. On entering he saw Astynome's eyes had closed again.

'I've brought the stew,' he said. 'If it tastes as good as it smells –'

The nurse brushed past him and knelt at Astynome's side. There was an urgency in her movements that made him feel suddenly, horribly sick. She placed a hand over Astynome's brow, then took her wrist in her other hand and pressed her fingertips to the soft skin. Eperitus placed the bowl on a table by the doorway, his fumbling hand spilling some of the contents.

'What is it?'

The nurse looked at him for a moment, then her gaze dropped to Astynome's motionless chest. Eperitus knelt down by his wife and pressed his hand to her cheek. It was cold.

'Astynome. Wake up. Wake up, my love.'

He was not aware of the nurse rising to her feet and laying a gentle hand on his shoulder as she parted. Blinded by his tears, he could barely even see Astynome's pale face as he kissed her for the last time and sank down beside her.

The next day was the seventh since the sacrifice. The sun crept out of the ocean into clear skies. Eperitus felt it on his skin as he stood amid the long grass of the dunes and heard the jubilant shouts of the Ithacans on the beach below, knowing that with the

storm gone they could sail for home. It was a joy he could no longer share. His emotions were exhausted and flat, his hollow heart
incapable of either ecstasy or despair. His mind, too, seemed empty
of thoughts. There was no future and no past, and to think of the
present was torture. For a while it was easier to stand in the daze
of grief and simply let his senses slump from one sound to another,
from one smell to the next, as if lingering on the distant lowing of
Hyperion's remaining cattle or the smell of wet stone drying in the
sun could provide an escape from the void within. But it could not.
Eventually he turned his back on the bright morning and returned
to the nearby hut.

Astynome's corpse lay where he had left it. His eyes flickered over her, indulging the faint hope that something might have
moved – a slight turn of the head or repositioning of a hand that
would indicate life had returned. But she was exactly as she had
been. He knelt beside her and stroked her hair, soft with the illusion
of life and yet the scalp beneath cold, horribly so because once it had
been warm and lovely to touch. His red-rimmed eyes were too dry
to shed more tears, but something continued to sink within him as
if his heart and lungs and liver were slowly contracting in on themselves. And he felt afraid. More afraid than before any battle he had
fought. Afraid that soon he would be parted from her forever; that
once he had buried her corpse he would never be able to look on her
again, beautiful even in death; that eventually he would forget what
she looked like, even as he had forgotten Iphigenia's face; and that
all that would remain would be the aching gap where their love had
been. The tears returned at the thought and he bowed his head in
submission to them.

After a while he took her body up in his arms and carried her
to the hill where he had buried their child. He laid her on the grass
beside the small mound and took her cold hand in his. She looked
as if she was sleeping, but as he touched her cheek the deception was
revealed. Her spirit had gone to Hades, leaving behind all memory
of their short time together. He spoke his last farewell and laid the
blanket over her pale, lovely face.

When he returned to the camp, his hands rough and bloodied from the stones he had placed over her, he saw the galley already resting in the bay with most of the crew aboard. Odysseus was in the stern, but he turned away as he saw Eperitus coming across the sand. The last few men waited for him in the small boat and then rowed out to the ship. Not caring that every eye was upon him, he sat down on one of the benches and hid his face in his hands. With his eyes closed he could pretend the world around him did not exist, and after a while his mind drifted to thoughts of Astynome. Then someone sat down beside him.

'I'm sorry, Eperitus,' Omeros said.

Eperitus nodded.

'Odysseus is too.'

'He told you that, did he?'

'He didn't have to. On the surface he's angry – with all of us – but beneath he hurts for Astynome and for your grief.'

'To Hades with him.'

Omeros sighed. Eurybates shouted for the anchor stones to be hauled in and the oars to be lowered. Eperitus and Omeros were joined by another man and together they slid the long pine blade into the water and began rowing. Before long the galley was out at sea with the wide hump of Thrinacie visible in its entirety behind them. A westerly wind was blowing, and after a discussion with Eurybates, Odysseus called for the oars to be withdrawn and the sail unfurled. It caught the breeze with a snap and soon the ship was moving swiftly at an angle across the direction of the low waves.

'He won't carry out his threat,' Omeros said. 'To cast you off on the mainland, I mean. He doesn't know what's facing him at home so he'll need his best men at his side when he gets back.'

'I'm not *his* man any more, Omeros,' Eperitus answered. 'I want nothing more to do with him. And if he tries to keep me around until he gets back to Ithaca then I'll take a boat to the mainland.'

'And do what? You need him every bit as much as he needs you, especially now that –'

'Now that I don't have Astynome?'

Omeros looked away. 'Yes. You've lost one of the two most important people in your life. If you lose Odysseus, too, the last twenty years of your life will have been for nothing. Can't you see that?'

'All I see is that he killed Astynome. Just as he killed Polites and Elpenor, the closest friends you had.'

'Elpenor was a traitor.'

'No more than I am for sacrificing those cows for Astynome's sake. Odysseus decided to stop at Thrinacie instead of sailing on to this other island Circe spoke of, Phaeacia. The woman I love would still be alive if he'd had the will to keep going, rather than letting himself be overruled by his own crew.'

'Your grief has distorted your judgement,' Omeros said, laying his hand on his shoulder. 'Odysseus made the best choices he could, better than any you or I could have made. Without him we would be dead anyway.'

'No, it's *his* presence that has cursed us. When he and I first met, the Pythoness gave us each an oracle. She warned him against ever going to Troy, saying that if he did he would not find his way home for twenty years. Twenty, Omeros, not eleven or twelve or however long it is now since he left Ithaca. And that wasn't all: she said that if he came back he would be alone and destitute. Whatever happens to him, *we're* doomed anyway.'

A change in the wind brought something to his senses that made him look up. Behind the galley to the east a bank of dark cloud had appeared in the otherwise clear skies. It was moving with an unnatural rapidity that made him stiffen. Odysseus was in the helm beside Eurybates and noticed Eperitus sit up and look. He glanced over his shoulder and alerted Eurybates to the approaching danger.

Eperitus rose from the bench and walked to the stern.

'We need to turn around,' he said. 'Thrinacie is just over the horizon; if we turn the ship about now we might make it back in time to save ourselves.'

'We're not going back,' Odysseus replied with a scowl.

'That cloud is not natural. Look at the speed of it! It's a storm sent by the gods to destroy us.'

'Because you slaughtered those cattle against my explicit orders! *You* brought this on us.'

'Then *I'll* save us,' Eperitus replied through gritted teeth. 'Eurybates, turn the ship around.'

The helmsman looked at Odysseus, who shook his head in response. The cloud now slipped across the face of the sun, turning the light grey and the air cool. A squall of rain swept the deck, pursued by a blast of wind that pushed out the sail so hard it strained the forestays. Eperitus pulled Eurybates's hand away from one of the rudders and took hold of it. Before he could seize the other, Odysseus grabbed him by the chest and shoved him across the deck, where he fell among the Trojan women huddled below the mast.

His melancholy at Astynome's death now turned to sudden and terrible fury. Tearing his sword from its sheath he charged through the pouring rain at Odysseus. The king drew his weapon and their blades met with a ringing clash. Lightning flashed, followed by a boom of thunder so loud it felt like the sky was being torn in half. Eperitus lunged at Odysseus's stomach, a blow that would have taken his life. Odysseus parried and returned with a thrust that spelt out his own murderous intentions. The blade glanced off Eperitus's belt and again the two men threw themselves at each other on the plunging deck. Then a new gust of wind snapped the forestays and tore the sail from the cross spar, whipping it up into the angry skies like a rag. A loud crack followed. Odysseus looked up, then threw himself at Eperitus's waist, knocking him to the deck just as the broken mast fell lengthways across the galley. It landed on Eurybates, crushing his skull and sending him toppling overboard into the churning sea. Women screamed and men shouted in terror. Eperitus rolled aside and tried to stand, but the deck dropped suddenly beneath his feet and he was thrown against the bow rail. Steadying himself, he looked for Odysseus but could distinguish nothing through the driving rain. A man's body lay on the deck before him. Wiping the water from his eyes, Eperitus saw that it was Omeros. His forehead was gleaming with blood and his eyes were closed, so that Eperitus could not tell whether he was alive or dead. Then the sea fell away beneath the galley and he was pitched headfirst across the deck. His hand found a bench and seized hold of it with what strength he could muster, but all around him he heard screams as others toppled overboard into the hungry sea.

Zeus's anger was approaching its zenith. The skies erupted with a second deafening boom and a flash of intense light. A loud, splintering crack followed and the air was filled with the stench of sulphur. Eperitus felt the ship that had carried them through so many ordeals give a last groan, then disintegrate beneath him. The deck split into two and sank rapidly into the tumultuous sea. Everything went dark as he plunged into the water, sinking deeper and deeper amid the black, falling shapes of broken oars, benches and other bodies. His senses were muffled and confused, alive only to the coldness of the water as the heat and immediacy of life was sucked from him. He considered surrendering to the quick death that was but a few heartbeats away. There would be the brief panic of drowning as his body died, then his soul would go to join Astynome. But he knew that would never be. As soon as he had drunk the waters of the River Lethe he would no longer love her, just as she would no longer love him; two more strangers in a kingdom where the only emotion was regret.

There was something else, though. Something forgotten. Something he had to do.

The falling stopped and he felt the pressure of the water buoy him upward. Below him was a black abyss, above him a lesser darkness punctuated by twisting shadows. Suddenly, as he felt the air in his lungs expiring, he knew he had to live. He kicked hard and pushed his hands before him, propelling himself upward. His lungs began to burn and he kicked again and again, all the time resisting the instinct to open his mouth and drink in the air that was not there. He could hear his heart pumping furiously and his already dark vision darkening further. Then he broke the surface, took a gulp of air and was swallowed up by a wave. He pushed through again, glimpsing grey clouds and the countless heavy drops of silver rain falling from them, before being submerged by another swell. The third time he wrestled free of the sea's clutches he saw the high waves and the flotsam being tossed about on them. Near at hand was a piece of the deck with a man clinging to its broken edge. He snatched a mouthful of air before the next wave engulfed him. Opening his eyes, he saw the dark shape of the wreckage above him and the legs of the man hanging on to it. He reached out, grabbed the wood and used what little strength remained to him to pull himself on top.

Immediately a wave broke over the wreckage and would have thrown him back into the sea had he not grasped the edge of the platform and hung on to it. He wiped the water from his eyes and saw that the man had been swept away. Looking around, Eperitus saw the galley had completely disappeared, though its broken remains were spread across the undulating surface of the sea. There were a few bodies, too, mostly of the Trojan slaves and their children who had not been pulled down by the weight of armour or muscle. All were dead, kept afloat for a while by pockets of air in their clothing, but this soon escaped and one by one the corpses sank from sight, leaving Eperitus alone on the water. Its work done, the storm rolled away almost as quickly as it had arrived. The waves grew calm again and the sun reappeared, its warmth making steam rise from Eperitus's sodden clothing.

The revenge of the gods had been absolute. Hyperion's cattle had been paid for in Ithacan blood, while Poseidon had avenged Polyphemus's eye by taking Odysseus down to the seabed. Eperitus lowered his head and wept, his misery complete. Why had they fought ten long years at Troy and overcome such fantastic obstacles since, only to perish at the last? He understood the gods were the gods and the lives of men were insignificant. But even the gods had their favourites, men and women whose strengths and weaknesses gleamed like gold amid the earthly mire. They populated the songs that Eperitus had heard since he was a boy, and he had been privileged to fight alongside or against many of them in the Trojan War. Of these, Odysseus was the greatest of all. The humble ruler of an insignificant nation, he had walked with gods and counselled kings, conquered the greatest of cities and sailed beyond the known world, even to the realms of the dead. Now his great friend had returned to Hades forever – if indeed Eperitus could call him friend any more. As Ajax had spurned Odysseus in the Underworld, would Odysseus turn his back on him should their souls meet again? It was as much as he deserved. And yet death was not what Odysseus had deserved. The gods had cheated him, just as they had cheated Astynome. Just as Eperitus felt they had cheated him, too. Why had Ithaca always been just beyond the next horizon? Why had the gods robbed him and Astynome of home and family, and Odysseus of the loved ones he had fought so hard to return to? He wanted to shout his anger at the skies, but he knew the gods would not listen. They never listened.

He lay down on the raft and closed his eyes. The water moved gently beneath him, lapping at the edges of the broken wood as it bobbed up and down. He wondered whether he would be taken back to Thrinacie, or onward to Phaeacia, or whether he would just die of thirst on the raft. He could not last more than a day or two. The sooner the better, he thought. Then, as he drifted into sleep, something took hold of his raft and almost tipped it over. Startled, he sat up and looked at the man trying to pull himself onto the unsteady platform.

'Odysseus!' Eperitus exclaimed, taking hold of the man's forearms and pulling him aboard.

But it was not Odysseus. Instead, Eperitus found himself staring into the pig-like eyes of Eurylochus.

Chapter Forty-Two

AFTER THE STORM

The room was dark and smelled fusty. Heavy curtains hung across the window that had once allowed daylight to fill the room. Now only a few fingers of sunshine penetrated the gaps, capturing countless particles of dust in their narrow beams. Argus sneezed and then looked up at Penelope, as if to ask why she had come to the deserted bedroom. She patted his grey head and ordered him to lie down.

White sheets covered the furniture, though Penelope remembered every piece. Beneath the window was a couch that she and Odysseus used to share in the evenings as they looked out at the stars. Over against one wall was her dressing table and here and there were a few chairs, anonymous beneath their pale covers. The bed in the centre of the room was also covered, but for its four posts. These were made of olive wood and inlaid with intricate patterns that twisted up to the ceiling. They were grey with dust now, but Penelope knew their designs intimately.

She walked over and put a hand on one of the posts. The dust came away beneath her thumb to reveal a gleam of gold and silver. But the rich ornamentation her husband had put there was not its only secret. He had built their bedroom over a small courtyard beside the palace, where an olive tree had stood; this particular post had been carved from the bole of that tree, the roots of which still ran beneath the floor of the bedroom. It was a secret only she and Odysseus knew. Or perhaps it was now hers alone.

Every king who had survived the war had either returned home by now or had perished. Only Odysseus's fate remained unknown.

In his absence Eupeithes and his allies had regained the confidence they had lost after the news of Troy's fall. The old serpent had reasserted his authority over his son, but Penelope did not know how long that would last for. And though Antinous had not threatened Penelope with rape again, she felt his eyes on her constantly. As if he felt it was just a matter of time before she was his.

She sat on the mattress, raising a thin cloud of dust. Argus sensed her sadness and came to lie at her feet. His brown eyes looked up at her as he lay with his head on his paws, wondering what was on her mind. She smiled and rubbed his head.

'Time, Argus, that's what I need. To buy time for your master's return.' The dog's ears pricked up slightly. 'There was an old oracle that said if he went to Troy he wouldn't come back for twenty years. I hated that oracle, but now it's all I've got left. The promise that he'll return one day. That his bones aren't at the bottom of the ocean, or that he hasn't given his love to another woman. I couldn't bear either, but it's more unbearable not knowing anything.'

She looked around at the room. It was just a place of memories now. The couch where they had looked up at the stars was just a couch; the bed where they had made love so many times was just a bed. Without Odysseus they were meaningless and held nothing but pain for her, which was why she had abandoned the room to dust and darkness. If she knew that he had perished it could become a place of grieving and slowly fading memories, where she would go through the process of letting go. Until then it was a place of sadness, somewhere to be avoided. She should not have returned here.

'Come Argus,' she said, rising to her feet. 'Let's return to the world of the living.'

Odysseus lashed the broken mast to a part of the keel and tied himself to the makeshift raft before collapsing with exhaustion. When he awoke it was to darkness. He pushed himself up onto his knees and looked around. The sky was filled with stars from horizon to horizon, but the ocean was black and empty. He scoured the surface for a long time, hoping to spot wreckage from the galley with men clinging to it. But there was nothing. The gods had obliterated his ship and taken his crew with it.

And yet he still lived. Had they overlooked him? Not Zeus, who never missed an opportunity to punish. Then had Athena pleaded that he be spared? Or perhaps it was the others who had been spared, while his punishment continued. Like Sisyphus continuously pushing a boulder up the same slope in Hades, or Tantalus taunted by food and drink he could never reach, was he doomed to drift from one place to another for eternity with Ithaca and his family always just beyond the next horizon? The thought was terrifying, and for a moment he contemplated the cold comfort of the surrounding waters. He only had to jump in to end his torture. But the ever-present voice of his sanity argued that his fate might be to survive and reach Ithaca after all; that this might be just another test of his worthiness, or a final step towards redemption. And if not – if the gods had decided that he must indeed spend eternity lost – then would they not contrive a way to pull him out of the water and throw him up on the next strange shore?

He sighed and lay on his back with his arms stretched out, looking up at the distorted constellations. The skin of water he had grabbed as the galley had disintegrated around him was strapped over his shoulder and there were some dried strips of beef from the sun god's cattle in the pouch on his belt. Remembering them, he felt the sudden dryness in his mouth and the gnawing hunger in his stomach. But he knew that if he was to survive he would have to eke out his rations until he found land again. And surviving, he thought dryly, was something he excelled at.

'Somehow I never thought I would make it without you, Eperitus,' he said. 'I just assumed we would go on together, even if everyone else perished. But you've gone too. Abandoned me when I needed you most.'

His face pulled into a sudden snarl and he felt the tears burning their way out of the corners of his eyes. It felt like anger but he knew it was grief. His friend was gone and they had parted as enemies, with clashing swords and murder in their faces. Damn the gods, he thought. Damn their mockery. Damn their unassailable detachment. Damn their grand games and petty schemes, pitting men against the impossible. Damn them for making him the instrument of their revenge. Damn them for making him betray everyone he had ever cared about, one by one, until there was no-one left any more. He rolled onto his side and pulled his knees up to his chest, sobbing like a child.

He woke drowsily to bright sunshine and shadow. He could smell wet rock and hear the roar of breakers, as if they were part of the dream he was still half rapt in. Then he realised their meaning and sat up.

He was passing between two great bulwarks of rock, the skirts of which were lost in a fine mist from the waves crashing against them. Through this narrow gateway he could see a large circle of water surrounded by cliffs. He recognised the place at once by the cave high up on one side, the same den from which Scylla had snatched up six of his crewmates. Any moment she might appear over the threshold of her cave and seize him too. But the current pulled him away from the cave and to the right, where the waves splashed and lapped against the smooth base of the cliff. Then he realised what was drawing him that way. Ahead of him the water was bubbling and frothing like the contents of a great cauldron. The perverse luck that had led him away from Scylla was now sending him into the mouth of Charybdis.

He looked at the cliff wall, but there were no jutting rocks that he might swim for or cling on to. Charybdis's mouth opened with a roar of sucking water and the raft spun rapidly towards it. Odysseus saw the overhanging boughs of the olive tree that clung tenaciously to the cliff face and leapt up. He seized hold of a branch just as the raft was pulled out from beneath his feet and down into the throat of the vortex. The branch sagged under his weight and as he hung there the sound of rushing water was deafening. The mist from it drenched his hair and clothes and he felt his fingers slipping as they gripped the wood. The white rocks of the monster's teeth gleamed below him and he could see the blackened ribs of wrecked ships' protruding from the blue-grey sand. With terrifying suddenness his interlaced fingers slid apart and he fell. In the same instant, with a crash of water and a jet of spume, Charybdis's jaws snapped shut. He hit the surface with a smack that momentarily concussed him. As he came to, his limp body was being drawn down by the last of the swirling current. Kicking out with new strength, he forced himself to the surface and gulped in a lungful of air.

As he looked around at the smooth, uninviting cliffs, he called on the name of Athena. A moment later his raft bobbed up just a short way ahead of him. He pulled his weary body towards it and climbed on board.

Eurylochus had fallen into a deep sleep from the moment he had crawled exhausted and naked onto the raft. Taking pity on the wretch, Eperitus had thrown his cloak over him as he lay face down on the piece of wreckage they shared. After all, they were all that remained of the six-hundred-strong army that had sailed from Ithaca so many years before. Several times Eperitus had checked to see that he was still alive, fearing his soul might have slipped away in the night. But when the chariot of the sun climbed out of the far reaches of the ocean the next morning he was still breathing.

'Where are we?' Eurylochus mumbled, raising himself groggily on one elbow.

'I don't know,' Eperitus answered.

'Are we the only ones left?'

'Yes.'

'There must be other survivors.'

'I've been scanning the horizon since dawn. There's no-one else.'

Eurylochus groaned and slumped back down on the raft.

'But why me? Why not one of the others? They're stronger and fitter than me –'

'Some were wearing armour. Some went down with the galley. Some couldn't swim, I suppose.'

'*I* can barely swim.'

'But you can float. Fat is lighter than water, or so Odysseus once told me. It kept you from drowning and it kept you warm during the night.'

'And what good will it do me if we don't find land soon,' Eurylochus grumbled, sitting up and wrapping Eperitus's cloak around his shoulders. 'I'll just starve, which is the worst death imaginable.'

'I'd starve before you: you've more fat than me.'

'So being a fat good-for-nothing finally trumps being a mighty warrior,' Eurylochus said sardonically.

'Not if the warrior decides to kill the good-for-nothing and eat him instead. But it doesn't matter either way; we'll both die of thirst long before we starve.'

Eurylochus shook his head. 'What I wouldn't do for a cup of sweet wine now. My throat's as parched as… Wait, what's that?'

He pointed over Eperitus's shoulder. Eperitus gave him a cynical look, but Eurylochus jumped to his feet and pointed, the cloak slipping away to reveal his nakedness.

'By all the gods, it's a sail!'

He began to wave his hands, his movements unsettling the raft. But Eperitus did not care if he tipped them into the water or whether he had seen a sail or not.

'What are those?'

'They're coming towards us. We're saved!'

'What are those marks on your chest?' Eperitus repeated.

'What? Oh –'

Eurylochus snatched up the cloak and threw it quickly about his shoulders.

'Look, Eperitus. Look, why don't you!'

Eperitus snatched the cloak from Eurylochus's shoulders. Four parallel scars ran across his chest, from his right shoulder to beneath his left nipple. Eurylochus threw his hand across them and shook his head.

'They're nothing. Old scars from –'

'A few days old at the most,' Eperitus said, pulling Eurylochus's arm aside with one hand and tracing the fingers of his other hand down the deep gashes. 'Who gave them to you?'

'One of the slaves.'

'It was Astynome, wasn't it,' Eperitus said, his voice quiet and firm. 'You attacked her.'

'Of course I didn't –'

Eperitus slapped him hard across the face.

'You attacked her, didn't you?'

Eurylochus shook his head and Eperitus slapped him again, harder.

'*Didn't you?*'

'*Yes!*'

Suddenly Eperitus's fingers were on Eurylochus's throat, crushing the windpipe until his fat face began to turn a deep purple. He took hold of Eperitus's wrist with both hands, trying desperately to prise himself free of the grip that was squeezing the life from him. Eperitus pulled one of the hands away and closed both his hands around his neck. Eurylochus's jaw moved quickly and a few sounds escaped his slobbering lips, but no words came out. He began to struggle violently, but Eperitus's hold was unrelenting. Even after Eurylochus's body had gone limp and his weight pulled him down to the surface of the ramp Eperitus refused to let go, squeezing harder until he was certain the man who had raped his wife was dead. He understood everything now, and knowing gave terrible strength to his anger, which Eurylochus's death did nothing to soften. The man had murdered his son and killed his wife and Eperitus had not been there to stop it. Even when the blood began to flow over his thumbs he could not stop himself. Eurylochus had taken all he had and the only thing he could do about it was to keep squeezing.

By the time the shadow of the galley's sail fell across him and the rope dropped onto the raft, Eurylochus's body had rolled off into the water and disappeared. Eperitus remained on his knees, aware only of the monotonous repetition of his own breathing.

'Take the rope, man,' a voice shouted.

After a moment, he fumbled for the leather rope and wound it twice around his wrist. Steadying himself, he let the crew haul him in until the small raft butted up against the side of the galley.

'Here, give me your hand,' said the same voice. 'I think we've got another of your crewmates on board.'

Eperitus looked up into a leathery face with a ragged seafarer's beard and long, braided hair. The man looked at him with kind eyes as he offered him his hand. Other men stood around him, and as Eperitus took the outstretched hand, several others joined together to pull him onto the deck. He fell onto his back and someone placed a skin of water against his lips, squeezing a few drops into his mouth before splashing his face with it.

'How long've you been out here?' said another voice.

'Don't crowd him,' said the first.

'What ship is this?' Eperitus asked, sitting up.

'A Phaeacian trader. Don't worry, you're safe; we won't harm you. My name's Proreus.'

'You said you'd got somebody else on board. Another survivor?'

'You tell us,' Proreus replied. 'We fished him off another piece of flotsam this morning, but he can't remember anything at all. He must be a shipmate of yours, though.'

'Where is he?'

Proreus took his arm and helped him to his feet.

'Over here. Do you know him?'

The ship was big and well made with a crew of perhaps two dozen. The Phaeacians were all large, muscular men browned by long years at sea. They watched him from the rowing benches or as they leaned casually against the bow rails on either side. Proreus took him to a figure sitting on sacks of grain with a blanket around his shoulders. It was Omeros. As Eperitus's shadow fell over the boy he looked up. It took a few moments for Eperitus to realise he was blind.

'Yes. He was a passenger on our ship.'

'Was he blind before you were wrecked?'

'No.'

'I thought as much. There's a deep cut on the back of his head, so whatever struck him has robbed him of his sight. It took his memory, too, poor wretch. Can't even remember who he is. But if you speak to him – tell him his name – perhaps something'll come back.'

Eperitus shook his head. 'I don't recall his name. Like I said, he wasn't one of the crew.'

'And your name?' Proreus said.

'My name doesn't matter.'

'Doesn't matter? A man's name is who he is.'

'I don't want to be anybody.'

'Well, stranger, I can see you're a man who's seen hard times and perhaps you're in no mood for talking. You can tell me your name when we reach Phaeacia. For now, I'll find you a blanket and something to eat.'

Eperitus nodded and sat down on one of the grain sacks. He looked at Omeros's unseeing eyes and the blank face that remembered nothing, and he envied him. If the gods had been merciful they would have left Omeros his memory and taken Eperitus's instead. But perhaps that was part of the joke: take the past from a young man who had nothing to regret, while leaving an old man with the ghosts of everything he had lost. He would not let them have their joke, though. He had let down those whom he cared for the most: Iphigenia; Arceisius; Astynome; Odysseus. His life had been a failure. But he had to move on. He had seen the Underworld and knew the eternity of misery that awaited him. He would not let that start now. Astynome would not want him to, nor would

Odysseus. For his own sake he had to leave his past behind, deny it and move on. Odysseus had once believed that the decrees of the gods could be reversed. He had to believe the same.

Reluctantly, Odysseus opened his eyes. He had been dreaming he was back home on Ithaca, hosting a feast in the great hall. Penelope and Telemachus were on either side of him and the other tables were filled with the kings and heroes he had fought beside in the war: Agamemnon, Menelaus, Diomedes, Achilles and even Great Ajax. Eperitus was there, as were Antiphus, Polites, Eurybates and many others who had since descended to Hades's Halls. But in his dream they were happy. Their faces were free from suffering, free from any memory of the trials they had faced. And he had wanted to remain with his family and friends. But some instinct had disturbed his contentment, nagging at him until he was forced to follow it into consciousness and the knowledge that what he had been enjoying was a fantasy. As he felt the rise and fall of the raft and the bite of the leather straps that lashed him to it, he remembered that he was alone and without help in a world that hated him.

He lay there a moment with his cheek pressed against the rough wood, wondering what had pulled him from his sleep. Then he knew. The smell of land. The sound of waves crashing against rocks. And he realised he was in mortal peril.

He unslipped his wrists from their bonds and knelt. Dark hills were rising out of the sea ahead of him, silhouetted by thousands of stars. Explosions of silver spray marked the island's jagged teeth, and knowing he would be dashed against them in moments, Odysseus leapt into the water and began swimming. He had seen a line of breakers from the raft and headed in their direction, hoping they marked a beach. He prayed the gods would give him the strength to reach the narrow spot before he was pulled to his death on the rocks. The gods heard him. Just as he thought his limbs would take him no further, a wave picked him up and threw him onto soft sand. He dragged himself up the beach on his elbows until he felt long grass between his fingers, then collapsed.

He did not dream, but when he awoke it was to a parched throat and the gnawing of hunger. He had been on the raft for nine days, the last five of which had been without any food and the last two without water. Rising to his feet, he saw by the early morning sunlight that he had found his way into a cove between two rocky headlands. A small misjudgement in direction or weakening in his stroke last night would have seen him swept to his death. Perhaps the gods had not finished with him after all. Brushing the sand from his tattered clothes, he entered a line of trees at the top of the beach and immediately found himself on a well-trodden path. Not so long ago he might have followed it with caution, but he no longer cared. He was starving and unarmed, and if the path's makers were hostile then he could do nothing about it. But something told him there was no danger here. Not mortal danger, at least. Instead there was a strange familiarity about the place. As he followed the path deeper into the trees he heard the sound of trickling water. Strengthened by his thirst, he stumbled on until the path was intersected by a small stream, where he threw himself into the cool water and drank deeply. When he had finished he waded to the opposite bank and sat on the lush grass. It was there that he saw the small white flower.

It was not a particularly beautiful flower. Indeed, it was quite plain. But it had a strong fragrance that he had not smelled for many years, and then only in one other place. Slowly and carefully he parted the grass on either side and scratched at the earth that nurtured it. Its fragrance and the shape of its petals were not enough, but as it yielded to his touch he saw the turtle-shaped root and knew it was a chelonion. A chelonion! The native flower of his homeland, found only in the soil of Ithaca and Kefalonia. He stared at it in disbelief as tears rolled down his cheeks.

'Who are you?'

Startled, he looked up and saw a young woman standing before him. She wore a long white dress that left only her milky white arms and neck exposed. Her hair fell in long blonde curls about her shoulders, framing a fine face with lips that were still slightly parted with surprise. Her pale blue eyes wore an expression that was both cautious and yet intrigued. Odysseus became acutely aware of his ragged tunic and – conscious of the irony that he might be the girl's king – felt compelled to bow his head before her.

'Forgive my appearance, my lady. I'm a mere sailor brought to this land by the misfortune of storm and shipwreck. Though I don't know which land this is.'

'You're no mere sailor,' she answered in a light voice. 'It takes more than brine and a few rags to hide a man's nobility. As for this place, you have arrived on the island of Ogygia.'

'Ogygia?' Odysseus replied, his voice failing. 'Are... are you sure?'

'Of course I am. This is my home and I've lived here alone for many years. In all that time I've only ever been visited by the gods, and yet here you are, brought to me by the sea.'

'But I thought this was Ithaca or... or maybe Kefalonia,' Odysseus protested. He held up the flower in his fingertips as proof. 'This plant only grows there –'

She took the chelonion and examined it briefly before tossing it aside. Then she knelt before him and folded his hands in hers.

'I've never heard of either of those places, and as for your little flower, it grows all over this island. But you are weary. Come with me to my home and be my guest. I will bathe and clothe you and then we will eat together.'

'But my lady –'

'Calypso. My name is Calypso.'

Her earlier surprise had disappeared and now she looked at him with kinder eyes. But the kindness came from hunger, the same hungry longing he had seen in Circe. It was a longing he felt himself – a longing that was born out of loneliness – and which only one woman could satisfy. But it seemed he was destined never to see Penelope again, and without her he knew he would always be incomplete.

As black despair settled in his heart, Odysseus allowed Calypso to take him by the hand and lead him into the woods.

AUTHOR'S NOTE

The Odyssey has enthralled and perplexed readers for around three thousand years. Of its twenty-four chapters, twenty are focussed on Odysseus's return to Ithaca and his fight to save his family and home from the ambitions of a host of would-be usurpers. The other four chapters relate the story of his fantastic ten-year voyage from Troy to the shores of Phaeacia, where he tells King Alcinous of his encounters with the Cyclops, Circe, the Sirens and other mythical beings. It is these four chapters, and the handful of events that precede them, that form the basis for *The Voyage of Odysseus*.

Scholars, both ancient and modern, have tried to impose Odysseus's wanderings over a map of the Mediterranean and come up with solutions to the many mysteries in Homer's poem, such as who were the lotus eaters, where was the entrance to the Underworld, and what was Charybdis. For the most part they have sought natural solutions to supernatural conundrums, an exercise which has to be futile. I've opted to accept Homer at his word and take up a different challenge: to fill the gaps in Odysseus's account of his voyage, and to relate the story to the events that took place after the fall of Troy.

As with the previous books in this series, I have attempted to remain true to the original myths while also taking a few liberties to help the stories fit together into a single coherent narrative. Calchas, the renegade Trojan seer, did not die at Troy, but in Asia Minor, where he expired from shame or grief after meeting a prophet greater than himself; or alternatively after a fit of laughter that caused him to choke to death. Odysseus did not find Little Ajax's body floating in the waters off Euboea, though it is generally said his fleet was wrecked there by Athena, as a punishment for his rape of Cassandra in the goddess's temple. Neither were the lotus eaters stirred to violence when Odysseus hauled his drugged countrymen back to the safety of their ship.

Homer does not suggest that Circe drugged the wine to keep Odysseus and his comrades from thinking of Ithaca – this is my way of excusing him for lingering so long when he should have been hurrying home to Penelope. Nor was Elpenor anything more than a poor fool in *The Odyssey*, who fell off Circe's roof after drinking too much wine. His role as an assassin is entirely my invention, while his fellow assassin, Selagos, does not appear in the original myths at all.

The same is true of Eperitus, a product of my imagination who provides an element of the unknown in a popular and familiar tale. Indeed, this story is as much Eperitus's as it is Odysseus's, and so we must wait until the sixth and final book of the series to see what the Fates have in store for them both.

42817739R00295

Made in the USA
Lexington, KY
20 June 2019